THE SWORDSMAN'S DESCENT

THE ROYAL CHAMPION
BOOK 2

G.M. WHITE

The Swordsman's Descent
G.M. White

Editor: Vicky Brewster
Cover design: Get Covers

Copyright © 2022 by G.M. White

All rights reserved.
No part of this book may be reproduced in any form or by any electronic or mechanical means, including information storage and retrieval systems, without written permission from the author, except for the use of brief quotations in a book review.

This book is dedicated to all those frontline workers that have kept the world going during the pandemic.

Special thanks go to the staff at Watford General Hospital for their care of my aunt, Carole Payton-Gresswell, during her last days.

AUTHOR'S NOTE ON SPELLINGS (AND AI)

Please note, the author is British, and so uses British English spellings throughout.

No AI was used in the writing of this book, it is the work of a human mind with all the frailties and faults that entails.

1

BELASKO TRAINED, ALONE. He was in the main hall at his academy. Once, before it was gifted to him by the late King Mallor, it had been the manor house of an important noble family. Their line had dwindled to nothing, and when the king had been looking to bestow the house and surrounding land on someone, his eye had alighted on his champion, who had recently proposed establishing an academy of the martial arts—to help improve the standard of training throughout the Villanese military and, ultimately, help choose his own successor. So the juicy prize had gone his way. Another reason for the nobles to hate him, the upstart son of a farmer. As they saw it, anyway.

From an open window, high in the wood-panelled wall, came the sounds of his students sparring, practising their drills, young voices raised in encouragement, derision and occasional laughter.

Belasko worked his way across the room, moving in the odd stuttering gait he had adopted to work around the pain in his damaged foot and other joints. A fighter adapts, and

Belasko had adapted his technique to take into account his physical ailments.

It was why he trained alone. Shrouded in secrecy, his students assumed he was developing a new technique. A new fighting style that they were all desperate to learn. He forbade them, insisting instead that they follow the drills and teachings of himself and their other instructors.

"Master the basics first, then you can branch out." His new motto, so often repeated that the students would start to chorus it before he got to the end of the sentence.

Few knew the reason why he trained alone, developing new techniques, was because his body was failing him. More and more, year by year, he was less the man he had been. War hero. Legendary duellist. Royal Champion.

Belasko snorted as he worked through a drill, sweeping his practice blade high and then low, countering multiple imaginary opponents. *A Royal Champion whose hands, some mornings, are so stiff they can barely hold a blade.*

His pace quickened, blade sending the motes of dust that hung in the air spiralling into new and interesting patterns. He still moved with some of his old speed. A lifetime of training and practice stood for something. When he did train with his students or other instructors, none could land a touch on him. When challengers came, they were defeated and sent away. Either on their feet or in a wooden box.

A knock came at the door. Belasko finished his drill, returning to a guard position, before calling out, "Yes? Come in." He wiped a bead of sweat from his brow with the back of his hand and frowned. "Come in, what is it?"

The door opened as Belasko moved to a table by the wall, revealing Denna. The wife of Belasko's oldest friend, Orren, she had taken over her husband's position as the steward of Belasko's Academy upon his death. Honey-blonde hair pulled back in a bun, clad in a sober gown, her mischievous eyes had taken on a more serious cast in the last few years. She no longer wore mourning black, but there was no doubting the depth of her loss.

"Good morning," she said. "There's a challenger at the gates."

Belasko sighed as he replaced his practice blade in its polished hardwood case, snapping the case shut with a long-practised motion.

"Good morning, Denna. Is it a serious challenger today, or another drunken young noble on a dare?" Belasko shrugged on a black jacket.

Denna rolled her eyes. "A rather serious young man, a Baskan. Come to seek vengeance for his father's death at Dellan Pass."

Belasko sighed again, pinching the bridge of his nose. Dellan Pass. The day that had made his name. Made him a legend. It had begun to feel like a millstone around his neck.

He straightened up, shrugging his shoulders. "Bring him here. Does he have a second with him? If not, ask one of the instructors—Ailvin perhaps—to stand with the boy. Please ask Byrta if she'll serve the same office for me."

Denna nodded and went out. Belasko eyed up his sword belt and rapier, which he had taken off to train and now rested on the table next to his practice blade in its case.

Denna appeared at the open door, followed by a Baskan man who looked to be in his early twenties, with the dark hair and olive skin that were common among his people. He moved well, and the blade that rode at his hip seemed well made and cared for, as did the sword belt and scabbard it sat in.

Filing in behind them came Ailvin, a slender redheaded

man who was relatively new to Belasko's staff, and Byrta, who wasn't

They had trained together under Markus, the previous Royal Champion, when he had been looking to appoint a successor. A former cavalry officer, she was one of the first instructors Belasko had recruited for his Academy, where she led on mounted combat and sabre techniques. Brown hair tied back in a long tail, a white shirt rather haphazardly tucked into riding trousers, she gave the impression that they had interrupted her at something and she was not best pleased about it.

The young man marched up to Belasko and offered him a perfunctory bow. "You are Belasko, the villain of Dellan Pass?"

Belasko nodded. "I suppose I am, from your point of view." He shrugged. "Although I was protecting Villanese territory from a Baskan invasion force, so our perspective on it is somewhat different."

The young man tilted his head to one side, a speculative expression on his face. "I thought you'd be taller."

Byrta couldn't hold back a burst of laughter at that, while Denna and Ailvin tried to keep their faces straight.

A faint smile touched Belasko's face. "I get that a lot. You are?"

His erstwhile opponent drew himself up to his full height, which was, in fact, taller than Belasko, hand now resting on the pommel of his sword. "I am Olbarin, son of Albarin, come to challenge you and avenge his death at your hands."

Belasko eyed him warily. "Are you now? Well, Olbarin, you aren't the first, and you certainly won't be the last, to cross my threshold and issue such a challenge." He turned

The Swordsman's Descent

to Denna. "Young Olbarin here is, what, our third challenger this autumn?"

"Fourth, actually." Denna replied.

"Fourth." Belasko turned back to his challenger. "I am sorry for your father's death. Many good people were lost during the Last War. On both sides. Are you so eager to join him? Would you heap more grief upon your family? What does your mother think of you coming here?"

A look of uncertainty clouded Olbarin's face.

"Ah. She doesn't know, does she?" Belasko shook his head. "Well then, are you determined to proceed along this path?" Olbarin nodded. "Then say the words."

The Baskan eased his sword in its scabbard. "I, Olbarin, challenge you, Belasko, to a duel."

Belasko walked to where his rapier waited and put on his sword belt, leaving the blade undrawn. "I accept. To first blood, defeat, or death?"

Olbarin paled a little. "To death," he whispered.

Belasko frowned, then shook his head. "No. I have no desire to send you back to your family in pieces. Try to kill me as you will, but I will fight to your defeat. Not death."

"Very well," said Olbarin, voice tight with anger and the colour returning to his cheeks at the slight. "To your death, then."

"Many have tried, young man. So far, none have succeeded." Belasko gestured to the centre of the hall, where a duelling circle was marked out with white paint. "After you. Ailvin here will be your second; Byrta will serve the same role for me. Denna is our witness."

Olbarin took up his place at one side of the circle, drawing his sword as he did so. Unbuckling his sword belt, he let it fall to the ground before kicking it aside. Belasko took his place across from the younger man. Still, he did not draw his sword.

Olbarin looked up, saw Belasko standing across from him, hands hanging easily at his sides, and his face coloured further.

"You insult me so, to enter the circle without a blade drawn? You think I will be so easily defeated?"

"I have no desire to send you back to your family in pieces. Your story is familiar enough to me. Would I add to their grief? Now come, show me what the Baskan military are teaching these days."

Olbarin roared in anger and leaped forwards, sword whistling round in a vicious blow to Belasko's neck. Except Belasko wasn't there. He had spun out of the way and used his momentum to bring his leg round in a sweeping kick to the back of Olbarin's knees. The young man staggered. Belasko backed away, waiting to see what his opponent would do next.

Olbarin pressed forwards, always on the attack, but Belasko was not there to meet him. He seemed to dance around his challenger, spinning, whirling, landing a series of glancing blows with his hands and feet. If he had drawn his blade, the boy would already have been cut to ribbons.

Olbarin fought on, undeterred, although he was tiring now. Belasko changed tack, barely moving at all—just enough to avoid Olbarin's attacks. When he did move, it was with an odd stuttering gait that was impossible to predict. The young Baskan became increasingly desperate in his own movements as he tried to counter this.

He launched another attack, a desperate thrust. Belasko leaned away from Olbarin's blade, then stepped into the young man's body. As he did so, Belasko finally gripped the handle of his own sword with his left hand and drew it backhanded in a short sharp movement that crashed the pommel of Belasko's rapier into the young man's chin without fully drawing the sword. Olbarin dropped to the floor, stunned, as Belasko slid his blade back home.

Belasko stood over Olbarin, tipping back his chin with the toe of his boot. "Do you accept defeat?"

Olbarin's face crumpled in sadness. "I accept defeat."

Belasko leaned over, offering him a hand up. Olbarin reached up and took it, and as Belasko pulled him up to standing, he shifted his grip on the young man's hand, so they were holding each other by the wrist. The warrior's grip.

Belasko leaned in close to the young man. "A word of advice: watch your weight on your front foot. You overextended, and it allowed me an opening."

Releasing the Baskan, Belasko beckoned Ailvin over. "Can you take him to the infirmary? That blow to the jaw will start to swell soon. We'd best get something on it."

The redheaded instructor took Olbarin by the elbow and started to lead him away. "Come on, this way. We'll get you checked over."

Confusion was writ large across Olbarin's face as they led him out the door. "He's not what I expected..." he was heard saying to Ailvin as he walked out.

"I'll say." Byrta slapped Belasko on the back of his head. "Going into the duelling circle without drawing your weapon. What fresh idiocy is this?"

"I have to agree, that was spectacularly stupid, even for you. What has got into you lately? Are you not taking these challenges seriously at all?" Denna frowned at him, hands on her hips.

"I didn't need to draw my blade to defeat that young man." Belasko pursed his lips. "Although he has promise, with the right training..."

"Oh no." Byrta threw her hands in the air. "No. We're not adding Baskans to the waifs and strays you collect, no matter what promise they show!"

"I have to agree," said Denna. "I don't think the Queen would be terribly pleased. Do you?"

"No. No, she wouldn't be pleased." Belasko sighed. "Not that I know what would please her these days."

"If you spent a bit more time at court instead of moping here, maybe you'd know." Denna shook her head. "You have friends, Belasko. The Queen used to be one of them, didn't she?"

"That was before the high and mighty Royal Champion here decided to cut himself off from court life and half of those who love and care about him, wasn't it?" Byrta snorted. "Listen to Denna, you fool. You have friends, me included. Whether you like it or not." She clapped him on the shoulder. "Now I'm off to do the job you pay me for: putting those students through their paces." She sauntered out of the room, calling back over her shoulder, "Don't forget your friends, idiot. Maybe we can train together sometime. Like the old days."

Denna went to follow her out. "I have work to do as well. But, Belasko, you need to take these challenges seriously."

"Denna, I..." She stopped in the doorway, turning back to him. "I need pen and paper. Can you have some sent to me? When that boy leaves our infirmary, it will be with a letter of introduction to Ambassador Aveyard in his pocket." She said nothing, but a questioning look crossed her face. Belasko frowned. "I said the boy had potential; I would see it fulfilled." Denna arched an eyebrow. Belasko looked away. "Damn it, I killed his father. It's the least I can do."

She turned around and walked away, boot heels clicking on the floor, leaving Belasko alone in the hall.

2

THAT NIGHT, BELASKO worked late in his study. A neat room, with a place for everything and everything in its place. The walls were lined with bookshelves that held tomes on combat techniques and military history from a variety of nations and traditions in multiple languages. There were translations as well, but Belasko struggled on in the original tongues when he could, knowing that, otherwise, there might be a missed nuance in meaning. Something a warrior would see that a scribe might miss.

Many of the books and scrolls had been gifts from Queen Lilliana and her father, King Mallor. Belasko had felt uncomfortable with keeping the late King's gifts at first, after his true nature had been revealed when he poisoned his own son, Prince Kellan. The tumultuous days that had followed, when he had set loyal Belasko up to take the blame, added to the sting. Thoughts of the old King could sour Belasko's mood for days, and the gifts Mallor bestowed on him had seemed tainted.

It was Queen Lilliana herself who had pointed out that the gifts, no matter who they came from, had value in them-

The Swordsman's Descent

selves. It wasn't the books' fault that the one who had given them had turned out to be a treacherous, murderous, villain.

"Although, Belasko, if you ever decide to part with some of your collection..." Queen Lilliana had looked around the room on one of her increasingly rare visits to the Academy, a faint smile playing across her lips. "They would be gratefully received back into the royal library." She had laughed then. "Forgive me, my friend, you know my fondness for old tomes on any subject."

Belasko smiled at the memory before returning his attention to the paperwork in front of him. He squinted in the lamplight. *Wonderful, now my eyes are going, too.*

He sighed and brought the paper closer to his face. A knock came at the door, and, with some relief, he replaced the paper on his desk. "Who is it?" he asked.

"It's Denna," said a muffled voice through the door. "Can I come in?"

"Please do," Belasko said. He smiled at her as the door opened and she entered. "And save me from all this work." He gestured at the pile of letters and papers on his desk. "It never seems to decrease, no matter how much I do."

Denna returned his smile as she took a seat opposite him. "That is the nature of work, I'm afraid."

Belasko pursed his lips. "You're right there. Now, what can I do for you?"

She paused for a moment, hesitant. "I, um. I was wondering..."

He leaned forward. "Yes, Denna, what is it?"

"I was wondering... How are you? We see so little of you these days. You keep yourself apart from everyone. We don't talk like we used to. I worry about you."

Belasko sat back in his chair, expression becoming coldly neutral. "I'm fine. You don't need to worry about me."

Denna shook her head. "Maybe I don't need to, but I do. Since that business with the old king, since..." She looked away for a moment, taking a deep breath. "Since Orren died you've not only cut yourself off from everyone at court, but from your friends too. You don't need to be alone, Belasko. There are people who care about you, who love you. Right here, under these roofs. Don't be afraid to turn to them."

Belasko's face only grew colder. "I'm not afraid. Thank you for expressing your concerns. Now, if there isn't anything else?"

Denna sat for a moment, looking at her hands in her lap. Then, so quiet he almost couldn't make it out, "I know you loved him. Orren. We've never spoken of it, but I know. I've always known."

Belasko held his breath, deathly still. Denna looked up, meeting his gaze.

"He loved you, too, you know, if not in the way you would have wished. The thing is, Belasko, you deserve love, too. To have your love returned. Which will never happen while you keep everyone at bay. You don't have to do everything yourself. You can't solve every problem alone. There are people around you who are capable. Who care about you. Let them in."

They sat in silence for a long moment, eyes locked. Belasko looked away first, coughing to clear his throat.

"Thank you, Denna, for your thoughts. Your counsel is always welcome. Now, if you'll excuse me, I do have to get through all of this." He gestured at his heavily laden desk. "Maybe not all tonight, but sometime before I die."

She stood, chair scraping across the flagstone floor.

"Very well. I'll leave you to your work. And your thoughts." She turned to leave.

"One more thing before I go." Denna turned back, retrieving a letter from the pocket of her ever-present apron. "A letter for you, from the Queen. Delivered by a messenger who wouldn't stop, not even for refreshments. She rode straight back to the city, so I suppose an answer isn't required."

Belasko took the letter from her hand, breaking the wax seal with his thumb. He scanned it, frowning, before looking back up at Denna. "It's a summons. She expects to see me at the palace tomorrow afternoon."

"Well then," said Denna, "you'd best not disappoint her."

3

BELASKO RODE UP to the palace gates alone. He had brought some staff with him to the city but left his retinue at his city home. Queen Lilliana hadn't specified that they meet alone, but their meetings sometimes veered onto personal matters, and so discretion was often the best course.

He approached over the same bridge he had used when escaping from the palace dungeons four years before. Of course, he had used the bridge many times before then, and since, but ever since that day, it always came to mind when he crossed.

I wonder what sort of reception I'll get today. The Queen wasn't clear as to the reason for this meeting, so it's difficult to say.

Years of palace intrigue, and of warfare before that, had made Belasko wary of venturing into unknown situations. The terrain was familiar, of course, but the motivations for his summons... That was another matter.

He pulled up at the gatehouse, and after exchanging a few words with the guards on duty—a grizzled veteran called Tanit and a young woman named Vilette—was admitted entrance.

Belasko dismounted and walked further into the palace complex. Seeing his horse stabled in the stall kept for his use, he met Captain Majel at the entrance to the palace proper. She had been alerted to his arrival by the gate guard.

The young officer was now the head of the Queen's private guard, an elite unit within the palace guard. Belasko had overseen its formation when palace security was overhauled following his successful infiltration on the last day of the old king's reign.

Captain Majel wore her responsibility well, a serious expression now permanently settled on her face. Her short-cropped dark hair framed sharp features, and she cracked a smile at Belasko's arrival. Both were dedicated entirely to the Queen's protection, albeit by different means, and usually got along well.

"Hello, old man, how are you today?"

Belasko scoffed. "'Old man', is it? I could still teach a bright thing like you a thing or two." He returned her smile as they clasped hands. "I'm as well as ever, Majel. How are you? How is the Queen? Do you know why I've been summoned?"

She laughed as they entered the main palace building through decoratively inlaid but steel reinforced doors. They crossed a large airy portico, light falling onto marble floors and wood-panelled walls. Decorative and finely made tapestries hung on the walls and exquisitely crafted tables were spaced along the walls, each holding items of art and craft that were as expensive as they were tasteful and beautiful to behold.

"So many questions this morning! I'll reply in order. I am fine, thank you. The Queen is in fine spirits, although she received a letter yesterday which put a grim expression on her face. You know the one, I'm sure. Deathly serious, but with a speculative air about it."

Belasko nodded. "Oh yes, that's what I call her 'something terrible has happened, but I sense opportunity in it' face."

Majel snorted. "You're braver than me if you've said that to her directly."

"I've known her since she was a child, I'm allowed a little leeway. I'm guessing that letter is the reason I'm here."

They passed a pair of guards stationed along the corridor, who saluted. Both Majel and Belasko returned their salutes.

Majel shrugged as they continued on their way. "I'd be willing to hazard a guess as to that effect, but I don't know the contents of the letter. The Queen wouldn't be drawn on it."

They made their way further into the palace proper, exchanging salutes with guards as they passed, deep in conversation and catching up as they moved through the circuitous and confusing corridors of the palace.

Eventually, they reached the Queen's study, where she held meetings of a private but official nature. Two guards were stationed outside the door, as was the Queen's secretary. A personable young man by the name of Parlin, he shared the Queen's love of learning and took his responsibilities extremely seriously.

He stood up and came out from behind his small writing desk to greet them. Parlin was of slender build, but tall. His bright red hair spiked up into tufts no matter how neatly he tried to style it.

Parlin gave them a warm smile. "Belasko, sir, Captain Majel, ma'am, so good to see you this morning. The Queen is still with her previous appointment, but I have a feeling they may want them present for your meeting as well. Let me just see..."

He went to the door and rapped on it with his knuckles, opening it at a muffled command from inside. There followed a muted exchange of words before Parlin turned to them and opened the door wider to admit them.

"As I suspected, the Queen would like to see you now. With her previous guest. Would either of you like any refreshments? I can send for them now if you like."

Majel shook her head. "Not for me, thank you."

"Or me," said Belasko. "But thank you for the offer."

"Of course. If either of you change your minds, I'm just outside." Parlin gestured for them to go inside.

Belasko led the way into the room. What he saw there drew him up short in surprise. Standing behind the Queen's shoulder, poring over documents open on her desk, was Ambassador Aveyard, the Baskan ambassador to the Villanese court. She looked up at their entrance, nodded a greeting, and went back to her reading.

Queen Lilliana stood, and her golden hair caught in a beam of light from a high window and seemed to glow. She smiled and held her hands out in greeting. Belasko regained his momentum, offering the Queen a bow before walking up to her desk and kissing her hand in greeting.

"My Queen. It's always a pleasure to see you. I will admit to some curiosity as to the reason for my summons, and to the company I find you in."

The Queen laughed, accepting Majel's bow and kiss before gesturing for them to take the seats on the other side of her desk. "Please, sit. I have some news for you both." A rather mischievous smile hovered about her lips for a moment. "I must admit, it was enjoyable to see your surprise, Belasko."

"I beg your forgiveness, majesty, but I thought my days of being ambushed by Baskans were behind me."

Ambassador Aveyard snorted, brushing her dark hair back behind her ears. Clad in military uniform, she had a Baskan's olive complexion, married to sharp features and a sharper mind. "The war is in the past, Belasko. Leave it where it belongs."

"With all respect, majesty, Madam Ambassador," said Majel, "why are we here?"

"We have had news from Bas. The old Baskan King has died without leaving a clear line of succession. There has been a bit of disagreement over who should replace him." Ambassador Aveyard snorted again at that. Queen Lilliana gave her a look. "Perhaps that is underselling it somewhat. Baskan politics is a little more, um, openly bloody than our own. We understand that discussions became quite heated. Fighting broke out on the streets of the capital as rival factions tried to sort it out amongst themselves. In the end, one name was chosen to succeed. Lord Edyard, the former Baskan General, is now King Edyard." Queen Lilliana turned again to the Baskan ambassador. "I will, of course, write to King Edyard officially, but please do convey my congratulations to your uncle privately."

Ambassador Aveyard inclined her head. "Of course, your majesty."

"The ambassador confirmed this news for us, as well as making an overture on behalf of the new king. That is why she, and you, are here. Ambassador?"

Ambassador Aveyard cleared her throat. "My uncle has written to me to extend an invitation to Queen Lilliana to visit the Baskan capital with the aim of signing some new

The Swordsman's Descent

accords between our people, to put the war behind us once and for all. He has mentioned several other people he would like to attend, figures from the Last War, as he feels their presence would lend some weight to the occasion. Your name is among them, Belasko."

Belasko leaned forward. "He wants me there? Why?"

Ambassador Aveyard shrugged. "It's not just you. My uncle wants prominent people from both sides of the conflict to be present and part of negotiations. I wouldn't want to speak for him, but I think he feels that it would show a united front."

"And give an opportunity to settle some grudges. It risks reopening old wounds." Belasko snorted. "I'm not sure as to the wisdom of this, majesty."

"Be that as it may, an open wound might never heal. Perhaps it's time we cleaned that wound and applied some fresh bandages." Queen Lilliana inclined her head to the Baskan Ambassador. "Thank you, Ambassador, for bringing us the invitation and frank discussion. If you wouldn't mind, I'd now like to discuss this with my councillors in private."

Ambassador Aveyard nodded. "Of course, your majesty. I'll leave the letters for you to go over. I am, of course, at your disposal if there is anything further you wish to discuss." She walked towards the door, turning back to offer the Queen a respectful bow. "Your majesty." The other two got a brusque nod. "Belasko. Majel." She rapped on the door with her knuckles, it was promptly opened from the other side, and she was gone.

They waited until the door was firmly shut to continue talking.

Queen Lilliana gave them both a frank look. "Well, what do you think?"

"I don't like it," said Majel, blunt and direct. "We go to

the Baskan capital, where we'll be surrounded by Baskan soldiers, where members of your retinue are hated by the people... It's risky. No, more than risky. It's outright dangerous. We would be placing our lives, your life, majesty, in the hands of a man we don't know and whose true intentions we can only guess at. No, I don't like it at all."

Queen Lilliana nodded. "Very well. Belasko?" She turned to her champion, a questioning look on her face.

He thought for a moment, cradling his hands and tapping his forefingers together. Then he shrugged. "I think you can guess my mind, majesty. I agree with Majel. It's dangerous for all the reasons stated and more. Winter is on its way. If we were to go, we would need to leave soon in order to get over the mountain passes between our kingdoms. Winter snows will close them off before long, meaning if we tarried too long in Bas, we would be stuck there until the spring thaws. Something General—sorry, *King* Edyard knows only too well. The man is a master strategist, one of the finest military minds in the world. I would think very hard about all the angles before agreeing to anything. Why should we go to him? Have him come here. Or better yet, find a neutral nation willing to host the talks. That way, we can each bring an agreed-upon retinue, the same amount of soldiers, so no one is at a disadvantage."

Queen Lilliana nodded. "There is something to what you say, but I can see several reasons for Edyard inviting us to come to him. He's trying to cement his power, so would not want to leave a vacuum for others to plot in. There are many in Baskan society who hold him responsible for their loss in the Last War. By bringing us to him and forging a lasting peace between our peoples, he puts that past behind him and sets his country on a new path. It would be the defining act of his reign." The Queen paused for a moment. "You've met him, Belasko. What was he like?"

Belasko sighed. "That was a long time ago." A memory stirred in him of an old soldier with salt and pepper hair, a uniform of high rank, with a sharp smile and bright eyes. "You've both heard the story of that day more than enough times. He acted honourably then. Will he now? Time can change a man."

"Yes, but what was he like? How did he carry himself?"

Belasko thought for a moment. "As I say, he behaved honourably. Honestly, I liked the man. A good leader who didn't want to throw away the lives of his people, who kept to the old ways. Who kept his word. That says a lot." He gave the Queen a rueful grin. "That being said, I still don't think you should go."

The Queen stood, pushing back her chair and turning to the window behind her. She looked out for a moment, seeming to study the patterns in the clouds while deep in thought. Then Queen Lilliana nodded to herself, a decision made. She turned back to them.

"Thank you both for your honest counsel. The decision rests with me. I know there are risks involved, but I think there is much to be gained here. We will go to Bas." She walked back to her desk, leaning over a map that was spread out on it. Queen Lilliana traced a finger along the map's surface, mouthing silently to herself. She looked up at them. "You're right, Belasko. We do need to go soon if we're to make it there and back before the passes close. We could take a sea voyage, but overland is the most direct route. I won't command you to come with us, Belasko, but I would value your company almost as much as your counsel. Majel, if you and Belasko can start planning this immediately, I'd be grateful. Speed is of the essence."

"Of course, majesty." Majel knew when she was being dismissed and stood, offering her Queen a respectful bow. Belasko made to stand until the queen waved him back into his chair.

"Stay a moment, Belasko. There's something else I would talk to you about. Majel can make a start without you."

"Of course, majesty," said Majel. Then, to Belasko, "I'll get the relevant maps sent up to my office. Along with some refreshments. Join me there when you're able." She offered the Queen another bow, strode to the door, and was gone.

Queen Lilliana pursed her lips, eyeing Belasko speculatively.

He laughed. "What is it? I feel like the prize goose being weighed up for the midwinter feast."

She smiled. "It's something of a personal nature, although it does relate to your position. Tell me." She paused, trying to find the right words. "How is your condition?"

Belasko sighed. "You know as well as I. I'm sure Maelyn reports to you." The Royal Physician had been treating Belasko's physical ailments for some years now.

"She does, but not everything. I know things are worsening."

Belasko nodded slowly. "That's true. It's not just my foot, either. To be frank, there's not a part of me that doesn't hurt. Some mornings my hands are near useless until I've been up a while. Things worsen."

The Queen gave him a sad smile. "You are my champion, Belasko. What I will say next may be difficult to hear, but it needs to be said." She took a rep breath. "You need to find your successor, and find them soon. Before you are unable to carry out your duties."

Belasko blinked. "Yes, ma'am."

The Swordsman's Descent

"Don't 'ma'am' me, Belasko. This day has been coming for some time. I need you to be fit to carry out your duties, but you are my friend, dear to me. You are a hero, a phenomenal swordsman, still most likely the best blade in the country. But for how long?" She turned away, wiping something from her eye, going back to the window. "Don't think I'll let you off easily once you have found your replacement. I still have work for you, if you'll do it."

"Majesty?"

She turned back to him. "Belasko, you're more than just a swordsman. I know we have grown apart these last few years, but I value your mind, your counsel. You have lived a different life to others at court, brought another perspective. Most importantly, you have a good heart, which cannot be said for all at court. I would ask that when you have chosen a successor, you come back to court to serve on my inner council. While I cannot compel you, as I will not command you to come with me to Bas, I would hope that our friendship means something to you. I know you will do your duty, but I ask as your friend."

There was silence between them then—a long moment as they looked at each other before Belasko nodded slowly. "I will work to find my successor more quickly, majesty. As to the rest... I will think on it. You know you are dear to me, although life at court is not."

Queen Lilliana smiled. "That is all I ask. Think on it. We will have time to talk on the journey to Bas, if you choose to come. Now, go to Majel. Put your heads together and see how quickly you can arrange things. Pay special consideration to the security arrangements. I might think the trip is worth the risk, but I wasn't born yesterday."

4

"WHAT DO YOU think?" Majel poured Belasko a brandy from a decanter on her desk and passed him the glass. She poured another for herself and then put the decanter back to work as a paperweight, holding down one corner of the map that had been unrolled and spread across her desk. The other corners were weighed down by an old dagger, a porcelain figurine, and a thick book on cavalry tactics.

Belasko smiled his thanks for the drink, taking a sip and rolling the brandy around in his mouth. He swallowed and made an appreciative face, then peered at the glass.

"I think they've been letting you have the good stuff since your promotion."

Majel rolled her eyes. "Not the brandy, Belasko. What do you think about this? A trip into the heart of Bas, where we hold none of the advantages and will be surrounded by an unfriendly populace at the worst possible time of year."

The smile left Belasko's face. "Yes, well, I was trying not to think about that for a moment." He sighed. "It's not quite the worst time of year. Winter closing in will mean we can't tarry long. Hopefully negotiations can be closed quickly, and we can bring the Queen home soon."

"'We'?" Majel sipped her brandy. "So, you are coming with us?"

Belasko shook his head. "I'm not decided yet. I believe the Baskan people are not fond of me. The ambassador herself has told me so many times. Many, many times. Did you know I still get challenged by Baskans looking to avenge a death at Dellan Pass? We had one turn up at the gates yesterday." He looked at the map, casting his eye over terrain familiar from years of war and military service, and over the border to Bas and other lands he had not yet travelled. "If I go to Bas, I might well be challenged every step of the way."

"Is that so bad? You're still Royal Champion for a reason. The finest sword in the kingdom."

"Yes, well..." Belasko looked at her for a moment. "How much does the Queen tell you? You have earned her trust. How frank is she with you?"

Majel tilted her head to one side as she looked at him. "She's frank. Doesn't tell me everything, of course, but I know a little about your difficulties. Why?"

"Things are getting worse, Majel. I'm in constant pain from my foot and a score of other places. My joints are weak. Some mornings my hands are too stiff, too cramped, to hold a sword. I'm reaching the point where I won't be able to function as the Queen's Champion."

"Oh, Belasko, I'm sorry." Majel's voice had dropped to a whisper.

"Don't be." Belasko knocked back the rest of his brandy. "Can I get some more of this?" He held out his glass, which Majel refilled. "Thank you. No, don't be sorry. It's not like I'm dying. Just outliving my usefulness. Anyway, the Queen knows all this and has asked me to accelerate my search for a replacement. I'm not sure how that tallies with a jaunt into former enemy territory."

Majel thought a moment, tapping her finger on the side of her glass before nodding to herself. "It could work. Why don't you gather your best students, tell them you'll be making your decision about your replacement when you return from Bas, and have them redouble their efforts while you're gone? Is there anyone at the Academy now who shows promise?"

Belasko frowned. "Several. There is something to your suggestion." His expression lightened. "Of course, you were a promising student yourself, not so long ago. If you'd stayed at the Academy..."

"Oh, no," Majel laughed. "I was never that good, although it's kind of you to say. My secondment to the Academy was enjoyable, but my duties with the palace guard took precedence."

"I might follow your suggestion. If I come along on this trip."

"Speaking of which..." Majel gestured at the map. "What do you think? Best route?"

Belasko leaned forward, tapping his finger on the map. "It makes sense to cross the mountains here if we're going overland. The main trade route has the best roads, so we might as well use it. If we move quickly it'll take us, what? Seven or eight days to get up into the mountains and to the border, and about the same to reach the Baskan capital. Which isn't all that far south of the mountains. In fact, it's only about a day or two's ride from the entrance to Dellan Pass, which is one of the reasons I think Edyard tried to use it as he did in the Last War." Belasko stood pack, gesturing at the map. "Those trade roads take a winding route. A few people on horseback could travel much more swiftly, more than halve that travel time, but we'll be with the royal retinue after all. Of course, we won't take the whole court with us. This is an ambassadorial mission, not a royal progress. They'll know we're coming, so no point in being sneaky. Not with our main body of troops, anyway."

"Fair point." Majel raised an eyebrow. "Main body of troops? How many are you thinking we should take? We need to protect the Queen, project strength, but we don't want to look like an invading army."

"No, that wouldn't do. I suppose." Belasko looked at her. "The Queen's personal guard, under your command, obviously."

Majel nodded. "Obviously."

"I'd say a detachment of the royal guard as well. Baskans are a martial people, they respect strength of arms, so I'd suggest at least a company or squadron from all branches of our military. Infantry, cavalry, engineers—make sure everyone's represented. Just to remind them what waits across the border if their territorial ambitions were to rise again."

Majel laughed. "You're not exactly subtle, Belasko."

He shrugged. "I'm no diplomat. Other people will be doing the talking; we'll have to find other ways to get our message across." His hand came to rest on the hilt of the sword at his side. "Hopefully, my own skills won't be needed on this trip. If I go." He held up a single finger. "I still haven't decided."

"As long as you promise to think about it. It'd do you some good to get away from your academy for a while."

Belasko nodded. "I will think it through. So we're

looking at about four hundred fighting men and women, give or take, plus the queen and her attendants, courtiers and their staff. Now, we need to discuss logistics. Just how this trip will be managed."

"Oh yes, the enjoyable stuff. The responsibility of leadership really isn't any fun at all." Majel sighed.

5

QUEEN LILLIANA SAT in her study, poring over some documents that required signing. She reached for her pen, dipped it in ink, and dashed off her neat signature in the appropriate places. She reached for a pull that hung down next to her desk, setting off a little bell outside the door, which opened to reveal an expectant Parlin.

"Yes, ma'am, how can I help?" he asked.

"I've signed those documents. Can you get them sent out for me? They're to go to the northern garrisons. Wait, I need to seal them."

As Parlin crossed the floor, she took her sealing wax and signet from a desk drawer, picked up a candle, and melted the end of the wax. Dripping some over the edge of the folded documents, she quickly pressed the royal seal into the wax, leaving the recipient in no doubt that they had come from her hand. While they waited for the wax to set, Parlin spoke.

"Ma'am, if I may be forgiven for asking, how did your

meeting go? I take it your champion and Captain Majel were not all that pleased?"

Queen Lilliana laughed. "How do you know that? Have you been listening at the door?"

A slight smile cracked Parlin's serious expression. "No, ma'am, but it hardly takes an expert to interpret Belasko's mood. He's not exactly subtle."

"He can be, when called for. But no, the Royal Champion is not always best suited at hiding his feelings." Queen Lilliana sighed. "It went as well as I'd hoped. They weren't pleased, but I think they both realise the necessity of our upcoming trip. You'd best pack soon, Parlin. Prepare to take this show on the road." She eyed her young secretary. "I noticed your informality with Belasko. I've not forgotten he recommended your services when I was looking for a secretary. Do you know him well?"

Parlin shrugged. "Not especially. As you know, ma'am, I was a student at his academy when this post became available. He thought the work would suit me, which it does, and put in a good word. I have much to thank him for. As for informality, well, he invites it, doesn't he?"

Queen Lilliana nodded. "He does that, at times. It used to seem that he wanted to be everyone's friend, and he's always been popular with the common folk. He used to set some of the nobles' teeth on edge, though. Here." She passed him the documents. "These are dry and ready to go. What's next?"

He took the documents from her. "Thank you, your majesty. I'll see that these are sent out at once. What's next? You have a meeting with the Aruvian ambassador in half an hour—he wants to discuss tariffs on the spice trade—and then you have some cases that have been brought to you for adjudication."

"Very well. I'll take some tea before the meeting with the ambassador, and preemptively draft a letter to the Grand Duchess of Aruvia along the lines that no, we won't be changing our tariffs at present, but we always welcome constructive feedback on how we may improve trade with our friends and neighbours." The Queen looked at her secretary. "Is there something else?"

"Oh, no, majesty. It's just, I was wondering…" Parlin looked down at the documents in his hands. "When you said that Belasko sets some of the nobles' teeth on edge, is that why you want him back at court?"

"It has something to do with it, yes." Queen Lilliana smiled. "Look, Parlin, Belasko is one of the few people who hold a position at court and isn't of noble birth. He can provide excellent insight, a different point of view. Also, he won't hesitate to tell me what he thinks is the right course of action. I've missed him these last few years, and the court has missed his wisdom and experience. So, yes, I would like to have him back at court. I'd like him at my right hand. Not least because he sets some people's teeth on edge." She winked at him. "But you didn't hear that from me, all right?"

Parlin gave a slight bow. "Yes, majesty. I'll see about that tea."

6

BELASKO RODE THROUGH the gates of his city home, hooves clattering on the cobbles of the courtyard. He left his horse in the care of the groom in his stables, crossed the courtyard, and entered the main building.

He had spent the best part of the day cloistered with Majel, trying to work out the requirements for the Queen's proposed trip. He had left the palace as night was settling in and was aware that the rest of the household would be finishing up the evening meal. On another night Belasko might have tarried a while at one of the taverns he knew, but there was too much to do for him to spare the time.

A member of the household staff hovered by the front door. A young man by the name of Telemann, he was one of Denna's most able members of staff. Blond hair was pushed back from his eyes as he approached Belasko. "Hello, sir. I hope your visit to the palace went well."

"Thank you, as well as could be hoped. Would you mind asking Byrta to meet me in my study when she's finished her dinner? No need for her to rush. I've got something to tell her when she's free."

"Of course, sir. I'll go down the dining room myself." He paused. "Should I be discreet?"

"Always, my dear Telemann. Always."

Belasko left Telemann to his task and went to his study. He let himself in and walked across to his bookshelves, pulling out books on Baskan culture and customs, their martial traditions, and some maps of his own. Although not as well-stocked as the library at his academy, he still kept useful information to hand at his city home. You never knew when it might be needed. Spreading the maps out on his desk, he began to flick through the books, unsure of exactly what he was looking for.

After a short while, there was a knock at the door, which opened to reveal Byrta. "You wanted to see me?"

"Yes, yes, please come in."

Byrta entered the study. She peered at the books on his desk and raised an eyebrow. "Books on Bas? We're not back at war, are we?"

Belasko shook his head. "No. The opposite, with any luck. Close the door behind you." The door clicked shut behind Byrta.

"Right. No messing about. The Queen wanted to talk to me about two things. The one that has most bearing on us here is this: she has asked me to hurry up and pick my successor." He gave a wry smile at Byrta's expression. "Not in quite those words, mind you. It is time, so I'd like you to think about your students, and I'll ask the other instructors as well. Who are the most promising? Who would you put forward to try for my position?" He held up a hand. "I don't need suggestions now, but think about it. The second thing is that there is a new king in Bas, and he has written to the Queen suggesting they meet for negotiations to set in place new accords between our peoples."

Byrta's frown deepened. "And why does that involve you?"

"The new Baskan King has invited me to attend these negotiations. The Queen hasn't commanded me to go but has left the decision up to me. I'm still unsure, but if I do go, I will tell those most promising students that I will choose my successor on my return and ask them to push themselves further in their training while I am gone. So, you can see that I'll need those recommendations quite soon. If I choose to accompany the Queen, then I would leave Denna in charge." He smiled. "She runs everything anyway, so it makes sense." Byrta laughed. "Byrta, I haven't yet decided whether I will accompany the Queen, but if I do, I would like you to come with me. How do you feel about that?"

Byrta pursed her lips. "I'm not exactly fond of Baskans, but you'll need someone to keep you out of trouble. So, I accept."

He smiled. "It's trouble I'm worried about. We'll be travelling on horseback, and you're the best mounted warrior I know. I want you with me in case anything happens on the way. That might be to fight, organise a retreat, or spirit away the Queen to a place of safety. Who knows? Everything might go perfectly, but we have to expect the worst and plan accordingly."

Byrta nodded. "Fine by me. Whatever you need. Anything else?"

"Not tonight. You're free to go. I'll return to my planning." He gestured at the desk. "What a fun evening I have ahead of me."

Byrta grinned. "You're the boss. That's why they pay you the big purses. Night, Belasko."

"Good night Byrta."

Then she was gone, the door closing behind her. Belasko sighed, opening a book on Baskan court traditions.

I'm not sure those purses are big enough.

7

LATER THAT NIGHT, Belasko was relaxing in his rooms, sipping a glass of wine in front of the fire in the small but comfortably appointed lounge that was attached to his bed-chamber. He sighed, drawing a weary hand down his face.

A long day, a lot of thinking, but still no decision made.

There was a knock at the door. He sighed again. "Yes?"

The door opened a crack, and Telemann poked his head around it. "Sorry to disturb you, sir. You've got a visitor."

"At this hour? Can't you put them off until morning?"

"A bit tricky as I'm stood right here," a booming masculine voice called out, muffled slightly by the door.

Telemann made an apologetic face. "Sorry. He was quite persuasive. It's your friend. From the docks." He frowned back over his shoulder at the unseen figure. "Said he had some urgent shipping news to discuss with you. Something about a voyage."

"It's all right, Telemann, let him in. Can you see if anyone's still about in the kitchens? If so, get them to send up a plate of something. Our friend enjoys his food, and I'll wager he's a little peckish at this time of night."

"You wager correctly, Belasko," called the voice, "which is why I'm not a gambler. Not without loading the odds in my favour, anyway."

"Very well. In you come, sir." Telemann opened the door fully and took a step back. "I'll see what the kitchen can rustle up."

As he disappeared from view, a barrel-chested man appeared in the doorway, dressed in the sober clothes of a dockworker. Long black curly hair tumbled down his back, a little silver at the temples. He dripped jewellery, ears and fingers festooned with rings, and cracked a broad smile.

"All right, Belasko? How are things?"

Belasko stood, going over to the man and gripping his hand. "I'll wager again that you already know how things are. They're a damn sight better for seeing you, I can tell you. Come in, pull up a chair."

The Water King grinned. "Don't mind if I do." He swaggered over to the chair across the fire from Belasko's and threw himself into it, leaning back and putting his booted feet up on a small table. Belasko went over to a decanter that stood on a table by the wall and poured a glass for his visitor, topping up his own in the process. He took the drink over to his guest, then retook his own chair with some relief. He did not bother to hide his limp.

The Water King raised his glass. "Your health," he said before taking a long swallow. "Ah," he said, grinning at Belasko, "you like that Centrian red I sent you, then?"

Belasko returned the grin with a smile of his own. "It's a fine wine. Your palette is, as ever, exceptional. I won't ask how you came by it."

"That's probably best. You'd not like the answer if it was

through dishonest means, and I'd not like to tell you if I came by it honestly. A man has a certain reputation to uphold, you know." The Water King pointed at Belasko. "Speaking of your health, how's the foot? I couldn't help but notice your limp seems worse."

Belasko sighed. "That's because it is." He shook his head. "The pain is constant, now, and only worsening with time. My other joints plague me. I won't be able to carry out my duties before long. I saw the Queen today, and she told me to find my successor, quickly."

"Good," said the Water King. "Oh, don't look at me like that. You know you should have picked your replacement long ago. You're a good man, but a stubborn one, with an over-developed sense of duty. Pick a successor and enjoy the life you've earned."

Belasko nodded. "You're right. Direct as always, too."

The Water King shrugged. "Just because I'm a criminal doesn't mean I'm dishonest. No time for dancing around the point in my game, or someone might stick something pointy in you while you're messing around with niceties."

Belasko downed the rest of his wine. "Enough of my woes. What can I do for you? What's this about a voyage?" He got up to refill his glass, bringing the decanter back to the fireside and topping up his guest's glass in the process.

The Water King nodded his thanks. "It's to do with what I believe brought you to the palace today. I understand you might be taking a little voyage? To a land where blood flows like water, and you're not well-liked?"

Belasko stared at him. "How do you know that?" He shook his head. "Never mind, I don't want to know. If you heard that, then presumably you know about the regime change in Bas?" The Water King nodded. "Of course you do —why did I bother asking?" Belasko sipped his wine. "The

The Swordsman's Descent

new Baskan King, Edyard—" The Water King raised an eyebrow. "Yes, that Edyard—has decided he wants to negotiate new accords with Villan, settle a lasting peace. Only, he wants to do it in Bas, and he wants me there. I am somewhat suspicious of his motives, although my memory of him is as an honourable man."

"I'd be suspicious, were I you." The Water King scratched the side of his nose with a long finger. "Are you going?"

Belasko shrugged. "I haven't decided yet. What's your interest in this?"

"Oh, I might just have some business to attend to in Bas. The sort of thing that requires the personal touch. They're not fond of people just wandering across their borders, though, Baskans, so I was hoping I might ask you for that favour. The one you owe me for helping you out with that business a few years ago."

Belasko sat for a moment, looking at his guest, who met his gaze with a bland one of his own. "I'll honour my word as I gave it then. As long as your actions will bring no harm to the Queen or the Villanese people, I'll return the favour you granted me. What is it you ask?"

"Oh, not much." The Water King swirled his wine around in its glass. "Just, if you go, that myself and several of my people travel with you disguised as your servants." He held up a finger. "I promise that we will cause no trouble and do all the tasks expected of us in the roles that we play."

Belasko frowned. "You're a smuggler. Why not just smuggle yourselves into the country?"

"A fair point. We could do, but it would be more time-consuming. Sometimes it's easier just to sneak in right under someone's nose."

"All right." Belasko pointed at the Water King. "If I do go

—*if*—then you and your people can accompany me. On one condition: that if things go sour, you help me get the Queen to safety. It's not that I don't trust the Baskan king, I just…"

"Don't trust Baskans generally? I can understand that, although I personally have found them not much different to deal with than your typical Villanese. A bit more direct, perhaps, but that suits me." The Water King grinned once more. "Now that's all agreed, let's get good and drunk."

"That sounds like a plan to me. Now, I'm trying to remember the topic of conversation the last time we saw each other." Belasko squinted at his guest.

The Water King sighed. "You were trying to trick some secrets of my past out of me, I believe."

Belasko laughed. "It's a fun game to play, when you have such a mysterious friend. I remember, you were telling me how you first entered into a life of crime. You said it was in your childhood, if I remember correctly."

"That's right. Ah well, when can you tell old stories if not with a glass of wine by the fireside." The Water King scratched the side of his nose with one finger. "Yes, I think I can tell this one without giving too much away."

Belasko leaned forwards. "Go on then, what was the start of your great criminal career."

The Water King, eyes distant as if he was lost in memory, rubbed his chin. "Smuggling ducks."

Belasko blinked. "What?"

The Water King sat up a little, grinning once again, and met his eyes. "That was it, smuggling ducks. You see, where I grew up the local landowner, who I worked for, had these incredibly expensive rare breed ducks. Notable for their colourful plumage. They were carefully guarded, although the occasional one was lost to a fox or other predator. Can you guess who had the care of these particular ducks?"

The Swordsman's Descent

"Hmm, was it you by any chance?"

"Yes, it was. Along with a friend of mine." The Water King nodded. "I haven't thought of him in years... Well, one day this friend of mine and I had an idea. These ducks were much more valuable than the others which the landowner possessed, a breed with plain white plumage. Some of which we to market fairly regularly. If we could line up a buyer, and smuggle out one of these rare breed ducks, we could earn ourselves a pretty penny. As long as we didn't get greedy we could make out they were killed by a predator."

"How did you do it?" Belasko had a faint smile on his face as he sat back in his chair, curiosity piqued and enjoying the Water King's storytelling.

"Ah, well, that part was fairly straightforward. One lot of ducks was colourful, one was white. The cages we took them to market in were fairly flimsy things, and the ducks were visible. We wagered that if we could disguise one of the rare breed ducks and hide it in the centre of the others, right in the middle of the wagon, then the landowner wouldn't notice."

Belasko frowned. "How do you disguise a duck?"

The Water King laughed. "In this instance, with something common to farm yards everywhere. Whitewash."

"You painted a duck."

"That we did." The Water King's ever ready grin lit up his face once more. "We painted them white, put their cage in the middle of the others, and prayed to the gods above and below that no one would notice."

Belasko grinned too, the Water King's humour infectious. "Did they?"

"Oh no, not at first. We carried out the duck smuggling operation successfully a few times, never too often or too close together as we didn't want the landowner getting

41

suspicious." He sighed. "Of course, like many juvenile criminal enterprises it was destined to fail."

"Oh no, what happened?" Belasko found himself leaning forward again, hanging on the Water King's words.

"One day, on the way to market, something unforeseen happened. It started..." The Water King paused, drawing out the moment. "It started... To rain."

Belasko caught on. "Oh. Oh no." His hand went to his mouth.

"Oh yes. It started to rain. And the whitewash, well it washed right off." The Water King's big laugh boomed out. "And there were we, caught red handed, looking as sad as painted ducks in the rain."

Belasko's took his hand away from his mouth. "What happened? What did the landowner do?"

The Water King shrugged. "He would have wanted us whipped, and dragged before the local elders. My friend and I had other ideas. The market that day was in a port town, we got away from the landowner while he was still gawping at his ducks and ran to the quay as quickly as we could." He smiled fondly. "We ran down to the nearest ship, that was just letting slip its moorings, and jumped aboard. Lucky we didn't end up in the drink. We were shouting for sanctuary, offering to work our passage, and the captain took pity on us. Said her crew had all needed a fresh start at one time, and took us on."

"That sounds like it must have been an exciting afternoon." It was Belasko's turn to grin. "What sort of ship was it?"

"Yes, yes it was a rather exciting moment. The ship? She turned out to be a smuggling vessel, her crew all pirates, and so our career really got going."

Belasko picked up the decanter and, leaning over,

topped up the Water King's glass and then his own. "What happened to your friend?" he asked.

The Water King sighed. "He took a cutlass in the guts a few years later, fighting off another crew. It has been a long time since I thought of him."

Belasko raised his glass. "Then here's to him, and all old friends."

The Water King raised his own glass, and they both drank deeply. After wiping the back of his hand across his mouth, The Water King looked at Belasko.

"One thing about this new venture we're embarking on together, Belasko."

"Oh yes, what's that?"

"Make sure my disguise is better than a whitewashed duck."

8

"REALLY, MAJESTY, I can understand the reasons for taking such a trip, although it seems foolhardy to me to venture so far into formerly hostile territory." Lord Beggeridge paused, peering at her, light glistening on his liver-spotted pate. "Far be it for me to second guess our monarch, of course. I only mean..."

Oh, yes, far be it for you to second guess me. So why do you do it so often then, my lord?

Queen Lilliana kept such thoughts to herself, her face blank and impassive as the elderly lord prattled on. She had agreed to see him in her study, although now she was beginning to regret it.

"...as you know, the other nobles look to me. Both as a senior member of their own number, and also as something of a, um, steady hand on the tiller these last few years. Guiding you as you found your way as our Queen. Which you most assuredly have! If you can help me better understand than perhaps I can win them around to your new mission, hmmm?"

If it wasn't for his seniority I wouldn't have to put up with the old dullard, or his insinuations. He'd never say outright that a young woman isn't fit to rule, though, because then I could dismiss him. Or have his head.

She smiled at the thought because it was so far from something she would do. Her smile seemed to unsettle Lord Beggeridge, and his speech temporarily slowed—until he hit on another subject to remonstrate with her about.

"The other thing that occurs to me: why on earth take the swordsman? What can he possibly bring to the negotiating table?"

Now Queen Lilliana's smile turned cold. "Firstly, my lord, because the new King of Bas has personally invited Belasko, so it would be rude not to extend that invitation and let him decide for himself if he will come. Secondly, that swordsman, as you put it, is still my Royal Champion. The monarch has historically been attended by their Champion when they travel. One never knows when one will need their services. When someone may overstep the mark, and one's honour need defending. As you just said, *you* would not second guess your monarch. Perhaps others need a more obvious reminder of who commands their allegiance and the possible consequences of disloyalty."

Lord Beggeridge blinked at that. "If Belasko is to attend in his role as Champion then perhaps he should have been attending to those duties here at the palace, instead of absenting himself from court these last few years."

The Queen leaned forward. "An absence that you advised, in the time after my father's death."

"Yes, well, it was necessary. With his part in that whole sordid affair, you needed to distance yourself from him, your majesty."

She nodded. "That's true. I did. And if he chose to stay away, can we blame him? There are some—I mention no names, of course, my lord—who have never made him feel welcome at court despite his many years' service to the crown. Why come back somewhere he feels he is not wanted when he has his academy to occupy his time? No, Belasko has served us well, and I will hear nothing more said on the matter. What other names are on the list? Who should we bring?"

"Ah, yes, let us see... Young Carlin, of course. He may seem a bit of a boorish sort, but his family have land along the Baskan border, and he's used to dealing with them. Lady Fenelia—she has a sharper grasp of figures than most and an eye for profit that would put a market stallholder to shame. Then there's..."

The elderly man rattled off a list of names, some of whom gladdened Queen Lilliana's heart. Most of whom did not. She sighed. *One cannot always keep the company one would like when one is Queen.*

It took her a moment to realise that Lord Beggeridge had stopped talking. She looked up at him to see a questioning look upon his face.

"Yes, my lord?"

"Are you well, your majesty? Only, you sighed a moment before. When I was reading out the names of those who might accompany you."

"Oh yes, my lord, I am well. I was only sighing because of a notable absence on that list: your good self. Surely you will be accompanying me to Bas?"

The elderly lord blinked. "Me, ma'am? To Bas?" He swallowed.

"Yes, of course. Where would I be without your sage counsel? You must come."

Lord Beggeridge blinked once again. "Yes, your majesty, of course. I'll start making preparations at once."

The Swordsman's Descent

"Very good. Please leave that list for me to look over. Parlin will see you out." Queen Lilliana pulled the cord that hung next to her desk. The little bell tinkled its song outside the door, which opened immediately. Lord Beggeridge, realising his audience was over, bowed deeply to his queen and left. The door closed again behind him, and Parlin crossed the floor on silent feet.

"Your majesty, is there anything I can get you?"

Queen Lilliana drew a weary hand across her eyes. "No, Parlin, unless it's a way to undo my invitation to that dull old windbag. He's going to bore me every step of the way to Bas, isn't he?"

Parlin chuckled. "That he may, ma'am. But he is well-versed in trade agreements, as you have impressed upon me on several occasions."

She sighed. "Yes, you're right. Beggeridge has forgotten more about trade deals and peace negotiations than most of us will ever know. In truth, I found his counsel astute and helpful in the period after my father's death. Now, though... I feel like I need to remind him that I'm not that young woman anymore. I know what I'm doing."

"That you do, your majesty. And you demonstrate that every day. Lord Beggeridge is old and set in his ways, but he is loyal. How do things go otherwise, ma'am? Is there anything I can help you with?"

Queen Lilliana lifted the golden circlet she wore so she could rub her brow. She held it up a moment. "Wear this for me?" She smiled. "No, all is well, thank you, Parlin. I will admit I am nervous about this upcoming trip. I said before that it will be the defining act of King Edyard's reign, to bring in a lasting peace between our nations. But it may well be the defining act of mine, too." Her face grew more sombre. "A great many lives may rest on us getting this right. I only hope that I am up to the task."

"I have every faith in you, your majesty. As do the rest of your subjects. If anyone can do this, you can."

"Thank you, Parlin. That will be all for the moment. I need to go over this list and start making decisions."

The red-haired secretary bowed and turned to go. He paused by the door. "And if I took the liberty of sending for a pot of tea for you, your majesty?"

She smiled once again. "Thank you, Parlin, that would be most welcome. You anticipate my desires before I know them myself."

He returned her smile. "That is what you pay me for, your majesty."

9

"THIS ISN'T WHAT you pay me for, boss."

The Water King grunted at Borne, the large man who normally watched the comings and goings of the crime lord's underground kingdom. He was broad of chest and of shoulder, tall, too, and immensely strong. But he was a gentle soul, so not much use as muscle in the Water King's criminal schemes. His love of reading meant he was happy to sit and watch secret entrances and exits for as long as he had his head in a book.

The big man shook his head, dun-coloured hair swaying in his eyes. "No, sir, I'm not sure about this."

The Water King leaned forward and tapped Borne on the crossed-sword insignia picked out on the chest of his new jerkin—the crossed swords that were Belasko's insignia as Royal Champion. The Water King had brought Borne to one of his safe houses in the city to try the new clothes on. It was a property he kept for emergencies, but it was little used. Sparsely furnished and a little run-down, it was the perfect out-of-the-way place for a clandestine meeting.

"Listen here, big lad. I pay you to do as I tell you. And

I'm telling you to put on this uniform and get to work in Belasko's household here in the city. He'll shortly be taking a trip, and we'll be going with him."

Borne raised an eyebrow. "We will, will we? How interesting. A trip where?"

"To Bas, if you must know. We're going to their capital. I have business there."

Borne perked up at this. "Oh, well, now that is interesting. Did you know that Albessar, the Baskan capital, has been the site of a city for over a thousand years? It predates the current kingdom of Bas by at least a millennium. In fact, I—"

"Yes, Borne, I did know that. I've been there before. Your knowledge is one of the reasons I'm bringing you. Don't make me regret it."

"No, boss, no fear of that. When do we leave?"

"Yeah, when do we leave?" The twin urchins, Nobody and No One, wandered into the sparsely furnished room. "When do we leave, and where are we going?"

The Water King sighed. He turned to them. "This is why I didn't want to say anything until we were all together. Right, for the first and last time, here is what is going on: we are going to Bas, disguised as members of Belasko's household. Borne is coming because of his encyclopaedic knowledge of, well, everything. You two—" He pointed a finger at them. "—are coming because I'm going to need runners and messengers. Appropriately sneaky ones. Can you be trusted to do as you're asked?"

"Oh, yeah, trustworthy. That's us." Nobody grinned, eyes twinkling under dark brows.

No One, as fair as Nobody was dark, had an equally mischievous grin. "Definitely trustworthy. What do we need to do?"

The Swordsman's Descent

The Water King held up a parcel of clothes in each hand. "First of all, I need you to put these on. See if they fit. Then we're going to present ourselves at Belasko's house. He's told them to expect some new staff." He threw the parcels to them, and they were deftly caught.

"Okay," said Nobody, "sounds good."

No One nodded. "What are we stealing, and when are we stealing it?"

The Water King rubbed his brow. "No, we're not stealing anything. At least not yet. We're going to Bas to see if we can come to an arrangement with my counterpart in the Baskan capital. Something mutually beneficial. We need our disguises to get into the country, so don't do anything to put our positions at risk. That means no stealing at Belasko's house and no stealing when we're on the road. Got it?"

The twins looked at each other. "No stealing," said No One.

"Playing at being humble servants," said Nobody. They both grinned.

"Could be fun," they said in unison.

"Why do I have a bad feeling about this?" the Water King muttered under his breath.

"No idea, your aquatic majesty," said Nobody. "Perhaps I could run milord a bath?"

"Or make him a pot of tea," said No One. "Nobles like that sort of thing, right? That's the sort of thing a good servant would do, right?"

"I'm going to need something stronger than tea if you pair carry on like this."

"Sorry, boss," said No One. "We're only messing. You can count on us."

"Yeah," said Nobody. "Just pulling your leg."

"How about you stop pulling legs and start pulling on

those clothes?" Borne's deep voice rumbled. "If I've got to put on this get-up, so have you."

"All right, big man, keep your hair on!" said Nobody.

"What happened? Someone lose your place in your book?" asked No One.

Borne sighed. "No, although I'll probably have to set that aside and concentrate on some more suitable literature. Get myself in the right frame of mind for a trip to Bas."

"You do that," said the Water King. "But before you go searching for the perfect tome, let me tell you who we are. I've got the identities all worked out. So you, Borne, are..."

As he laid out who they were to be for the next few weeks, possibly months, his people paid attention. For all the joking around, they were very good at what they did and were totally loyal.

10

AMBASSADOR AVEYARD LOOKED at the man who sat across from her—Jonteer, her secretary and almost certainly a member of the Baskan intelligence service. She'd never been able to catch the balding, closed-faced man out. He played his role as her secretary to perfection, but she knew he had another master.

They were in her study at the Baskan embassy, discussing the arrangements for their journey.

"It was good of the King to call you home. Do you think your uncle has a different role lined up for you?" Jonteer's eyes gave nothing away as he probed with questions.

It's a good thing that I know he's loyal to Bas, if not whoever happens to sit on the throne at any given moment.

She shrugged. "I don't know what my uncle's thinking or what his plans are. But it will be good to see home, even if it will be for only a short while."

Jonteer smiled, and for once, it seemed to reach his eyes. "That it will. It's been a long time since I've been home. You too, Ambassador."

"That's right. You're from Albessar originally, aren't you,

Jonteer? I'd almost forgotten that. You must be looking forward to getting back. Do you have any friends or family you might catch up with while we're there?"

Just like that, his expression was once again unreadable. "None that I'm planning to see, Ambassador, but you never know who you might bump into."

"That is true. One can only hope it is an old friend you care for deeply, rather than someone you owe money to. Now, I think that's mostly organised, isn't it? We'll take a few of the soldiers stationed at the embassy with us, some diplomatic staff, and servants, too. Are we missing anything?"

Jonteer shook his head. "Not that I can think of, but if anything occurs, I shall let you know." He paused. "I have been wondering, do you know who will be in the Queen's party?"

Ambassador Aveyard shrugged. "I don't know for certain. There'll be a number of soldiers, of course, various staff and hangers-on. Some of the more senior courtiers and advisers to assist with the negotiations... Oh, and Belasko. If he decides to come."

Jonteer blinked. "Belasko?"

"Yes, didn't I say? My uncle invited him personally. Something to do with uniting figures from the Last War to lend weight to the negotiations and help to put the past behind us. He sees Belasko as part of that process."

"That is interesting. I hadn't thought of that." Jonteer rubbed his chin. "Yes, interesting."

Ambassador Aveyard leaned back in her chair. "Is it? A bunch of tired old warhorses clapping themselves on the back and discussing their old feats of valour? I can think of a few words to describe it. Interesting might not be one of them."

"No. He isn't well-liked in Bas. He knows this, yes? He's

likely to receive challenges. If something were to happen to him, it might upset the talks. I believe Queen Lilliana is supposed to be fond of the old swordsman."

Ambassador Aveyard shrugged. "Perhaps, although they're not as close as they once were."

"Be that as it may, there is much to ponder."

"Then please, feel free to ponder it. Meanwhile—" She gestured at her desk and the abundance of paperwork thereon. "—I have much to occupy my time."

Jonteer nodded. "Yes, Madame Ambassador. One thing, before I go. It might be advisable if I keep a low profile on the journey, stay out of the way of the Villanese. My visit to the palace the day Prince Kellan was killed caused some difficulty previously, although Belasko's unveiling of the person responsible cleared my name. Best not to remind the Villanese of those past tensions, as we're looking to build a peaceful future. Now," he pushed back his chair and stood, "I shall get on with my own duties. With your permission?"

"Of course, don't let me keep you."

Jonteer snapped off a crisp salute, which Ambassador Aveyard returned in a more relaxed fashion, and left the room. The ambassador watched the door close behind him. *Now, what is going on in that head of yours, Jonteer? Sometimes I wish I knew.*

11

IT WAS SEVERAL weeks later that Belasko and the people he had chosen to accompany him were surrounded by the hustle and bustle of a royal progress getting underway in one of the palace's largest courtyards.

You can only rush a royal trip so much, and even so, some of Queen Lilliana's courtiers were sniffy at what to them seemed undue haste. In truth, it had been organised with military efficiency in order to make it over the mountains and back before the winter snows made them impassable.

The Queen's carriage stood in the centre of the courtyard, the calm at the eye of the storm. Stationary, horses waited patiently in their traces, while all around them made ready.

The courtiers and their baggage would travel at the centre of their train, the Queen's personal guard, and then the accompanying division of the palace guard arranged around them. They would pick up their accompanying military escorts on the way to Bas. One of the only pillars of the Villanese state not represented was the Inquisition.

The Swordsman's Descent

They had fallen far from favour after it emerged that one of their own had been involved with the poisoning of Prince Kellan.

Belasko was talking with Byrta and Majel as the horses were readied and the final checks undertaken. "I'd watch the spacing out on the road," he said to Majel. "It's been a while since the guard have been out on manoeuvres. They may tend to stand too close to each other, hampering their movements should we need to form up."

Majel sniffed. "Thank you for the unasked-for suggestion, Belasko. A reminder to you, though. You've been long absent at court. Your position as Royal Champion carries weight, and the fondness I have for you adds to that, but none here are required to obey your orders—other than your staff, that is. I command these troops. Don't undermine that. You've been at your academy too long. You're used to people carrying out your wishes." A junior officer caught Majel's eye, beckoning her over to observe something. "I need to attend to my duties—I know you can see to yourselves. I'll check in with you when we halt for lunch." With that, she left to see to her tasks, entering into animated conversation with the officer that had called her over. Belasko watched her go.

"What shat in her breakfast?" asked Byrta.

Belasko shook his head. "No, she's right. I'm used to dealing with her in private, informally. Where we're friends. Here, she is the commanding officer, and I need to treat her accordingly. Remind me to ask if my opinion is welcome next time before I offer it."

She snorted. "Okay, I'll do just that. Although getting you to pause before offering an opinion is about as futile an endeavour as I can think of." Byrta watched as Belasko started checking the straps of his saddle one last time.

"What made you choose this course? Going with the Queen to Bas?"

He sighed, tightening a strap slightly before turning back to her. "The sooner we get this journey over and done with, the quicker I choose my successor. I can rid myself of court life and return to my work at the Academy. That's all."

"Court life isn't so bad, is it? Good food, excellent wine, nice accommodation... The Queen asked you to advise her. You and she are fond of each other, are you not?"

"The Queen is dear to me. I do have some friends here. It's just that..." Belasko shook his head. "Politics. You can't be at court without being mired in it, and politics is about as pleasant as wrestling pigs in hip-deep excrement. I grew up on a farm, remember, so when I say that, you know what I'm talking about." He pointed a finger at her. "That's the other thing: most of the lords and ladies can't stand the fact I'm a commoner and waste no time in reminding me of the fact."

"Don't look now, but I think one of those lords is coming over here... I don't think you'll mind this one, though." A broad grin spread across Byrta's face. "Anerin, you old bastard, come here and give us a hug."

She launched herself at a finely dressed member of the nobility who was walking up behind Belasko and grabbed him in a fierce embrace. The newcomer's fine clothing was at odds with his coarse features, made coarser by the ruddy complexion and bulbous nose of the seasoned drinker. He winced at "bastard" but returned Byrta's embrace. "Careful with words like that around us nobles, Byrta, you old she-devil. We tend to be rather sensitive about issues of legitimacy."

"She-devil I'll accept, but old?" Byrta held him out at arm's length. "I should challenge you for that."

Anerin laughed. "Please don't. I think I'm still sore from

the last drubbing you gave me in the training circle, under Markus's tutelage all those years back. What is it now, twenty years ago? Anyway, you haven't aged a day. You're looking well, too, Belasko."

Byrta released Anerin, and he stepped towards Belasko. They clasped hands, wrist to wrist in the warrior's grip, then pulled each other into a tight embrace.

"It's good to see you," said Belasko. "What are you doing here? I thought you were still travelling the world, acting as a trade envoy for your family's interests."

Anerin stood back then. It was in truth a long time since the three old friends had been together, but Belasko knew him well enough to pick up an undercurrent of sadness to his friend's mood.

"You haven't heard then?" Anerin asked. "Why would you have? You're hardly at court." He sighed. "My older brother died, childless, so I'm now head of the family. I've come back to Villan to take on my duties and—" He mock-shuddered. "—*responsibilities*. It's a revolting development, but what can you do when duty comes calling?"

"Run in the opposite direction?" offered Byrta.

Anerin gave her a wry smile. "I was tempted, believe me."

"In all seriousness, Anerin, I'm sorry for your loss," said Byrta.

"Me too, Anerin. I'm sorry." Belasko reached out and put a hand on his shoulder.

Anerin snorted. "Don't be. My brother and I weren't overly fond of each other." He smiled ruefully. "Still, it'll be good to see more of you two."

"You're coming on this little trip then?" Belasko asked.

"Oh, yes. I've had dealings with the Baskans before over trading relationships, that sort of thing, so the Queen asked me to accompany her as part of the delegation. We'll see how that goes."

"It's good to see you, Anerin," said Byrta. "I need to see to my horse, make sure some idiot hasn't loosened my saddle. Catch up with you later?"

"Please," said Anerin. "I'd like that." He leaned in towards Belasko as Byrta went in search of her mount. "Belasko, why don't you call by my tent when we've stopped for the night? We can catch up over a glass of wine."

"I'd like that," Belasko said, smiling. "It's been too long."

Anerin returned his smile. "Later then." He clapped Belasko on the shoulder, then turned and started walking back to his own party. "No, no," he called out to someone. "That doesn't go on the wagon. It's fragile. Put that with my personal things. What back alley molly house did I find you in? Honestly, you can't get the staff these days..." His voice drifted off, lost in the clamour and calls of a sizeable number of people getting underway.

12

SO IT WAS that night, after their group had come to a halt, set up camp, and had their evening meal, that Belasko paid Anerin a visit at his tent.

A servant was stationed at the entrance, wrapped up in a thick woollen cloak. They took Belasko's name and disappeared inside, barely rustling the tent flap. It was an impressive tent, large and brightly coloured. *Only the Queen's is larger*, Belasko thought to himself.

The servant reappeared, ushering him in. "He'll see you now. Quickly, don't let the heat out."

Belasko slipped inside, the servant exiting and smoothly fastening the tent flap in one quick movement.

"He's well-practised at that," Belasko remarked to a seemingly empty tent.

"We spend a lot of time on the road. Well, we did." Anerin's voice, muffled slightly, came from behind a screen.

The tent really was large, sectioned off into separate areas by screens of patterned silk stretched over wooden frames. There were several braziers about the place, warming the tent up nicely.

"He was right not to want to let the heat out. It's lovely and warm in here."

Anerin appeared from behind one of the silken screens, dressed in a simple robe, a decanter in one hand and two glasses held loosely in the other. "When you spend as much time travelling as I have, you learn to make yourself as comfortable as you can afford."

"Yes, and you can afford a lot. I'd forgotten how wealthy your family is." Belasko traced the pattern on one of the silk screens with an index finger. "I thought outside that only the Queen's tent is larger. And only slightly better appointed, I think."

"That's by design, not accident. I couldn't very well go around upstaging our beloved monarch, now, could I? Here." Anerin gestured to a table and two chairs set up by one of the braziers. "This is as comfortable as I can make us." He placed the glasses on the table, pouring them each some wine from the decanter. "Please, sit."

Belasko did so, accepting the offered glass of wine. "Thank you. How are you? It's been a long time. I must admit, I'm surprised to see you on this venture. I hadn't heard about your brother. Thought you were off travelling the length and breadth of the known world."

"I have been, these last few years—the known world and some of the hazy bits around the edges. Developing my family's trading relationships, sometimes acting as an unofficial ambassador for the crown. Doing my bit to further Villan's interests as well as my own. Until my brother had to go and ruin everything by dying."

Belasko leaned over and touched the back of Anerin's hand. "I am sorry, Anerin."

His friend gave a bitter laugh. "Don't be. We really didn't get on. My brother didn't approve of my 'lifestyle', as he called it. I didn't approve of him stuffing his face every chance he got. Well, the fat fool ate himself into an early grave, so here we are. I'd not been back in the city long when the Queen asked me to come along on this trip. She seems to think my experience of dealing with Baskans in trade might be of some assistance."

"I'm sure she's right. She usually is. A mind sharp as a razor, our Queen. Sometimes as cutting, too." Belasko sipped his wine. "Anyway, I'd love to hear some stories of your travels. I haven't been far from my academy these last few years."

"So I've heard." Anerin scratched his chin. "I really must come for a tour. When we get back. I'd love to see what you've built. I've heard that it's really quite something. Before I start spinning yarns, lying furiously to make trade talks and negotiations sound interesting, I need to offer my condolences to you, too, Belasko. I heard about Orren's death. I know what he meant to you."

Belasko avoided Anerin's eye, playing with the stem of his glass. "Thank you. I know it's been four years, but the wound still feels fresh."

"The loss of a loved one never truly heals, I think. We just come to bear the pain. With time it becomes bittersweet, our happier memories tinged with sadness. I'm just sorry I didn't write to you at the time. The news was months old by the time it caught up to me, and I had thought I'd see you in person long before now." Anerin raised his glass. "To Orren, and all those we've loved and lost."

Belasko silently joined him in the toast. They sat for a moment in companionable silence before Belasko broke it. He cleared his throat. "So, what does your future hold, now that you've returned home? You must have a lot of responsibilities as head of the family."

Anerin snorted. "My younger sister is intent on marrying me off. Finding some suitable young woman to help me produce my own heir. She knows she's barking up the wrong tree on that front, but she is rather insistent."

"What do you plan to do?"

"Live long enough to make good on the trade deals I've made. I've no intention of getting married or producing offspring—I'd have stood aside for my sister if her husband wasn't a grasping little toad. No, I intend to be as positive an influence on her children as I can until they're old enough not to be under their father's sway and can help their mother. Then I might stand aside. Pack myself off to a little cottage in the countryside where I can host my pick of confirmed bachelors. Somewhere on one of our vineyards would be nice. Plenty of wine on hand."

Belasko smiled. "That sounds nice. Your family, however, sound, um, interesting."

"It's the way of things for the nobility." Anerin shrugged. "We rarely marry for love, but for power, position, or politics. It's possible to grow up barely knowing your siblings, or your parents, as you're raised by various servants and educated separately."

"Sounds lonely."

"It can be." Anerin gestured at the surrounding opulence. "The fabulous wealth helps, but it's a hollow thing."

"Money can't buy happiness, or so they say."

"Yes, I've heard. It can, however, afford you a better class of misery." Anerin raised his glass again. "Cheers to that." He took a long swallow of wine, then topped up both their glasses. "This became maudlin rather quickly. How about you, Belasko? What does the future hold for you?"

Belasko smiled at him. "Not much cheerier, I'm afraid.

The Swordsman's Descent

Queen Lilliana has asked me to find my successor, and soon. I'm getting older, slower. Part of my reason for coming on this trip was to help speed that process. The sooner it's done, the sooner I can retire from court life completely and concentrate all my time on the Academy."

"I see. At least that would mean the opportunity to put down the heavy burden of your duty. Have you..." Anerin coughed delicately. "Had any romantic entanglements?"

Belasko snorted. "No. A few assignations with people met at certain, um, taverns in the city. You know the sort of places I mean, where you're free to be yourself. But no romance, no lasting relationships. You know why, too. A duellist can't allow that. It's what Markus told me long ago. Death is a possibility for a soldier; for a duellist it's an inevitability. In the end. I'd rather not leave someone behind to suffer the grief when a faster, better opponent eventually comes along. Besides, I've been consumed by my work."

"Oh yes, I know the sort of places you're alluding to." Anerin chuckled. "Where all are welcome, nobody judges who you might go home with at the end of the night, and all keep each others' secrets. I was surprised when I got back to the city to see those particular venues being more open. More public. Much has changed since the queen took to the throne and progress marches on apace. Which is most welcome. Perhaps one day, soon, we nobles may live as openly as others already seem to. Yet old prejudices and traditions are slow to fall away." He paused in a moment of reflection and looked to Belasko as if he was about to say something else. Then he shook his head, and carried on. "But I digress, and feel the need to point out two holes in your logic." Anerin put down his glass and ticked off the points on his fingers. "One, death is an inevitability for us all, in the end. A duellist's profession may hasten theirs, it's true, but that's all. Two, if you are soon to retire, then surely those restrictions won't hold true?"

Belasko gave him a sad smile. "You know as well as I that a duellist never really retires. There will always come challenges, and opponents who won't take 'no' for an answer. You remember what happened to Markus after he retired as Royal Champion, don't you?"

"I do. You tracked down the person who killed him and cut them to pieces, didn't you?"

Belasko nodded. "Markus had earned his peace after years of service to the crown. I took his death rather personally."

"Understandable. But here's the thing." Anerin leaned forward. "You are not Markus. You've more than earned your peace, and you've years yet to live that need not be weighed down by duty."

Belasko smiled sadly. "Would that were true. However, speaking of duty, I must go. We'll need to be up at first light to help get things underway."

"Of course. Call on me again, won't you? You're welcome anytime."

They both stood, and Anerin walked Belasko to the tent's entrance.

"Likewise," said Belasko. "My accommodation isn't so fine, but the wine's good. I'll aim for more cheerful conversation next time. Good night, Anerin. It really is good to see you again."

"You too, Belasko. Good night." The aristocrat pulled Belasko into an embrace, which he returned warmly. Belasko felt his heart begin to race as they held each other for what seemed longer than was strictly necessary, and a flush came to his face that was not just from the wine. He cleared his throat and broke the contact, turning to open the tent flap.

"Bye, see you tomorrow," he said over his shoulder. With a rustle of canvas, he was gone.

Anerin went back to the table and refilled his glass. He knocked it back quickly, then poured himself another.

13

"EXCUSE ME, SIR?"

Belasko looked up from his breakfast. It was early the following morning, and the camp was getting ready to move. He could have taken his morning meal in his tent, but he preferred to eat with Byrta and his staff, and so they had gathered around a communal cook fire as dawn broke. There was a lot of ground to cover and not much time, so it would be early starts from here on out.

Belasko swallowed his mouthful of porridge. Standing just outside the group was the young Baskan who had challenged him the day he had received the Queen's summons. He was now dressed in the military uniform of the Baskan diplomatic corps.

What was his name? Olbarin, that's it.

"Good morning Olbarin, how are you? Please, come closer. Don't make me shout this early in the morning."

Flushing, the young man came forward. The rest of Belasko's retinue made room for him until he stood next to Belasko, who was perched on a low stool.

The Swordsman's Descent

"Come on, lad, drop down a bit. You'll put a crick in my neck."

Olbarin lowered himself until he was crouched, sitting back on his heels.

"That's better. Now, what can I do for you?"

The young Baskan started. "Oh, no. You've already done so much for me. That's why I'm here, to say thank you."

Belasko shook his head. "For what? There's no need."

The younger man seemed hesitant, a little shy—not the firebrand that had knocked on Belasko's door demanding vengeance.

"The letter of recommendation you wrote for me. To Ambassador Aveyard? She's taken me onto her staff, reinstated my commission, and brought me into the diplomatic corps as a Lieutenant." He flushed again. "Not quite what I imagined would come of my trip to Villan, but I warrant it will make my mother happy."

"As what you imagined was a foot of steel in my guts or your own death in the attempt, I'm very happy to have disappointed you." Belasko set down his now empty bowl and picked up a wooden cup full of tea. "I'm also glad if it brings your mother happiness, as I wager from what you told me that I have been the cause of much unhappiness in her life. And your own."

A sad look crossed Olbarin's face. "My father was a soldier. He knew the risks." He looked away, visibly struggling with emotion. "He may have died by your hand all those years ago, but blaming you, seeking revenge, was foolish. You were both soldiers in a war not of your making, following your orders." Olbarin looked back at Belasko. "There's an old saying among my people: 'you may as well hold on to a burning coal as try to hold on to hatred; you'll harm only yourself'. It's time I let my anger go." He held out a hand. "Thank you, Belasko."

The older man clasped his hand and shook it firmly. "You're welcome, Olbarin. The uniform suits you. I hope the work does, too."

When the Baskan made no move to leave, Belasko asked, "Is there something else I can do for you?"

A sheepish look crossed Olbarin's face. "I'm hesitant to ask, but I was wondering..." He trailed off.

"Yes, lad? Out with it."

Olbarin cleared his throat. "I was wondering if I might train with you? Just while we're travelling."

The hubbub around the cook fire died down. Everyone was now looking at the two men.

Belasko blinked, more than a little surprised. "You'd like to train with me? That's not... I mean, the express purpose of my academy is to strengthen the Villanese military. We've had visiting instructors before, but our students have always been Villanese. Why do you want to train with us?"

Olbarin looked down at his hands. "I've always thought of myself as a good swordsman, but you took me down in moments. It was, um, embarrassing, to be honest." He held out his hands, palms out. "I know it's an odd request, but it would just be while we travelled. I clearly have a lot more to learn than I thought."

Belasko looked at the faces around the campfire. Most were unreadable, but he could see surprise, disgust, even anger on some features—apart from Byrta, who looked faintly amused. The Water King, in his guise as one of Belasko's servants, had a speculative expression on his face.

"It's definitely irregular. Let me think about it. I'll come find you later. I'll give you an answer then. Is that all right?"

Olbarin nodded. "Of course." He stood to leave. "Thank

The Swordsman's Descent

you, sir. I hope the day's travel is pleasant for you." He nodded to the rest of the group. "Good day, all." With that, he turned and left, disappearing into the crowd.

Conversation immediately sprung back into life. Belasko shook his head, disbelieving. "What do you make of that?" he called across the circle to Byrta.

She shrugged, grinning. "Why not? Go on. It'll be good for a laugh. This whole trip's about forming closer ties with the Baskans, right?"

"I'm not sure this is what the Queen has in mind."

Byrta shrugged again. "So ask her, see what she thinks. One silver crown says she encourages it."

Belasko nodded. "You know, I think I'll do just that. I'll go see her now." He drained his cup of tea, stood, and headed off into the bustling camp.

14

BELASKO MADE HIS way to the royal area of the encampment. Parlin, was stationed in a little antechamber to the Queen's tent. Belasko smiled at the sight of him, working at a battered folding desk, the mirror of his usual position outside the Queen's study.

Parlin looked up as Belasko entered. He smiled. "Hello, sir, how are you finding our little jaunt so far?"

"It's been a while since I spent this many hours on horseback. A fact my back was loudly reminding me of yesterday, and my backside joined its remonstrations this morning. Is she free? I have something I'd like to ask her."

Parlin nodded, scanning the diary open in front of him. "No appointments in the book. I know her majesty is alone just now. I'll check, but I'm sure she'll be happy to see you." He got up and walked to the entrance to the main tent, ringing a little bell that hung from the ceiling. A muffled call came from within, and Parlin opened the way far enough to admit his head. After a few words were exchanged, he opened the tent flap all the way and stood to one side.

"Her majesty will see you now."

Belasko went to walk in. As he passed, Parlin put a hand to his shoulder. "Please don't keep her too long," he whispered. "We'll need to get underway soon. All this takes quite a long time to break down and stow away—if I can persuade her majesty to pause in her own work long enough to let the staff do their jobs."

Belasko smiled. "That's our queen. I promise not to be too long." He patted Parlin's hand and went in.

It was a fabulously appointed tent. Similarly to Anerin's, silk screens stretched over wooden frames divided up the space. Everything was larger, though. Grander, made of more expensive materials. Belasko could appreciate how carefully Anerin had pitched his tent, as it were, making sure he displayed opulent wealth but in no way overshadowing the monarch.

The Queen was sat at a table of finely polished wood, her breakfast things to one side. She was dressed for travelling in a panelled riding skirt. Queen Lilliana looked up from a book she was reading and smiled to see Belasko. "Dear Belasko, how are you this morning?"

He offered her a bow. "I'm well, your majesty. All the better for seeing you."

She laughed. "Flatterer. Please." She gestured to a chair across the table from her. "Join me. Parlin said you had something to ask me. What can I do for you?"

"Thank you, ma'am." Belasko eased his aching body into the seat. "I've had a request this morning which I'd like your opinion on, if I may."

Queen Lilliana smiled. "Of course. What's the matter at hand?"

Belasko put his hands together on the table in front of him, taking in the scars from nicks and cuts of blade work, earned in battle and training. The callouses and rough skin bestowed by many hours of hard work. He looked back up at the Queen.

"The day you brought me to the palace to discuss this trip we're now on—the Baskan situation, all of that. I had a challenge that morning from a young Baskan man, name of Olbarin."

The Queen nodded. "Yes, I've heard."

"Then you've no doubt heard as well that he came seeking vengeance for his father, slain by my hand at Dellan Pass. I defeated the lad easily enough but something about him..." Belasko shook his head. "Perhaps I was in an overly contemplative mood that day, or I felt guilty for my part in his father's death. For whatever reason, I sensed some promise in the boy. Or perhaps I just felt sorry for him. So, after I'd sent him to the infirmary I penned a note of recommendation for him to Ambassador Aveyard and sent him on his way with it in his pocket."

The Queen nodded. "Yes, I'm following so far." She lifted a crystal decanter. "Apple juice?"

"Thank you, please, ma'am."

Queen Lilliana poured them both a glass, passing one to Belasko. "So, what happened next that brings you to me this morning?"

Belasko lifted his glass to the Queen. "Your health, ma'am." He took a sip. The juice was delicious. Cool and sweet but slightly tart. "I didn't think anything more of it until this morning. The young man presented himself at my campfire this morning. Dressed in Baskan uniform. The Ambassador has taken him onto her staff."

"That's good, isn't it? You wanted to do the man a kindness, and it looks like it worked out." The Queen took a delicate sip of her apple juice. She sighed. "I really must write to the keeper of the royal orchards. The new varieties they've grown are showing much promise." She looked back at Belasko. "Sorry, go on."

"While I'm pleased that things have worked out for him, it's what Olbarin came to ask that has thrown me somewhat."

"Which is?" The Queen arched an eyebrow.

"Sorry, I'll get to the point. He's asked to train with me while we travel."

"Ah. I see." Queen Lilliana's brow furrowed in thought. "Yes, I can see how that might present some difficulties."

"Some?" Belasko shook his head. He leaned back in his chair, drumming his fingers on the table. "My academy was founded to further Villanese martial prowess, to develop the skills of our military. Not to help those of another country. I'm not sure what to do."

The Queen also sat back in her chair. She tapped a delicate finger against her chin. "We are no longer at war with the Baskans. This trip is meant to ensure that we never find ourselves in that position again. Denying his request isn't the best way to start that off."

"I know," said Belasko. "I can't help but wonder if the Ambassador has a hand in this—if it's one of her schemes." He lifted up a hand as if to ward off what the Queen might say next. "I know, I know, but Aveyard has a mind like a trap and is always plotting, as much as she claims to hate politics. Wheels within wheels, schemes within schemes—what if this is a plan of hers?"

"To what end?" The Queen shook her head. "No. I can't see what she would gain from this, other than an insight into your training methods. I think we have to accept, or at least act as if we accept, that the young man's request is genuine."

Belasko sighed. "Then I still don't know what to do.

Shall I take him on for this trip? We may no longer be at war with his people, but memories run long. Not just mine. Some of the soldiers that accompany us may be too young to remember the war personally, but a number will have fought in it. We all lost friends, loved ones, in that war." He drained the rest of his juice, wiping the back of his hand across his lips. "Also, his desire for revenge drove him to travel all the way to my gates, thirsting for my blood. I defeated him easily, no doubt denting his pride. Are we supposed to believe he set all that aside in a matter of days?"

"Perhaps not. Or perhaps he realised that the thing he sought was not what he expected it to be. That you are not the person he imagined. Or perhaps he wants to learn from you so he can challenge you again." The Queen leaned forward. "You're a good judge of character. Do you detect anything underhand in him?"

Belasko shook his head. "No. My instinct tells me he's an honest young man who wants to improve his skills."

"Then treat him as such. Teach him, get to know him. Maybe it will help you put to rest some of your own feelings hungover from the war. Treat him as you would wish to be treated in his place."

"Right. Then that is what I shall do. Thank you, your majesty. If I have your permission to depart?"

The Queen nodded. Belasko stood, bowed to her, and headed for the tent flap.

"Where are you going next?" asked the queen.

"To see Ambassador Aveyard. A member of her staff will need to be excused his duties twice a day, so I'd best ask her permission first."

"One thing, Belasko," said the Queen.

He turned back towards her. "Yes, your majesty?"

Queen Lilliana tapped a forefinger on her pursed lips.

"It occurs to me that there is an opportunity here. Why not run training sessions for our own troops? We can see who's interested, come up with some sort of rota, so people can take their turn and not miss too many duties. What do you think?"

Belasko smiled. "An excellent idea, your majesty."

Belasko left the Queen's tent, nodded to Parlin, and made his way over to the Baskan portion of the camp.

All about him, people were scurrying about, getting things packed up and stowed away, readying themselves for the day's travel. The camp was like a hornet's nest, buzzing with activity.

He quickly found himself by the Baskan lines, receiving some odd looks as he gained admittance from the guards they had posted. He found the ambassador outside her tent, inspecting her horse and preparing for travel. Her secretary, a thin, balding man, went over to her, whispering something. She looked up, surprise on her normally passive features. Her expression quickly settled back into its usual neutral state. She passed her horse's reins to a member of staff and walked over to Belasko.

"You are the last person I expected to see this morning. What can I do for you?"

He smiled at her. "It's about what I can do for one of your staff. Olbarin, his name is."

Something flickered across her face too quickly for Belasko to register it. "Oh? What about him?"

"I was as surprised as you are now when he visited my campfire earlier. He had a request to train with me while we all travel together." A look of irritation made its way onto Ambassador Aveyard's face and settled there. "Did you know about this?" Belasko asked.

"No, I did not." She turned to her secretary. "Jonteer, can

you please fetch Lieutenant Olbarin?" He nodded and disappeared among the tents. Ambassador Aveyard turned back to Belasko. "That was bold of him, I must say."

"Yes, I thought so. After some thought, I have decided to accept his request. I've come to ask he be relieved of his duties at first light and again after we have stopped for the day, so that he might train with us. The Queen has suggested I take this as an opportunity to run training sessions for our soldiers as well."

Ambassador Aveyard made no attempt to hide her surprise, her eyebrows climbing up her forehead. "That is not the reaction I would have expected."

Belasko grinned at her. "I'm glad I can surprise you from time you time. Or perhaps you don't know me as well as you'd like to think."

Jonteer returned, Olbarin following him with a sheepish expression on his face.

Ambassador Aveyard pointed to the ground between her and Belasko. "Lieutenant, come here. Stand to attention."

The young man did as she asked, coming to a perfect parade ground halt. Arms by his sides, heel stamping into the mud, he peered into the distance and rattled off a crisp salute. "Ma'am, yes, ma'am."

Ambassador Aveyard pointed at Belasko. "Queen Lilliana's Champion here informs me that you sought him out this morning, not to challenge him as you have previously, but to request that you be allowed to train with him. Is this correct?"

Olbarin kept his eyes forwards, face expressionless. "Ma'am, yes, ma'am."

She walked back and forth in front of him, hands clasped behind her back. "It's interesting that you, so new in

The Swordsman's Descent

my service, wouldn't seek my permission before doing such a thing. Why is that?"

Olbarin swallowed. "Didn't think he'd say yes, ma'am."

"Well, luckily or unluckily for you, he has. Belasko here has come to ask that you be relieved of your duties twice a day while we travel to Bas, so that you may train with him and his students. What do you think of that?"

Olbarin's eyes widened, flickering over to Belasko's face, before resuming their study of the horizon. "Quite surprised, ma'am, to be honest."

Ambassador Aveyard laughed. "I like you, boy, you're bold. You'd better be hard working as well, as I'm going to grant Belasko his request. To make up for missing your duties twice a day, you will be taking on additional responsibilities the rest of the time. Does that sound fair to you?"

Olbarin swallowed. "Yes, ma'am. More than fair."

"I'm delighted you're pleased by my magnanimous nature. Now, go back to your work while I think of something particularly unpleasant for you to do in recompense for throwing my morning off course."

"Yes, ma'am." Olbarin saluted Ambassador Aveyard, then marched off to resume whatever he had been doing.

The ambassador turned back to Belasko. "There you go, you have a new student. Temporarily." A quizzical look played across her face. "What are you up to, Belasko?"

He laughed. "Damned if I know, Madame Ambassador. Just trying to get through the day."

"Yes, aren't we all?" she muttered. "Now, if you don't mind..." She gestured at the bustling camp around her.

"Of course, lots to do."

Ambassador Aveyard sighed. "Too much, and no rest this side of death."

15

MAJEL WASN'T SURPRISED when Parlin rode up to speak to her. He often acted as a go-between to the Captain of the Queen's personal guard, bringing her messages and instructions from Queen Lilliana. This time, the request was to drop back and ride alongside the Queen.

"Any idea what she wants to talk about?" she asked the Queen's secretary.

Parlin shrugged. "Her majesty didn't take me into her confidence on this occasion."

Majel snorted. "You could have just said 'no'. No need to be so formal."

"Sorry. Shall we?"

Majel nodded, and they turned their horses, peeling away from the column and riding back down its length towards the Queen. Queen Lilliana smiled and waved at Majel as she approached, indicating for the captain to fall in alongside her.

"Thank you, Parlin," she called to her secretary as he took up a discrete position a short distance away, where he could not easily overhear their conversation. He nodded and smiled in reply.

"How are you this morning, your majesty?"

Queen Lilliana let out a breath. "All the better for getting away from palace life for a bit. This fresh air is bracing, isn't it?"

Majel smiled. "If it's 'bracing' you're after, wait until we're up in the mountains. Once winter sets in, the air's bracing enough to freeze in your lungs if you're not careful."

The Queen gave Majel a smile of her own. "I'm sure you're exaggerating, if only slightly."

"Your majesty knows me only too well." Majel's expression was deadpan. "What can I do for you this morning?"

"I had a visit from Belasko earlier about something odd that happened, and I'd like your opinion."

"Of course, ma'am, whatever I can do to help. What happened?"

So, Queen Lilliana told Majel how Olbarin had approached Belasko for training and that she had given her permission given the nature of their mission. "What do you think?" she asked her captain. "Did I do the right thing?"

Majel nodded slowly, considering. "I think so, ma'am. Given the nature of our trip, it seems hard to say 'no' as we're trying to improve relations with the Baskans. What if it's a ploy, though? I sense Aveyard's hand in this. What if the boy, Olbarin, is acting under her command? Trying to get close to Belasko, and by extension you? Eavesdropping on things he shouldn't? It is a concern."

Queen Lilliana smiled. "Then we are agreed. It was the right thing to do, but there are some concerns. I'm glad. What do you think we should do to combat those concerns?"

Majel shrugged. "I'd suggest setting someone inside

Belasko's training sessions to watch Olbarin. Not obviously, but just to keep an eye on him. Make sure he's not getting into things he shouldn't."

"Then we are agreed again. I'm so glad. I was hoping you would be my observer—join Belasko's training sessions, keep an eye on things?" The Queen frowned as Majel stiffened in her saddle, face expressionless. "Unless that's problematic for you?"

Majel shook her head. "No, ma'am. Not problematic. I like Belasko and trained with him in the past. I just..." She sighed. "It's hard to hear that and not immediately feel like you think I need further training, not that you just want me to keep an eye on the Baskan youngster."

Queen Lilliana waved her hand, dismissing the suggestion. "Oh no, not at all. I know you have your own training regimen, and I have the utmost faith in your abilities. Still." She gave a gentle smile. "Every blade needs sharpening, does it not? This wouldn't be an order—if you'd rather not do it, I'll find someone else. I thought you'd be suited to it, that's all."

"It's just a moment of self-doubt, ma'am, think nothing of it. I'll be happy to be your observer."

"Oh good, that's settled then. Thank you, Majel. I appreciate it."

16

LATER THAT SAME day, after they had made camp for the night, Olbarin found himself walking up to Ambassador Aveyard's tent. She had summoned him to attend her, and he was fairly sure he could guess what she wanted to talk about.

He arrived at her tent and, unsure of himself, hovered for a moment before reaching out a tentative hand to ring the bell that hung on a post outside the tent's entrance.

His hand had only alighted on the bellpull, not even pulled it, when the entrance to the tent was pulled aside to reveal Jonteer. His inscrutable, sharp features were thrown into even sharper relief by the darkening evening light. Jonteer observed Olbarin for a moment, and the young man felt his mouth go dry.

The secretary, slight of build, shorter than he, his hair thinning, unnerved Olbarin. There was something to him, an edge that told Olbarin that this was someone you wanted to keep on your side. The cold calculating gaze that warned Olbarin that there was more to this man than he could see.

Jonteer eyed him a moment longer. "Well?" he said,

eventually. "What are you here for?" There was wry amusement in his dry voice. He knew that he unsettled Olbarin and clearly enjoyed it.

"The Ambassador, um, she asked me to come." Olbarin found himself hesitant, unsure; he didn't like it.

"Oh yes, that's right. I'll let her know you're here." Jonteer disappeared back into the tent. Olbarin waited, standing at attention until the ambassador herself came striding out of the tent. She stopped short when she saw him and sighed. "At ease, Olbarin, we're not on the parade ground here. Come with me. I'm going to take a walk around the camp, and I'd like to talk to you while I go." She started off, then turned back when he didn't immediately follow. "What, do I have to tell you to fall in? Come on."

She set off again, and Olbarin scurried to keep up. They started walking around the perimeter of the Baskan camp, Ambassador Aveyard nodding to soldiers and staff as they passed by. After a while, she spoke.

"That was interesting this morning. You going to see Belasko. It surprised me, something that doesn't happen all that often. A military career followed by a political one saw to that. Mostly, I'm surprised that you didn't talk to me first. Why didn't you? Why didn't you ask me? For someone so recently in my employ, that is a very good way to go about leaving it."

Olbarin swallowed. "I thought you might say no. Tell me I couldn't."

"A reasonable assumption. Here, hold a moment." The Ambassador stopped by a tent with sagging guy ropes. She called to the soldier nearby who was clearly billeted there, remonstrating with them over the quality of their work. Shamefaced, and with Ambassador Aveyard's condemnation ringing in their ears, they started setting it right as Aveyard and Olbarin moved on.

"Yes, a very reasonable assumption." The Ambassador stopped, turning towards Olbarin, who almost tripped over his own feet coming to a stop, so quickly did she do so. "Why did you go to Belasko? You challenged him to a duel just days ago. Are you not still interested in your revenge? Does your blade not thirst for his blood? He killed your father, did he not?"

Olbarin rubbed his hands together, pulling at his fingers nervously. "Um, that's a lot of questions. Let me see..."

Ambassador Aveyard grabbed his hands, pulling them apart. "Stop that. Answer the first one first, then. Why did you go to Belasko?"

Olbarin sighed, not meeting the Ambassador's eye. "It shamed me how easily he bested me. I thought I could handle a blade well enough, but... I didn't stand a chance."

"There's no shame in that. For all that he can be a sanctimonious prick at times, he's the best with a blade I've ever seen. While he grows slower every year, he becomes more wily. More tricky an opponent. There's nothing wrong with losing to Belasko. He's never been beaten. So, what? You want to learn from him?"

The young man nodded. "Yes, I do. Aren't we taught to seek improvement at the military academy? I clearly have much to learn, and I think Belasko can teach me."

"All right." Ambassador Aveyard tilted her head to one side, then turned and continued her walk. Olbarin once again rushed to keep up. "So, learn from him and then challenge him again? Have you so easily forgiven him for killing your father?"

"No, of course not. You could say I've had a change in perspective." Olbarin leaped to avoid a mound of horse dung that lay, fresh and steaming, in their path. "All that time I was fixated on Belasko was a waste. What good did it do me? I gave up my commission to go and challenge him, and if he hadn't taken mercy on me, I'd have died for it. What good would that have been to the rest of my family?"

"Perhaps the important question is, what good would it have done your people? Whether Belasko took pity on you or saw promise in you, you do have something to offer us. You couldn't serve us dead, could you?" Ambassador Aveyard stopped, looking out towards the Villanese side of the camp. "You can serve us now, if you're willing."

"Of course, Madame Ambassador. What can I do?"

"I've given permission for your training because I think it will be useful to have an observer in the Villanese camp. While you are training, you are to be my eyes and ears. How does that sound?" The Ambassador turned to him once again. "Are you willing to serve?"

Olbarin hesitated. "Of course, I'm willing to serve, but... I'm no spy."

Ambassador Aveyard snorted. "I half wondered when Belasko sent you to me if you were *his* spy. That's what politics does to you: you see spies everywhere. I know you're not a spy—that much is clear. I doubt you've ever had a thought that wasn't immediately paraded across your face. All you have to do is keep your eyes and ears open and report anything interesting back to me. Well, to Jonteer. I'm sure they'll be wary of you to start with, but after a while, their guard will drop." She looked at the expression on his face and sighed. "I'm not asking you to do anything other than go and train with them. Be yourself, but be open to what's going on around you. Can you do that?"

Olbarin nodded slowly. Still unsure. "Yes, Madame Ambassador. I can do that."

"Good lad. Jonteer will debrief you every day somewhere out of the way. Quiet. The location will change regularly. We don't want anyone wondering why you're meeting my secretary do we? He'll be keeping a low profile on this journey anyway." Ambassador Aveyard caught Olbarin's questioning expression. She sighed. "He was present in the palace kitchens the day Prince Kellan was poisoned. He was only helping to make sure some Baskan dishes were properly prepared for an upcoming feast, but it raised awkward questions at the time. Thank the gods Belasko discovered the true murderer, otherwise we could have had a major diplomatic incident on our hands! You'll only see me in relation to your task if I have questions for you. Which I might if anything particularly interesting crops up. All right? Excellent. Now..." Ambassador Aveyard looked about her, frowning. "I need to find my way back to my tent. I could murder a glass of wine."

17

THE FIRST TRAINING session was held the next morning. Olbarin was in attendance, as was Majel, much to Belasko's surprise, as well as a mixed group of Villanese soldiers. There had been a lot of interest in the sessions, so a rota had been implemented, as the Queen suggested, to make sure that all those who wanted to attend could do so, in turn.

Eager to set the tone for these sessions, Belasko pushed his new students hard. Nothing was good enough for him. He picked apart their timing, their movement, everything about the way they fought. His students marvelled that he could recount details glimpsed from the corner of his eye during a group training session, but when it came to swordsmanship, there was very little that escaped Belasko's notice.

That morning, as others struck camp, the trainees worked by the light of the rising sun. Belasko walked among his students, adjusting a stance here, correcting a movement there. In some ways, he resembled a dancing master, although a misstep in this dance could be fatal.

"No." Belasko shook his head, touching Olbarin on the

shoulder. "The sword needs to be an extension of your arm; its weight is part of you. Until you feel that, you will fall just shy of what you could achieve. But you are doing well."

He moved over to a young Villanese infantrywoman. "And you, what are you doing? You're leaving yourself open on almost every move." Belasko looked around at his students. "You all show promise, but you're also making rudimentary mistakes. Perhaps a demonstration is in order."

He called Majel over from where she was working, alone, as she ran through some exercises. Olbarin looked on, intrigued. "Majel, come here. You can show what I mean." To the other students, Majel seemed the only person at the training session who Belasko was pleased with. "Run through the forms. Everyone else watch."

The others present stood back, giving Majel room to move. She started from a guard position, flowing seamlessly into one attacking move after another as she worked her way across the makeshift training ground. Then backwards, defensive move after defensive move as she retreated back to her starting point. She stopped, relaxing, and turned back to Belasko.

"Like that, you mean?"

Belasko clapped his hands. "Yes, exactly like that. Now, can you do it again, but at half speed?" Majel nodded and launched into the attacking moves again, slower this time. "Everyone look. Look at the way Majel moves from one position to the next. Her weight is perfectly balanced. She's using the sword's weight, not working against it. Each of her attacks moves easily into the next—the defensive moves, too. This is what you're aiming for. The level you have to achieve."

"It's all well and good on the training ground, but what about during a fight?" Olbarin said. "You're not going to be able to rattle off the forms while people are trying to kill you."

Belasko shook his head. "No. The point is that you take the time on this now, learn these forms, so you will use them instinctively when needed. It's a way of working on your core skills while developing the movements that will save your life in a real fight. Let us show you. Majel, would you spar with me? Training swords, of course."

Majel paused in her movements. "It's been a while since we've crossed blades. Why not?"

So, she and Belasko readied themselves in the circle that had been marked out in the mud, training swords held at the ready, waiting for the call to begin.

Byrta gave the command, and they leaped into action.

The students' mouths dropped open at the masterclass that unfolded in front of them. They could see the forms at the heart of the combatants' movements, but they were using variations built up from years of experience, reacting to the actions of their opponent. Belasko and Majel almost danced around the circle, movements flowing around each other as they tried to strike, tried to catch their opponent with their blade.

Belasko was assessing Majel's movements the whole time they fought. After a few minutes, he spoke. "Interesting. You've improved since your time at the Academy," Belasko said, parrying a blow so that its weight was sent off to the side, opening Majel up to a return thrust. She followed the redirection of her attack, letting it pull her away from Belasko's riposte. "I couldn't help but notice you've made some adjustments to the forms I taught you."

"It's been a few years. I haven't been standing still." Majel attacked again, a high thrust that dropped low, trying to get under Belasko's guard. With a twist of his wrist, he sent her thrust towards the ground, stepping onto her blade as he brought his own up to rest at her throat.

"I can see that," Belasko said, quiet enough that the others couldn't hear. "There's more to it, though. That last attack, you knew what I would do. Why throw away the bout so recklessly? Why hide your obvious quality?"

Majel's face darkened. "I don't want your job, Belasko. I've worked to improve my sword skills so I can do my own job better. So I can protect the Queen."

"What is it you think I do, Majel?" A sad smile twisted across Belasko's face. "Ultimately, that's my job, too."

Majel opened her mouth to reply, then stopped. She shook her head, dropped the training sword, and turned and walked away. Leaving the circle and the training area behind, she walked off into the busy camp. Belasko watched her go.

"Sir, should we continue?" asked a Villanese infantrywoman. Then again, when no reply came. "Sir?"

Belasko was still looking in the direction Majel had gone. His eyes narrowed. "No. That's it for this morning. Think on what I said and what you saw in Majel's practice of the forms. I'll see you again this evening."

The rest of the students exchanged puzzled glances, then began tidying things away in preparation for the day's travel.

Oblivious to them, lost in thought, Belasko stood looking in the direction the departed guard captain had taken. *Has she always hidden her quality?* he thought to himself. *If so, why? What purpose would it serve?*

18

BELASKO STRUGGLED TO fit in with the courtiers as their journey continued towards the mountains. He saw them, for the most part, as spoiled brats writ large, unaware of their wealth and privilege. They saw him as rough and uncouth, a commoner with his feet under the table, despite the fact that he had over the years adopted courtly manners and was now a refined gentleman of means. They knew he had saved the kingdom and had never forgiven him for it. "What use is a dog that turns on its master?" they whispered amongst themselves. The fact that he had slain the King he was sworn to serve in single combat was always at the front of their minds.

This came out in little ways: sniping here and there, cutting comments, outright hostility at times. Things came to a head on the third night on their journey. At a dinner with the Queen, to which only a select few had been invited.

Belasko was late because he had been training with his students, which got things off to a bad start. The nobles were annoyed that he had kept the Queen waiting, while the Queen herself didn't mind at all.

"Glad you could join us at last, Belasko," said the elderly Lord Beggeridge, waspishly. "The Queen might not mind the delay, but some of us..."

"Need to be wrapped up with a glass of warm milk nice and early, eh, Lord? Some of us don't mind a late night, although I'll wager you're not one of them, Belasko. Not with your early starts. Such dedication you show to our Queen in your quest for constant martial superiority," Anerin interjected, rolling his eyes at Belasko before shooting meaningful looks at the others present.

The wealthiest of all of them and, for all he sends himself up, he wears his privilege lightest of all. Except when he uses it to browbeat the other nobles into line, Belasko thought, smiling to himself.

"I am sorry, your majesty, and everyone. A student was having some difficulty, and I wanted to make sure they had mastered the technique we were working on before we stopped for the night." Belasko bowed to the Queen. "My old friend rather over eggs it a bit, but my work can be all-consuming. My apologies, ma'am."

Queen Lilliana laughed, a bright sound that cut the tension like a knife. "That's quite all right, my champion. It allowed us some stimulating conversation, didn't it, my dear Lord? Now, let's sit." She offered her elbow to Lord Beggridge, who was only too delighted to escort the Queen to the table.

Unfortunately, that was far from the only awkward moment of the evening. Queen Lilliana's goal of bringing Belasko back into court life seemed further away than ever, as Belasko and her other counsellors fell out at every turn.

The Queen interjected again as Belasko and a young noble named Carlin bickered over matters of military training over the after-dinner brandy.

"Why, I think we spend far too much on training our soldiers as it is. What more do we need do than hand them a blade, tell them to stick the pointy end in the enemy, and let them go?" Carlin was red-faced, his crystal glass weaving in the air.

"You have served then, Lord Carlin? To be an expert in such matters? Perhaps you need it explaining to you that not everyone has access to fencing tutors from a young age. We won the last war. If you want to win the next, then training needs to be a bit more detailed than 'poke them with the sharp bit'. Left to you, our military would be a laughing stock." Belasko was red-faced also, but not with drink. His barely suppressed rage beat off him like heat from a forge.

The Queen cleared her throat, and both of them fell silent. Although they still glared at each other.

"That is enough, gentlemen. Why, who needs enemies when we are at each other's throats?" She turned to Carlin. "My lord, you forget yourself in drink. I will forget your words tomorrow, and I suggest everyone else do likewise, but I would also recommend you tread carefully. Think before you anger my champion. I know you don't believe what you have said tonight, so can only assume that you have done so to elicit a response from him. That, my lord, is beneath you."

She turned then to Belasko. "And you, my champion, need to keep that cool head that has seen you overcome so many obstacles. You are not at your academy now, and this is not your table. I expect you to keep a civil tongue in your head, even if others do not. If someone truly offends you, I know you have other ways of seeking satisfaction, although I can't think of anyone here that would wish to face you in the circle." Queen Lilliana turned, surveying the gathered lords and ladies with a delicately arched eyebrow. "No, I

The Swordsman's Descent

thought not. Well, ladies and gentlemen, I think that's enough for one night. I would urge you all to try to get along better. I have need of your service now and in the future. Tonight I am embarrassed for all of you. Do better; I need you to."

With that, the Queen stood, and all knew that dinner was at an end. Those gathered stood and, in a low murmur of conversation, started to make their way out. Belasko waited, not wanting to leave with the nobility. He looked to the Queen, but her expression was closed, her face an unreadable book to him. He bowed to her, then turned and left.

Belasko could feel the flush on his face, anger at the behaviour of the nobles and his own treatment by the Queen. He stalked off to his own tent, ignoring the footsteps of someone behind him until a hand landed on his elbow. Belasko whirled around, grabbing the person that had touched him by the front of their shirt.

"If you want to finish what you started in there..." he growled, trailing off when he realised that it was his friend, Anerin, he had by the shirtfront.

Anerin coughed. "Not particularly. The conversation I got stuck into with Duchess Morlake was dryer than my old nanny's baking. Um, do you mind?" He gestured at the fine fabric of his shirt and jacket, wrinkled and creased in Belasko's fist.

"Oh, yes, of course." Belasko released him and stood back, shaking his head. "I'm sorry, I thought you were that idiot Carlin come to start an actual fight."

"Are you mad?" Anerin laughed. "Did you see his face when the Queen mentioned you seeking satisfaction? I thought the little fool was going to wet himself."

Belasko smiled, although his heart wasn't in it. "Yes, well.

Be that as it may, that was as painful an evening as I've had to endure in a long time. What the Queen said..."

"Was quite right." Anerin flinched at Belasko's expression. "Come on, you left her no choice. You're her champion. You need to behave yourself at the dinner table. You represent her, as do we all, and none of us did a good job of that tonight. We all need to get our houses in order before we arrive in Bas. We must present a united front." He moved closer to Belasko. "You need to work *with* the nobility. Find a way forwards." Anerin reached out and took Belasko's hand. "You have friends there, you know. More than just me. If only you'd see it. You're as bad as them in some ways, seeing us all as the same. We're not all the same. You know that."

Belasko squeezed Anerin's hand and sighed. "I know. You're right, you're right, it's just... I've never forgotten how some of them treated me when I was made Champion. And since. King Mallor himself confirmed it when I confronted him."

Anerin stepped a little closer. "Some. Not all. Don't forget your friends."

Belasko was aware of his friend's physical closeness, could feel the heat of Anerin's breath on his face. His heart was racing, that nervous feeling in his stomach once again. Then Belasko sniffed and smiled. "You still sweeten your breath with cloves?" He let go of Anerin's hand and took a step back. "Good night, my friend. I have an early start in the morning."

Belasko turned and left, continuing on his way to his tent. He was aware that Anerin stood and watched as he disappeared into the darkness.

19

QUEEN LILLIANA SAT alone in her tent, servants dismissed. The guests had all departed, the detritus from dinner had been cleared away quickly and efficiently. She sat back in her chair, swathed in blankets and warmed by a nearby brazier, and sipped at her tea—a herbal concoction introduced to her by the Royal Physician, Maelyn, to help her sleep.

Sleep did not come easily these days. She felt the weight of responsibility on her more than ever before, and her mind raced with thoughts and possibilities. Lilliana was more than up to the task of being queen; she just found it difficult to switch off. She took another sip of her tea.

This is so important, this trip. I was only a child at the time of the Last War, but I have no desire to see such bloodshed occur again in my lifetime. We have lasting peace within our grasp, not just the tentative truce of these last years.

Lilliana sighed, placing her tea down on a small table that sat beside her, picking up some paperwork that Parlin had brought her earlier. If I can't sleep, I might as well do something useful. She leafed through the papers but found herself unable to focus on them either. *Damn it.*

She stood, pulling the blankets tighter around the robes she wore, and went to the door of her tent. She slipped outside, startling the guards that Majel had set at either side of the entrance.

"Is everything all right, your majesty?" asked one of the guards.

"No. I can't sleep. And I can't work. So, I'd like to go for a walk. Will you accompany me?"

"Of course, ma'am, anywhere." They looked across to their comrade. "We should probably get some more guards if you're going out. We shouldn't leave the tent unattended."

Queen Lilliana waved away the suggestion. "There are plenty of guards around, and we're surrounded by allies and friends. It will be safe. I just want to stretch my legs for a few minutes. We won't be long or go too far."

"If your majesty insists," said the second guard, a sceptical look on their face.

Queen Lilliana smiled at them. "My majesty does. Come on."

She set off, and the guards followed. Despite her command, quiet words were exchanged with other guards as they left the perimeter around her tent. Two more guards walked back to the tent, and several others peeled off to follow behind. Queen Lilliana sighed.

What's the point in being queen if people won't do what you say? She smiled to herself. *They're more afraid of Majel than they are of me.*

There were few people about at this hour. Most of the camp was safely abed, resting for the morrow's journey. One or two people, night owls or guards patrolling the camp, were startled as she walked by, throwing off hasty bows or salutes as they did their best to get out of the way. The Queen nodded to them, exchanging smiles and a few words with the people she recognised.

For some reason, her feet carried her to Anerin's tent. She was a little surprised to see him sat on a stool outside, gazing up at the night sky while taking occasional sips from a flask in his hand. He looked over as she approached and got to his feet—not too steadily, she couldn't help but notice—and bowed.

"Your majesty, I didn't expect the pleasure of your company again this evening. May I invite you to sit?" Anerin gestured at another stool next to his.

"You may indeed, thank you." As Queen Lilliana moved to the stool, her guards faded into the background, taking up positions around Anerin's tent. She pointed at the flask he held. "What is that, may I ask?"

Anerin grinned at her. "Baskan Fire. A spirit I developed a taste for during my business dealings there. Would you like to try some? It's pretty potent." He held out the flask.

"Why not? It might help me sleep." Queen Lilliana took the flask, then a tentative sip. The spirit had a pleasant fiery quality in her mouth, leaving a warm trail down to her stomach as she swallowed. There was a surprisingly delicate aftertaste that she enjoyed. She took another sip before handing it back. "Very nice. I'm impressed."

Anerin took the proffered flask and another sip himself. "Yes, one of the nicer things to come out of Bas."

They sat for a moment in companionable silence. Queen Lilliana broke it.

"You've spent a fair amount of time in Bas, haven't you?" she asked. Anerin nodded in affirmation. "What do you make of our mission? Does it have any chance of success? Be honest."

Anerin thought for a moment, taking another sip from his flask before offering it again to the Queen. "I think it is a bold move of the new Baskan King to invite you to these talks, but from what I have heard, Edyard is a good man. An excellent general, who prefers peace, if that makes any sense. I'm sure there are parts of Baskan society that are not happy with peace. They have their counterparts among our own Villanese people, as well. Although their voices are quieter." He shook his head. "I didn't serve in the Last War, although I have friends who did. From their stories... War is to be avoided at all costs, the last resort of kings. And queens, of course. If we can achieve lasting peace, then it is worth trying for. It worked with our other neighbours, eventually."

Queen Lilliana passed the flask back to Anerin. "That's good to hear. I'm sure we're on the right track, but sometimes I need a little reassurance. When you talk of friends who have known war, do you mean Belasko? You and he trained together under the previous Royal Champion, Markus. Didn't you?"

"Oh yes, that we did." A sad smile appeared on Anerin's face. "Belasko and Byrta, the former cavalry officer that travels with him. We were good friends once. It is good to see them again. My work on behalf of my family took me away for a long time. Too long, I think."

Queen Lilliana sighed. "I'm not sure what to do with him—Belasko. I'd like him by my side. I trust him implicitly and know he will only ever tell me the truth as he sees it, but he has to get along better with the other members of my court."

"Oh, he will, in the end." Anerin chuckled. "He's a good man, but sometimes he needs pointing in the right direction. It's not a bad thing that he and the other courtiers keep each other on their toes, but the antagonism between them has to stop. Belasko can take a while to see sense, but he is an excellent ally."

"Why is that, do you think? That it takes him a while?"

Anerin shrugged. "He's stubborn. He has a chip on his shoulder about class because some people at court have never forgotten, or forgiven him, for his roots." His expression darkened. "Like Ervan."

The Queen nodded. "That's right. You would have trained with him as well, wouldn't you? Moved in the same circles. He caused a lot of damage in the end."

"It's sad. I don't think he needed to be like that. He was a product of his environment, his family, and couldn't take being beaten by a commoner to the role of Royal Champion. He wasn't always like that, you know. We did move in the same circles. Used to play together at gatherings when we were younger. If he'd been raised differently..." Anerin shrugged again. "Don't mind me. I'm getting maudlin in my cups."

"That's all right. We all do from time to time." Queen Lilliana reached for the flask, which Anerin handed over. She took another sip, and they sat in silence for a little while.

"What were you doing out here, when I walked up earlier?" the Queen asked after some time had passed.

Anerin tilted his head back, once again looking up at the night sky. "I was looking at the stars," he said quietly. "Something I got into the habit of on my travels. There's something constant about the stars. It helped me to look at them when I got homesick or missed people too much." He ran a hand through his hair, mussing it up. "My father taught me the constellations when I was younger. We didn't always get on, particularly as I grew up, but I find comfort in them."

"My father taught me about the constellations too, when I was younger," said Queen Lilliana in a soft sad voice.

Anerin coughed. "And what are you doing up and about at this hour, ma'am?"

Queen Lilliana made a face. "I have trouble sleeping sometimes. The weight of my responsibilities can be more than a little pressing, and it's difficult to switch off. To stop my thoughts from racing."

"Ah," said Anerin. "I've always found alcohol handy at such times, although I suppose that only delays the inevitable." He sipped from his flask. "Of course, I haven't had much in the way of responsibilities until recently. That came as a bit of a shock."

"Oh yes, I know that feeling. Nothing prepares you, does it? Especially when you're the second born. You always think your older sibling will be there to save you from such things." She held out her hand for the flask. Anerin passed it to her wordlessly. Queen Lilliana took a healthy swig and sighed before passing the flask back. "Would you mind if I sat with you for a while, and we looked at them together?"

Anerin smiled at her. "Of course, you may. Nothing would make me happier." He shook the flask. "Although I may need to fetch more drink."

Queen Lilliana smiled in return. "Not too much more. We have more journeying to do tomorrow."

"Ah, my queen clearly hasn't mastered the art of riding while half asleep. I'm more than happy to teach by example on the morrow. Now, what can we see?"

And they passed the time quietly, pointing out stars and constellations to each other, both taking comfort from it.

The Swordsman's Descent

Later, much later than was proper for a responsible monarch that had an early start the next morning, Queen Lilliana walked back to her tent. Her guards trailed behind her, as silent as they could be in their armour, and she was deep in thought.

As they neared her tent Lilliana could feel tiredness reaching up to claim her. She yawned. "I'll be going to bed as soon as I get back," she said to the one of the guards that accompanied her. "I dismissed my staff for the evening earlier, I hope you and your colleagues are due a shift change soon."

The guard smiled. "In an hour or so, your majesty. We'll see you safely settled and resume our posts."

She yawned again. "As long as you get your rest, my apologies for dragging you out into the night."

"Think nothing of it, your majesty. It was nice to stretch our legs."

They arrived at the tent and one of the guards went to open the flap. It was dark inside, lit only by the faint glow from a brazier. Queen Lilliana frowned. "That's odd, I swear I left a lamp on low for when I got back. Let me see..."

Two of the guards accompanied her as she went inside. Queen Lilliana looked about her, trying to remember where the tinderbox was kept. With it were the wooden splints she could light from the embers of the brazier and then use to relight her lamps.

She laughed. "This is the problem with having everyone do things for you, you lose all sense of where everyday useful items are kept. I'm sorry to ask, but could you help me locate the tinderbox?"

"Of course, your majesty. I'm just trying to think where it would be put."

The guards and Queen Lilliana moved into the tent, the

queen pushing aside a silk screen and going to the chest at the foot of her bed.

"Now if I were a tinderbox, where would I be?" she mused to herself as she opened the chest.

As she did so, Queen Lilliana caught a movement out of the corner of her eye. She turned as a shadow detached itself from the gloom beside her bed and launched itself towards her. The queen had a moment to let out a startled yell as she caught sight of something gleaming in the low light. A blade.

It seemed to Queen Lilliana as if time slowed then. She still had the blankets wrapped around her that she taken for warmth when she left her tent earlier. In that short moment before whoever or whatever was in her tent made contact, she shrugged them off one shoulder, took hold with both hands and pulled the blanket out in front of her. As the shadowy figure collided with her, the blade they carried was tangled in the blankets. The queen wrapped them around it as best she could.

She fell backwards, the shadow on top of her, the blade caught in the blankets between them, as her guards came crashing past the silk screen she had only moments before slid aside.

"Your majesty!" cried one of the guards.

"The queen is attacked, raise the alarm!" called the other, as they tried to grab hold of whoever was atop Queen Lilliana.

The queen was struggling with the figure that had her pinned to the ground, both of them trying to gain control of the weapon trapped between them.

They're small, Queen Lilliana thought to herself, *smaller than me.*

One of the guards got a hand on her attacker as shouts

could be heard outside, and pulled at them, trying to lift them off the queen. This had the unfortunate effect of freeing the weapon from the blankets, and the attacker swiped at the guard, catching them on the back of the hand. The guard yelped in pain, and Queen Lilliana felt something warm and wet drip onto her face. *Blood, it must be blood.*

The guard remained steadfast and would not let their opponent go, as they caught the assailant's wrist with their other hand and worked with their fellow guard to haul them off the queen.

The shadowy figure hissed, writhing in the guards' grip, and somehow freed themselves. Queen Lilliana heard them curse under their breath. *A high pitched voice, a woman?*

The attacker leaped over the queen and raced towards the tent's entrance. As they pulled the tent flap open Queen Lilliana caught a glimpse of a sharp featured face framed by long black hair, and then the attacker was gone.

Queen Lilliana struggled to her feet, throwing off the blankets, and went to the entrance. She was beaten there by her guards who bid her to wait and, with swords drawn, opened it and stepped outside. The queen joined them, and was pleased to see that her assailant hadn't got far. More torches had been lit around her tent as the rest of her guard had come, responding to the calls from inside the tent.

The attacker could be clearly seen in the torchlight. A woman, she was slight and short of stature. The knife held in their hand had a dark smear down one side of the blade. She was surrounded by guards, with no way out. Her eyes flashed in the night as she grimaced.

Majel, clearly roused from her sleep by the commotion, was with the guards that surrounded the mysterious woman. Her eyes lit up with relief when she saw the queen, then with concern.

"Your majesty," said Majel, "are you well? That blood on you–"

"Isn't my own, thank you Majel." Queen Lilliana looked towards the injured guardsman who stood beside her, sword out and levelled at the attacker, blood running freely from a gash on the back of their other hand. "You get that seen to as soon as possible."

"Yes ma'am," the guard replied, not taking his eyes off the woman who had attacked the queen.

Queen Lilliana's gaze followed his "As for you, you might as well give yourself up. You have no hope of escape now."

The woman turned hate-filled eyes on her, and bared her teeth. Then, not breaking eye contact with Lilliana, she raised her knife up.

"Good, you'll drop that if you know what's good for you," said Majel.

The woman's gaze did not shift, and remained locked with Lilliana's, as instead she drew the blade across her own throat.

∼

That moment replayed itself over and over again in Lilliana's mind. The way the woman's flesh had parted. Blood that welled up and then poured from the wound. Her attacker's eyes as they rolled up in their sockets and she collapsed to the floor. The shouts from the guards as they rushed towards her, all too late for any action to be taken.

I think I'll be seeing that in my nightmares for some years to come, thought Lilliana.

She shivered, and became aware of Majel barking orders

as she rushed to her queen's side. "Search the tent, now! I want to find out how that woman got into Queen Lilliana's tent. Then search the camp, working out from here, make sure there are no accomplices lurking." She was beside the queen now. "Your majesty, are you sure you're alright? What happened in there."

"I'm fine, Majel, honestly." Queen Lilliana could feel herself shivering, not just from the cold. *That statement might not be entirely accurate.* She recounted for Majel what had happened inside the tent as her guard captain listened intently.

"Well done, your majesty. Your own quick actions saved your life, thank goodness you had those blankets over your shoulders."

Queen Lilliana shook her head. "The actions of these two guards as well, they moved quickly and placed themselves in harms way."

Majel grunted. "Not before the attacker got to you ma'am." She eyed the two guards who had been with Queen Lilliana in the tent, and pointed to the wound on one of their hands. "Best get that seen to, now. I'll debrief the pair of you later. Go together to the healers' tent, then return here."

"Yes, captain." The guards bowed to the queen. "Your majesty." Then they were off into the night.

Majel leaned in closer to Queen Lilliana. "Where did you go, your majesty, if I may ask?"

"I was consulting with Lord Anerin. Now, shall we take a look at the body?"

Majel hesitated. "I'm not sure you want to see it, your majesty. I think you may have seen enough blood tonight."

"I'm afraid I'm going to have to insist." Queen Lilliana tilted her head slightly as she regarded Majel. "There was something about their face when I glimpsed it, I might recognise them, be able to identify the body."

At that moment Parlin appeared through the ring of guards, concern writ large across his face. He saw Lilliana and the look of concern turned to one of relief, and then back to one of concern. He hurried over. "Your majesty, are you well? That blood—"

"Isn't my own, Parlin, I am unharmed." She smiled at him. "Thank you. Now, Captain, shall we take a look at the body?" The queen looked at Majel expectantly.

Majel nodded. "Of course, your majesty. Let us see what we can determine." Majel turned and led them back to the body. Guards surrounded it. At a word from Majel they stood back and allowed the queen to step closer.

The women, small of stature and sharp of feature, was otherwise unremarkable, apart from the gaping cut across her throat. She had dark hair and pale skin. Paler now that the blood which surrounded the body had left her veins.

"Bring that torch closer," Queen Lilliana gestured to one of the guards. They did as they were bid, holding it up high over the corpse. The queen peered down, and frowned.

"I don't recognise her, but there is definitely something about the face... Parlin?"

Her secretary crouched down over the body, examining it as closely as he could without getting blood on his clothes. He looked up at Majel. "Judging from the angle of the cut, and the blood all over her hand and blade, she used the knife on herself?"

"Yes," said Majel. "Remarkable really, she must have been a very disturbed individual."

"Or a remarkably committed one," Parlin muttered as he resumed his examination. He shook his head. "To take one's own life, in such a fashion, that isn't something you see often."

He looked up at Queen Lilliana. "I know this woman, your majesty. She's one of the household staff, only recently employed. She wasn't due to come on this journey until one of the more senior servants took ill."

"Do you know where she was billeted?" asked Majel, even more intent than she had been moments before.

"No," said Parlin, "but I can find out. Her majesty's steward would know."

"Then let us rouse the good steward from his bed and see if we can find out a little bit more about this assailant."

They looked up at the sound of raised voices. Now Belasko pushed his way through the guards, face pale and sword at the ready. "What the bloody hell is going on here?" He took in the scene in front of him, the blood on Queen Lilliana's face. "Your majesty, are—"

She sighed. "I'm well, Belasko, the blood isn't my own. You know, can someone please get me a cloth? Otherwise I'm going to be repeating myself all night. In fact, I'll repeat myself again. Shall we rouse my steward and find out what we can about this woman?"

~

That turned out to be very little. The woman, Dielle by name, had been quiet and kept to herself. She had made no friends amongst the other people in the camp, and attended to her duties admirably. So well, in fact, that she had been asked to helped prepare the queen's bed that evening as her last task of the day.

"That's where I recognised her from," said Queen Lilliana. "There was quite a flurry of activity this evening, clearing things away and whatnot, and a lot of staff in and out of the tent. How did she get back in though? There were guards stationed all around."

They had retreated into the queen's tent, once it had been thoroughly searched and then returned to order, to get out of the chill and discuss the evening's events.

"Perhaps she didn't leave," said Belasko. "There was no sign of forced entry, no cuts made in the tent fabric, nothing disturbed. She was small, could she have hidden? None of the other servants report seeing her after attending to you, your majesty."

Queen Lilliana shivered. "That's a terrifying thought, I was alone in here for some time before I went for my restless walk. If she was in here with me..."

"...she could have struck at any time." Majel's face was grim as she finished the queen's thought. "From now on, only servants with many years service are allowed near the queen. Guards will be with you at all times, and your tent is to be searched thoroughly by them before you settle down for the evening."

Parlin, entered with a pot of tea on a tray and three cups. "I hope you don't mind, your majesty, I thought a little something to keep the cold at bay would be welcome."

Queen Lilliana smiled. "You're right, as always, Parlin. That is most kind."

Her secretary busied himself placing the tray on a side table, before pouring it out, Passing a cup to the queen, then Belasko, and finally Majel.

He sighed. "I'm afraid my enquiries among the staff have got no further, your majesty. This Dielle was seemingly unremarkable. She was a solitary sort, made no real friends, and it seems no one knows much about her."

"Nothing at all?" asked Belasko. "Nothing of her

thoughts and feelings, why she may have wanted to attack the queen?"

"No, nothing." Parlin shook his head. "It is most strange."

"What of her background?" asked Majel, frowning. "Do we know where she was from, any associations she may have had outside of her work at the palace?"

"Again, I'm afraid not. She claimed to be from a small town in southern Villan, lured to the city by the prospect of better paid work. But can we even take that as true?"

"She will have given references when she applied for work at the palace," said Belasko, "previous employers, things like that. They would have been checked."

Queen Lilliana sighed, then took a sip of her tea. "Perhaps she was simply a disturbed individual, as you put it Majel. Seeking attention, or revenge for some imagined slight."

"Or perhaps she was the agent of a foreign power. Or a hired assassin, playing a long game in order to get close to you, your majesty. Seizing their opportunity when it presented itself." Belasko let out a deep breath. "We might never know,."

"Some things we can't look into until we get home, we can recheck her references and investigate, so for now our answer has to be increased vigilance." Majel tapped her fingers on the side of her teacup. "I'll double the guard on you, your majesty, and we'll carry out more regular sweeps of the camp." She drained her cup of tea, and looked to her queen. "Your permission to withdraw and set that in motion now, your majesty?"

"Granted," said Queen Lilliana, "but do try and get some rest before sun up, captain."

"I'll do my best, your majesty." Majel bowed deeply to

the queen, nodded at Belasko and Parlin, then turned and strode from the tent.

"I think you should follow your own advice, your majesty." Belasko said, before a poor attempt at stifling a yawn.

Queen Lilliana smiled at him. "As should you, Belasko. And you Parlin, thank you for your help in these small hours of the night. You should go find your bed."

Parlin bowed to her. "Yes, your majesty." He stood, nodded to Belasko, and left.

"Belasko," said the queen, "I can't help but notice you are still here."

"Yes, majesty." He coughed. "I just wanted to say, the way you used those blankets to defend yourself from the assailant's blade. That was well done."

"Thank you, Belasko. From you that is high praise indeed." She paused. "Is there anything else."

Belasko looked a little shamefaced. "I'd like to apologise, your majesty. For my behaviour earlier, at dinner. I don't know why I let my emotions get the better of me, or why Lord Carlin was able to rile me so." He shook his head. "I use other's anger against them in the duelling circle, usually my own is kept in better check."

"Thank you for the apology, but I do expect better from you." She eyed him over the rim of her teacup for a moment. "It's not like you to lose your temper, Belasko."

Belasko sighed. "You're right, of course, your majesty. I have been prone to foul moods of late. I will do better, you have my word."

"Then let that be an end to it." Queen Lilliana looked at her champion, then smiled. "And thank you for coming so quickly when you heard the commotion outside."

"You're welcome, your majesty. I would be nowhere else at times of danger, but at your side."

"That is reassuring. Goodnight, Belasko."

"Goodnight, your majesty." Now it was Belasko's turn to bow to the queen, before turning to leave.

Alone once more in her tent, the scene of the attack such a short while ago, Lilliana looked around her.

Despite the hour, despite how exhausted I am, I think sleep will not come easy this night. What remains of it.

When she did take to her bed, she kept a lamp burning low on the table beside her.

20

THEIR JOURNEY CONTINUED after the attempt on Queen Lilliana's life, albeit with an even more watchful guard and further security precautions in place. Although the queen must have been disturbed by the attempt on her life, only those who knew her would have noticed the occasional hesitancy in her actions. She was very adept at putting on a brave face.

Belasko found that in the aftermath of the attack, and without the pressures of palace life, he and Queen Lilliana enjoyed each other's company and would sometimes ride together. Although she often used her carriage, the queen enjoyed riding, and when the weather was pleasant enough, she would have her horse brought up, and she and Belasko would ride along together. Their conversation ranged widely, from her hopes for their current mission to shared memories. They avoided the topic of her father and brother as best they could, as it was awkward and painful for them both. Queen Lilliana, ever curious, never missed an opportunity to probe Belasko about his life and experiences.

They were riding together on a crisp and clear morning

The Swordsman's Descent

on the sixth day since they had left Villan, and for some reason that he couldn't put his finger on Belasko was feeling apprehensive.

Queen Lilliana looked around as they rode, taking in the scenery of snow-topped peaks marching away into the distance. "Belasko, you grew up in these mountains, did you not?"

He nodded. "Yes, your majesty."

"What was it like?"

Belasko laughed. "A difficult question for anyone to answer. It was a long time ago and the only childhood I've known." The Queen regarded him with a questioning look, one eyebrow raised. Seeing she would not be deterred, he thought for a moment, then shrugged.

"As I say, it was a long time ago. But I'd say it was happy enough. What was it like? To answer that, you need to understand the life of a smallholder. We were poor, although I didn't know it. The farm provided us with what we needed. Almost everything we had was made or mended by my parents' hands. Apart from my schooling. I was despatched to the nearest village once a week so the local priest could teach me my letters."

"Was it a hard life?"

Belasko shrugged again. "I suppose so. The work was constant, always something to do. The only respite was in the evening, after supper and before bed, when we'd sit by the fire, and my mother would sing. Or my father would tell stories. Even then, their hands were busy. Mother spinning wool, father mending something. It was a simple life, but a good one."

Queen Lilliana tilted her head to one side. "So, why did you leave?"

Belasko sighed. "I wasn't brave enough."

Laughter burst from Queen Lilliana's lips. "You? Not brave enough? I think you're the bravest person I know."

"You don't know many farmers, do you? It might do you well to meet some, understand their lives a little. No, ma'am, farmers are among the bravest folk I know. I've been to war, fought in battles, faced skilled warriors across the duelling circle, but I wasn't brave enough to farm."

The Queen frowned. "Explain, please."

"All right. A farmer toils from dawn to dusk, working their land to provide for themselves and their family. Work that might come to nothing if the weather's bad that year or some sort of blight or pest comes along. In many ways, despite all the hard work, your fate and that of your family is in the hands of the gods. A poor harvest, and you'll all go hungry." He shook his head. "No, give me something where the outcome depends on my skills, on the work I can do myself. When I step into the duelling circle, I know I have prepared, that I have trained. Victory is mine for the taking. If I lose, it is because I have met a more skilled opponent. Not because the wind changed direction, or the rains never came."

They rode in silence for a while. "It all sounds a bit grim," the Queen said after some time had passed.

Belasko smiled. "Don't mistake me, it was a good life. Growing up, I had this as my playground." He gestured to indicate the world around them, the soaring cliffs, snow-topped, and tumbling ravines. "I learned to climb almost as I learned to walk. I had friends from nearby farms, from the village, and we used to go climbing together when we were old enough. Sledding in the winter. There was joy here, too."

"Was it far from here, then, where you grew up?"

"No, ma'am. In fact, we should pass the track that leads up to my parents' farm some time tomorrow."

The Queen turned in her saddle and stared at Belasko. "What? We're passing that close by your parents' home, and you didn't think to tell me."

"I didn't think it mattered." Belasko looked away, taking in the landscape of his youth. "I haven't been home in a very long time. You see, your majesty, it wasn't just the lifestyle that made me leave. I was... Different. Not many like me in my village, if you take my meaning."

The Queen looked at him for a moment. "Yes, well. Be that as it may, you have given me something to think on. Will you point it out to me tomorrow, when we pass the track?"

"Yes, ma'am. If it would please your majesty." Belasko sketched the best bow he could manage on horseback.

A smile touched Queen Lilliana's lips. "Yes, it would please my majesty. Now, tell me about climbing. How on earth do you go about climbing something like that?" She pointed out a particularly vertiginous cliff face across the valley.

"With a great deal of care, ma'am."

The rest of the day passed easily, the two of them enjoying each other's company until they stopped for the day, and Belasko went to find that day's students.

As the Queen had requested that he point out the track to his parents' farm, he rode with her again the next day. It was mid-morning when they rounded a corner in the road, and there it was before them. A narrow, unprepossessing track, unpaved like the main road and only just wide enough for a cart. Belasko felt an ache in his chest, a physical manifestation of an old sadness.

"Majesty, forgive me for interrupting, but there it is. The track that leads to my parents' farm."

The Queen, who had been mid-discussion about the flora and fauna of the region sparked off by the sighting of a bird with most spectacular plumage, looked where Belasko was pointing.

"That track there?" she asked. Belasko nodded. "Very well." The Queen brought her horse to a stop, and the whole column with it in a slow clanking process, as word was passed along the caravan that the Queen had halted.

Queen Lilliana turned in her saddle. "Captain Majel?" she called to the commander of her personal guard, who rode not far behind. "We're going to attend to that little task we spoke of last night. Gather the guards you'd like to bring and the supplies we discussed."

"Yes, your majesty." Majel saluted and rode off into the column, calling out orders as she went.

Belasko stared at his queen. "Your majesty, what's going on?"

Queen Lilliana peered up the track to his parents' farm. "How long a ride is it to your parents' farm?"

"Your majesty, I..." Belasko trailed off, a heavy, leaden feeling settling in his stomach.

She turned to him and raised an eyebrow. He sighed. "A few hours on horseback. If we set off now, we'd be there by this afternoon."

"Good. I'll make sure Majel has organised enough supplies. We'll probably have to stop overnight before returning, so we'll need to bring tents."

"Your majesty..."

Queen Lilliana gave him a brilliant smile. "This is your idea really. You said I should meet some farmers. Why not start with your parents? The rest of our party will make camp and wait for us until we return. Belasko, you're going home."

Belasko began to feel nauseous, his heart racing. He swallowed. "Yes, your majesty."

Once Majel had returned with the ten handpicked members of the guard she had selected, along with the necessary supplies, they set off. The track was steep in places, which made for slow going, but they rode two abreast with Majel alone up front. She turned back and called to Belasko. "It's just straight up here, no turnings or branches?"

"That's right," he called back. "It leads straight there."

She turned forwards again, satisfied.

The Queen had been looking at Belasko out of the corner of her eye for a while. Now she turned to him.

"Are you all right, Belasko? You don't seem yourself."

"I'm fine, ma'am. Just a little nervous, that's all."

She gave a most unladylike snort at that. "You, nervous? I didn't think that happened to you. You always seem so confident, so sure of yourself."

He winced. "That might be how I come across, but this is different. I haven't been home in a long time, I'm... I'm not even sure I'll be welcome."

"Whatever for? Surely, your parents will be glad to see you after so long. Unless you had a falling out? Was that why you left in the first place?"

Belasko shook his head. "No, majesty. Not a falling out, as such. I just... Let's just say that I didn't fit in. There aren't many people like me around here—I said as much yesterday. At least openly."

"I see." The Queen waited with an expectant air, clearly wanting to hear more on the subject.

Belasko sighed and carried on. "I never felt quite right,

up here in the mountains. Not so much when I was a boy, but as I got older... I was uncomfortable. People kept trying to pair me up with girls at dances and celebrations in the village and didn't understand when I wasn't interested. Then the recruiting sergeant came through, with his splendid uniform and tales of glory, and that was it. I was off."

"Have you ever been home since?"

"Yes, on leave during the war, and again a few times after. Things never felt right between us, my parents and I. I wrote, sent money and gifts, but it seemed easier not to come back. So eventually, I stopped."

The Queen frowned. "I have to say, Belasko, that I'm a little disappointed in you."

Belasko looked down at his gloved hands on his reins. "You can't feel more disappointed with me than I do with myself, majesty."

"I have to say, as someone with no parents left in this world, that I hope you repair that relationship. Make it work, Belasko. You never know how long they'll be here." Queen Lilliana coughed, voice thick with emotion. Belasko looked over to see she had tears in her eyes, unshed. "It'll be a larger source of regret for you if you don't."

"Yes, majesty. I expect you're right."

She gave a delicate little laugh and dashed the tears away with the back of her hand. "Of course I'm right. I'm very wise, you know. Comes with the crown." She tapped the slim gold circlet with the tip of one finger.

"Oh, is that where it comes from? I had wondered." Belasko smiled at her and felt a little of his tension ease. "One thing, your majesty."

She smiled at him. "Yes, Belasko?"

He pointed at the guards that rode before and behind

them, at their bulging saddlebags. "You had Majel bring supplies with us, I presume for the soldiers and ourselves?"

"And for your parents, too, of course."

He frowned. "Better to offer to share with them, supplement their food with our own." Queen Lilliana gave him a quizzical look. Belasko sighed. "My parents are proud, ma'am. They will be offended if it seems you offer them charity. Guest rites are respected here in the mountains, even for unexpected callers. My parents wouldn't expect a guest to bring their own food to supper. But catering for this many might empty their store cupboard."

The Queen frowned. "I see. The last thing I want to do is offend your parents. I'll let you handle it as you see best."

Belasko snorted. "Hopefully, I won't make a mess of things as I normally do with them."

"Have faith in yourself, Belasko. I do."

He inclined his head in acknowledgement. "Thank you, your majesty." Then it was his turn to look at her out of the corner of his eye.

"If I can ask, your majesty, how did you get Majel to agree to this? Taking an unexpected detour so soon after the attempt on your life?

"Oh, that was simple. She objected, of course."

"Of course," murmured Belasko, "I'm not surprised."

"But then I pointed out that I would be with her, guards handpicked by her, you, and your parents. I do think threats are unlikely to come from those quarters, don't you?"

"I do, your majesty. I do."

They passed the next few hours in idle conversation, Belasko trying his best to hide the rising tension that grew in him with every passing mile.

Eventually, the forest around them grew sparse, and as they turned a corner, a sheltered valley was revealed. The land on one side was terraced for farming, the other hillside dotted with sheep. At one end, sheltered by the cliffs rising behind, was a small cottage, a drift of smoke coming from its chimney.

The Queen gasped. "Belasko, it's beautiful."

He gave a sad smile. "Perhaps you can see why I prefer my academy to city life. As much as I love my role as Champion, part of my soul always longs for the open air. Come, let's ride on. They'll see us approaching."

Belasko was correct. As they neared the little cottage, a lone figure came out to stand by the gate post. A tall man with steel-grey hair close-cropped, he looked to be in his mid sixties and had the ruddy weather-beaten skin of someone who spent a lot of time outdoors. Back slightly stooped, as if he spent a lot of time working bent over, he nevertheless stood as straight as he could.

He raised a hand in greeting as they drew near, stony face expressionless, deep-set eyes giving nothing away. "Hello, son. It's been a while."

Belasko dismounted and walked over to his father. "The fault for that lies with me, Father. We were passing and thought it rude not to pay our respects."

His father grunted, eyeing the people Belasko travelled with and giving them a respectful nod, frowning slightly as his eyes passed over the Queen.

"Where's Mother?" Belasko asked.

"Preparing dinner, although we'll need to set out a few more places now." He leaned closer to Belasko, whispering, "What are you doing bringing so many to our table as winter sets in? We need our stores to get through the next few months."

"It's all right, Father," Belasko replied, just as quiet. "We have our own supplies for the journey. Let us share them." A look of sudden anger appeared on his father's face. "Not charity, Father. Fellowship. Let us share what we have in fellowship. My employer would not want our visit to cause you hardship."

Belasko's father frowned, looking again to the Queen. "Employer?"

Then Belasko's mother appeared at the front door. Shorter than her husband, her hair still retained most of its chestnut colour. Her cheeks held a rosy glow, and the lines around her eyes gave the impression of having their source in smiling. She seemed confused for a moment, until her eyes alighted on Belasko's face. With a cry, she sprang forward, seizing Belasko in an embrace.

"Oh, son," she said, "it's been too long." She kissed him soundly on both cheeks, to the shared amusement of the guards still mounted behind him, then looked over his shoulder.

"I know, Mother, and that's entirely my fault. I'm sorry. We were passing on the road at the bottom of the valley, and my employer reminded me of my manners. So, we decided to pay a visit."

She peered at the people behind him, eyes coming to rest on Queen Lilliana, who smiled and gave a little wave. "Employer?" she said haltingly, before gasping and turning white as a sheet. She turned to Belasko's father and swatted him on the shoulder. "It's the Queen, you idiot, bow!"

Belasko's father, startled, got to one knee, lowering his head, while Belasko's mother sketched a deep curtsy.

Queen Lilliana dismounted and walked over to them.

"Your majesty," said Belasko, "may I introduce my parents? My mother, Drina, and my father, Edrik."

The Queen smiled. "I honestly can't tell you how pleased I am to meet you both. I've known Belasko since I was a little girl, yet his past has always been something of a mystery. But please, get up." She put a hand on Drina's elbow, gently encouraging her to straighten. She lifted Edrik's chin with a dainty finger until he looked her in the eyes. "I, and our country, owe your son many debts of gratitude. Far too many to repay. We owe those debts to you, too, for you raised an extraordinary man. Please, up on your feet, and never stand on ceremony with me again." Her brow wrinkled. "Unless we're at court—one does have to keep up appearances somewhat."

"Yes, your majesty," said Drina.

Edrik grunted and levered himself back to his feet. Belasko felt a pang at how much more difficult this was for his father than when he last visited. In truth, age had set its hand upon both his parents. He felt his face flush as the shame he had been feeling for years deepened just a little bit more.

"Would... Would you like to come in, your majesty?" Drina asked.

Queen Lilliana beamed at her. "I would be delighted. I hope you don't mind if we stay for supper?"

"No, of course not, your majesty." Drina took in Majel and the ten guards just starting to dismount and tend to their horses. She swallowed. "We have enough to go around, though I dare say it won't be the sort of fare you'd get at the palace."

"It will be a most welcome change, I assure you. I understand that you observe the guest rites most strictly here in the mountains, which I respect. However, where I am from, it is unbecoming for a guest not to bring a gift for their host. We have travel supplies, more than we need, so please let us add them to your larder and see what we can come up with.

The Swordsman's Descent

Pool our resources, as it were. That won't be a problem, will it? I'll be terribly put out if you don't let us contribute."

Edrik and Drina merely looked at each other, Edrik nodding his acceptance.

"Good. Majel?" Queen Lilliana called to the commander of her guard. "Can you bring our travel supplies inside, please? I'm sure Drina will direct you."

Majel nodded, calling a few orders to the guards, who quickly set about stripping packs and panniers from their horses. They filed up to the door, looking expectantly at Drina, who looked a little flustered.

"Of course," she said. "Come with me, through here." She led the way inside, the guards and Majel filing in after.

Queen Lilliana smiled at Belasko. "I'll just see if there's anything I can do to help." She followed the others, leaving Belasko alone with his father.

An awkward silence grew. "Do you not want to go inside?" Belasko asked.

Edrik grunted, looking away. "There's a few chores to do yet before I'm free to entertain guests."

Belasko forced a smile. "Let me help you, then. I'm sure I remember how."

His father nodded. "All right, let's be on with it then."

Edrik led the way, and Belasko followed. After an initial awkwardness, they soon settled into a routine from long years before. They gathered animals in, distributed feed, made sure all the outbuildings and gates were closed and locked, finally collecting water from the well to be used in cooking.

Although they worked in silence, by the time they were heading back to the cottage, carrying a large pail of water between them, something had thawed a little between them, and the silence was a companionable one. One that his father broke.

"It's good to see you, son. Good to see that city life hasn't softened you to a bit of proper work, too."

Belasko smiled. "It's good to see you as well. I'm sorry it's been so long."

Edrik grunted. "You should be. Your mother's missed you something terrible. It's shameful."

"I know." Belasko bowed his head. "I've felt ashamed for a long time, putting it off. Always something to do—students to teach, an academy to run... Excuses to put off something I should have done long ago."

They had reached the front door to the cottage and set down the pail of water.

Edrik turned to his son. "Why did you stop coming?"

Belasko swallowed. "It's hard to say. Perhaps I should talk about it with both you and Mother. I..."

Just then, the cottage door opened, and Majel stepped out. She looked up, surprised to see them so close. "Sorry to interrupt. I wanted to find a spot to set up our tents."

"The southern pasture over there by that barn," Edrik said, pointing the way. "That should do nicely."

"Thank you, Master Edrik, I'll take a look." She walked around them, heading to the gate. Majel turned as she opened it. "By the way, Belasko, you might want to step inside. The Queen is insisting that she help with dinner, and I think your mother is about to have a fit."

Belasko and Edrik exchanged glances. Their conversation would have to wait. They picked up the pail and hurried inside, but carefully so as not to spill a drop.

As they moved through the front room of the cottage, fire already lit in the hearth, Belasko looked around. The room remained much as it had in his childhood: the tiled floor that his father had laid himself, chairs drawn up in front of the fireplace, table by the back wall. Shelves lined the walls, full of this and that—some of his father's tools, wood to be whittled and shaped, his mother's knitting and sewing materials. Her spinning wheel stood by the fire. There were books, too, and bundles of papers that caught Belasko's eye. Before he could investigate them further, they had passed through the front room into the back of the cottage, which housed the kitchen and larder.

He had never seen the room so full. Guards had been set to work on every available surface, chopping vegetables, weighing out flour and grain, slicing meat. The activity came to a halt as they walked in, Drina raising her voice to be heard above the clamour.

"Thank you, thank you, that's enough. It's very kind of you all to help, but now the preparation is done, don't you all have tents to put up or some such? Once you've seen to your duties, call by the front door and we'll make sure you all have enough beer to slake your first."

One of the guards threw her a crisp salute. "Yes, Mistress Drina. Please let us know if there's any other way we can be of assistance." They turned to the Queen. "Your majesty, do we have your permission to withdraw?"

Queen Lilliana waved her hand. "Of course, thank you for the help. I'm sure Majel will have jobs for you to do. Send her back inside once she's able."

The guards all trooped out, nodding and smiling at Belasko and his father.

Drina had gone bright red. She turned to the Queen. "Oh, your majesty, I'm sorry. It's hardly my place to be ordering your soldiers about."

The Queen smiled. "Mistress Drina, this is your kitchen.

It is precisely the place for you to be ordering people about. Speaking of which, how can I help?"

Drina swallowed. "If your majesty is sure?"

"My majesty is. Where do we start?"

Drina rolled up her sleeves, putting on an apron as she passed one to the Queen. "I don't want you to make a mess of your fine clothes, your majesty."

Queen Lilliana took the apron, donning it swiftly. "Lilliana, please."

Drina flushed again. "All right then, Lilliana. I was going to use the ham you brought to make a chicken and ham pie, so we'll need to make the dough for the pastry. Edrik, dear, pass me down the sack of flour from that shelf, would you? Belasko, fetch me the bowl—the big one, you know."

Belasko went over to a shelf and got down the large glazed pottery bowl his mother always used when baking. It had been a fixture of his childhood, and his mother had inherited it from her mother. No one knew how old it really was. As he picked it up, a wave of memories washed over him. Helping his mother in the kitchen when he was small. Making dough, rolling and kneading it out for pastries. The smell of delicious treats baking that would permeate the house.

He turned, swallowing, and passed it to his mother. Belasko smiled at her. "Here you are. It's nice to see you still have the same one."

Drina returned his smile. "Yes, I don't know where I'd be without it." She turned to the Queen. "When he was little, Belasko would help me bake. Just as I helped my mother, using the same bowl. I always hoped..." Here, her smile faltered a little. She cleared her throat. "Never mind. We've the flour and the bowl. Edrik, did you two fetch in some water? Ah, lovely, thank you. Now, we need to get the measurements just right."

Drina set to her work, talking Queen Lilliana through every step as she assisted.

"What can I do to help, Mother?" Belasko asked.

Drina looked up from her mixing bowl. "Hmm? Oh. Well, those soldiers have done most of the preparation for us. Can you see to them, make sure they're settled?" She frowned. "I'm not sure we'll be able to get them all around the table. Edrik, dear, can you get out the trestle table we use to feed the farmhands at harvest time? We'll need the extra crockery and cutlery too, I've already set the large oven going. Hopefully it'll get up to temperature in time."

"The guards will certainly be all right outside, although it might be nice if Captain Majel were to sit with us tonight. Ma'am?" Belasko directed this last question at the Queen, who looked up from what she was doing with an absent-minded expression on her face.

"Oh, yes, that would be nice." She blushed a little. "If that would be all right with you, Mistress Drina, Master Edrik? I've no right to decide who should sit at your table."

Edrik coughed. "If it please your majesty—" The Queen raised an eyebrow. "—that is, if it please you, Lilliana, then we're happy to accommodate our guests however you think best." He turned to Belasko. "You're sure the guards will be fine outside?"

Belasko smiled. "They've probably already erected a shelter somewhere out of the way. Majel's an efficient sort. Come on, let's go check on them. Ladies, we'll be back to see if you need anything shortly." Then he and his father left the ladies to their undertaking.

As they made their way outside, this time via the back

door in the kitchen, Edrik cuffed Belasko gently round the back of the head.

"Hey, what was that for?"

Edrik gave him a hard look as they walked back around the house in search of the guards. "All these years, no visits, your letters stop coming just as you did, and now you bring the Queen to our door? The bloody Queen!"

Belasko sighed. "I know, I know. I'm sorry. We were passing and..."

Edrik snorted. "'We were passing', don't give me that! You weren't out here." Edrik waved an arm, trying to encompass the vista of snow-covered mountains that reared up and surrounded them. "You weren't out here on a jaunt. The Queen. The bloody Queen! I'm surprised your mother didn't have a fit." Now, he grinned. "Still, it'll give us something to talk about at the midwinter dance. If we're not snowed in again this year."

They rounded the cottage and went in search of the soldiers.

"Why don't you tell me what you're really doing here? Not here, with us, but passing through the mountains? Or is it some secret business you can't tell your old father about?" Edrik gave Belasko a sly look.

"It is, actually, but if we're successful, you'll hear soon enough anyway." Belasko cleared his throat. "We're on our way to Bas, to their capital, to meet the new King. He wants to negotiate new accords and a lasting peace between our countries. I..." Belasko faltered, coming to a stop, aware that his father had stopped walking a pace or two behind him. He turned to Edrik, who had gone white as the flour Drina and the Queen were working with in the kitchen. "What is it? What's wrong?"

Edrik stalked up to him, almost quivering with anger

and something else Belasko couldn't quite work out. He cuffed Belasko again, and not so gently this time, then seized him by the shoulders. "Are you mad? Going to Bas? To Bas! Those people hate you, son. I don't think you know how much. Setting foot in their country may as well be a death sentence. Are you a fool, boy? I didn't think we'd raised an idiot."

Edrik's face was white, his eyes wide, and Belasko could now place the emotion he saw there. *It's fear. My father is afraid for me.* He smiled at his father, putting a hand on his shoulder in return. "It's all right. We go in peace under the Queen's banner. An attack on any of her party, including me, would be an act of war. Nobody wants that. At least, no one sane. I might get a few personal challenges—I had one just before we left on this trip—but I can see those off easily enough. I might be feeling my age, but I'm still pretty handy with this." He patted the sword at his hip with his free hand. "I can look after myself."

Edrik sighed, pulling away and turning to look out over the valley. "I don't know how you can treat your own life so recklessly."

"It's not reckless, it's calculated risk. I'm good with a blade, very good, and I train every day to keep it that way. When I step into the circle with someone, I know I've done everything I can to prepare. Win or lose, it's on me." He paused. "In case you hadn't noticed Da, I've never lost."

"Not yet." Edrik turned back to him. "It might be a calculated risk for you when you draw your blade, but it's not just your own life on the line. It's your mother's heart. Mine as well. If anything was to happen to you... All these years, we've never stopped worrying about you." He pulled Belasko into a rough embrace. "Just be careful, all right? Whatever you do, be careful."

Belasko, feeling awkward at the sudden display of affection, patted his father on the back. "It's fine. Nothing's going to happen. We're going to have some very boring meetings, with some very boring people. I promise to keep any dangerous or exciting stuff to an absolute minimum. Is that acceptable?"

Edrik pulled away as rapidly as he'd embraced his son. He turned and carried on walking towards the soldiers' little encampment. "Good. See that you do."

Belasko sighed, shook his head, and followed.

Majel was working with her troops. She looked up from hammering in a tent stake as they approached. She nodded to them, giving the stake one final hit with the hammer, before standing. "Belasko, Master Edrik. How go things inside?"

"Well, thank you, Majel." Belasko grinned at her. "The Queen has rolled up her sleeves and is currently helping my mother make a chicken and ham pie."

Majel laughed, spinning the hammer in one hand. "Well, I never. The Queen is a curious one. Always seeking out opportunities to learn. I wonder if she'll take this newfound interest in preparing culinary delights into the palace kitchens when we return?"

"Oh my, old Pellero would have a fit, wouldn't he? Still, I can't see the harm."

"If you think it's odd, imagine how we feel, putting the Queen to work for her supper." Edrik swallowed. "Bloody odd day, all around. I'm glad to see you, son, but some warning wouldn't go amiss next time. We're getting a bit old for these sorts of shocks."

Majel changed the subject. She gestured to their small encampment. "I hope I've chosen a suitable spot for us to put up our tents, Master Edrik? It's only for one night, so the disruption to the pasture will be minimal."

"Just Edrik, please. And yes, you've chosen well. Captain Majel, we've not room for all of your soldiers around our table, so I'm afraid most will have to have their dinner outside, but the Queen has asked that you join us for supper, if that's all right?"

Majel sketched a bow. "It would be my pleasure. I hope you have lots of embarrassing stories of Belasko's childhood to share."

Edrik arched an eyebrow at his son. "Oh yes, one or two, one or two." He smiled as Belasko pulled a face. "If you wanted those kept to ourselves, then you should have visited more. Not sure we'll be able to stop them coming out. In all our excitement at reminiscing, you understand."

"Oh, I understand. I understand perfectly." Belasko kept a dry, serious expression on his face for a moment before returning his father's smile. "No less than I deserve." He turned back to Majel. "On that note, please do join us inside when you're ready, Majel. We'll bring out refreshments for the guard shortly."

Majel looked around, tossing the hammer up in the air so that it spun one full revolution before the handle landed back in her hand. She shrugged, threw the hammer back up in the air and this time, as it landed, struck it so that it diverted off to the side and landed neatly in the kit bag at her feet with a soft clink. "I'm just about done here. Let me come with you now, and we can fetch these reprobates something to drink." She turned to the guards, who were now setting out guy ropes for their tents. "All right, you lot. Once this is done and all the kit is stowed, you're at ease. We'll be keeping watch in pairs tonight, in two-hour shifts, so decide who's going first amongst yourselves. I'll be back out shortly with something for you to drink."

They made their way back to the house, where Majel watched with wide-eyed wonder as the Queen, be-aproned and with sleeves rolled up, rolled out and cut pastry. Her hands and forearms were dusted with flour, as was her forehead where she had absentmindedly pushed back a lock of hair. She looked up at them. "Are the guard well? Happily situated?"

"Yes, your majesty. Just finishing setting up the tents and stowing their gear now. We thought we might take them out something to drink."

"Mistress Drina has already thought of that." The Queen nodded towards several pitchers that sat on the kitchen table. "Beer and some fruit juice for those that don't drink alcohol."

Majel sketched a bow to Drina, much like the one she had offered Edrik outside. "Ma'am, you are as wise as you are beautiful. On behalf of my troops, I thank you."

Drina blushed. "You're most welcome, but flattery won't get you extra helpings at dinner tonight. Now, you three, those pitchers won't carry themselves, will they? Have you got the table and extra crockery out yet?"

"Not yet, we'll do that now," said Edrik. "Come on, you two, you heard the lady. We've got jobs to be getting on with."

So they took out the drinks to ten very grateful members of the guard, dug out the trestles and long piece of wood that served as a table when Belasko's parents had farmhands. They refreshed the guards' drinks, after which Belasko, Edrik, and Majel themselves stopped for a drink.

They stood outside the cottage, leaning against the trestle table. Majel took a sip of her beer and made an appreciative face. "Very nice, Edrik. Do you make it yourself?"

Belasko's father nodded. "Yes indeed, an old family recipe."

"Belonging to the brewer who lives down the mountain. Come on, you're many things, but a master brewer isn't one of them." Belasko smiled into his own cup.

Edrik frowned at him. "Cheeky pup. Just for that, I'm telling Majel about the time you wet yourself at the midsummer fair."

"Oh, come on, I was five!"

Edrik nodded. "You were. It's still a good story, though."

They finished their drinks and went inside to see what else needed to be done. The kitchen had been a hive of activity, settling down now as the last few dishes bubbled away. There were several pies cooling on the kitchen table, meat in gravy, bowls of steaming hot greens, and more besides.

Belasko blinked. "Wow. Mother, you've conjured up a feast."

Drina smiled over her own cup of beer. "Not just me. Lilliana has a lot to do with it."

The Queen looked up from where she was stirring something in a pot over the fire. "Oh no, it's all Drina's work. I just did as I was told." Even with the apron she had been provided, she had still managed to get somewhat covered in food, and the streak of flour across her forehead remained. Queen Lilliana had clearly set to her tasks with the enthusiasm and dedication that was her hallmark.

Drina shook her head. "You're a fast learner and a hard worker. I could do with that helpful extra pair of hands more often. Thank you."

"My pleasure, Drina. Now, what's next?"

Drina drained off the rest of her beer. "We're ready to start serving. If you three wouldn't mind carrying out the soldiers' portions, these here, we'll bring plates and whatnot. Then we can sit down to our meal once they're settled with theirs."

They sprang into action, all moving as Drina directed, and carried out dinner to the guard. The Queen came last, carrying plates and cutlery.

Once outside, Majel called the guard over using her best parade ground voice as the others set the table. The guard approached, carrying their pitchers of drink and making appreciative noises at the sight of all the food that was set out for them. A few stared openly at the Queen helping to set the table for them.

"Come on, you lot, be seated and help yourselves. You don't expect the Queen to serve you as well as help cook, do you?" Majel said with a smile.

The guardsmen and women fell in swiftly, voicing words of appreciative thanks.

"You're all very welcome. Now, are you all right for drinks? Let's get those topped up for you." Drina took a couple of empty pitchers and went back inside.

Once Drina and Edrik were satisfied that the soldiers were settled and had everything they needed, they set their own smaller table inside and sat down to eat. Edrik had fetched up and tapped a small barrel of wine from the cellar, filling a glass decanter that was placed on the table. He poured a glass for all of them, serving the Queen first, before sitting at the head of the table.

Edrik raised his glass. "To visitors," he said, "and sharing food with friends."

"To visitors and friends," they chorused before sipping from their own glasses.

The Swordsman's Descent

Belasko made an appreciative noise. "This is very nice. Much better than what you used to drink."

Edrik grunted. "We had to spend all that money you sent over the years on something, son. Little treats and luxuries to make life easier, mostly. Decent wine, better quality glasses to drink it out of, things like that. Now please eat, all of you."

So they did, and the food was delicious. Plates piled high, they set to with enthusiasm, and for a moment, all was quiet except for the sounds of contented eating.

After a while Edrik spoke again. "It has been very helpful, especially as we're not getting any younger." He spoke around a mouthful of food, then looked at the Queen and hastily swallowed. "Begging your pardon, ma'am." She raised an eyebrow. "Lilliana, I mean." Edrik looked at his son. "It's as I said, we've spent a little on things to make life a bit more comfortable. Small luxuries around the house, hiring a few hands to help with things around the place now I'm getting on. But otherwise..." He held out his hands to indicate the cottage they sat in. "What do we need with money? We grow, make, or mend most of what we need and trade for the rest. Don't get me wrong, we're not ungrateful, and we're proud that our son has become a man of wealth and influence. So the rest is lodged with a bank as security against any, um, unforeseen circumstances."

"Unforeseen circumstances? Such as?" Belasko took a sip of his wine, then stood and topped up all of their glasses before refilling his own and sitting down.

Edrik raised his glass in thanks and took a sip himself. Then he shrugged. "Illness, accident, that sort of thing. If we ever needed to sell up and move on."

Belasko frowned, shooting his father a quizzical look.

Edrik's face took on a more serious cast. He looked at

Drina, who shook her head slightly then sighed when he carried on. "Surely you must realise that being your parents has repercussions? After that business a few years ago, we feared reprisals, should you get up with court intrigue again. It wouldn't be difficult to find us." He glanced at the Queen. "Begging your pardon, Lilliana, not from you, obviously, but if things hadn't gone as they did..."

Queen Lilliana gave a sad smile. "No, I'm sorry. That you ever felt that way. I wouldn't have thought my father capable of such a thing, but then I never thought he would have poisoned my brother or framed his most loyal subject for the murder."

Her smile was a bright, crystalline thing. Like a thin skin of ice over a frozen lake, everyone at the table could feel the depth of sorrow that lay beneath it. Her hands sat on the table, clutching the edge of her plate, her glass, anything tangible that she could hold on to. Formality forgotten, Belasko reached over and placed a hand over hers and gave it a squeeze. That human contact seemed to ground the Queen, and her smile shifted, becoming something warmer as she turned her gaze on Belasko. "Thank you," she whispered, eyes glittering with moisture. She cleared her throat, retrieving her hand, and looked back at Edrik. "I'm sorry, Edrik, you were saying?"

"All right. It's not just politics. A number of Baskans have passed by, not all looking to cause trouble, but if they had, or if they'd come in number, there's not a lot we could do to stop them."

"Baskans have come here? Why?" Belasko was both concerned and curious. "What could they gain from coming here? Do they come often?"

Edrik snorted. "Why? Who knows? They come less often than they did, in fairness, but it seemed almost like a sort of pilgrimage to some. On their way to challenge you, those ones. I suppose they found it reassuring. Seeing you came from what they'd think of as humble roots, humble stock—perhaps it eased their minds. That you are only human, beatable. Not the monster their stories make you out to be." He took another sip of his wine. "Some of their traders tried to make life difficult for us a few years back, refusing to take our goods or those of people who associated with us." He grinned. "More fool them. Once word got out, no one in the mountains would trade with them. They did themselves out of a lot of business."

"I have to say, seeing something of Belasko's roots, meeting you both of course, has been very interesting to me." The queen smiled at Belasko. "Although he has been a great friend to me over the years, in many ways my champion has always been something of a mystery to me. Learning more about his early life, before he came to court, has been eye opening. I'd love to know more about it, about life in these mountains."

"Agreed," said Majel, "I'd like to hear more stories of Belasko's youth. There must be lots of embarrassing tales you can tell us."

"Well," said Drina, "there was that time he was trying to show off at the winter fair, down the mountain. He climbed the tallest tree in the village to retrieve someone's scarf that had blown up there, and slipped and fell into the pond beneath. Soaked to his smallclothes! We had to bundle him into the inn and strip him off in front of the fire, so he didn't catch cold."

"I'd forgotten that," said Belasko. "Or at least, driven it from my mind."

"That's the sort of thing," said Majel, grinning at Belasko. "Tell me all about it."

They passed the rest of the evening telling family tales, laughing and joking, drinking and playing silly games.

This has done all of us a world of good, Belasko thought to himself as he looked at Queen Lilliana, deep in conversation with Drina, while Majel entertained Edrik with a series of ribald and increasingly impossible jokes. *She really is wise.* He smiled. *I'd almost forgotten what family felt like.*

***

Later that night, after Queen Lilliana and Captain Majel had sought their beds, Belasko helped his parents tidy up. Belasko and Edrik set to clearing the table, while Drina stood behind her husband replacing now-clean glassware on a shelf. Belasko paused in what he was doing and looked across the table at his father. He cleared his throat. "What you were saying earlier, about those Baskans giving you trouble." He shook his head. "I'm sorry I've brought those difficulties on you. I never thought…"

Edrik banged the edge of the table with his hand, his face screwed up in a sudden flash of frustration and pain. "No, you never did. But you didn't bring anything on us. Those idiots acted of their own accord. And they can come again and again, as far as we're concerned, because we'll never shy away from who our son is. If anyone tried to harm us, everyone in these mountains would take up arms against them. Because the mountains are as proud of our son as we are."

There was silence then. Belasko and his mother shocked by Edrik's outburst. Belasko stared at his parents, from one to the other. "You're proud of me?" he asked in a whisper.

"Of course, we are, son. Who wouldn't be?" Drina said quietly, moving to stand beside Edrik. "The truth is, we thought you were ashamed of us. Once you were moving in the circles of the high and mighty."

"Ashamed of you? I thought you were ashamed of me. Because of... Because of what I am. Who I am."

"Never." Drina was fierce now. "You're our son, and we love you, no matter what."

"I love you both, too. I thought that..." Belasko faltered.

"Because you prefer men?" his mother finished for him.

He nodded. "Yes, because I prefer men. Because the life I have chosen is a lonely one, as Champion. Because of these things, you would never have grandchildren. I thought..."

"You thought wrong," his father said, quiet but with a forceful tone.

"We thought you had outgrown this place, us, your roots. That we didn't know how to talk to each other anymore. We thought you ran away to war because of us."

"Because of you?" Belasko blinked, then shook his head. "No, no. I ran away to join the army because I was afraid. I couldn't work the land like you, so I became a soldier instead. I've always been proud of you. So all these years, the difficulty between us..."

"Has been because of a misunderstanding," Drina said. "One that could have been resolved if only we'd talked sooner, more honestly."

Edrik grunted. "Instead, we all assumed things. Assumed we knew the mind of the other. How foolish we all are."

"I'm glad we're talking now. I just hope I can make up the years lost to foolishness. My own most of all." Belasko shook his head, then began to laugh. Gently, a chuckle at first, then increasingly loud, his shoulders shaking. Eventually, he came to a stop, taking deep shuddering breaths. "I was just thinking," he said, "about how lowlanders call us mountain folk stubborn." He started laughing again, and first Drina, then Edrik, joined him.

Belasko walked around the table, throwing an arm around each of his parents and drawing them into a deep embrace. "Let's not be so foolish again. We have a lot of catching up to do." He gave his parents a squeeze. "Let's clear the air properly."

After the chores were done, the three of them drew up chairs by the fire and talked long into the night. When it was time for bed, Belasko made his way up still familiar stairs to his childhood bedroom. He opened the door and stopped.

It hasn't changed. Not a bit.

His parents had kept it as he'd left it, all these years, ready for when he came home. Belasko crossed to the bed, a low frame of simple construction that his father had built, and sat down. Looking up, he caught sight of the shelf above where he had stored his childhood treasures. Interesting rocks he'd found while climbing, colourful feathers, toys his parents had made. Rising, his hands ran across these things. An eagle feather he'd been especially proud of. A wooden boat his father had carved for him from a single piece of wood. A doll in the shape of a bear that his mother had started knitting when she learned she was with child. A doll that had been placed beside him in his cot when he was born.

Years I slept with this thing next to me. He smiled. Everything is neat and dust free. Even an unused room can't escape mother's diligence.

Belasko sat back down on the bed, still holding on to the doll. Kicking his boots off, too tired to undress, he lay back on the bed fully clothed. Doll still in hand, his eyes gradually closed and he fell into a deep and dreamless sleep.

***

The next morning saw them set off early, after Drina had prepared them all a hearty breakfast. The farewells were tearful, and the others stood back a little as Belasko said goodbye.

He smiled. "I'll be picking my successor soon, so I'll have more time for travel."

"And fewer excuses not to visit." Drina's smile took the sting out of her words as she pulled her son into one last embrace.

"Come back soon, son," said Edrik, clapping Belasko on the shoulder. "Be careful in Bas. Promise us."

Belasko nodded. "I promise, I'll be as careful as I can." He gave his father a hug, then turned and strode to his horse. He mounted, waved to his parents, and set off. The rest of the party joined him.

When they got to the far end of the little valley, Belasko stopped his horse and turned to look back. He could just make out two figures stood by their gate, watching. Belasko stood up in his stirrups, waved one last time, then sat down and rode on. The twisting track out of the valley almost immediately hid his parents from view.

Belasko rode alongside the Queen in silence for a while, until he gave a little cough and cleared his throat. Queen Lilliana looked at him quizzically.

Belasko looked across to the Queen, eyes wet with unshod tears. Happy ones. "Thank you, ma'am, for insisting we take this little detour. Last night, after you left us, my parents and I reconciled. Would you believe the distance between us, these years of difficulty, it was all because of a misunderstanding?"

Her smile was warm. "My pleasure, Belasko. I can't tell

you how happy I am to hear that the three of you not only reunited, but resolved your problems. It's everything I hoped for when I suggested we pay them a visit." She tilted her chin, so she was looking down her nose at Belasko, a mock-imperious expression on her face. "One *is* rather wise, you know."

"Oh yes, I heard that the other day. It must be the crown." He grinned at her, before his expressions settled into a more serious cast. "But I really can't thank you enough. For taking the time out of our trip to force an old fool to correct his mistakes."

"Think nothing of it, Belasko. I enjoyed it very much. If we've time on the return leg of our journey, we must stop by again. Perhaps see if we can bring your parents some gifts from Bas."

They passed the rest of the journey back down the track in companionable conversation.

21

IT WAS A grey foggy day, the day after they had rejoined the main party. The world around them was shrouded in opalescent mist, quiet and still. Belasko had taken to spending some days riding with the vanguard of cavalry that led their way into the mountains. It reminded him of his early days, scouting for the army in what had been, in many ways, a simpler time for him.

He smiled at a memory of a particular scouting mission with his friend, Orren, when Orren hadn't for once properly hobbled his horse for the night, and the poor creature had worked its way free and made a bid for freedom. They'd spent the small hours of that night trying to corral it and get it back to camp, Belasko on his regular steed and Orren mounted on their packhorse—the small stature of which made Orren, a bear of a man, look like an oversized child on a too-small pony. His smile faded, all of these memories bittersweet since Orren's death.

Belasko was brought back to himself by the shout of one of the forward scouts, who came galloping back to the line.

"There's a bear up ahead, in the middle of the road. If it

won't move. We might have to fetch spears and deal with it," the scout reported breathlessly.

"If I may?" Belasko asked the cavalry squadron's Commander, who nodded their assent. "Bears will rarely attack unless it's a female and their cubs are nearby. They are, however, incredibly strong and fierce. If we provoke them, we risk losing people in the process. What sort of bear is it? The black bears that live in these mountains are fairly placid. Their bigger cousins less so."

The forward scout wrinkled their nose. "Not much of an expert on bears, sir. This one was white and a little bigger than a man."

"White? There's no white bears hereabouts, although I've heard tell of such far to the north." Belasko frowned. "But those are accounted to be much, much larger than a man." He addressed the commanding officer. "Do I have your permission to ride forward and examine this bear for myself? I know the creatures of these mountains, and there's something not quite right about this."

The officer thought for a moment, clearly weighing up her options, before nodding again. "I'll need to take a look myself, help decide the best course of action. You might as well come with me."

So they rode forward together, Belasko, the Commander, and the scout, until they reached a bend in the road. The scout twisted in the saddle to address them. "It's just up ahead, around this corner. We're upwind of them, so it shouldn't smell us. Go quietly so as not to spook it."

They rode forward slowly, as quiet as they could. As they rounded the corner, Belasko peered through the fog, trying to catch a glimpse of the bear. A slight breeze parted the grey curtain, and there, ahead of them, was a white bear, stood in the centre of the road as if waiting for them.

Belasko squinted. The bear was larger than most men but not of the stature of the northern white bears he had heard of, which could grow to be twice a man's height. There was something about the posture that wasn't right—it stood too straight compared to the mountain bears he had encountered in his youth.

"That's not a bear," he whispered.

"What?" said the Commander.

"I know what I see," said the scout.

"I don't think you do. Let's draw a little closer and see if I'm right."

They rode forwards again, their eyes on the creature in front of them. Belasko was right; it wasn't a bear, but a man in a bearskin.

He was huge, a mountain of a man and the biggest person Belasko had ever seen. He wore the skin of a white bear, its skull as a cap, the rest over his shoulders as a cape, huge platter-sized paws crossed over his chest. The clothes he wore underneath were fur-lined black leather. The man's skin had the weathered look of someone who spent a lot of time outdoors, his hair jet black. His arms were bare under his bearskin cloak and corded with thick muscle.

"Hello, friend," called Belasko. "How does the day find you? We're riding through here with our company."

The giant of a man stared at Belasko impassively for a long moment. Then he spoke in a deep voice, the words from his mouth in a guttural tongue that Belasko didn't understand.

"I'm sorry," Belasko said. "Do you speak the common tongue?"

The man stared at him, heaved a great sigh, then repeated himself, pointing down the road as he did so.

"All right. Hold on a moment while we find someone

who can talk to you." Belasko turned to the others. "I don't suppose either of you speak Vargassian? It looks like we've happened across one of their shaman, although what they're doing here I don't know."

"No, of course I don't," snapped the Cavalry Commander. "Let's just force him from the road and have done with it."

Belasko shook his head. "You don't want to do that. He looks difficult enough to deal with, but I've heard tell of these shamans from people I trust. They have uncanny abilities."

"Abilities? Poppycock," sneered the Commander. "Let's force him aside and have done with it."

"I really wouldn't do that if I were you. Wait." Belasko snapped his fingers. "One of my men used to work with a Vargassian. He might be able to communicate." He turned to the scout. "Can you ride back and find a man called Jofar? He's travelling with my people. Bring him back here as fast as you can." Belasko described the Water King to the scout.

The scout looked to their Commander, who frowned. They shook their head. "It's against my better judgement, but very well. See if you can find this Jofar and bring him here. Quickly, now."

The scout snapped off a crisp salute and, setting their heels to their horse's flanks, galloped back the way they had come.

The shaman stared at them impassively while they waited. Taking occasional sips from a skin bag that hung from their shoulder, the man would swill whatever the liquid was around his mouth for a moment before swallowing.

"What, um, abilities are these shaman supposed to have?" the Commander asked after a while.

"Different people say different things. I think it's supposed to be linked to the animal skin they wear." Belasko nodded at his person in front of them, who was now swaying slightly. "So this chap, for example, would probably be able to perform prodigious feats of strength."

"I think he'd manage that anyway," murmured the Commander. "He's huge."

"There are other things, if you believe the stories. They can communicate with each other over great distances, move things with their mind... One person I met insisted they could take on animal form for short periods of time. Swore they'd seen it for themselves, although they were drunk at the time."

"Speaking of which, does this particular shaman look a little this worse for wear to you?"

The shaman was swaying in a more pronounced manner now. He took another swig from his skin and yelled something in his own language, once again pointing up the road as he did so.

"They do have a reputation for drunkenness, it's true. It's all right," Belasko called to the shaman. "We're getting someone who can talk to you."

The sound of approaching hoofbeats reached their ears.

"Here we go," said Belasko, "and not a moment too soon."

The scout rounded the corner, the Water King in his guise as Jofar right behind him. The two men rode up to Belasko and the cavalry Commander.

"What do we have here?" asked the Water King, eyebrows raised.

"What Belasko assures me is a drunk Vargassian shaman, blocking the road," said the Commander.

"They don't seem to speak the common tongue. I

remember you saying once before that you used to work with a Vargassian. I hoped you might be able to find out what's going on," said Belasko.

The Water King dismounted, handing his reins to the scout. "I see. And has he been drinking?"

"Steadily," said Belasko, "since we got here. Why do you ask?"

"It means he anticipates using his powers soon, which could be bad."

"Powers?" The Commander had a scornful look on their face.

The Water King ignored them and addressed Belasko. "It's to do with focus and relaxation, apparently. They need to unfocus the mind in order to access their powers, abilities —call it what you like. I always thought it was an excuse for a drink, but they seem to believe it. I do speak some Vargassian. Let me see what I can find out."

He stepped forward, arms wide in as unthreatening a posture as he could adopt. The Water King paused and called something out in the same guttural tongue the shaman had used. A broad smile split the Vargassian's face, and they called back, continuing in their language as they gestured up the road. The Water King laughed, nodded, and turned back to his own party.

"What does he say?" asked the Commander.

The Water King smiled. "First, he said that it was good to hear a civilised tongue. Then he asked what kept us. He's been waiting all day for us. There's been a cliff fall up ahead which has covered the road, and he's been sent to clear it for us."

"Sent?" Belasko frowned. "By who?"

The Water King turned back to the shaman, saying something in a questioning tone. The shaman shrugged, touched his bearskin, and pointed to the sky before saying a few words.

"He said the world sent him. He says we're on a quest that could do much good, and he's been sent to assist us."

"Okay. Can he show us the rockfall? Then we can send for some engineers to help clear it."

"That might not be necessary. I'll ask him to show the way. Then we can watch while he goes to work." He spoke to the shaman, who nodded and beckoned for them to follow as he turned and walked up the road.

They all dismounted and followed on foot, leading their horses. As they came further around the corner and through the fog, it became clear the Vargassian was right. There had been a rockfall, and several large boulders now blocked the road, the weight of them having crushed the stones of the road to powder beneath them.

Belasko whistled. "Yes, this does present a bit of a problem. How does he propose to help?"

The Water King relayed this to the shaman, who grinned and cracked his knuckles. He said something in reply before taking a swig from his skin.

"He says 'watch'."

So they did. The shaman closed his eyes and began muttering to himself, his words rising to become a droning song as he began some ritualistic movements. He gestured with his hands, moving his arms as though he gathered unseen forces. His considerable muscles tensed with the effort as he brought his hands together in a clap. The shaman shuffled his feet, sweeping them across the gravel of the road and leaving patterns in their wake that were obliterated moments later by his next movements, before touching his bearskin and pointing to the sky. Then he began the cycle over again, faster this time.

The cavalry Commander gave a sceptical snort, which the Water King shushed. They glared at him.

"Wait," whispered Belasko, "something's happening."

Something was indeed happening. As the shaman worked through his ritual, Belasko began to feel a strange tingling sensation on his skin and a feeling as if pressure was building in the air. It seemed to Belasko that the fog that surrounded them had begun to glow with a faint white light

The shaman's singing got louder and faster until finally he brought his hands together in a loud clap and gave a roar that echoed off the mountainside. All was quiet for a moment. Then a faint sound could be heard. The pitter-patter of gravel falling as a series of pebbles, stones, and small rocks began to roll down the cliffside over and around the boulders that blocked their way.

Then those boulder began to move also. Slowly at first, they slipped and rolled their way across the wide road, splitting and pushing the smaller stones with them. A few of the smaller rocks and stones started to roll more freely. Then it seemed like the momentum was with them as they scraped and rattled their way to the cliff edge and then over. A rattling cascade of rock and earth roared as it poured over the edge of the road and further down the cliff, until the road, cracked and damaged, was clear.

The sound of the rocks crashing into the valley below echoed before eventually returning to silence. Belasko and his party were stunned, apart from the Water King, who looked as if this was the sort of thing he witnessed on a regular basis.

"Now that's something you don't see every day," said the cavalry Commander.

The shaman turned back to them, sweat pouring from

his bare flesh, and took another swig from his skin. Then he grinned and said something to the Water King.

"Ah," he relayed, "now we come to the matter of payment."

"Payment?" asked the cavalry Commander. "For what? All he did was shout and trigger another landslide. We're lucky we weren't killed!"

"Ah, but we weren't, were we?" said the Water King. "Whichever way you look at it, he did clear the road. And quickly. He's saved us a lot of time."

The shaman called out to the Water King, who replied with some words in a pacifying tone.

"What did he say?" asked Belasko.

"That if there is any issue with the quality of his work, we are welcome to inspect the rocks at the bottom of the valley to see if we could have done better. He'll even help us on our way."

Belasko chuckled. "Please tell him that won't be necessary. If he comes with me, I'll arrange suitable payment." He turned to the cavalry Commander. "I'll send forward a detachment of engineers to make sure the way forward is safe." Then, to the Water King, "Ride back with us. I'll want a translator."

As the shaman made his way over to them, Belasko whispered to the Water King, "Did he do anything? I thought I felt something in the air, but the cavalry Commander is right. It could just be coincidence."

The Water King shrugged. "It's hard to say exactly. What they claim to make happen usually happens. Wouldn't that be magic, though? To control coincidence?"

They made their way back to the lines, where it transpired the best form of payment was a rather nice barrel of brandy from Belasko's personal stock.

The shaman spent the night around their campfire, drinking, gambling with dice, and telling wild stories through his translator. The next morning, when Belasko woke early to start training, he was gone. Without a trace. The only proof he had been there at all was the sore heads and lighter purses of those who had gathered around their fire.

22

IT WAS LATE at night in the Baskan camp. Olbarin picked his way carefully between the tents, careful not to trip on any ropes or pegs. He was on his way to his regular debriefing with Jonteer. The ambassador's dry little secretary had a nondescript tent he worked out of for these things, away from Ambassador Aveyard's tent. *Probably so she can claim no knowledge of his activities. Of course,* Olbarin thought to himself, *if he is Baskan intelligence, then she probably doesn't know half of what he's up to.*

He found the tent and, checking the position of the moon in the sky to make sure he was calling at the right time, plucked an agreed-upon signal on one of the guy ropes.

The tent flap opened slowly to reveal Jonteer's face, the light of the moon reflecting in his deep-set eyes. Something like a smile flickered across his face, although there was no humour in it.

"You're on time for once. Good lad, come on in."

Olbarin stooped to get through the low entrance and stepped into the tent. A brief look told him the inside was as sparse as ever. Two low stools perched on either side of a small oil lamp. The tent contained nothing else. He'd never seen Jonteer take any notes during their meetings—not that Olbarin had been able to offer anything of use. He could only assume that the man committed everything to memory.

How many secrets are rolling around that head of yours?

With a start, he realised that Jonteer was already sat on one of the stools and looking up at him expectantly. Olbarin quickly took the other.

"Are you all right? You paused a moment there?"

Olbarin hesitated but remembered that the older man seemed to be able to sniff out truth from lie and that telling the truth from the start was the easiest path. "I was just thinking that I've never seen you take a note of anything in our meetings. That you must retain it all in your memory. It's remarkable."

Jonteer's smile was a little more genuine this time. "Maybe you're not so hopeless after all. There are exercises, tricks one can use to improve your memory or retain certain information. If you continue along this path, then you may find them useful." He paused. "Of course, you haven't yet given me any information worth keeping."

Olbarin sighed. "I know, I'm sorry, but it's not like Belasko and his people are spilling state secrets. They're training sessions in swordplay. The conversation, such as it is, is kept to the subject in hand." He shrugged. "If I had heard anything interesting or useful, I'd relay it."

Jonteer nodded. "Such is the way of it. We cast out our net, and we wait. These things come to us. Something you may think inconsequential may provide a small piece of a larger puzzle. So, please, talk me through your time in the Villanese camp."

So Olbarin told him. Of the training sessions he'd attended that day. Who else had been there, what they had discussed, what he had seen on his way through the Villanese camp. Jonteer asked questions, teasing as much detail out of him as possible, but eventually, he sighed and shook his head.

"It is as you say, little that seems of any import." Jonteer frowned at Olbarin, his bald pate wrinkling. "So little of import that it makes me wonder if you are holding out on me. Has Belasko won you over?"

A chill ran through Olbarin. Tales were told about what the intelligence service did to people who betrayed them, and he had no desire to end up in one of those stories himself. "No, sir, I am loyal. I will admit, against my better judgement, that Belasko seems likeable. He works tirelessly with his students, me included, it seems for no other reason than to help us improve. Be better. He delights in our progress."

Jonteer leaned forwards. "And how does that make you feel?"

Now, it was Olbarin's turn to frown. "Guilty, in a way. This is the man who killed my father. I'm not supposed to feel anything but hatred for him. Yet I can't help but be grateful for his tuition and, yes, to like him for it."

"The fact you find yourself beginning to see him in a positive light—that isn't affecting your reporting? You're not holding anything back?"

Olbarin shook his head in denial. "Gods no, nothing."

"Good. I would hate to think you disloyal."

Olbarin actually shivered at the gleam in Jonteer's eyes. "No, sir, I'm loyal. I swear it."

"Well, I'll need something useful from these meetings. Or I might have to consider that you're lying to me."

"No, I'm not."

"Give me something then, boy." Jonteer leaned further forward. "It might be a detail you think inconsequential, that your mind has skipped over until now. Think."

Olbarin nodded and closed his eyes. He ran through the last few training sessions again in his mind, picturing them, trying to go over the details. He frowned.

"Yes, boy?" said Jonteer. "What is it? Something has struck you."

Olbarin opened his eyes. "It might be nothing. It's only..." His frown deepened.

"Only what, boy? Out with it."

"I'm not sure if this is the sort of thing you're looking for, but now that I come to think of it, Belasko himself doesn't train with us every day. He talks us through things, asks his friend Byrta and the Guard Captain Majel to demonstrate, but rarely joins in. He does, but not often. And..." Olbarin shook his head.

Jonteer's expression was carefully masked. He merely raised an eyebrow, and Olbarin blurted out the rest of his thought.

"He moves differently. Some days he seems slower than others. Now that I think of it, it could be that he's favouring one foot over the other. When he does lead exercises or show us examples, he seems fine, but on the days he doesn't, there is definitely something different about him." He shook his head. "I'm sure that's not useful, but it's all I can think of."

Jonteer regarded him for a long silent moment. "It's definitely interesting. I wonder what ails the swordsman? Keep an eye out for this specifically when you are with him. Perhaps the great Belasko's powers are waning. That could be very interesting indeed."

Olbarin sat for a moment. Then, when Jonteer indicated the tent's exit, he realised that their meeting was at an end. He stood. "Right. I'll do that. I'll report back tomorrow, but in the meantime, I'll keep my eyes and ears open, particularly on Belasko."

"You do that. Until next time."

Olbarin took that as his cue to leave, ducking back out under the tent flap. As he turned to close the tent behind himself, Olbarin caught a brief glimpse of Jonteer. A cold and hungry smile was spreading across the secretary's face.

23

IT WAS A clear day when they reached the border with Bas. Sun shining, although the air in the mountains still had a certain bite to it. Winter was on its way, after all.

The column moved at its usual pace, but Belasko couldn't help but notice a wary air about his travelling companions. They rode cautiously, eyes scanning their surroundings. The awareness that they were leaving their own territory and entering that of those who had recently been enemies was strong.

For most of the soldiers and guards that accompanied the Queen, it would be the first time they had ever left Villan. The first time their feet had trod on foreign soil. These were as excited as they were nervous, sharing glances and jokes with their comrades until commanding officers reminded them of the need for decorum.

"We'll soon be encountering Baskans, albeit in a peaceful capacity. Let's show 'em what real soldiers look like," said Captain Ricker, who led their infantry. He smiled and then a bit more seriously said, "We represent Villan today. Let's do our people and our Queen proud."

His soldiers called enthusiastically back before launching into a spirited marching song that had gained popularity after the Last War, the lyrical content of which mostly concerned trouncing Baskans.

Belasko smiled to hear it, although the words always made him a little uneasy. The realities of war could not be reduced to a simple tune. He was riding with the Queen and her retinue that morning, as she wanted him to be one of her representatives when they met their Baskan escort.

Queen Lilliana smiled. "Not the first time you've heard that, I'd wager."

"No, definitely not. I'm not overly fond of the song, but if it helps the troops put one foot in front of the other..." He shrugged. "We might want to ask them to quiet down when we get within shouting distance of the border. This is a peaceful mission. Rubbing Baskan noses in their defeat might not be the most politic way to start."

Ambassador Aveyard, who rode with them in anticipation of meeting the Baskans, snorted. "That's not bothered you before, Belasko. Are you calming in your old age?"

Belasko smiled at her. "Oh no, Madame Ambassador, nothing of the sort, I assure you. When I needled you in the past, that was for my own enjoyment. Today I represent the Queen and all of the people of Villan. It wouldn't do to make a bad first impression."

Ambassador Aveyard returned his smile with a bland expression. "Don't worry. I'll tell them what you're really like."

"Ambassador, my Champion, although this is in good humour, I'd rather you not exchange blows today. Verbal or otherwise." Queen Lilliana's slight smile took the edge off her words. "This is an important day in a mission to broker a historic peace. Let's behave appropriately. Agreed?"

Belasko and Ambassador Aveyard exchanged glances, then nodded their assent.

"Good. Now how far is it to the border?" The Queen stood up in her stirrups, peering at the way ahead.

"Not far now, your majesty," said Ambassador Aveyard. "Perhaps another hour's ride."

Queen Lilliana sat back in her saddle. "Have you ever been in Baskan territory, Belasko?" she asked her Champion.

Belasko frowned, stroking his chin. "Yes, but not far in. Borders got a little, um, permeable during the war. It all gets a little hazy up in the mountains anyway. You can't always be sure whose land you're treading on. This is one of the few roads where the border is actually marked."

"My compatriots will be waiting just the other side of the border, I believe." Ambassador Aveyard looked at the mountains around them. "Yes, I'd judge it to be about an hour's ride away."

"To pass the time, Ambasador, tell me what you know of those we're about to meet," Queen Lilliana said.

Ambassador Aveyard frowned. "I'm afraid I haven't been given much information, other than the fact we'll be met by a squadron of cavalry. I haven't been told who's in command."

"The sooner we get there, the sooner we'll know. Let's pick up the pace a little." Queen Lilliana nodded at Majel, who gave the command using a cavalry horn she had hung from her saddle. The call was echoed up and down the column, and then the whole column, infantry and mounted troops, began to move a little faster.

The Swordsman's Descent

It was as the Ambassador had said. About an hour later, they reached the border and their Baskan escort.

A squadron of cavalry, waiting patiently in formation, armour polished, and their mounts' coats brushed until they gleamed, they were clearly disciplined and well-organised.

Word was passed back to the Queen's secure position in the centre of the column, which slowed to a halt as the Queen and her party made their way to the front.

Two Baskans waited a little apart from the others, between the two groups on the road. Both sat atop their horses well. One carried a banner, which fluttered in the chill breeze. The other, laughing at something the banner bearer had said, raised his hand in greeting as Queen Lilliana arrived.

"Interesting," said Ambassador Aveyard.

"Oh? Care to illuminate us, Madame Ambassador?" Queen Lilliana arched an eyebrow.

The Ambassador nodded towards the pair who waited a little way before them. "That banner, it's my uncle's house arms. With the royal crest newly added. Whoever's been sent to escort us is one of the royal family."

"Any idea as to who?" Belasko squinted at the banner. He could make out a golden sun, a black crown at its centre.

Ambassador Aveyard scratched her chin, musing on it for a moment. She peered at the figure ahead of them. "I can't be sure at this distance, but it's likely my cousin, Beviyard. He's a cavalry officer, although it looks like he's jumped a few ranks."

"Sudden elevation to royal status enhancing his career prospects, perhaps?" Queen Lilliana smiled.

Ambassador Aveyard nodded. "Most likely. He'd have

got there in a few years under his own merits; he's really very good. His father's son."

"I suppose we should go and greet them, as they're waiting so patiently. Ambassador, please come with us to make the introductions. Belasko, join us. We'll take no more. We don't want to outnumber them."

They rode forward, leaving the Queen's guards behind. Majel had a face like thunder, but Belasko didn't think the Baskans would try anything against their greater numbers or in defiance of their new King's wishes.

As they neared the Baskan forces, Belasko could make out that their leader was a young man, handsome with the olive skin and dark hair that marked him as Baskan. The banner bearer was a woman, slightly older, with stern features.

Ambassador Aveyard called out as they approached. "Queen Lilliana, the rose of Villan, I have the pleasure to introduce my cousin Beviyard. Knowing him, he wears his new royal status lightly."

"Your majesty, the tales of your beauty have, if anything, been understated. I am delighted to make your acquaintance." Beviyard essayed a fine bow from his saddle.

That's his first mistake, Belasko thought. Although she uses both to great effect, Lilliana would rather be praised for her mind than her appearance.

Queen Lilliana's lips pursed a little at the compliment. "I'm afraid word of your handsomeness hasn't reached the Villanese court, your highness. We'll make sure to tell people when we get home. It's a pleasure. Thank you for coming to meet us."

Prince Beviyard blinked, unsure how to respond. He cleared his throat. "Your majesty is too kind." He looked at Ambassador Aveyard. "Cousin. It's good to see you."

She nodded. "You, too, cousin."

The Prince now turned his attention to Belasko. "And who do we have here?"

"I am Belasko, the Queen's Champion."

A shadow flitted across Prince Beviyard's face. His companion's face had turned stonily expressionless.

"Ah, yes, Father did say you'd been invited." The Prince remembered himself enough to smile. "He has spoken highly of you in the past, for all that you only met once." He frowned. "Although I have to say, I thought you'd be taller."

Belasko sighed while Queen Lilliana tried to hide her amusement without much success. "I get that a lot. I've always thought highly of your father, too."

"As much as I'd like to spend all day telling each other how highly we think of one another, there is still some way to go." Ambassador Aveyard gave a wry smile. "Are you to escort us, cousin?"

Prince Beviyard flushed. "Yes, cousin. You are correct. My squadron will lead the way. We have a few days' travel until we reach the capital." He addressed Queen Lilliana. "I hoped that we might ride together at least some of that time, your majesty, if that isn't too presumptuous?"

Queen Lilliana smiled. "That would be most agreeable, your highness. There is much I would ask you about Baskan society, the functioning of the court and civil society. I would understand your people better to help me build bridges between our two nations."

Prince Beviyard nodded. "That is my hope, too." He turned to Belasko. "I hope you will spare me some time, too, sir. There is much I would ask you about the Last War."

"No need to call me 'sir', your highness. Belasko is fine. I don't normally enjoy picking over old wounds, not least because people are usually disappointed that the truth of events doesn't match the bards' and troubadours' tales too closely." Belasko glanced at Queen Lilliana, who raised a delicate eyebrow. "But as we are trying to build bridges between our people, and out of respect for your father, I would be happy to."

Prince Beviyard flashed a smile. "Not out of deference to my rank as a prince? I'll take your company however you choose to justify it."

"Don't forget, cousin, Belasko is a commoner. He spends half his time annoying the nobles of the Villanese court. Rank isn't something he defers to." Ambassador Aveyard glanced at Belasko. "It might be why I've always liked him, against my better judgement."

"I think we're getting off the point somewhat," said Prince Beviyard. "We'll rejoin my squadron and lead the way out of the mountains. Once we're on level ground and can spread out a little more, then I'll send word, your majesty, and either I'll drop back to ride with you, or you can bring your guard forward to me. You, too, Belasko. Now, if you'll excuse me, I should go and lead the way. Your majesty." He bowed in his saddle to the Queen. "Belasko." A friendly nod. "Cousin." This last said in a warning tone but accompanied by a wink. Then he turned his horse and rode back to his squadron, his banner bearer just behind him in perfect formation.

"That went well," said Belasko.

"Yes," Queen Lilliana murmured. "An auspicious start." She turned to Ambassador Aveyard. "I am curious about something, Ambassador. Your names. Aveyard, Beviyard, Edyard. They all have that same ending, why is that?"

Ambassador Aveyard blinked. "Oh, well. Our names are patronymic. Or matronymic. After the person who founded

our family line. It's not the same for all Baskans, but it's the habit of noble houses in our region."

Queen Lilliana nodded. "I see, that is interesting. Now I do have a bone to pick with you, Ambassador."

"Oh yes, your majesty, what's that?"

"You could have mentioned that you had such a handsome cousin. Really, Ambassador, I am quite put out."

The ambassador shrugged. "I suppose he is, at that. Beviyard's the least annoying of my cousins, too. Shall we rejoin our people? No doubt the newly crowned prince will want to set off soon."

24

IT TOOK ANOTHER day or so to continue their journey down out of the mountains onto the Baskan plane. The road was narrow in places, although equally as well-kept as the Villanese roads. Their long caravan of uneasy travelling companions made its winding way through the Baskan side of the glorious peaks.

Once they were down into the foothills below, it became a little easier, the road a little wider, and there was more interchange between the two groups. Each was wary of the other. The two nations having been at war in recent memory, many had reason to dislike or fear their counterparts. The importance of the mission to those leading the expedition had obviously been impressed on all, as everyone was on their best behaviour.

Several times, Prince Beviyard dropped back, accompanied by one or two of his squadron, and rode with the Queen. Several times, the Queen rode forward with her guard and joined the Prince. They seemed to enjoy each other's company, Queen Lilliana and Prince Beviyard exchanging questions about each other's people and cultures. The Queen seemed to have met her inquisitive match. Queen Lilliana had a mind like a trap, endlessly curious about the world. Prince Beviyard answered her questions happily, posing plenty of his own in reply.

Sometimes Belasko accompanied the Queen at these times, other times not. Whenever he did, he was acutely aware of the eyes of the Baskans, for they watched him openly, some staring, some hostile, others curious.

The day came that Prince Beviyard sent for him, asking Belasko alone to accompany him as they rode.

"Do you want some company?" Byrta asked him.

Belasko shook his head. "I'll be all right," he said. "You keep an eye on things here."

Byrta raised an eyebrow. "You're going to go amongst a group of heavily armed Baskans? On your own?"

"They won't harm me. I'm sure of that."

Byrta snorted. "I wish I had your confidence."

"Confidence, idiocy, call it what you like. They're the ones suing for new treaties and an improved relationship between our two countries. An attack on me would jeopardise that. Say what you like about the Baskans—and I know you have—but they're disciplined soldiers. If they've been ordered to leave me alone, they'll leave me alone. Prince Beviyard is intelligent enough to realise that."

Belasko urged his horse on with his heels, moving up through the column until he approached the rear of the Baskan squadron. He bore the letter of invitation, Prince Beviyard's seal prominently displayed, as he rode.

At first, those at the rear of the Baskan group ignored him, not making way so he could pass through. Belasko slowed to meet their pace, holding up the letter.

"May I pass? Your Prince has invited me to ride with

him, and I'd hate to keep him waiting. Or have to tell him why."

The two cavalrymen that were holding him up exchanged looks and heeled their horses over to the side to let him through.

"Thank you, most kind." Belasko rode forwards and was not held up again. Soon he was at the front of the column, riding next to Prince Beviyard and his banner bearer.

"Your highness," Belasko said as he rode up, "it's good to see you again." He turned to the Prince's banner bearer. "I'm afraid we haven't been properly introduced, I'm—"

"I know who you are." The banner bearer gave him a look that could cut steel. "Emilynn, Prince Beviyard's banner bearer."

"And about the finest warrior with a sabre I think I've ever seen," said Prince Beviyard.

"Oh really?" Belasko looked at Emilynn. "I should introduce you to my friend Byrta, as I would say the same about her."

"Perhaps we could find a quiet moment to carve pieces out of each other, see who's best," said Emilynn drily. She looked to her prince. "Permission to drop back, your highness? I need to inspect a few things."

"Of course," said the Prince, "permission freely given."

She bowed to her Prince, nodded to Belasko, and slowed her horse, falling back through the squadron.

"It's nice to see you, too, Belasko. Don't mind Emilynn. She's got a dark and dry sense of humour." Prince Beviyard scratched his chin. "At least, I think she was joking." He squinted. "She's not overly fond of the Villanese, so it's hard to be sure."

"I know some people that feel the same way about Baskans. I won't take offence if you don't."

They rode in silence for a moment, before Prince Beviyard broke it. He looked at Belasko. "And how do *you* feel about Baskans?"

Belasko shrugged. "The ones who haven't tried to kill me have always seemed all right to me."

This caused the Prince to let out a deep laugh. He grinned at Belasko. "Fair enough. You fought us in a war, will have lost friends to our blades. You hold no resentment?"

Belasko shook his head. "I've never blamed the common soldier for their part in the war. They just went where they were told and followed orders, same as me. Ask any old soldier, and they'll tell you war's a terrible thing. A waste of good lives. But how else do we defend our people when aggressors come? The people who order those aggressors? That's another matter."

"People like my father, you mean?" There was a glint in Prince Beviyard's eye that Belasko found difficult to interpret.

"Oh no, your father was a soldier, too. He may have had more medals and shinier buttons than the people on the front lines, but he, too, was following orders. No, if I were to blame anyone, it would be the people who ordered him to war. The fact that your father now reigns means that they are dead and buried, but they were foolish to order your forces into a war that was too evenly matched."

There was silence again as they rode.

"I think my father would agree with you," Prince Beviyard said quietly. "Would you mind if I asked you some questions about the war? I've never spoken to anyone with a Villanese perspective on it."

Belasko nodded. "Of course. I'll do my best to answer

your questions. Forgive me if there are some I can't answer for you."

And so they passed the time quietly discussing the events of the past, both Belasko and the Prince trying to see through the bias of their different nationalities and think about things from the other's perspective.

After a while, the conversation came round to the events of Dellan Pass, which Belasko had held single-handedly against the forces of then General, and now King, Edyard, before defeating the Baskan Champion in a duel to decide the day. The Prince was most curious about this part of the war, when Belasko made his name. They went back over those events several times until Belasko finally had to put up his hand.

"I'm happy answering your questions, your highness, but I think we've gone over this ground enough times."

"Of course, I'm sorry. It's just..." Beviyard shook his head. "I could never quite believe that one person could hold that pass, all day, alone... My father said you were a remarkable man. I see now that he was right."

Belasko coughed to clear his throat, averting his eyes from the young prince's gaze. "Thank you, your highness, but I was just another soldier, doing my duty as best I could."

"That's precisely what a remarkable person would say. Or have I found your weakness: you can't handle compliments?" Prince Beviyard smiled. "Thank you, Belasko. It's been an illuminating discussion. If you don't mind, I'd like some time to think about what you've said."

"Likewise, your highness. Seeing the same events from a different perspective has been... Interesting. I'll take my leave of you now, but if you'd like to talk again, you have only to ask." Belasko paused. "As I rode up to join you, I couldn't help but notice I'm the subject of some attention from your squadron. Whenever I go amongst them, I'm stared at."

Prince Beviyard gave him a sad smile. "Ah, yes. Not everyone shares mine and my father's outlook. My people tell the tale of Dellan Pass a little differently to the Villanese. According to our stories, you're the person who broke our dreams of empire. A demon of the battlefield that killed hundreds of our soldiers in a single day. Your name is used to scare our children into behaving. You are notorious. Whereas in Villan you are a hero, in Bas you are a villain. They hate you, Belasko, even though they've never met you."

"I see. Thank you, your highness." Belasko turned his horse around, riding back through the Baskan force. He felt the weight of eyes on him, heard the whispers, and kept his own eyes straight ahead. Anything else might be misconstrued as a challenge. There was a prickling sensation between his shoulder blades, as if he expected to feel the blow of a Baskan blade at any moment.

He let out a sigh of relief when he rode back through his own lines. He found Byrta and settled back in beside her. "How was it?" she asked.

"The prince was fine, but I'm not going there on my own again." Belasko shook his head. "I didn't realise the depth of the Baskan people's dislike for me."

Byrta tilted her head slightly. "Multiple Baskans turn up at your door every year looking to kill you. How had you not realised it?"

"I'm just dense, I guess. Here, Prince Beviyard said that his banner bearer, Emilynn, is the finest warrior he's ever seen with a sabre. I suggested the two of you meet, as I'd say the same for you."

"Oh yes, and what did this Emilynn say about that?"

"That you could go somewhere private and carve pieces off each other, see who's best."

Byrta grinned. "I wouldn't mind going somewhere private with her." She laughed at the astonished look Belasko gave her. "Don't be like that—she's a fine looking woman. I'm just doing my bit to improve Villanese-Baskan relations."

Belasko laughed. "I'm not sure that's what the Queen had in mind, but go ahead. I don't know how amenable she'd be to your advances."

Byrta shrugged. "It's worth a shot. Hey, fancy a drink at my tent tonight?"

"That would be nice." Belasko stretched in his saddle. "As much as I didn't want to come on this trip, I have to admit I'm enjoying being on the road. It's been a long time since I left the Academy."

"It's good to see you loosen up a little. You're a good employer, but I'm starting to see a little of my old friend on this trip. Thank you for asking me along." She reached across from her saddle, squeezing his hand.

Belasko squeezed back. "I'm glad you came, old friend. What are we drinking tonight?"

Byrta grinned. "I won a rather nice cask of brandy off that Vargossian shaman in a game of dice the night he stayed in our camp. I thought we might as well crack that open."

"Serving my own drink back to me?" Belasko laughed. "Very well, that sounds ideal."

25

QUEEN LILLIANA AND Prince Beviyard were riding together. They were positioned between the two groups on the road, a mix of Queen Lilliana's personal guard and Prince Beviyard's best cavalry troopers arranged around them as protection. They were lower down in the mountains now, wending their way through thickly forested slopes as they moved towards the Baskan plain that would take them to the capital.

"What do you think of Bas so far, your majesty?" asked Prince Beviyard.

Queen Lilliana smiled. "Well, your highness, it seems much like the Villanese side of the mountains, if truth be told."

He laughed. "That is true, I'm sure. You will find the scenery changes as we make our way further south. The climate, too. My country is warmer than your own. Something our buildings and settlements reflect."

"I have read as much. I love the books in my library, but it is nice to get out and see something with my own eyes for a change."

"Have you not travelled much beyond Villan?"

Queen Lilliana sighed. "No, I have not. My father seemed to want to wrap me up and keep me safe when I was a child. I think..." She hesitated for a moment.

"Yes, go on?" Beviyard tilted his head questioningly.

"My mother died when I was born, and Father often said I reminded him of her. I think he wanted to keep me safe because he hadn't been able to protect her. So I didn't travel as much as he or Kellan." She looked wistfully into the distance for a moment, as if she was looking into another time and place. "Perhaps that's why I spent so much time in the library. Books were my gateway to the world." She blinked and returned her attention to Prince Beviyard. "And you? I suppose your work as a cavalry officer must have taken you to some interesting places."

Prince Beviyard shrugged. "I suppose, but mainly to different military camps around Bas. Now Father is King, I think he'd like to put me to work. Send me to other courts as an emissary of some sort. Who knows? My older siblings are serving in that role now, out and about doing the rounds of foreign courts." He smiled at her. "I like books well enough myself, but if I'm curious as to what's on the other side of a hill, I ride there and take a look."

"Oh, to be so footloose! I think that is likely to come to an end now that you're a Prince of the Realm. Royal status comes with obligations as well as privileges."

"I'm sure. If all my obligations are as enjoyable as escorting you, then they will be none too onerous."

Queen Lilliana laughed. "I'm not sure many ladies would be delighted to be referred to as an obligation, but I take your point—and the compliment hidden within it."

"Oh, I... Oh dear. Yes, that didn't come out well at all, did it?" Prince Beviyard looked a little shamefaced.

"I wouldn't worry, although you may want to work on your diplomatic language somewhat before acting as your father's emissary." Queen Lilliana smiled at him. "Do you know where he might send you first of all?"

Prince Beviyard returned her smile warmly. "I've no idea. Hopefully, father might give me some indication when we get to Albessar. I would like to visit Villan one day, though. Speaking with you and with members of your court has been most enjoyable and made me curious to see both the city, and the country, for myself."

"Perhaps that is something we could discuss as part of our negotiations. If there is a need for further talks, I would be only too happy to host." Queen Lilliana frowned. "Please forgive me for prying, but what of your mother? I've heard no mention of her, either in the invitation your father sent or from anyone else. Is she still living?"

"Ah, yes. Mother. A difficult subject." The smile had fallen from the prince's face.

"Oh, I'm sorry. Please, forget I asked."

Prince Beviyard shook his head. "That's all right, it's no secret." He sighed. "My mother didn't react well to father's loss of face after Dellan Pass. She began to spend more and more time at our country estates, less and less with him. In the last few years she has become unwell. Perhaps that was the first sign and we all misread it. She's rarely herself these days."

"That sounds like a difficult situation for all concerned," said Queen Lilliana. "Something similar happened to an old family friend. In fact I—"

As she spoke, something to the side of the road caught Prince Beviyard's eye. He frowned, then his eyes widened in surprise. He called to his troopers, "shields up!", and drew his sword, causing exclamations from the Villanese Royal Guard as they reached for their own weapons.

Prince Beviyard's cavalry troopers moved with the discipline that only hours of drilling could bring, their long shields unstowed and raised in one smooth movement. Prince Beviyard used his shield, not for his own protection, but for Queen Lilliana's, as he leaned out of his saddle to cover her.

Majel, who had been riding at the head of their small formation, turned at the commotion, and seeing Prince Beviyard's blade bared, brought her horse around and kicked it into a canter as she rode back towards them.

"What is the meaning of this? What is going on?" she asked as she drew her own sword.

Prince Beviyard frowned, peering into the forest that surrounded them. "I saw figures in the tree line, too many to be woodsmen. I thought I saw at least one holding a — there!" He heeled his horse to the side, yelling, "Lilliana, get down!" as he did so. His larger war horse nudged her own mount, making Queen Lilliana fall forward onto the neck of her horse.

It was then the attack came.

26

ANERIN AND BELASKO were both riding with the Villanese vanguard, behind the Queen and Prince Beviyard's party. They broke off their conversation as they became aware of a commotion up ahead.

"What is going on?" Anerin wondered.

Then an arrow came whistling out of the trees and buried itself in the flank of Queen Lilliana's horse. Belasko kicked his horse into a gallop and raced towards the Queen. After a moment's hesitation, his reflexes not quite so sharp, Anerin did the same.

The stricken animal reared, whinnying in fear and pain, while the Queen, an excellent horsewoman raised to the saddle from an early age, tried to calm it. Belasko and Anerin galloped up through the combined Villanese and Baskan guards while Belasko roared. "We are attacked! Protect the Queen!"

Majel's expertly trained guards were already moving, and in moments they had separated Queen Lilliana from Prince Beviyard and encircled her, shields raised to offer her what protection they could. Although it would be precious little if any arrows came from above.

The Baskans moved equally quickly to protect their Prince, and soon the two separate groups were peering into the woods and at each other with suspicion.

"Are you all right?" Prince Beviyard called to Queen Lilliana.

"I'm fine, but my poor horse..." Queen Lilliana leaned forward in the saddle, stroking her mount's neck and whispering into its ears. The horse was trembling as blood ran freely down its flank. Queen Lilliana was doing her best to control it, but the stricken animal kept trying to turn. Wanting to get away from the source of pain in its hindquarters.

Majel frowned at the forest boundary by the road. "Where did that arrow come from?"

"Out of the forest, from over there." Prince Beviyard pointed. "I saw some people in the tree line, watching us. Enough of them to get my hackles up."

"Did anyone else see, to confirm?" Majel asked.

Belasko nodded. "Yes, we were looking forward and saw it happen. The Prince is right. If I'm not mistaken, the arrow came from just inside the tree line."

"All right. Whoever loosed the arrow is probably long gone, but I'll send a few guards into the trees to check. Fetch trackers, we'll want to find whoever did this if we can. I have some questions for them." Majel began instructing her guards, and five of them left the shield wall to start searching the forest. The others adjusted to their absence immediately.

"Let's work together, see if we can flush any remaining attackers out of hiding." Prince Beviyard gestured to Emilynn. His banner bearer called out some commands, and an equal number of Baskans left their group and advanced towards the forest.

"Go carefully," Belasko said. "There might be more."

"Yes, yes, this isn't our first tussle." An annoyed expression crossed Majel's face. "We do know what we're doing, Belasko."

He held up a hand. "I know, I know. Old habit. Sorry."

Majel looked to the Queen. "I'm going to suggest we get you out of the open and into your carriage, ma'am. The roof should provide some protection. I know you prefer to ride, but I have to insist."

Queen Lilliana shook her head. "You'll get no argument from me. Let's go." She called to Beviyard. "It's all right. Let's continue our conversation when the danger has passed."

He nodded his assent, although Belasko thought there was something wistful to his expression as they rode away.

They rode back to the main body of the Villanese column. The Queen dismounted from her injured horse, laying a hand on its neck in a tender display, before they began to move towards the carriage.

As they did so, shouts could be heard in the forest, and the sound of steel on steel. Belasko grinned at Majel. "Told you."

"All right, old man. No need to be smug about it." Majel rolled her eyes. "I'm sure my guards can handle them, but we'll send reinforcements in a moment. I bet you've got an old war story that fits this..."

As she spoke, more noise could be heard. Shouts came from the front of the column and from the rear, screams, and the crash of weapons.

"Everyone, be on your guard; it sounds like the whole column's under attack." Anerin loosened his sword in its scabbard. "I don't like this at all."

When they arrived at the carriage, Queen Lilliana was ushered inside. Two guards climbed up to sit beside the driver, protecting him with their shields. The guards, joined by more of their comrades, surrounded the carriage and reformed their protective shield wall around it.

Majel, Anerin, and Belasko were all left on the outside of the shield wall. "I hope you don't mind—my troops are the last line of protection for the Queen. If anything happens, we'll do what we can out here, and they'll deal with anything that gets through us." Majel had a fierce glint in her eye, the prospect of battle awakening something in her.

Belasko felt the rush of blood in his veins, too, the familiar feelings before a fight. "That's all right. Let's hope it doesn't come to that." The sounds of fighting were already fading away ahead and behind them. "If we—"

Belasko didn't get to finish his sentence as a group of men and women rushed out of the trees on either side of the road. They wore ragged clothes in dull colours and had little discipline in their movements, but the sharp steel in their hands told its own story.

Belasko and Anerin rode to meet the attackers nearest them, swords in hand. Belasko had drawn a cavalry sabre he kept strapped to his saddle for fighting from horseback, and Anerin his longsword. Majel stayed back, eyeing the attackers and calling instructions to her guardsmen and women.

As Belasko and Anerin closed on the attackers, they heard the rumble of hooves behind them. A brief glance gave Belasko a sight to make him glad: Byrta and some cavalry were galloping up from their position further back in the column. Byrta leaned low in the saddle, her sabre flashing in the sun, teeth shining in a savage rictus grin.

Byrta and the cavalry squadron split, moving around the

The Swordsman's Descent

circle of guards as they closed on the enemy. Byrta caught up with Belasko and Anerin as they rode into the line of attackers, getting to work with their blades.

"Just like old times," Byrta yelled as a blow from her sabre opened an opponent's neck.

Anerin's blade weaved an intricate pattern in the air as he defended himself from an attacker before striking with lethal speed. His opponent crumpled to the floor. Anerin let out a breath. "I have very different memories to you."

Then they were in the thick of it, surrounded. Belasko lay about him with his sword, striking to either side with no time to talk. His horse reared up, kicking an enemy in the face while a blow from Belasko's sabre nearly beheaded a man to his right. They collapsed to their knees, blood pouring from their neck as their body slumped to the side.

The trio fought on, their opponents fought silently, with a grim determination, but in dwindling numbers. In appearance they were typical of the people in these border lands, not distinctly Baskan or Villanese, and their ragged clothes marked them out as bandits. They seemed focused on the royal party, the boldness of their attack bleeding into desperation as they struggled to reach the queen. Finally, at a shouted command from somewhere in their ranks, they broke and ran, fleeing for the safety of the trees. Dragging their injured with them. Byrta pulled out a cavalry bow from somewhere, loosing arrows after them but hitting no one. She turned to the others and shrugged. "I'm not much of a shot, but it was worth a try."

"A shame you didn't wing one of them. We could have used a captive to tell us what the hell they were doing." Belasko looked around. Dead enemies lay on the ground around them, around the shield wall protecting the Queen, up and down the road. "I don't think we'll get anything useful out of these. We should check the bodies, see if any are only injured but playing dead." He frowned. "It's unusual not to have taken a single captive, but they almost threw themselves onto our blades in recklessness to reach the queen. It all happened so quickly."

Anerin dismounted, leading his horse by the reins as he approached a fallen attacker. He used his foot to roll them onto their back. It was a woman, with hair dark, face ashen. She had bled out from a wound to her throat. Anerin knelt over the body. "They still might be able to tell us something." He examined the corpse. "Look, her clothes are very poor quality, patched and ragged. They all look like common bandits. But the weapons..." Anerin picked up a sword that lay on the ground nearby. "Simple enough, but good steel and finely made." He shook his head. "Finer weapons than these wretches could afford. And why attack against well-armed, well-trained soldiers in superior numbers? It doesn't make sense."

Majel approached from where she had been fighting on the other side of the shield wall. "There is one explanation that makes sense. Someone armed these people and set them against us." She frowned down at the corpses. "Do they look Baskan to you?"

Belasko shook his head. "It's difficult to say. Some people this high in the mountains don't look much like your typical Baskan or Villanese. They're their own people and don't take much notice of which side of the mountain belongs to which country." He looked at Majel. "The Queen?"

"She's well and asking for you."

The Swordsman's Descent

They gathered by the Queen's carriage. Queen Lilliana looked almost serene, untroubled by the attack. Only someone who knew her as well as Belasko did could tell that she was unnerved beneath.

Luckily, none of Byrta's reinforcements or Majel's guards had been killed in the fighting. As reports came in from the rest of the column, it was clear not everyone had been so lucky.

"Fifteen of our own dead, to fifty of theirs." Majel sounded disgusted. "They were poorly trained rabble. We shouldn't have lost a single life."

Belasko sighed. "You're right, and on a level battlefield that would have definitely been the case. They had the advantage of surprise."

"Well, no more surprises," said Queen Lilliana. "From now on, we double the scouts to the sides of the road as well as ahead. Somebody clearly wants our mission to Bas to fail. We won't let that happen."

Ambassador Aveyard had joined them, bringing word from Prince Beviyard. The Baskans had suffered losses of their own. "I wonder at their purpose, your majesty. They couldn't have hoped to succeed against our greater numbers and training. While it seems like you were the target, they may also have been aiming for my cousin. Either way, if they'd got lucky in their attack, then the peace talks may have been called off."

"The question remains, who armed and sent these people? Both Villanese and Baskan forces have suffered losses. It doesn't seem like the answer would lie with either country." Anerin leaned against a carriage wheel, careless of the mud on his breeches, rubbing his chin in thought.

"There are always extremists, those for whom their goal is worth any cost." Ambassador Aveyard shrugged. "I can't think it would be any of my people, to go against my uncle like that... Well, they can't fear death if they have, let's put it like that. Although he is new to his reign, he would not stomach an attack on one of his children. The retribution would be swift and deadly."

"Let's see what we can find out from the corpses—their clothes, what they're carrying. Then we move on." Queen Lilliana was steely in her determination. "Whatever their goal, they have succeeded in delaying us." She turned to Majel. "Speak to the other commanders, have them bury our dead not far from the road. Mark the spot, and we will collect the bodies on our way home to reunite them with their families. They should come home with us."

"Yes, majesty," said Majel in a quiet voice.

27

Nobody and No One were crouched behind a tent, out of view of passers-by.

"Right," said No One, "let's take a look."

Nobody emptied a small bag onto the ground. A host of valuable items tumbled onto the grass. They started stirring through them with one finger, giving an appreciative nod. They grinned at their twin. "Shiny."

Both jumped as a meaty hand landed on one of their shoulders. "Oh dear," came Borne's deep voice, his tone mournful. "What have you two been up to?"

"I'll tell you what they've been up to," the Water King said as he walked around the corner of the tent. "They've been trying to scupper our disguise, that's what." He frowned at the twins, who were trying to put on contrite expressions. "Put that lot away and come to our tent. I can't give you the telling off you deserve in public. Borne, I don't think they'd do a runner, but keep hands on just to make sure." He turned and walked off.

"We wouldn't run," said Nobody, their tone hurt.

"Yeah, what does he think of us?" asked No One.

"If you two feel upset, imagine how the boss feels. He brings you along, of all the people he could choose, on this important mission, and this is how you repay his trust?" Borne shook his big head. "He's not happy."

The twins looked at each other and swallowed. "Best get this over with then," said No One. Nobody only nodded glumly in reply. They started to gather up the items they'd pilfered, under Borne's watchful eye, then walked back to the tent that was shared between the four of them. Borne crouched low to open the tent flap to admit them, staying outside himself.

They entered to find the Water King sat in the dim interior, cross-legged on his bedroll, his face impassive. He indicated the bedroll opposite, and the twins sat down there, wordlessly.

The Water King didn't take his eyes off them. "Borne, keep an eye, will you? Make sure we're not interrupted."

"Yes, boss," said Borne, straightening up with some relief and fastening the tent flap.

There was silence inside the tent for a moment. Then the Water King shook his head. "What am I to do with the pair of you?" Nobody started to open their mouth, but the Water King held up a finger. "That was by nature a rhetorical question, young one. I shall tell you what I'm to do with you." He sighed. "Maybe it's my own fault. I've been too lenient on you both. Perhaps I saw something of myself in you and let a few too many things go."

"Lenient?" No One spluttered. "I remember the time we mucked up the numbers on that jewellery shop robbery, and you tanned our hides."

"No less than you deserved," said the Water King. "You didn't do it again."

"How about that time we played a prank with the

takings from a week's picking pockets? Another beating," said Nobody.

"Perhaps 'lenient' is the wrong word then. I have allowed you both too much leeway, so that when I give you a simple instruction, you cannot follow orders. You must do as I say, particularly when we are far from home."

"Why?" asked No One.

The Water King scowled. "*Why?* Because we are away from our base of operations, you idiots. Away from the control that gives me power. What do you think would happen if you were caught stealing?"

"We'd never be caught," said Nobody.

"You taught us yourself, you know that. We're too good to be caught," said No One.

"On a long enough timeline, everyone gets caught," said the Water King. "Whether during the robbery, or going through the loot, if you were spotted here... You risk throwing our whole disguise. Because there's nothing I could do to stop justice being exacted, short of dropping the pretence and asking Belasko to intervene. Or breaking you out and making a run for it, both of which would put paid to our own mission to Bas."

"Why are we going there again?" asked Nobody.

"Yeah, I still don't get that bit. You control all the crime in Villain. What does it matter to you what happens in Bas?"

The Water King growled in frustration, leaning forwards. "It matters because I say it matters. Look, we're going to meet my counterpart in Albessar to discuss some mutually beneficial arrangements. Regarding the transport of goods and services, shall we say, across borders. We can make life easier for each other and therefore, more profitable for everyone concerned. Is that simple enough for you? And you two have jeopardised that, and our lives, with this foolishness."

Nobody and No One looked at each other. "Our lives?" they asked.

The Water King pulled a weary hand down his face. "We're travelling with the military, although this is a mission of peace. Do you know their punishments for theft? Let's just say that they are harsh to discourage potential offenders. Tensions are high after the attack. I'm sure they'd be happy to take that out on someone."

"Oh," said No One.

"Right," said Nobody.

"Yes, right," said the Water King.

The twins looked at each other again.

"What are you going to do to us?" asked Nobody.

"How can we make it up to you, boss? We're sorry. Honest. We weren't thinking," said No One.

"Damn right, you weren't thinking. You two need to use your heads more before you lose them." The Water King shook his own head, his long curly hair bobbing as he did so. "No punishment, not yet. I'll think of something suitable for when we get home. But you are going to put back every item you stole where it belongs. Unpick those pockets and purses, young ones. Return things to the tents from whence you stole them. And do it without being caught."

"We can't do that!" said No One.

"That's far too hard," said Nobody, "there's no way we can do that without getting caught."

A vicious grin spread across the Water King's face. "Nonsense, I know you can do it. I know just what you're capable of. I taught you myself, remember?"

The Swordsman's Descent

"Again," said Parlin.

Queen Lilliana and her secretary were at work in her tent, furniture pushed to the sides in order to give them more space. She felt the grips in her hands, a long-bladed knife in each, and resumed the guard stance Parlin had drilled into her.

He was similarly equipped with a pair of knives, and lunged for her with the one in his right. Queen Lilliana shifted her weight, letting her left side drop back and away from Parlin's thrust as she diverted his blade with her own and brought the knife in her right hand to bear in her own attack.

Parlin and the Queen worked their way backwards and forwards across the tent in this deadly dance, until he caught her out with a feint, and she stopped short, his knife at her throat.

"Again," said Parlin.

Queen Lilliana sighed. "Come now, we've been at this for quite some time. I'm tired, and I have other work to attend to. Can we not pick up again tomorrow?"

Parlin nodded. "We can, once we've finished here for the night. We still have more to work on."

With a flutter of her sleeves, the Queen's knives disappeared. "No, Parlin, that's enough for tonight."

Her secretary looked awkward for a moment before his own knives vanished with a flick of his wrists. "Your majesty, I am your most obedient servant, you know that, but during our lessons, I am the master and you are the student. That was the agreement. One of the reasons Belasko suggested me for the role as your secretary was that you'd expressed an interest in learning to protect yourself. You've come a long way in the last few years, of that there is no doubt, but I feel we have got lax in our practice on this journey, and there are a few things I would like to correct. Particularly following the attempt on your life, and now the attack by those bandits. I do not feel I would be doing my duty otherwise."

Queen Lilliana smiled at Parlin. "Your steadfastness is one of the things I like most about you. Your dedication and the seriousness with which you take your work. Being able to defend myself is important, but look where we are. We are at the centre of a ring of steel, with my personal guard, the royal guards, divisions of infantry, cavalry, all arrayed for my protection. Besides, no knife work under Aronos's golden sun would have kept that arrow from my chest if the archer's aim had been true."

"Perhaps," Parlin nodded, "but Prince Beviyard's intervention may have helped there. Good reflexes and a willingness to act can turn the most hopeless of situations around. What are the chances that someone would find their way to you here, in the middle of the camp? But yet that has already happened once on this trip. Good luck and your own quick actions saved your life that night. You may not be so fortunate again. All it takes is one blade. One blade wielded by a foe you thought a friend or carried in secret. You must be prepared."

Parlin moved then, quicker than Queen Lilliana had ever seen him. A glint of light on steel was the only hint that he had retrieved his knives, and she brought hers out as quickly as she could, only to find that both her blades were blocked and held down low by the one in Parlin's left hand. The blade in his right hand now rested at her throat.

At least he has the decency to look apologetic, Queen Lilliana thought to herself.

Parlin cleared his throat. "I am sorry, your majesty. I know you're tired, but we have more to do tonight. Once more through that particular form and its variations, and then we can rest."

Queen Lilliana sighed. "Of course, my dear Parlin. Although I do wonder what the point is in being queen if people won't do as I say."

"I would be doing you no service if I shirked in your training, your majesty. Even at your own instruction. Again."

Queen Lilliana took a few steps back and assumed the guard position. "Again," she said.

28

TWO DAYS LATER, they spotted the Baskan capital in the distance. A signal went up from Prince Beviyard's squadron, and a murmur ran through the column. Belasko, who was riding with Byrta and Anerin, stood up in his stirrups, craning his neck to see the spreading blot on the horizon that was the distant city.

"What can you see?" asked Byrta.

"Not much yet, but it's there. I don't know much about the place, if I'm honest. Anerin, you've been here on business, haven't you?"

Anerin, who was nursing a particularly vicious hangover that morning and had been riding in something of a doze, opened his eyes and squinted blearily at his friends.

"Yes, several times." The sun came out from behind a cloud, and Anerin narrowed his eyes further, as if in pain. "I wish someone would do something about the light."

"You could always try praying to Aronos; he is the sun god, after all." Byrta's grin was as vicious as her friend's hangover, for all that she had been one of the key architects of Anerin's current misfortune.

"What do you think I've been doing all morning? If someone could do something about the light and stop my horse from swaying quite so much, that would be marvellous." Anerin let his eyes close again.

"I don't know why you drank so much when you knew we'd be arriving today. And you were about to tell us about Albessar, our intended destination." Belasko stood in his stirrups again, craning for another view. "All I know is that it's an old city, very old."

Anerin sighed. "We won't go into the city today. We'll stop a short enough distance away so that the Queen can be readied for a suitably splendid arrival tomorrow and look fresh as a daisy when we appear at the city gates." He cracked one eye open, peering at Belasko. "Which is why I drank so much last night. From tomorrow, I have to be sharp, on my best form as part of the negotiating team representing the interests of the Villanese people. From now until we leave, I'll be taking nothing more than watered wine. If you see me with anything stronger in my hand, please do take steps to stop me drinking it."

Belasko stared at his friend. Anerin chuckled. "What? I know my vices, old friend, and alcohol is chief among them."

"I didn't know it was that bad," Belasko said quietly.

Anerin shrugged. "I don't know if it's bad or good, exactly; it just is. Now, Albessar." He scratched his chin. "Yes, it's an old city, much older than Villan. Grander, too, in some ways, although more dishevelled. It dates back farther than people can remember, and was the seat of an ancient empire, if I recall correctly. It became run-down, ill-used by the various warring principalities that made up this land."

"So, how did it come to be the capital?" Byrta was intrigued, leaning in to hear Anerin's description.

He squinted at her. "When those warring principalities were unified, bloodily, as the nation we now know as Bas, the first King wanted somewhere for his capital that hadn't belonged to any of the different factions. Aware of its history as the seat of an empire, he chose Albessar and set about restoring it to something of its former glory."

"But what is it like?" Belasko asked.

Anerin let out a breath. "Beautiful. Confusing. A deadly maze of cobbled streets, squares, and narrow alleyways. There's been a city there so long that it's mainly made out of itself. Old stone repurposed, new buildings and streets built over old. Old streets became the sewers and catacombs of their new children above. Like someone dug a rabbit warren into an ants' nest and filled it full of intrigue." He grinned. "I rather like it."

~

The rest of that day passed without incident, and they made camp for the night an hour or two's ride from the city walls. Prince Beviyard despatched a rider from his squadron to go ahead and give word of their arrival. Proper preparations were needed on both sides, it seemed.

The camp was a hive of concentrated activity that evening, as uniforms were readied, boots and buttons polished until gleaming, horses' coats brushed until glossy. Even though everything would have to be checked and gone over again in the morning, the activity lent purpose to the evening and was a good way to dispel any rising tension or nerves over the next day.

Many of those who had fought in the Last War felt uneasy at riding into a Baskan stronghold—Belasko had to admit he was one of them.

The Swordsman's Descent

He gathered at the Queen's tent with senior nobles, advisers, and the commanding officers of the forces they had with them.

That was itself a hive of different activity as the Queen's own armour was chosen. Dresses chosen, then discarded, then reexamined. Different options were laid out depending on what weather the morning brought them. Accessories were carefully selected for all possible eventualities. Queen Lilliana was determined to appear every inch a queen. In truth, she had grown into that role. Belasko smiled. *The little girl I met when I first came to the palace has grown into a formidable woman. I couldn't be prouder.*

"And what are you smiling about?" Anerin asked, having sidled up to Belasko's shoulder.

Belasko jumped slightly, making Anerin laugh. "You must have been deep in thought if I was able to catch you unawares."

Belasko smiled at him. "I was just thinking of an inquisitive, fiercely intelligent little girl I used to know and marvelling at the impressive woman she has become."

"She has at that. I'm not sure the Baskans know what they've let themselves in for. They'll be lucky to escape the negotiating table with the clothes on their backs." Anerin grinned.

"And what are you two gossiping about?" Queen Lilliana called from where she was looking over an assortment of necklaces, pendants, rings, and earrings. She nodded to Elladine, her mistress of the wardrobe, a slim delicate finger darting out to indicate the items she was wanted. "This, this, and this, to go with the white, I think."

"Your majesty has a fine eye. Those would have been my own suggestions." The mistress of wardrobe closed the cases she held with a snap. "I shall ensure all are made ready for the morning."

"Thank you, Elladine," the Queen murmured as the older woman withdrew. "Well?" This last directed at Anerin and Belasko, a twinkle of amusement in her eye. "You haven't answered my question."

"Your apologies, majesty." Anerin gave a florid bow. "We were marvelling at your splendour, sure to strike the Baskans dumb at the negotiations."

Queen Lilliana gave a most unladylike snort. "I'm sure you were. It's tiresome that women are judged on their appearance so much more than men, but if it must be so, then I will use it to my advantage as and when I can. Now, ladies and gentlemen, gather round. We need to discuss the order of procession tomorrow. How best to make an impact. Who will be travelling with who."

She took a deep breath as those assembled drew closer, letting it out slowly.

"By now, I don't need to impress upon you the importance of our trip. I was a child at the time of the Last War. I know some of those here who fought it in it, defending Villan and her people. I've heard the tales, yes, of honour and glory, but also of death and pain. The stench of ruptured guts on the battlefield, the many lives lost. So many lives. Too many." Here she quieted, lost in a moment of reflection. Those gathered hung on her every word.

Queen Lilliana stood taller then. She looked around and met the eye of everyone present as she spoke. "We have the opportunity here to ensure that doesn't happen again. We can bind the Baskans to us, with promises of trade, in peace and prosperity, and enable future generations to sleep soundly in their beds. It may be hard work, detailed and dull, at the negotiating table, but I am determined we see it done. Are you with me?"

"Aye!" those assembled cried as one.

The Queen nodded. "Good. Thank you in advance for your efforts as we strive for peace. Your loyalty will not be forgotten. Now, let us turn to tomorrow." She cleared her throat. "I will, of course, ride with my guard arrayed in formation around me. With me will be Lord Anerin, Lord Beggeridge, Duchess Morlake, and those who will be regularly attending negotiations. Belasko, as my Champion, you will also be with me. Now we must turn our attention to the arrangement of our forces, for both discipline and impact as we arrive and travel through the city. I'm prepared to hear suggestions."

On this, Majel and the other commanders drew nearer, discussing the merits of various formations.

Anerin leaned closer. "A lovely speech from our Queen. It's almost a shame she works so hard for peace; she'd be an inspiring war leader."

Belasko nodded. "Aye, she would at that."

Anerin looked at Belasko out of the corner of his eye. "It's good to know loyalty will be remembered. What of disloyalty, though?"

"Oh, I wager the Queen will remember that, too." Belasko patted the hilt at his side. As Champion, he was one of the few allowed to carry arms in the Queen's presence. "Remembered and swiftly dealt with."

～

The next morning, the column formed up, apart from some of the servants and a few soldiers who were left to guard the camp and their supplies in anticipation of their return journey. Those venturing into the city looked if anything even more splendid than when they set out through the streets of Villan. Uniforms were smart and perfectly presented, boots, armour, and weapons all gleamed. The infantry marched in lockstep, and the cavalry kept perfect formation, the coats of their mounts gleaming and glossy.

Most splendid of all was the woman who rode at their centre, surrounded by her guard, the object of their protections. Queen Lilliana was a vision in white and gold. She wore a white panelled riding dress chased with designs in gold, white fur at the collar and cuffs and lining her short riding cape. Even her saddle, reins, and horse's tack were white leather, also decorated with gold designs. Her hair had been artfully styled around the slim gold circlet that sat on her brow and which caught the sun and dazzled the eye of any onlookers. This circlet was more decorative than the one she normally wore. A hunting scene was etched into its surface, the stag of the royal house rising from her brow

Riding side-saddle had still been in fashion for noble ladies when the Queen was younger. When she started to learn to ride, then Princess Lilliana had declared riding side-saddle to be "silly, uncomfortable, and just plain daft", and would have none of it. She set a trend, and now only older ladies of the court rode in the old-fashioned style.

Belasko rode at her right-hand side, as was customary for the Royal Champion on such official occasions.

Where the Queen was all white and gold, Belasko was in black and silver. His riding boots were polished and gleaming, black hose under black breeches with silver piping. The black doublet he wore was plainer than he would wear at home, the only decoration the stag picked out on one breast in silver to show his loyalty to the royal house, and two crossed swords on the other denoting his position. A black velvet cape was fastened with a pin in the same design, two crossed swords in a circle.

"It's a shame Prince Beviyard couldn't ride with us. I was going to ask him questions about the city." A slight frown marred Queen Lilliana's expression.

"I believe his father asked him to lead you into the city, so he felt he had to do so from the front of his squadron. He seems the sort of man who takes his responsibilities seriously," Belasko said.

"I rather like that about him," said the Queen.

"Me, too. He seems cut from the same cloth as his father, a good man," Belasko said.

"It sounds as if you like him, Belasko."

The swordsman nodded. "I do. I'm coming around to the idea that not all Baskans want to kill me."

"Just most of them." The Queen grinned at him.

"They just need to take the time to get to know me. Then I'm sure they'd be less interested in sticking sharp objects into me."

She nodded, a solemn expression on her face. "Once they've sampled your wit, they may be less inclined towards violence. Or perhaps more. Humour is so subjective."

"As your majesty knows only too well. Once you've found some, let me know."

Queen Lilliana's laughter rang out, causing a few heads to turn in their direction. "Oh, my impudent champion. You'll have to guard your tongue better than that once we're inside the city walls. We're about serious and important business, you know."

Belasko winked at her. "Just getting it out of my system, ma'am. That's all."

They rode on, passing the time in idle conversation as a darkening mark on the horizon revealed itself to be

Albessar, the Baskan capital. As they drew closer, the scale of the city became apparent. It was vast.

Belasko whistled. "I knew the city was older than Villan. I wasn't expecting it to be so much bigger."

It stretched out, filling a valley between several hills, the wide Bess River bisecting the city. As they got closer, some detail resolved itself, and Belasko began to realise just how high the city walls were.

"I wouldn't want to have to lay siege to that. Look at the walls. You'd need a vast army to encircle the city, too." He shook his head.

"Well then, it's a good thing we're here in the name of peace and not war, isn't it?" Queen Lilliana smiled.

"As someone who's seen both, I have to agree." Belasko sighed. "I hope our mission here is successful. I might be a warrior, but nobody who's seen war hungers for it again. No one sane, anyway."

A rider from Prince Beviyard's squadron dropped back to join them as they approached the city. Majel's guards let him through, and he approached Queen Lilliana. Bowing his head slightly in respect, he said, "Your majesty, our orders are to relay you straight to the palace. King Edyard is waiting there to greet you."

Queen Lilliana inclined her head. "Thank you for letting us know. How long do you think until we get to the palace?"

The rider scratched his chin. "Probably about an hour or so. People will clear out of the way when they see us coming, so it won't take too long once we've reached the city walls."

Queen Lilliana nodded. "Of course." She smiled. "Please tell Prince Beviyard that I'll be taking note of any interesting buildings and quizzing him about them later. He hasn't escaped my questions by riding ahead."

The rider looked confused. "Yes, your majesty. I'll rejoin the squadron now and pass that on." He bowed his head to the Queen and offered Belasko a respectful nod before turning his horse around and heading back to his own lines.

She and the prince are definitely getting along well. Belasko felt a little uneasy at this, peering ahead to see if he could make out Prince Beviyard amongst his riders. He could only just make out his banner near the front of the body of cavalry. *It can't be coincidence that the new King sent his youngest son, still unmarried, to escort us.* He cleared his throat. Queen Lilliana looked at him.

"Yes, Belasko?"

Belasko opened his mouth, then shut it again. He shook his head. "Sorry, ma'am, I was just thinking. What exactly is going to be on the table for these negotiations?"

She shrugged. "Trade agreements, efforts at mutual cooperation and understanding, establishing permanent peace. We'll have to see how things go. Why?"

He coughed slightly. "It's nothing, I'm sure. I only... I was wondering if the Baskans had broached any other way of cementing an alliance."

The Queen had a puzzled look on her face before realisation dawned. She chuckled. "Oh, you mean marriage. That's not a subject that's been broached. Not something I've thought about yet, in any case." A more serious expression crossed her face. "Although I do need to produce an heir at some point. I've been concentrating on finding my way these last few years. Perhaps it's time I started thinking more towards the future. My future." She sighed. "If life has taught me anything, it's that you never know what's around the corner. I'll give it some thought."

"It's not necessarily something to think about now, your

majesty. I just wondered at the thinking behind sending Prince Beviyard to escort you. That's all."

Queen Lilliana regained her smile. "Whatever the thinking, he's a pleasant companion." Her smile took on a mischievous quality. "Pleasant to look at, too." Belasko sighed and rolled his eyes, making the Queen laugh. Once again, people turned to look at them.

They rode on until they reached the city walls. Prince Beviyard's squadron led them through a vast gate, an edifice of finely carved marble that seemed more recent than the ancient walls in which it sat.

"The Unification Gate," Anerin said as they approached. He had come forward and rode on the other side of the Queen to Belasko. She had welcomed his knowledge of the Baskan capital, and he would do his best to fill in for the absent Prince Beviyard.

"It looks new. Or at least, newer than the walls," Belasko said.

Anerin nodded. "That's because it is. Or rather, the marble cladding is. Once he'd unified the warring city-states and principalities hereabouts into one country, the first Baskan King took Albessar as his capital and started a series of building works that are still ongoing." He pointed to the carvings that adorned the gate. "This was one of the first things he commissioned. The existing gates were widened, as was the road beyond, and the marble decoration added. Suitably martial scenes—a reminder to his recently conquered people of his victories. And that he would do whatever was needed to hold his new country together."

"A warning, then?" asked Queen Lilliana.

"Very much so. Bessar was a ruthless general and a merciless one at that. Fear of his reputation and possible reprisals for rebellion is what held Bas together in those early years. His new armies, made up of conscripts from his recently conquered foes, always marched in and out of the city by this gate, passing by the scenes of their parents' and then grandparents' defeats on a regular basis. Obedience was thus encouraged. Within a few generations, those links to the past were broken, and there came a feeling of pride in Baskan achievements. Their military might turned outwards. Even now, it is tradition that Baskan armies use this gate to leave or enter the city."

"You know a lot about it," said Belasko as they passed under the shadow of the gate.

Anerin shrugged. "I keep my eyes and ears open."

As they rode through the gate, it became obvious that the way ahead had been made ready for their arrival. The road was cleared, barricades holding back the pedestrians that thronged the pavements.

Moving into the city, Belasko could see what Anerin had meant about the nature of the place. Grand buildings with colonnaded marble-clad porticos and walkways rubbed up alongside much more crudely built constructions. The last much newer, but clearly made with ancient and much worked stone. Narrow alleyways cut between buildings and disappeared into shadow.

I wouldn't want to find myself lost here, the city is a maze. Belasko looked around, trying to take it all in. The architecture is different to Villan. Much is designed to give shade. Windows are smaller and higher up, as if to protect from the sun, he thought to himself. His gaze travelled upwards, taking in the many domes and cupolas of the city's rooftops. The tiles too, red instead of our grey slate or wooden shingle.

The Baskan citizens cheered as Prince Beviyard rode by. He stood in his stirrups, waving to the people in acknowledgement of their greeting. This only spurred them on to greater heights.

The cheers stopped as the final riders of Prince Beviyard's squadron gave way to the forerunners of Queen Lilliana's forces. Most of the Baskan citizens lapsed into wary silence as the Villanese rode past.

What do these warlike people make of our mission of peace? Belasko wondered. Do they see it as a weakness?

There was a smattering of applause, the odd call from the crowd, but it was clear that the people didn't know what to make of their presence.

Belasko's eyes swept the crowd, always alert to the possibility of risk to his Queen. After a moment, he realised that his gaze brought silence with it, as the crowd stilled further when they caught sight of him. Dressed in his champion's regalia, riding at the queen's right hand side. They knew who he was. He could see people pointing, make out lips moving as members of the crowd whispered to each other. *Are they afraid of me?* The prince's words came back to him, and he observed fear in the looks he met—fear with a good measure of hate.

With clear roads ahead of them, they made good time, although it was clear that Queen Lilliana would have liked to linger at some tumbledown temples and other sites of interest in the ancient city.

It was ancient, yet modern, too. The seat of an empire a thousand years before Bas was founded, its bones were old, but no expense had been spared on rebuilding the ancient city and adding new structures. The roads were straight, and as clean as they could be in a city this size, and it wasn't long before they were approaching the palace.

This was the fortified heart of the city, gardens and

porticos and different wings spreading out from the old fort that the city had risen up around all those long years ago.

There was a large square in front of the main gate, and it was here King Edyard waited for them. The gates themselves were wide open, and King Edyard waited on foot, with a division of his household guard arrayed behind him.

Prince Beviyard peeled off from his squadron, accompanied by his banner bearer, as they formed up in ranks on one side of the square, and rode up to greet his father. The Prince threw himself down from his horse, pausing to bow before embracing his father.

King Edyard returned his son's embrace before taking him by the shoulders and holding him out at arm's length. The older man smiled. "You look well, son, if a little weary from the road."

Prince Beviyard returned his father's smile. "It was mostly uneventful, apart from one moment of excitement. The company was good, which helped." He flashed a quick grin over his shoulder at Queen Lilliana.

"I'm sure. Your trouble with the bandits in the mountains, though, if that's what they were. That worries me." The King frowned. "I have Count Veldar working on it, seeing what his network can find."

"That old spymaster." Prince Beviyard made an indelicate sound. "You know my feelings there."

"Yes, although perhaps you should avoid voicing them quite so publicly." King Edyard looked past his son, catching sight of Queen Lilliana. A smile of genuine warmth appeared on his face, and it stayed there when he took in Belasko next to her. The new Baskan King nodded to his one-time adversary, and a moment of mutual respect passed between them. Then the King strode forward, pausing just short of the Queen's guards. His eyes drawn to Majel as the figure of command, he offered her a respectful nod before bowing to the Queen.

"My dear Queen Lilliana, thank you so much for accepting my invitation. I can't tell you how it gladdens my heart to see you here. All of you, welcome."

Queen Lilliana dismounted gracefully, walking towards King Edyard, hands outstretched in greeting. Her guards parted, allowing her through, and King Edyard took the proffered hands.

"My brother King, thank you for your kind welcome. I welcome you, too, to the family of monarchs that govern the nations of the world. You are a welcome addition to our number, and I bear congratulatory missives from several others of our select group."

King Edyard bowed his head over Queen Lilliana's hands before looking up into her eyes. "Thank you, Queen Lilliana. That is most heartening to hear. Now, please, we have an army of stablehands and stewards poised to settle your horses and see your people to their quarters. Will you join me for some refreshments while these things are seen to? Then, once everything's squared away, I hope you'll take some time to settle into the apartments we've provided for you before joining me for a small informal meal this evening." He released her hands and smiled again, eyes twinkling. "The heavy business of negotiations and statecraft can wait until tomorrow, as can the no less heavy business of state banquets." He winked at the Queen. "I'm finding it quite difficult to keep in shape, with all the food the palace kitchens keep putting in front of me."

"You are in shape, Father." Prince Beviyard called out. "Round is a shape."

Queen Lilliana couldn't help herself and burst into laughter before delicately covering her mouth with one gloved hand. "My apologies, your majesty. Your son rather fancies himself a wit."

"Doesn't he just?" King Edyard rolled his eyes. "Dratted boy, no sense of decorum. I don't know where he gets it from." He stood back, gesturing towards the palace gates. "Now, if I may escort you and your retinue inside, those stablehands and stewards are itching to get to work."

So they dismounted and were led in through the central palace gates. Belasko winced as his weight settled onto his bad foot, imperceptible to any who didn't know him. Anerin was close by and shot him a questioning look, which Belasko ignored. He focused on his breathing, using an old technique to ride out the pain.

They emerged into a large courtyard with covered walkways along each side. It was decorated with fountains and statuary, some of which seemed quite ancient. Anerin leaned in towards Belasko. "Some of this collection date back to the days of the old empire. Very valuable." He looked at the swordsman. "Are you all right? You didn't seem quite yourself for a moment back there."

"On the contrary, I feel more myself with every passing day." Belasko shot his friend a meaningful look. "Something to discuss later, in private." Anerin nodded, understanding.

The promised stablehands and stewards descended, various members of the Villanese royal household staff and military going with them to ensure animals were properly cared for and belongings properly stowed away. The Villanese hadn't brought their full strength into the city with them, as many of the servants and household staff that accompanied them would not be required while they were relying on the hospitality of their hosts, and so had been left with a small guard to maintain their camp ready for their departure from the city. The infantry and cavalry they had brought with them were shown to their respective barracks. The military of both sides seemed on edge, puzzled and unsure at their meeting, although they were far too disciplined to let it show overmuch.

Queen Lilliana, Majel and a few guards, Belasko, Anerin, and a few of the higher up lords and ladies who attended the Queen on her journey, were brought through into a welcome hall. Tall ceilings were held up by slender marble columns, and somewhere a water feature could be heard trickling away. Staff appeared carrying trays of food and drink, moving through those gathered with an efficiency and grace which spoke of long practice. Members of the Baskan court were there to greet them.

Anerin leaned into Belasko once again. "Ah," he said, "our first opportunity to take the measure of our opposition."

"I thought our purpose here was friendly? Why opposition?"

"Sword fights and war are your field of expertise; the negotiating table is mine." Anerin's grin was savage. "And it is no less a battlefield."

～

They were introduced to an array of nobles and dignitaries, while staff swept efficiently around and between them bearing refreshments. Belasko murmured niceties, all the while keeping one eye on Queen Lilliana. She seemed to be charming the Baskans, judging by the smiles and laughter that followed her around the room.

The reaction to Belasko's presence was quite different. Curiosity at best, hostility at worst. Some just wanted to lay eyes on the one they thought of as the villain of Dellan pass.

I shouldn't have come. Even if King Edyard extended a personal invitation. Belasko shook his head. *What was I thinking? At best my presence will distract from the queen's mission; at worst...*

It was then that a figure appeared at his elbow. A slender man of middle years, he was swathed in clothes of purple and black, dark hair turning silver at the temples. The typical Baskan olive skin was pale, as if he spent much time indoors.

"Greetings, Belasko. I hope your journey here progressed smoothly. Other than that one, um, moment of excitement, as I believe Prince Beviyard called it."

Belasko frowned at the man. "Well enough, thank you. And yes, other than that attack, everything went as well as could be expected. You have the advantage of me, knowing my name when I'm afraid I haven't a clue who I'm addressing."

A cold smile appeared on the man's face. "I'm Count Veldar. I look after certain concerns for the crown. Tell me, Belasko, how goes the search for your successor? We hear of such things even here. You've made no secret of your desire to find your replacement. To be free of court entanglements."

Belasko paused. There was something in this man's manner that he didn't like. A certain knowing attitude that was destined to rub him the wrong way. "It moves along. It's no simple thing, to find the person with the skills and dedication for the role. But I'm confident they will soon be found."

Count Veldar nodded. "Of course. I'm sure that Queen Lilliana will miss your counsel at court."

Then King Edyard appeared at Belasko's other side. "I hope you're not bothering our guest with too many questions, Count. Your inquisitive nature will get you into trouble one day." A smile, although not particularly warm, took the sting out of the King's words.

Count Veldar bowed. "Your majesty is quite correct, I'm sure. Belasko, I'll leave you be, but I do hope we get the chance to talk further during your stay. Your majesty." He nodded to King Edyard, then turned and moved into the room in search of other conversation.

"Sorry about him. Head of our intelligence service. An insufferable tit, if you ask me, but he knows what he's about." King Edyard smiled. "I'm glad you came, Belasko, truly. That day at Dellan Pass, it... Well, it's what set both our feet on the paths that brought us here. I told you then you were a remarkable man. It looks like I was right."

Belasko shrugged. "I've been lucky, I suppose. Then and now."

"Has your luck held then, Belasko? That's a rare gift." King Edyard looked over Belasko's shoulder. "Ah, I'm being signalled. My presence is required elsewhere." The King put a hand on Belasko's shoulder. "I'd very much like to talk more while you're here. Let's make time for it. I'd like to see a bit more of the man you've become—see if I judged you right all those years ago. Until then." The King clapped Belasko on the shoulder and was gone. Belasko watched him walk away then, turning, his eyes locked with Count Veldar's across the crowded room, and Belasko shivered as if he felt a sudden chill.

Has my luck held? I'm beginning to think it's run out.

A bell set off a faint ringing in the distance, and a uniformed servant in palace livery approached the King. They whispered in King Edyard's ear, and he nodded. He turned to address the room.

"Honoured guests, your quarters have been made ready.

If you'd like to take the time to settle in, we'll see some of you again at dinner."

King Edyard turned and left the hall while more liveried servants appeared to lead the guests to their different quarters.

Anerin appeared at Belasko's shoulder. "Well then, shall we go and see how high we rank in our host's estimations?"

29

QUITE HIGH, IT turned out. The closest members of the Queen's retinue were housed along a corridor high up in the palace, their rooms leading off from the hallway that led to the Queen's own impressive suite of rooms. It was a grand part of the palace, decorated with fulsome carpets and marble statues.

Anerin leaned against the door to Belasko's room. He peered inside. "I think they like you more than me. I'm sure your rooms are bigger. They obviously hold you in high regard."

Belasko frowned, looking around at the lavish room he would sleep in for the next few weeks. "Edyard maybe. I don't think the rest care for me much. Did you meet that Count Veldar? He made my blood run cold."

"I did. Careful of him, he's a wily fox. Head of the Baskan intelligence service." Anerin grimaced. "We've met before, not in entirely pleasant circumstances."

Belasko turned to him. "Oh, tell me more."

"It was the early days after the war. My family was amongst the first to try and reestablish trade links with the

Baskans. Plenty of people were suspicious, on both sides of the border." Anerin looked a little sheepish. "I may have got a little drunk one night, offended one or two of the wrong people, and spent a few nights in the cells." He sighed. "I gave them the excuse that put me in there, but it gave Veldar and his people the opportunity they needed to keep me there, supposedly investigating claims I was a spy."

"What did they do?"

"Nothing drastic. No torture or anything like that. Relentless questioning. I think they were trying to see how loyal I was to the crown, if they could turn me as a spy in their service." He shrugged. "Once they realised that wasn't going to happen, they let me go in fairly short order. Said all my papers checked out, and I could leave. Veldar himself led the questioning. I suppose I should be honoured."

"I'd have been surprised if they'd harmed you. The peace was a fragile thing then, and your family are one of the most prominent in Villan. Torturing you could have been all that was needed to send us back onto the battlefield." Belasko raised an eyebrow. "Also, you? Getting drunk and causing offence? I'd have thought you knew better."

Anerin flushed. "I was young. I, um, misread what I thought were signals of another man's interest. It turned out that not only were they not interested but that I had impugned their honour. They wanted satisfaction in the duelling circle. If it hadn't been for being thrown in the cells, it might have been my blade that started a second war. I've mellowed since."

"Glad to hear it." Belasko looked around him once again. "What now?"

"We could call on the Queen, see if she has any instructions for us before dinner." Anerin stood up straight, stretching his back. "I've lived in the saddle for the last few years. I'll be glad of sleeping in a proper bed tonight."

"Me, too." Belasko flexed his bad foot and winced. "My various aches and pains don't enjoy much time in the saddle these days. I'm definitely feeling this journey. Come, let's do as you say and call on the Queen."

They left, Belasko closing the door to his rooms behind them, and they made their way along the corridor towards the Queen's rooms.

"Where have they put the rest of our party—the guards and soldiers?" Belasko asked.

Anerin scratched his chin. "In an old barracks, attached to the Baskan palace guard compound. You know, I think I'm going to have to shave before dinner."

"I'd rather have had them closer... I have an uneasy feeling." Belasko looked over his shoulder to make sure they were alone. "There's something about that Count Veldar. I don't like him much at all."

"Careful, Belasko, your prejudices are showing." Anerin smiled. "To be fair, if I was surrounded by a country of people who hated me, I'd feel a little uneasy, too."

∽

King Edyard was in his chambers, dressing for dinner. Although there were servants that could help him, he preferred to dress himself. The old fashioned military man was used to people taking his orders and instructions but wasn't yet comfortable being waited on hand and foot.

There came a knock at the door. Brodkin, his body man, who had been hovering in case the King needed any help with tricky knots or fastenings, went to see who it was. The stout servant, hair thinning at the temples, turned back to the room. "Count Veldar, your majesty."

King Edyard looked up from fastening a particularly fiddly cuff on his shirt. "Oh? I didn't expect to see him until dinner. Please, send him in. And Brodkin? Have a word with my tailor, will you? The holes on these cuffs are too damn tight."

"Yes, sir." Brodkin opened the door to admit the Baskan nobleman, then returned to laying out the rest of the King's clothes for the evening.

Count Veldar closed the door behind him before turning and delivering a respectful bow to his King. "Your majesty. Are there not people to help you with that?"

King Edyard laughed. "There are, but I prefer to do some things for myself. As soon as you become King, everyone seems to think you're incapable of basic tasks. I tell you, though," the King muttered through gritted teeth, "my old uniform was a damn sight easier to put on than all this court get up. Aha!" He had succeeded in fastening one shirt cuff and turned his attention to the other. He looked up at Count Veldar. "What can I do for you, Count? I wasn't expecting to see you before dinner."

The Count clasped his hands behind his back and rocked slightly on his heels, an indication he was in the mood to report or offer an opinion on something. "I, ah, had some first impressions I wanted to offer your majesty. About our guests. They may be of use in the negotiations."

King Edyard frowned, focusing on his final recalcitrant cuff. "Go ahead, I'm listening."

Count Veldar pouted slightly, as if about to say something distasteful or unpalatable. "The swordsman Belasko, I noticed he has a strong influence on Queen Lilliana."

King Edyard looked up. "Oh, and how did you notice

that? I can't imagine they were discussing anything of consequence at that drinks reception."

Count Veldar waved away the suggestion. "It's not in what was said, but how. A man of my profession learns to pick up these things. The way she listened to him, gave him attention... I'm not saying she hung on his every word, but what he said carried weight with her. More than the other Villanese courtiers present."

"That's not surprising, I suppose. The Queen has known Belasko most of her life. With her father and brother gone, he's almost certainly an important older figure to her. It's understandable she would listen to him." King Edyard fastened his last cuff, then looked up at Brodkin. "Brodkin, my doublet if you please."

The man-servant came forward, helping the king on with the doublet before removing himself to a safe distance while the King fastened the buttons and ties that ran up the side of the garment.

"I'm sure you're right, majesty, but I detected a certain amount of anti-Baskan feeling in Belasko during our conversation. If he's present at the negotiations, he may sway the Queen against some of our proposals. Especially if the subject of an alliance by marriage were to come up." Count Veldar held up his hands as King Edyard raised his eyebrows. "It is early to think of such things, but I'm sure I picked up on an attraction between Queen Lilliana and your youngest son. She may be amenable to such a suggestion. Belasko, I fear, would not."

King Edyard frowned. "I detected no anti-Baskan feeling in the man. Have you considered that he may have taken a dislike to you personally, dear Veldar, and not all Baskans? I trust Belasko as a man of honour, as he trusted me all those years ago. I believe he would not put his own feelings ahead of what is right, what is best for his people. He has put his own life on the line for them often enough, and is mature enough to know what is to be expected of monarchs. Still..." He spread his arms, and Brodkin scurried forward to pull the doublet straight, making some small adjustments to the fastenings before retreating once more. "I doubt the long slog of the negotiating table will suit a man of action such as he. It might be best if we found another way to occupy him, for his own sake. Perhaps a competition or exhibition?"

"Your majesty?" Count Veldar gave his monarch an enquiring look.

The King began to pace around the room as his idea took hold. "Yes, that's it. An exhibition of martial prowess with a competitive element. Between the Villanese soldiers that accompanied Queen Lilliana and the best the Baskan Military Academy has to offer. I'm sure he would be interested in that. Preparations and practise would keep him busy so as to remove him from the negotiations. Hopefully, he would find that more entertaining. What do you think?"

"An excellent suggestion, majesty. Perhaps we could propose it to the Villanese tonight. Now, if I have your permission to withdraw?"

King Edyard waved. "Of course, off you go. I'll see you shortly at dinner."

"Your majesty." Count Veldar bowed, turned, and let himself out.

~

The Water King, Nobody, No One, and Borne were making their way along a dark tunnel underneath the palace. They had discarded their servants' uniforms for nondescript workers' clothes in muted tones. Their way was lit only by the torches they held, and the damp sounds of the underground echoed eerily about them.

"Lucky for us, we weren't needed to help out with that big dinner," said Borne. "Although I am feeling a little peckish."

"We'll eat when we get back," said the Water King. "Making contact with our counterparts in the city below is more important."

"City below? Is that what they call it?" asked No One.

"What is it about criminals and underground lairs?" asked Nobody.

"Yeah, it's like everyone's heard the phrase 'criminal underworld' and taken it to heart," said No One.

"Hush you two," said the Water King. "I'm trying to pay attention. We need to make the right signal in the right place or..."

"Or what?" asked Borne.

"Or you'll step into a whole heap of trouble," said a shadowy figure that appeared in their path. Cloaked, they drew back their hood to reveal sharp features in the light of the torches. A lean young man, his complexion made sallow by much time spent out of the sun. His frame carried tension, like a strung bow waiting to be loosed.

"We're not after trouble. We have an invitation," said the Water King.

"Well, you missed your marker and your opportunity to make the signal, so I might just have to gut you where you stand." The young man pulled back his cloak to reveal a long knife that hung at his belt. He reached for it and drew it slowly, taking a step forward as he spoke. "So make quick with that signal or—"

Borne moved with a speed that belied his size, putting himself between the potential threat and the others. He

The Swordsman's Descent

dropped his torch as he did so and seized both of the young man's wrists in one large hand, his throat with the other, and before anyone else could act, was holding their would-be attacker suspended in the air.

"I abhor violence," said Borne in a mournful voice, "but threaten my friends again, and I may have to make an exception."

The young man was turning red and tried to choke out some words. Borne relaxed his grip slightly.

"Sorry, you were saying?"

Borne's captive glowered at him. "There's a half-dozen crossbows trained on you, you fool. Hurt me, and you'll be bristling with bolts like a pincushion. "

The Water King stepped forward, laying a gentle hand on Borne's arm. "Now, Borne, we're all friends here. This is just a small misunderstanding. I'm sure he was only drawing his knife to make the signal. Now, I'm going to draw the knife at my belt, tap out the agreed signal, we'll exchange the sign and countersign, and then we'll go see your employer, and no blood need be shed. All right?"

He slowly drew the knife at his belt, knelt on the rocky floor, and tapped out a rhythm with the hilt. An answering rhythm came out of the darkness, followed by a voice.

"The path to knowledge is never easy," said the disembodied voice.

"But the wise man knows the trip is worth the trouble," replied the Water King. He sheathed his knife and turned to the young man Borne still held in the air. "There, all done. Borne, put this good fellow down and let us be on our way."

Borne set the young man down on the ground, released his wrists, then gently smoothed the cloth of his cloak where it had bunched up in his meaty fist. "There," he said in an apologetic tone. "No harm done."

The Water King took the young man by the elbow and turned him in the direction they had been walking. "Is it this way we're going? Good, let's get on the way. Time is of the essence. I'll make introductions as we go." He threw an expansive arm around the young man's shoulders as they set off. "I'm known as the Water King, and these are my associates. The big man is Borne—he's gentle as a lamb, really. Unless he's riled. The two youngsters are Nobody and No One, and while they're overly talkative, they are incredibly sneaky. Excellent pickpockets and burglars, good to have around in a pinch. Whom do I have the honour of addressing?"

The young man rubbed his throat and swallowed, seeming overwhelmed by the force of the Water King's personality. "I'm Chapman. Pleased to meet you. I think. I work for—"

"Ah yes, your employer. Let us make haste. We don't want to keep her ladyship waiting."

30

EVEN WITH WINTER approaching, the Baskan sun carried some heat with it, especially when you worked as hard as Belasko worked his students.

They were in a small courtyard attached to the barracks building that had been given over to the Villanese military during their stay. No windows overlooked it, so it was a nice private place in which to practice. And practice they did, in earnest now, for there was something to prove.

Why hold this competition? Why did I agree to it? Belasko shook his head as he observed his students. I couldn't not, or it would have been a loss of face for us here, among these martial people. Their society respects strength, so we will show it to them.

"No, no!" he called out, stepping forward to correct two of his sparring students. "What are you doing? Nerys, if you overextend like that, Sysko could have had you. *Should* have had you." He turned to Sysko, who flushed under the examination. "Why didn't you? She left herself wide open! Start again and this time try to remember some of what we practised on our journey."

Belasko strode away, taking up another vantage point

from which to observe his students as they worked, the ring of clashing steel practice blades filling the air. He caught Byrta's eye as she adjusted someone's grip on their sabre. She gave him an imperceptible shrug, to which he rolled his eyes.

Turning, he leaned his back against the courtyard wall and resumed watching his students. He couldn't help thinking back to dinner on the night of their arrival.

He had been seated at the top table with the royals and most important members of their retinue. Anerin was beside him, Count Veldar and an elderly Baskan woman named Welmar, who was a retired general and a key adviser in military matters, sat opposite. Queen Lilliana, King Edyard, and Prince Beviyard were a little further up the table and deep in discussion. The Queen was asking many questions of things she had seen as they rode through the city earlier that day—points of history and culture.

Part of their conversation drifted over to Belasko. King Edyard was explaining something to do with the many temples they had passed on their way to the palace. "We worship the same gods, actually. Well, the old pantheon. One of your ancestors turned away from the other gods and demigods towards worshipping the sun god, who you call Aronos. They brought the rest of the pantheon under him as, what do you call them? Saints? Here they hold their original place alongside him."

Queen Lilliana speared a piece of delicately steamed fish on her fork, waving it in the air as she talked. "There was one temple in particular that caught my eye, on the corner of that large square just inside the city gates. Very different to the others. Blocky, severe, without the delicate columns and open frontage many of the other old temples here seem to share. Which god is that one dedicated to?"

The Swordsman's Descent

King Edyard and Prince Beviyard shared a look. It was the Prince who spoke. "That temple is, well, a difficult one to speak of. Somewhat taboo in our society." He smiled. "Although one thing I have learned in our travels is that nothing is off-topic when it comes to conversations with your majesty. It is the temple of the Lady of Night. The moon goddess, her name isn't spoken, for she is the goddess of death."

Count Veldar spoke up. "Forgive me for interrupting, but Queen Lilliana may be interested to know that there are old temples to the Lady of Night in Villan. I believe they have been given over to use as temples of the dead, resting houses for the recently deceased, but in Aronos's name."

Queen Lilliana perked up at this. "How interesting, I had no idea. And history is something of a passion of mine."

"The split happened long ago," said King Edyard. "I wouldn't be surprised if some records were suppressed in order to shift worship to Aronos. If there's time during your stay, I'd be happy to open the palace archives to you, so you can learn more."

Queen Lilliana's eyes gleamed at this, and Belasko laughed. "Forgive me," he said, "but there's little else our Queen loves more than old libraries and dusty archives. If you dangle that in front of her, you may find negotiations achieved in record time simply so she may spend some time there."

Queen Lilliana smiled at him. "Belasko knows me too well and, while your offer is sorely tempting, we must first attend to the matters at hand. I would love to look through your archives, if there's time."

"What about you?" Count Veldar asked Belasko. "Do you share your monarch's love of books?"

Belasko snorted. "Not quite. My life has been immersed

in the study of swordplay and martial matters. I have amassed quite a library of my own in that regard, but I'm not overly fond of trawling through dusty tomes in search of dry facts."

"More a man of action, eh? I understand that," General Welmar said. "You'd rather be getting your hands dirty. Me, too, if age didn't preclude it. Now I serve in another capacity and find a use for myself there."

"I serve where my Queen needs me. For now, that is as Champion." Belasko shrugged. "In the future? We shall see. I would like to concentrate on my academy, my students there. Pass on what I have learned."

Count Veldar leaned forward. "That's right, I heard you even took to training some people on your journey here. It's clearly a passion for you." He looked from Belasko to Welmar and back again. "I have an idea. General Welmar here is on the board of the Baskan Military Academy. You are the leader of your own academy. How about an exhibition or competition?" He smiled, an expression lacking in genuine warmth that brought to mind a predatory animal. "Something to keep the man of action interested, where dry meetings and long negotiations may bore you."

Belasko eyed the Baskan courtier warily. "What exactly do you propose?" He was aware that conversation up and down the table had ceased, and people were listening to their words intently.

"I'm not sure; the idea has only just come to me." Count Veldar pursed his lips, tapping his finger against his wine glass. Then he smiled. "How about this? Some bouts, in different disciplines, between the best of your new students and the best our Military Academy has to offer? We can have exhibitions from each side first, then competition between the two. What do you say?"

Belasko frowned. "I remember very clearly what happened the last time Baskan and Villanese blades crossed. I thought we were here to move beyond that."

Count Veldar waved away his suggestion. "All in good fun, the spirit of cooperation—not to open old wounds. What do you say? Welmar?"

The elderly general eyed Belasko, rubbing her chin. "I share the swordsman's reticence, but if it's in the spirit of cooperation, then I fail to see the harm. I'm sure something could be arranged."

Count Veldar turned back to Belasko. "Belasko?"

He sighed. "If my Queen allows it, I see no harm also. It might be a learning experience for all of us." Belakso looked up the table to see Queen Lilliana watching him intently, although her expression was unreadable. "Ma'am?"

She nodded slowly. "I'm happy to be led by you in this, my Champion. And I trust in you and those you are training to uphold Villanese honour."

And so it was that he and his students had been sweating in the Baskan sun every day, working and preparing to uphold the honour of their country.

The Queen herself spent her days closeted with her advisers, Anerin among them, as they negotiated and debated with their Baskan counterparts. Belasko had attended a few of these meetings when his thoughts on martial matters were welcomed, but in truth, he found them boring. It was difficult to concentrate on talk of border controls and trade tariffs, voices droning on and on as they quibbled over every minor detail. The talk of military de-escalation caught his ear, and it was here that his expertise was welcomed. Both parties wanted to decrease their military presence along their shared border but were concerned about increased danger to their border settlements from bandits if they dropped their numbers. Belasko had suggested joint exercises, patrols, and searches aimed at keeping the presence of bandits and outlaws to a minimum while fostering greater cooperation between their people—a suggestion that had gone down well.

Other than that, his work with his new students kept him too busy to attend more than a handful of meetings, although the Queen spoke to him most evenings and updated him on that day's progress. She would ask his opinion and advice on what had happened and what he thought of the topics they would be discussing the next day. He did his best to advise her, but more than once pointed out that he was a swordsman, not a trade envoy or expert negotiator.

"Don't do yourself down, Belasko. You offer a unique perspective. You grew up along the borderlands, you know the people and the problems that they face, and your military experience is exemplary. You have a keen mind." Here a little smile quirked her lips. "Somewhere, in that head of yours."

The evenings had been full of soirees and dinners. Belasko had tired of these almost immediately, as the highly spiced Baskan cuisine didn't agree with him and he himself was a curiosity that people peered at. Everyone wanted to say that they had dined with Belasko, drunk with Belasko. The same questions were asked again and again. "So, what really happened at Dellan Pass?" He was bored of it and sometimes regretted attending.

Belasko was brought back to the moment by the arrival of Majel at the courtyard. He had asked her to continue training with them, and she had led some sessions. Her work with rapier and dagger was exemplary, and she was due to take a couple of students through their paces this afternoon. Byrta was taking a session in the sabre, Anerin had taken advantage of a break in negotiations to help and had a couple of students working with longswords, and Parlin was taking some students through their knife work. Each worked on their strongest discipline.

"Welcome, Majel," Belasko called to her from across the courtyard. "Thank you for coming. I was hoping you'd take Nerys and Sysko through their rapier and dagger drills, perhaps some practice bouts as well."

"Of course, Belasko, I'm happy to help." Majel drew nearer, then said quietly, "Which are they again?"

Belasko pointed them out. Majel nodded her thanks and went over to them. "Right, you two, Belasko tells me you're handy with rapier and dagger. Let's see, shall we? You've warmed up, I take it? Good. Run through your solo forms for me, then together, then the real work will start."

Belasko oversaw it all, observing everything, missing nothing. Watching for any weaknesses the Baskans they'd face in competition might exploit; any strengths to be praised.

Byrta's sabre work was going well. Anerin needed to watch the footwork of the longsword-wielding students, and the timing of some of the knife work was a little off. Belasko intervened when necessary, making small corrections and offering praise where it was due.

He was most intrigued by Majel, however. He could see the quality in her movements, the flashes of brilliance and skill that had been apparent on their journey here but quickly hidden. *She's doing it again. Why hide her quality? She's the equal of anyone here, better than most. Why disguise that fact?*

When it came time for their water break, he took Majel to one side. "Majel, a word please, if I may?"

She nodded, drinking deep from her water cup. Sweat beaded on her brow and arms. She had removed her uniform jacket and was working with her shirtsleeves rolled up to the elbow.

Majel swallowed. "What is it?"

"It's a difficult thing to broach but..." Belasko sighed. "Why are you hiding your skill? Again, as you did on the journey here."

Majel stilled, eyeing him warily. "I don't know what you mean."

"Yes, you do. Why? I don't understand it. You're the equal of anyone here, you should own that fact."

She laughed. "Do you include yourself in that?" A look of surprise appeared on her face when he didn't immediately rebut the suggestion.

Belasko nodded slowly. "Maybe I do. I'll never know unless you show me what you can really do. You're better than any of my students with rapier and dagger. I was going to ask you if you'd be willing to take part in this competition we've been manoeuvred into. If you're willing. But I'd need to see your true skill. The Baskans will give no quarter. You will need everything you have to triumph. Are you prepared to do that?"

Majel didn't reply at first, looking into her cup. After a while, her eyes rose to meet Belasko's, a fierce determination in their depths. "What if I am? I would be honoured to represent Villan in this, to represent the Queen. If, as you say, I'm the best of your current and former students here present, then it behoves me to take part."

"Then show me. After this break, you and I will have a bout. Practice blades, no quarter given. Show me the real Majel, the warrior you are. Because I don't think I've seen her yet."

Majel nodded. "All right, let's do it. Now give me a few minutes' peace to prepare." With that, she put down her cup and stalked off to find some space to stretch and ease muscles already tired from training.

"All right, everyone," Belasko called to the group. "You've done some very good work so far today. You're going to get a bit of a longer break, as Majel and I are going to have a practice bout. Something of an exhibition for you. Then it'll be back to work for everyone."

A murmur ran through the group. Belasko rarely trained with others these days, only with a select group of his friends and instructors. His students thought this was to cultivate an air of mystique or because he was developing secret techniques. The truth of it was that he was trying to keep his physical ailments as quiet as possible. The more people who saw him fight, the more would realise something wasn't right with the Royal Champion.

Belasko moved apart from the others, warming up. He ran through some movements, stretching and awakening his muscles. He flexed his left foot in his boot, disguising a wince at the pain. *I've been pushing myself a harder than normal.* Belasko flexed his fingers as he held out his arms, rotating his hands from palm up to palm down. *At least I'll be able to keep hold of my sword.*

He went over to the case that held his practice blades, flicking open the clasps on the polished hardwood container with the ease of long use. Belasko took out his practice rapier and dagger, feeling their weight and balance. "Hello, old friends," he murmured, half to himself and half to the lengths of steel in his hand. "Let's put you to work."

Belasko turned and walked towards the duelling circle they had marked in the courtyard. Majel was already there, as was Byrta.

"I'll officiate, shall I?" asked the cavalrywoman.

"Thank you, Byrta." Belasko looked at Majel. "Are you ready?"

She only nodded in reply. The other students drew near, gathering around the circle. "Well then," said Belasko, "let's begin."

He and Majel took their places across the circle from each other. They bowed, showing the respect due to their opponent, and then assumed their guard positions.

"All right, let's do this. You both know what you're about. Fight to first touch, as if to first blood." Byrta looked from one to the other. "Begin!"

Majel exploded into motion, launching a blistering series of attacks. One movement flowing into the next, she moved with a beautiful and deadly economy. Belasko met her head-on, blocking every strike, deflecting every lunge. He didn't attack, not yet. He was feeling her out. He wanted to see what she would do. The Royal Champion was getting a feel for how she might compete against the best the Baskans had to offer.

They moved around the circle, back and fore in little sidesteps, feet flickering in movements almost as quick as their blades. Belasko thought his moment had come as he caught Majel's rapier on his dagger and twisted his wrist to hold the blade. He brought his own rapier up and around in an overhead strike, but Majel took the momentum of the pressure from his dagger, ducking under and away while his blow sailed uselessly over her back.

Majel whirled away, resuming her guard position across the duelling circle. Belasko followed suit, and for a moment, they simply watched each other, each waiting on the other to move.

You could have heard a pin drop in that courtyard. The

students and instructors gathered held their breath, dazzled by the display.

Belasko grinned at Majel. *It's been a while since someone pushed me this hard.* He pushed off and attacked again, feinting with his dagger to try and draw Majel's rapier out, his own flickering out in a strike that she calmly parried. Her riposte tore through the air by his face as Belasko, through an adjustment to his weight, leaned back just enough that it wouldn't catch him.

He brought his dagger up, using it to put his own force behind her blow, pushing her rapier wide as he lunged with his blade in a strike that should have caught her midsection. But again, she danced away. Now she was smiling, too.

They fought on, apparently evenly matched. Belasko was patient. He knew the time would come, a weakness would show itself, and he would strike. They were both athletes, with years of physical conditioning, but eventually, they would tire. Mistakes would creep in.

Belasko detected a pattern to Majel's attacks. Again and again, she did her best to put him in positions and moves that meant he had to put his weight on his left foot. His bad foot. Pain flared each time he did so, getting worse as the fight progressed. He attacked, and once again, her reply forced him onto the back foot. This time, the pain was bad enough that he grunted. Belasko frowned at her. Majel responded with a slight shrug, as if to say *you told me to show you my all, to fight to win.*

What did I expect? Again, she forced him onto his back foot. He winced at the pain that flared up, feeling it like red hot needles running up into his leg. *Best finish this soon.*

Belasko changed his style, adopting the odd stuttering gait he used to cover his limp when the pain was bad. It made it difficult for his opponents to follow or predict his moves. Majel frowned, staring at him from under her brows. *See, Majel? I can play too.*

As he anticipated, his new method made it difficult for her to predict his movements, his attacks, and he very nearly landed several blows. Belasko pushed forwards, relentless, determined to end this duel.

Both of them were sweating now, red-faced, smiles gone as they put their all into defeating the other.

Belasko took a gamble. He threw himself into a wild lunge, aimed not at hitting Majel but at missing her. Passing wide of her, he deliberately overbalanced, almost tripping himself up as he sped past. Belasko twisted as he did so, bringing his rapier around to catch Majel in the side. But she had, at the last moment, realised his intention and twisted with him, rapier sweeping behind her. The two of them locked eyes as both blades landed at the same time. A draw. Both had got a touch.

Majel's eyes were wide as she and Belasko returned to standing, facing each other, chests heaving as they caught their breath. "I landed a touch. On you."

Belasko smiled. "You did. It's been a few years since anyone managed that. You made use of my injuries, exploited them. That was wise."

The two of them spoke quietly, so the others in the courtyard couldn't hear them. The students were silent, watching on, shocked. None of them had ever known Belasko to lose or draw a duel.

Belasko moved a little closer to Majel. They were of a height, so looked each other in the eye. "Bring that level of fight to the competition, and the Baskans won't stand a chance. Will you fight? For the Queen. For Villan. For me?"

Majel swallowed, a strange expression on her face. "I will. But, Belasko... I've said it before, I'll say it again: I don't want your job. I'm not looking to join the ranks of those desperate to succeed you."

"I know. May I ask why not? I'm beginning to think you have what it takes."

Majel swallowed again. "It's just that, Belasko." She looked away, unable to meet his eyes. "You're so alone. I don't want that. I can't live that life." She looked up again, eyes wet with unshed tears. "I'm sorry."

The other students surrounded them then, congratulating Majel, firing off questions to Belasko about his odd technique. Belasko answered them as best he could, but he could still hear Majel's words in his ears.

I am alone. I choose to be. So why did it hurt to hear her say it?

31

OLBARIN PEERED UP and down the corridor, wanting to make sure he was in the right place. He was down in the depths of the palace's storerooms and basements, standing in front of a nondescript door that looked much like the others to either side of it. He squinted and could make out a faint mark scratched in the wood by the door handle. Olbarin knocked on the door and entered.

What had once been a store cupboard, and may well return to that use after their meeting, had become Jonteer's temporary office. The balding secretary sat behind a desk, three chairs arrayed in front of it. The room was dimly lit by oil lamps, and while Jonteer's desk was well-lit, the man himself was shadowed.

He looked up as Olbarin walked in and nodded. "You're on time. Good. Please sit." He gestured to one of the chairs opposite him with the quill in his hand, then returned to scratching out whatever note he was writing.

"My mother always told me that punctuality was a form of respect," said Olbarin as he took his seat.

Jonteer didn't look up from his writing. "A wise woman,

your mother." He finished writing, set aside his quill, and looked up at Olbarin.

"I had thought these meetings would be over with, now that we're in Albessar and I'm no longer training with Belasko," said the younger man.

"The intelligence service decides when we're finished with our resources, not the other way around." Jonteer leaned back in his seat. Steepling his fingers, he peered over them. "You may not be training with the Villanese anymore, but you are certainly still friendly with some of those other students, are you not?"

"I am," said Olbarin. "I thought that was the point of inviting Queen Lilliana here: to foster better relationships with the Villanese."

"Oh, yes indeed, especially when those relationships can be useful. You have seen some of those fellow students since our arrival in a social capacity."

Olbarin was aware this wasn't a question, and his skin prickled at the thought that he had been watched. "That is correct."

Jonteer smiled. It was typical of his expressions: cold and didn't reach his eyes. "I was wondering if they said anything that might be of interest to us. If anything curious had occurred during their training. Any information about their preparations that might be useful."

Olbarin sighed. "Not really. Belasko's been pushing them hard, working towards this competition. They're all very aware that they're not students from his academy, that they've been thrown together by happenstance, and that they'll be up against the best the Baskan Military Academy has to offer. They're determined to do well, not just for their Queen and country, but to make Belasko proud."

There was silence as Jonteer looked at him for a

moment. He leaned forward. "It makes you uncomfortable, doesn't it? Providing information on those you consider friends?"

"In truth, yes." Olbarin nodded.

"You like Belasko, don't you?" Jonteer's eyes gleamed in the lamplight.

"I do. To my surprise, yes, I do."

"Despite the fact that he killed your father. Astonishing." Jonteer tilted his head slightly, another smile quirking his lips. "I've never found him particularly likeable, and I have no personal loss to pin on him."

Olbarin shrugged. "I'm at a loss to explain it. I spent a lifetime building him up in my head, hating him, but the real man... He's not what I expected."

"Perhaps, but you owe him no loyalty. Your loyalty belongs to us. To Bas." Jonteer's tone was sharp now.

"Gods yes, my loyalty is with Bas, but it's not true that I owe Belasko nothing. He could have killed me the day I challenged him, easily. Instead, he sent me away with a letter of recommendation in my pocket. A letter that gave me the chance to build a life I was prepared to throw away. So I do owe him something. As do you, because that act of mercy set me on the path to being useful to you. Of being able to provide the information I have." Olbarin's tone was not defiant but simply forthright.

Jonteer stared at him for a moment, then nodded. "Perhaps it is as you say. Now, is there anything you can share with me? Any bit of information that your new friends may have let slip?"

Olbarin frowned. "There was one thing, although I'm not sure how useful it is. During a training session the other day, Belasko put on an exhibition duel with Majel, the

The Swordsman's Descent

teapot that sat on the table between them. They were in a snug little lounge that was part of the Queen's suite of guest rooms, close to her sleeping chamber. Although it was moving towards evening, the tall windows that ran along one wall let in a good amount of light.

"Thank you." Belasko waited while the Queen poured out two cups. He picked up the one nearest him, blowing gently on the contents to cool it to drinking temperature, then taking a sip. He made an appreciative face. "Very nice. One of Maelyn's blends?"

"That's right. This one is designed to soothe and calm me before bed. It has the benefit of tasting pleasant as well." Queen Lilliana took a sip. "How go the preparations for this competition? Are your students adequately prepared for tomorrow?"

"Yes. I believe they will acquit themselves well across the disciplines. Majel will also be fighting."

Queen Lilliana blinked in surprise. "Majel? She hasn't mentioned it. I didn't realise she was so skilled."

"Yes, well, she seems to like keeping things close to her chest." Belasko laughed. "She's been hiding her talent somewhat, or at least her hard work. Majel's done a lot to improve in the years since I taught her at the Academy. I certainly admire her dedication and craft. Yet she didn't want me to see her quality."

"Why would she do that?" The Queen was even more surprised now.

Belasko sighed. "I think partly because she loves her job. She has no desire to replace me. For... A variety of reasons. Didn't want me to even entertain the notion."

"Would you? Entertain the notion now? If she's good enough to represent Villan tomorrow..."

"No." Belasko shook his head. "You have to want this

role. To be the Royal Champion is... Well, it's all-consuming. If she doesn't want it, it's not for her. I, for one, am glad to know the head of your guard is so skilled. She is a formidable opponent. I'm glad she's dedicated to your protection."

"Me also. I have been since she took on the role when we adjusted the security arrangements at the palace. She's grown into it. I think she has potential for further development as well." The Queen sipped her tea. "I look forward to seeing her perform tomorrow."

"I think you'll enjoy it." Belasko grinned. "The Baskans won't."

33

THE NEXT DAY dawned bright and clear, with only the faintest breeze. Their hosts had built stands around the outer perimeter of a parade ground that lay just outside the palace walls. In the centre of the parade ground were a pair of duelling circles. As the Villanese could put forward two competitors for each discipline, it was decided that the initial bouts would take place at the same time, the winners of each bout facing each other after a brief rest period.

Belasko and Byrta arrived at the competition square early, wanting to get a feel for the place.

"Seems fair, apart from the advantage of performing in front of a supportive crowd. I don't see the Baskans getting any unfair advantage from the layout," said Byrta.

"No, that all seems right enough. They've offered half the places in the stands to people from our contingent, including some our soldiers," said Belasko.

Byrta frowned. "That's sporting of them. I wonder whose idea that was."

"King Edyard's, perhaps?" Belasko shrugged. "Or

perhaps Prince Beviyard. Both strike me as fair-minded. Come, let's join the others at breakfast. We'll want to make sure they eat properly. They'll need the energy later on."

When they returned later, the stands were filling. The clamour from the crowd was already loud. Baskans and Villanese eyed each other warily from their seats. Belasko saw the flash of money changing hands as bets were laid, coins glinting in the sun. Those gathered seemed in good humour.

I wonder how long that will last...

Belasko knew there was no way that everything would go their way today. He knew how seriously the Baskans took their martial prowess. He smiled to himself. *Still, I'd bet on these unexpected students of mine against most. In fact, I might have to lay a few bets on. Good thing I brought coin with me.*

Majel and Belasko's students emerged into the parade ground, taking in the spectacle before them, although they would soon be the spectacle themselves.

"All right, everyone, gather round. A little talk before things get going." Belasko waved the others over, and they came to him, surrounding him and Byrta in a loose circle.

"Now," Belasko said, regarding them each in turn, "I could say a lot of things today. I could say that you're here to represent the Villanese people. Thet you're here to represent our Queen and her honour, as well as your own. I could say that you must win. That only victory over the Baskans is acceptable, any other result shameful." He shook his head. "But that's all nonsense. When you step into the duelling circle, you represent one person: yourself. The object remains the same, no matter what's at stake. Get your opponent before they get you. That's it. It's that simple." He smiled. "Even though we were thrown together unexpectedly, I've never been prouder of a group of students. You

The Swordsman's Descent

control what happens today to the best of your abilities because of your training, your dedication, your craft. You've done everything you can to prepare. Unleash all of it on your opponents. Don't hold back. Give it your all. That's all I, your Queen, or your country, can ask of you." Belasko clapped his hands. "Best start warming up. Let's get to it!"

～

The first bouts were a fine display of knife work. The Villanese, in two close fought bouts, lost to the Baskans, setting up an all Baskan final. Parlin was particularly interested in this round, though he was sniffy about the technique of some combatants. The royal parties were together in the stands, watching the competition unfold.

"I mean, look at the Baskans," Parlin said to Queen Lilliana. "They won—their technique was efficient if brutish. But what of style? There was no finesse there."

The Queen nodded. "That may be true, but they still won. I'm sure I heard someone say once that style is all well and good, but it doesn't keep you alive."

Parlin looked at her out of the corner of his eye and only harrumphed in response.

Count Veldar smiled. "If that is all we can expect from our Villanese guests, then it will be a short afternoon.

Belasko's answering smile was grim. "Watch on and you might learn a few things yet, Count."

～

The second bouts were in sabre. Here the Villanese and Baskans won an opening bout apiece, setting up a tense confrontation in the final. Nerys, Byrta's prize pupil, made quick work of her on the final round, winning with a series of daring moves.

Belasko smiled. "Like student, like master. I've never seen better than Byrta with a sabre."

Prince Beviyard raised an eyebrow. "Oh yes, so you've said. I've never seen better than Emilynn—she's a devil with her sabre."

Emilynn and Byrta eyed each other up, a speculative air about them.

Queen Lilliana intervened. "Now isn't the time. If the two of you want to schedule a practice bout of your own later, that's your business."

～

The third bouts were in rapier and dagger. Majel made quick work of her opponent to progress to the final. Sysko lost to their opponent, Eldren, the star student of the Baskan Military Academy.

"Isn't that the head of Queen Lilliana's guard?" asked Count Veldar.

"A former student of mine. She's been training with us on our journey here and working with my other students. She had a thing or two to show them," said Belasko.

"I can see that," said King Edyard. "I think she and young Eldren might teach each other a lesson or two."

The final was a fierce fight, closely fought. At first, the combatants seemed evenly matched, until Majel imitated Belasko's technique. The odd, stuttering, and unpredictable gait confused her Baskan opponent, and she found her moment to strike. Eldren looked up from the point of Majel's blade in disbelief.

I'd be happier if she hadn't aped my technique. For some reason, that feels like mockery.

King Edyard leaned towards them. "Congratulations on your overall victory. That was well done."

"Yes," said Prince Beviyard, "for saying you hadn't worked with them all that long it's impressive."

The Count frowned, a sour cast to his features. "An odd technique. I've not seen it's like before."

"Something of my own devising, Count," said Belasko. "As I said, Majel has been training with us and has picked up a thing or two."

"It's a shame, then, that we didn't see the originator of such a curious technique perform it himself. It would have been fascinating to see the legendary Belasko fight."

Belasko turned on the Count, fire in his eyes. "I am not here for your amusement, Count. Nor are my students. We have been good-humoured about this contest, having been forced into it by your engineering. I will draw my blade, if you wish, but know this: if I draw my blade in my role as Champion, it is to draw blood as well."

The two men stared at each other, Belasko's face stony with rage and dislike for the Baskan courtier. Something colder settled on Count Veldar's face, but there was a hint of amusement in his eyes.

Queen Lilliana put her arm through Belasko's. "I'm sure that won't be necessary, my Champion. But come, let us congratulate the victors and the losers both. All fought well today and deserve our praise." She turned towards Prince Beviyard. "I believe there was also talk of refreshments?"

A disturbance from the duelling circles, raised voices, caught their attention and they turned back to look. Eldren, the young pride of the Baskan military academy, was calling up to the stands. Looking at the Villanese ruling party.

The crowd quieted, and they could hear his words.

"I challenge. I challenge the villain of Dellan Pass, who would hide behind his students, to face me."

~

Belasko walked up to the railing from behind which they had watched the bouts. He leaned against it as he looked down at the young man that had challenged him. Belasko opened his mouth to reply, but King Edyard beat him to it.

"Today is not about personal challenges, Eldren, but friendly competition. Take your defeat with good grace and learn from it. Majel, the guard captain you faced, is a most gifted opponent. Come, all of you that took part, there is a reception at the palace in your honour. I—"

"I will not be denied, your majesty," Eldren interrupted. "None can forbid or deny a challenge, even our king. So I challenge Belasko. Let him come and face me, with bare blades, and not hide behind his students."

King Edyard, face like thunder, turned to Belasko. "He's right," the king muttered. "I cannot order him to give up his challenge. Sorry Belasko, this puts you in an awkward position."

"I'll say," Belasko replied. "If I accept his challenge, and defeat him, that causes further bad blood between our people. Something we are here to prevent. If he were to defeat me, my reputation would be in tatters and I would lose the respect and fear of your people. Or I refuse his challenge, breaking the oldest traditions, which also makes us look bad in the eyes of your people."

"What are you going to do?" asked Queen Lilliana, her expression calm, but Belasko knew her well enough to see the concern in her eyes.

The Swordsman's Descent

"What I must. I'm a duelist." Belasko looked down again at the young Baskan who had challenged him. Eldren's face was flushed, he was clearly up for the fight.

Belasko called down to him. "Think carefully, boy. One of my students bested you, yet you would challenge their master? You can still withdraw, there would be no shame in it. Now, embarrassing your king by challenging one of his guests in so public a setting? Choosing a course of action that might unbalance the negotiations we are working towards? Being defeated after making such a rash choice? That really would be shameful. Think. Many have faced me across the duelling circle. I have beaten them all. Are you really so eager to be added to their number?"

Eldren's face had flushed further. "I do not recant. I challenge you, Belasko, here and now."

Belasko nodded. "Very well, I shall send for my training blades and join you in the circle. It will take—"

"No," said Eldren, his voice steely. "Enough of this play with dulled swords. We fight with bared blades. To the death."

All was silent now, no one else in the crowd dared speak. Belasko looked around him, taking in the crowd, the ranks of spectators all mutely looking to him for his response. He did not look at Queen Lilliana, for he did not want to see the trepidation in her eyes. He sighed. "So be it. If you are eager to throw your life away, I will have to oblige you. I'll join you in the circle."

Belasko made his way to the stairs that led down from the royal enclosure. Anerin caught his arm and Belasko looked up to see there was desperation in his friend's eyes.

"Belasko," he said, "you don't have to do this."

Belasko smiled sadly. "Yes, old friend, I do. I'm a duelist, there will always be challenges." He gave a sour laugh. "In all honesty, I'm not surprised. I thought a challenge would come long before now." And with that, he left to face his young opponent.

~

Belasko walked out onto the parade ground and towards the duelling circles. Eldren waited for him, having already discarded his training blades and collected a far more lethal rapier and dagger.

Belasko frowned. *That was quick. A little too quick.* He looked back up to the royal enclosure and locked eyes with Count Veldar. The count's cold eyes had a look of amusement about them. Belasko grunted. *I think this is a set up. The count will get to see me fight after all.*

Belasko crossed the duelling circle, paying little heed to the young Baskan he was about to fight. He went to a low table that was positioned to the side of the parade ground, removed his jacket, and set it down upon it. Then, drawing his rapier from its scabbard and his dagger from its sheath, he undid his sword belt one-handed and placed it atop the jacket. He walked back out onto the parade ground and started warming up.

Belasko could feel the eyes of the crowd upon him as he worked his way through a series of preparatory movements, warming and stretching the muscles he would soon call upon. He felt a familiar stab of pain from his foot as his weight shifted, but did his best to ignore it.

Some of Belasko's tension eased as he ran through the familiar forms. Tension he hadn't been aware he was holding. Never mind being on unfamiliar ground, or a potentially hostile audience. The duelling circle is my territory. The fight is my home.

His movements were fluid and blisteringly fast, despite

The Swordsman's Descent

the pain and stiffness in his joints, and when he stopped, he noticed there was still silence in the stands. Belasko looked up. All eyes were on him, including those of his opponent. He looked over to the young Baskan, and it seemed to Belasko some of the confidence had gone out of his challenger.

"All right then," he called to Eldren, "if you're ready?"

Eldren nodded and moved to take up position across the duelling circle from Belasko.

"Very well, let us begin," said Belasko.

∽

Belasko and Eldren circled each other, each trying to get the measure of the other. Eldren did not seem intimidated by the older man, but nor was he rushing in.

He's not so rash after all, thought Belasko. I just wish he was shorter. Damn those long arms.

He lunged, launching a probing attack that Eldren easily parried. *He's fast, I'll give him that.* Then it was Eldren's turn to test Belasko, with a feint that he parried easily enough. The younger man stepped in close to Belasko, twisting his blade to lock Belasko's own and using the momentum from Belasko's parry to push his rapier wide. Opening Belasko up to attack as Eldren's own sword arm crossed his body. Eldren took advantage of this and brought the dagger in his other hand up and over his sword arm to try ands stab Belasko.

The Villanese champion caught Eldren's dagger on his own, and for a moment the two were locked together. The taller Baskan tested Belasko's strength as he leaned into him, pushing down on his blades.

Eldren smiled grimly at Belasko. "I didn't realise you'd be so short."

Belasko grunted. "I didn't realise Baskans talked so much. Is that a new class at the academy?"

He relaxed a little, which took Eldren by surprise and caused the Baskan to stumble forwards. Belasko brought his head down, delivering a vicious headbutt to his opponent's nose, and the young Baskan swore at the pain.

Then Belasko twisted his blades free, spinning away on his good foot, and the sudden absence of resistance caused his opponent to fall forwards. Belasko gave Eldren a kick on the backside as he stumbled past, almost pitching him face first into the dirt.

Eldren growled, turning quickly to bring his blades back to bear on Belasko. His eyes watered, and blood trickled from his left nostril.

"Hurts, doesn't it? A lesson for you, boy, a blow to the nose always hurts and, if you're lucky, cause your opponent's eyes to water. Not that you'll live to put that lesson to use."

Eldren launched himself at Belasko in a speedy combination of attacks, all of which Belasko countered. Now the fight was on.

They worked their way around the circle, forwards and backwards. No quarter asked, and certainly none given. The pace of combat was intense, blows flickering almost faster than could be seen. Neither combatant seeming to have the advantage.

He does have one thing on his side, thought Belasko. Youth. I'm tiring already.

It was true. A lifetime of training had given Belasko incredible reserves of strength and endurance, but the intensity of single combat was burning through them and the pain in his foot was worsening.

Best try to end this quickly.

Belasko shifted technique, adopting the unpredictable

staccato movements he used when he wanted to work around his damaged joints.

Ordinarily, this confused opponents and victory came swiftly afterwards, but Eldren had only just faced Majel using the same technique and he was not so easily cowed.

The Baskan smiled at Belasko as he countered the attacks, falling into a rhythm of his own that was counter to Belasko's. "New tricks only work once, old man."

"Ah," said Belasko, "but you fought a student before, now you face the champion." He threw everything he had at the Baskan, picking up the pace with a series of attacks that had Eldren scrabbling backwards, as their rapiers and daggers beat a sharp rhythm against each other. But whatever Belasko tried, Eldren countered. Even if only barely.

Belasko broke off the attack and backed away. The two of them circled one another again.

Ordinarily there would be shouts of encouragement from the crowd at a duel, but the tension was too high. The crowd remained silent.

The two combatants came together in the centre of the circle, blades flashing in the sunlight as they clashed. The sound of steel on steel rang out across the hushed parade ground. Again, their blades crossed and locked as the taller man tried to lean on Belasko.

Belasko dropped backwards, bringing Eldren's weight with him, their blades still locked together. Instead of spinning away, as he had done before, this time he allowed Eldren to fall into him. Belasko swivelled as he fell, Eldren turned with him, and Belasko set his thigh into the back of Eldren's legs, turning their fall into a throw. He pushed his blades out wide as they both fell to the ground, and brought his own legs up so that, as Eldren landed on his back, Belasko landed with his knees on Eldren's arms, pinning them down. The Villanese champion was now at leisure to cross his blades at Eldren's throat. A puzzled expression settled on the younger man's face.

"How... We thought you were infirm. You weren't supposed to win."

Belasko smiled, but there was no humour in it. "You know, people have been saying that to me for years. I put it down to much practice, and a willingness to try unorthodox moves." He spoke quieter then, for Eldren's ears alone. "Do you yield? You challenged for a fight to the death, but now find yourself defeated. There is no shame in choosing life."

Eldren paled. "No, I issued the challenge knowing what it might mean. I choose death."

Belasko sighed. "As you wish." Then in one swift movement he took his dagger away from Eldren's throat, spun it around in his hand so he held it in a reverse grip, and brought the point of it plunging down into Eldren's eye and through into the brain beyond.

34

IN THE DAYS that followed the competition, Belasko felt even further adrift from the Queen and the negotiating party. If his flash of temper towards Count Veldar hadn't marked him out as unsuitable for the delicate art of negotiation, defeating and killing the cream of the Baskan military crop definitely cast a pall over things. Belasko felt it best to keep a low profile, so he trained and lurked in his suite of rooms. Avoiding all but the most necessary social engagements.

Perhaps I should have refused the challenge. Not risen to Count Veldar's game. Belasko was sure it was the Baskan intelligence who was behind the unexpected challenge. *I shouldn't have let that lickspittle get to me, but I know I was being mocked.* Belasko sighed to himself, enjoying the sun on his face as he looked out the long windows that graced the lounge in his rooms. They opened out onto a balcony, a feature of all of the rooms along this corridor, and he was just about to head out to enjoy a glass of wine when there came a knock on the door.

Belasko sighed, going to open the door. It was one of the royal guard, and behind them, the Queen.

"Your majesty," Belasko bowed to the queen, offering a quick nod to the guard. "Afternoon, Tanit."

"Anyone else here?" asked Tanit.

"No, just myself. I was about to take some wine out onto the balcony and enjoy a glass before dinner." Belasko looked over Tanit's shoulder at Queen Lilliana. "Would you care to join me, your majesty?"

Queen Lilliana smiled. "I would. There have been some interesting developments in today's negotiations that I would get your thoughts on, if I may?"

Belasko stood to one side, gesturing into the room. "Of course, you may. Please, come in. Tanit, would you like to wait here? I know you're on duty, but I can offer you some watered wine and somewhere to sit, rather than waiting in the corridor and guarding the door."

Tanit shook his head. "Thanks, Belasko. I appreciate it, but best stand at the door and keep an eye on the corridor." He grinned. "I wouldn't say no to some wine, though, watered or otherwise."

Belasko smiled in return. "Wait here then, and I'll bring you something to drink."

Queen Lilliana entered Belasko's rooms, heading out to the balcony, while Belasko fetched Tanit their watered wine. Once he had settled the guard outside the door to his rooms, Belasko went to join her.

The Queen sat on a delicately carved wooden chair, one of a pair on the balcony, positioned so that one could watch the setting sun. Queen Lilliana was gazing out over the palace grounds and the city beyond. She turned to look at Belasko as he approached.

"I understand why you've kept yourself apart these last

few days, but there's really no need. I had to reassure King Edyard that you hadn't taken offence. Apparently he had made it known that his guests were not to be bothered in such a way, part of securing a more peaceful future. King Edyard was most put out that you were challenged."

Belasko sighed. "That explains the lack of challenges on our journey. The way some of Prince Beviyard's squadron looked at me as we travelled here I was expecting one long before. Please extend my apologies to the king."

Queen Lilliana nodded, then turned her gaze back to the city. She took a deep breath, which she let out slowly. "It's beautiful, isn't it? In its way. So different to Villan, of course, and yet so similar, in its energy. Even the people aren't all that different, at heart."

Belasko pulled the other chair over and sat, joining the Queen in looking out over the city. "I've noticed the same can be said for most large cities. Each is different from the other, but there is something to be said for the vibrancy of such places." He chuckled to himself. "I'm a country boy at heart, ma'am. Our journey here reminded me of that. I didn't realise how much I missed the mountains. Thank you for that—for the opportunity to return home, even briefly."

Queen Lilliana smiled, sadly, sweetly. "You're welcome, Belasko. I was happy to do it, and to spend time with your parents. I hope we can call in again on our way home. I'll have to make sure to find them some suitable gifts."

Belasko smiled. "That would be nice. Be warned, they have little time for anything that's not practical."

"Then in that, they are much like their son, although it has to be said that you've come to appreciate the finer things in life."

"There's an argument to be made for the practical nature of good wine or brandy. A well-made sword is infinitely better value than one of cheaper make. In most things in life, you get what you pay for." He shrugged, then took a sip of his wine. "What can I do for you, your majesty? You said something about today's negotiations?"

Queen Lilliana looked away from him, back out over the palace and city beyond. "Can't you call me Lilliana? At least when we're alone. I miss the days when you could. It is a heavy burden, being Queen, and that little familiarity would take me back to easier times."

"Of course, ma'am... I mean, Lilliana. It would be my pleasure." Belasko smiled again, fondly this time. "Using your given name alone reminds me of the little girl you once were. Scabbed knees poking out from under your dresses, always with your nose in a book."

Lilliana sighed. "Sometimes I long for those days, when my largest problem was what trick to play on Kellan, or how to please Father with my studies. Now, my concerns are far greater, and I must think not just of myself but the needs of my country, of my people." She turned back to him. "Belasko, our negotiations are complete, the wording of the new accords agreed and settled upon. They would be ready to sign tomorrow, but a further matter was broached today, and I would hear what you think of it."

"Of course, Lilliana, please go ahead."

She sighed then, toying with the stem of her wine glass. "The subject... A traditional way of forming alliances between nations or, in this case, of sealing peace. Something that would bring our countries closer together. The possibility of... Marriage."

Belasko stared at her, lost for words. "Marriage, Your—Lilliana? Between yourself and who? A member of the Baskan royal family?"

"Prince Beviyard, yes."

The Swordsman's Descent

He blinked. "And you want to know what I think of it?"

Lilliana was staring into her wineglass now, not meeting his eyes. Belasko sighed. "Have you come to an understanding, yourself and Prince Beviyard?"

Lilliana nodded, glancing up at him, then sighing. "In a way, yes. We like each other well enough, and he's certainly nice to look upon. But royal marriages are not based on love, Belasko. They are based on alliances, on politics, on creating and fostering peaceful relations between nations. Do we love each other? Not yet." She smiled shyly then. "But I think love may grow, in time. Come, Belasko, tell me what you think."

Belasko swallowed a large gulp of wine. "Well, my opinion as your adviser is that it could be risky. Beviyard's is a new dynasty, still securing their power. Another coup and they could be out of favour, and your marriage to one of their house a cause for problems instead of solving them. There are many who feel strongly on either side, who remember loved ones and friends lost in a war that was not so long ago. It may not be popular with the people —at least, at first. But I can see the case that can be made for it."

Lilliana's face was still. "That's what you think as my adviser. What about as my friend? As my Champion?"

Belasko blew out a breath between his lips, surprised at a sudden heat, an anger, that surged within him. "This is all news to me, Lilliana, so I don't know. We sacrificed so much, lost so many to defeat the Baskans in the Last War. To have a Baskan, no matter how agreeable a fellow he seems to be, within reach of the throne... What did we fight that war for? Why did so many lay down their lives? What they tried to take by force, you will allow them to have by stealth!" His voice had risen until this last was almost a shout. Belasko stopped, shocked at himself, his hand rising to cover his mouth.

Lilliana stood then, chair screeching on the tiles. Belasko could see the hurt he had caused her, the shock in her expression. The pain in her eyes as she searched his face, as if seeing him for the first time. Pain that was hidden as the royal mask came down, her expression smoothed but far from serene, and her posture became one of command.

"You go too far. Perhaps allowing old familiarities was a mistake." There was fire in her eyes now. "I am not that little girl you once knew, but your sovereign, charged with making difficult decisions for the betterment of our people. You would do well to remember that. As well as to remember this: *you* serve at *my* pleasure, not the other way around. If you cannot control your temper, or your dislike for our hosts, then perhaps I should send you home." She paused, and the mask slipped for a moment. Belasko could see again the hurt she was now carrying from an injury his words had caused. She looked away from him, before nodding in resolve. She turned the power of her gaze back on her champion. Secure once again in her royal strength. "In fact, yes. Prepare yourself to leave. I will make my final decision in the morning once my anger has subsided. *If* my anger has subsided."

Queen Lilliana strode off the balcony and through Belasko's lounge, slamming the door behind her.

35

LATER THAT EVENING, Belakso was stood in those same rooms when there came a knock at the door, which opened to admit Byrta's head, peering around. She frowned at the expression on Belasko's face and stepped fully into the room. "What is it, Belasko? You've a face like thunder. Why weren't you at dinner?"

Belasko started to pace around the room, avoiding Byrta's eyes. "Earlier this evening, the Queen paid me a visit. Informally, wanting to capture the spirit of our earlier friendship, when she was just a girl." He sighed. "She asked my opinion of something—a matter that has arisen in the negotiations. I gave it to her, somewhat indelicately, it has to be said." He stopped, rubbing his eyes. "If I could take back my words, or at least their heat, I would. Sadly, I cannot. Let us just say that I displeased the Queen greatly, and she has told me that I may be dismissed and sent home. I was just about to come find you. We need to make ready to leave in the morning, although she won't make her final decision until then."

"Why me? What have I done?" asked Byrta.

"Nothing, but as my employee, my associate, if I leave, then you have to come with me."

"Leave in disgrace." Byrta snorted. "I don't know what you've done, Belasko, but undo it. This is our livelihoods and futures you've just put on the line with a moment's foolishness."

"I know, and I'm deeply sorry. But the words cannot be unsaid."

Byrta squinted at Belasko. "Can't they now? What was the matter you were discussing? What did you say?"

Belasko coughed. "I'll tell you, but this goes no further. In the negotiations, discussion has turned to a possible alliance. A union. Between our royal house and theirs."

"Marriage, then? Between the Queen and who? Prince Beviyard?" Byrta asked.

Belasko nodded. "That is what's being discussed, yes. The Queen asked my opinion, and I gave it. First as her advisor, on why the match may be both advantageous and disadvantageous. She pressed me for my own opinion, not as her adviser, but as her friend. I gave it, but not in the most temperate fashion." Belasko looked away.

Byrta stepped closer. "What did you say, Belasko? What words?"

"I said..." He sighed. "I said that what the Baskans tried to take by force in the Last War she would allow them to have by stealth."

Byrta looked away for a moment, then rounded on him. "You bloody idiot! What did you go and say that for?"

Belasko sighed. "I know, I know. In the moment... An anger I didn't know was in me rose to the surface. I damn near shouted the words."

"You're a fool, Belasko. Sword skills out of legend, brain of an inebriated ox." Byrta cupped his chin in one hand, bringing his eyes up to meet hers. "If a young woman comes to you to ask what you think of her potential marriage match, that isn't the sort of answer she's looking for. Did you even stop to ask her ho*w she* felt about it?" She sighed. "I suppose we'd best make ready to leave."

"I don't want to leave. I don't want to leave the Queen alone here." Belasko walked over to the tall windows that opened onto the balcony and looked out. "I've felt uneasy since we got here. I trust King Edyard's intentions, it's not that, but something is not right. Perhaps it's just the feeling on an old soldier who's too deep in enemy territory, but I think there are some around the King who do not share his lofty goals."

Byrta joined him by the window. "The Queen is surrounded by her guard, her own military units. She's hardly alone."

"No. But I am her Champion, and it feels wrong to leave her here in this viper's nest."

"You know what to do, then. You can still fix this." Byrta folded her arms, waiting until Belasko turned to look at her. "You can fix this by the simple expedient of going to the Queen and apologising."

Belasko shook his head. "You didn't see how angry she was. I don't want to upset her further. I can go to her in the morning."

"No, Belasko. Go now. Don't let this build between you. Go to her and apologise. Lay out your fears and whatever drove you to say something so…" Byrta waved a hand in the air. "Indelicate to our Queen. Go now. Be sorry. Be humble."

Belasko looked at her for a moment, then nodded. "Yes, you're right. I'll go to her." He went to go, turning back to Byrta when he opened the door. "But do prepare to leave, just in case."

∼

The two members of the royal guard stationed outside the Queen's chambers eyed Belasko warily as he approached. "I'm not sure you're particularly welcome at the moment, Belasko," said Tanit.

"What did you say to her?" Vilette, a younger woman with short-cropped hair, asked. "Don't think I've ever seen the Queen so angry."

Belasko sighed. "What did I say? Something I shouldn't. I let old anger speak for me when I should have held my tongue. I've come to apologise. Do you think she will see me?"

Tanit whistled. "You're brave, I'll give you that. Let me see." He knocked on the door before going inside.

Vilette looked at Belasko. "You've been at court a good few years now, Belasko. How have you not learned to hold your tongue?"

Belasko shrugged. "Born stupid, I suppose."

Tanit reappeared, opening the door and holding it open for Belasko. "The Queen will see you." As Belasko walked past him, Tanit whispered, "Make it a good apology."

Belasko walked through into the lounge in which the Queen received visitors. It was the mirror of his own, if larger. The same tall windows opened onto a balcony, but everything was bigger and grander. More opulent, as befitted Queen Lilliana's status.

The Queen was in a set of robes, obviously preparing to take to her bed for the night. A flash of irritation crossed her eyes. "Yes, Belasko, what do you want?"

Belasko coughed and shifted his weight. He sighed, crossed the room to the Queen, and knelt. "I've come to apologise, my Queen. Lilliana. My words earlier today, the

The Swordsman's Descent

way they were said... It was not my intention to cause you upset. That has never been my intention in all the years I've known you. I understand if you choose not to accept my apology, if you send me home in disgrace—my actions have earned me that. I can only hope that you have a little fondness for me and will allow me to equip myself better in your service." He bowed his head. When no reply came, Belasko looked up. The Queen was looking away from him.

Lilliana sighed and turned her head to look at him. The glint of tears in her eyes surprised him. *To think I have caused her hurt, that is the worst of it.*

"Of course, I have fondness for you, you great lummox. More than a little. I admit our relationship is complicated, but with Kellan gone... In a way, you are my oldest friend. One of the few who look at me and see *me*, not just my title. To be spoken to like that, it upset me."

"Oh, Lilliana, it grieves me more than you can know that I've brought you hurt or tears to your eyes."

She leaned forward. "Then why say it, Belasko? In such a way... Why say it at all?" She rolled her eyes. "And get up off the floor, you'll ruin your hose."

Belasko stood, looking at the hands he clutched together in front of him. "It's difficult to say. At your own words, the news... I felt a swell of anger in me, such as I haven't felt in a long time." He sighed. "War damages people, Lilliana, in ways that are often unseen. Not all injuries are physical. At the thought of you marrying a Baskan, no matter how agreeable a fellow I find him, it brought to mind all that we lost— all that *I* lost in the war. So many friends, so many dead... And suddenly, it seemed as though they and their sacrifice were forgotten."

Lilliana looked at him for a moment, eyes unreadable. The moment seemed frozen, and Belasko felt that something teetered on a knife edge. What? His relationship with the Queen? Their mission? After a long moment that seemed to stretch out painfully, she sighed. Belasko let out a breath he hadn't realised he was holding.

Lilliana spoke quietly, so Belasko had to strain to hear her. "It seems to me that their sacrifice would be forgotten if we stayed in the past. Reliving and fighting old battles, rekindling old hatreds. People gave their lives so that the Baskan invasion would be resisted, yes, but ultimately for peace. For the protection of our nation and the peace we now have. Ensuring a lasting peace, however it is achieved, is the best way to honour their memories more than anything else I can do."

"You're right, I know. It's just..." Belasko hung his head. "I'm an old soldier, and perhaps I've held on to too many things from my past. Marriage between royal houses is a traditional way to seal alliances. If that is what needs to be done, then you have my full support and my total apology for my earlier words."

"That's good to know, Belasko. If things from your past bother you, then it would do you good to talk to someone about it. Byrta, Anerin, old friends who want to support you. I'm happy to help if I can."

"Thank you, your majesty." Belasko sighed. "I didn't realise that I was holding on to so much from the war. I buried it deep. Coming here... It has unearthed those old feelings. I've killed many people in combat. Each life you take also takes something from you. You know, at Dellan Pass, I felt sick with it. To deal out so much death... It leaves a mark on you, no matter how just the cause." He looked up and met Lilliana's eyes. "It is no easy thing to kill. Nor should it be." He paused, remembering Byrta's words from only a short while ago. "Enough about me. I should ask *you* something."

Lilliana stood, going to a small table and pouring out two glasses of wine from a crystal decanter. She walked over to Belasko, passing him one. "Yes, Belasko?"

"You asked my opinion on the match between Prince Beviyard and yourself. I should have asked you, how do you feel about it? The idea."

She smiled. "I have to admit, I'm quite taken with the Prince. He's kind, amusing, and we share a curiosity about the world. It helps that he's handsome, of course. I think it would be a good match."

Belasko raised his glass in salute. "Then that is all that matters. The rest can be made to work, somehow."

Lilliana took a sip of her wine. "You know, with everything that's happened in the last few years, I haven't allowed myself to think about marriage. About what it would mean. I half thought I'd never marry, that it was the best way to ensure my own authority, but the need to secure the line to the throne is paramount. I need an heir, and there's only one way to make one of those."

Belasko coughed. "Yes, so I understand."

Lilliana laughed, a bright sound that lightened the atmosphere. "Why, Belasko, are you blushing?"

He smiled. "I've known you a long time, your majesty. There are some areas of conversation that perhaps I'm not comfortable with. As long as you are happy in the match, I will do what I can to support you. Am I forgiven, or shall I go and pack my bags?"

"Don't be silly. Of course, you're forgiven. But watch your tongue more closely in future, especially if we're in company."

"Of course, Lilliana, and thank you. I won't let you down."

Lilliana reached out and put a hand on his shoulder. "You never have, Belasko."

He put one hand over hers. "Thank you. How do the negotiations with the Baskans go otherwise? What does Prince Beviyard say on the subject of marriage?"

"A good question. It's been raised through intermediaries so far. We haven't had the chance to discuss it between the two of us. I think—"

They were interrupted by a knock at the door. Lilliana paused, raising her eyebrows at Belasko. She turned to the door. "Yes, come."

The door opened a fraction, and Vilette leaned through it. "Your majesty, sorry to interrupt. The Baskan Prince is here, Beviyard. He begs forgiveness for the lateness of the hour, but he asks for a moment of your time."

~

Prince Beviyard walked into the room, hesitating when he saw Belasko. "I'm sorry, your majesty" he said, "I thought you'd be alone."

"That's quite all right," said Queen Lilliana. "It's odd that you appear now. You had just come up in our conversation."

The Prince smiled. "Oh, really? Should my ears be burning?"

"Well," said Belasko, "our conversation had turned to the negotiations. Your name just came up."

"Ah." Prince Beviyard's eyes flickered from Belasko to Queen Lilliana. "It's about that, or something related to it, that I've come to speak to the Queen." He offered her a

The Swordsman's Descent

slightly lopsided smile. "I can come back another time, your majesty, when you're alone."

"Oh no, don't be silly." The Queen waved her hand airily. "Belasko is an old friend, as well as an adviser. You can say anything in front of him in the utmost confidence."

"I see." His eyes flickered once more between Queen Lilliana and her Champion. The Prince cleared his throat. "What I have to say is of a personal, somewhat private nature."

Belasko turned to Queen Lilliana. "Really, ma'am, I can go. I should let Byrta know that she can unpack her bags."

The Queen looked at Belasko, expression indecipherable, and gave an almost imperceptible shake of her head. "No, Belasko. I'd rather you stayed a moment." She frowned at the wineglass she held. "I've had enough of wine. Would you be able to make us some tea? I have one of Maelyn's blends over there."

Belasko nodded. "Of course, ma'am. I'll do that at once." He walked over to a little tea caddy that stood on a table to one side of the lounge, spooning some of the mixture into a delicate little teapot, before setting water to boil in a small pot over the fire that had been lit to chase away the chill of the night. Behind him, he could hear the low murmur of conversation.

"Well, dear Beviyard, what have you come to say?"

"It's difficult to find the words. I hadn't expected you to have company, and I have to admit that I hadn't thought through what I was going to say with any particular thoroughness."

"Is it about the negotiations? The matter that was raised today?"

The Prince gave a little cough. "Yes, yes it was. I didn't know they were going to bring that up, not yet. I wanted..."

"To back out now, before discussions go any further?" Belasko could hear the humour in his Queen's voice, but there was an edge there, too.

"No, not at all. Lilliana, I had hoped to discuss the matter with you privately before it was placed on the negotiating table. I wanted to apologise. My father's advisers can be somewhat cavalier. They forget there are people at the heart of these things. Or so it seems."

Belasko did his best to close his ears to the queen's private conversation, attending to the task at hand, readying a tray with cups and saucers, and placing the teapot on it. He was aware of the murmured conversation taking place behind him, and began to feel uncomfortable. After a few minutes that felt much longer, the water began to boil.

Belasko took the pot from over the fire, poured some water into the teapot, then replaced the other pot. He had always had a fondness for tea, but in recent years, he had come to appreciate the calming ritual of making it. Belasko stirred the tea with a long-handled spoon, taking the opportunity to breathe in the scent. *Ah, Maelyn's teas and tinctures. The woman is a miracle worker.* As he readied the tea things Belasko couldn't help but tune into Prince Beviyard's and Queen Lilliana's conversation once again.

"Beviyard, I understand only too well. I grew up surrounded by people who thought of me as a princess first, a person second. Please, go ahead. Say what you came to say."

"I... That is, I suppose..."

Poor bugger's tongue-tied. Lilliana can have that effect on a person.

Belasko turned back around, teapot and three little cups balanced on a tray of polished and inlaid wood. Queen

The Swordsman's Descent

Lilliana had the beginnings of a wicked smile curling her lips, while Prince Beviyard's face was flushed and flaming.

The Prince opened his mouth in another attempt to speak when, in a crash of broken glass and wooden frame, three figures in dark clothes smashed through the long windows and came rolling into the room.

"Assassins!" cried Prince Beviyard, pushing Queen Lilliana behind him and drawing the sword at his belt.

"Really?" said Belasko. He sighed. "I've just made tea." A momentary feeling of fatigue washed over him. Another fight. More death to be dealt. Then a lifetime of training and his instincts kicked in, and he swung into action.

Prince Beviyard kept Queen Lilliana behind him, moving back towards the door. His sword was out, ready for use, its point circling nonchalantly in the air as the Prince eyed the three figures before them. Their lower faces covered by black cloth, they wore nondescript clothes of dark colour and no armour. They carried short swords as they stalked towards the Prince and Queen.

Belasko took them by surprise. Roaring, he leaped forwards, swinging the tray in his hands in such a way that the teapot full of boiling hot water was catapulted directly into the face of the nearest attacker. They screamed and dropped their sword as they pawed at their eyes, which were now a mess of scalded flesh and broken shards of porcelain. Belasko swung the tray again, catching them across the back of the head. They fell to their knees, and as one of the two remaining attackers turned to face him, Belasko got the toe of his boot under the first attacker's dropped weapon and flipped it up into the air.

Belasko grabbed the hilt as the short sword rose up, bringing the weapon around in a quick slash that opened the throat of the injured would-be assassin, before bringing it to bear on his next opponent.

Stepping over the twitching body of his first kill, their hands pointlessly clutching at a throat that now spilled their life's blood upon the floor, Belasko called to the Queen. "My lady, are you well?"

"I'm fine, Belasko," said Queen Lilliana. "A little shocked, but fine."

Belasko stalked his new opponent, poised and ready. "I know how you feel. I'm angered at the misuse of a very fine pot of tea. Prince Beviyard and I will despatch these remaining assassins, and then we'll get you to a place of safety." He darted forward, lunging at his opponent, who took a quick step back. "Perhaps the Prince can explain why the royal palace itself isn't a safe location."

Prince Beviyard grunted, fending off a blow from his own attacker. "I'm as surprised as you are, Belasko. Our negotiations are in good faith."

"For you and your father, perhaps, but clearly not all the Baskan people are so happy we're here!" Belasko lunged again, grunting a little at the pain in his bad foot as he pushed off. This time the assassin parried the blow, attempting a retaliatory counter-attack that Belasko easily rebuffed. The clash of steel to his side told Belasko that Prince Beviyard was holding his own against the attacker.

His sabre has greater reach than the short swords these attackers carry. He should be able to finish the fight quickly, depending on how skilled his opponent is.

Belasko attacked again, launching a blistering series of strikes. His blade moved high to low, coming in at different angles, keeping the assassin on the move and on their toes —until they stepped backwards and tripped over a low footstool. Belasko was on them before they could even register their surprise, his short sword sweeping theirs aside as they lost their balance before he buried it a foot deep in their stomach.

The assassin screamed. Even the muffling face cloth they wore couldn't hide the agony in their voice. Belasko leaned over and cut their throat.

A belly wound is a painful way to die—I wouldn't wish that on anyone. At least a slit throat is a quick death.

He wiped his borrowed sword on the dying assassin's clothes before picking up their blade from the floor. Now, a short sword in each hand, he turned just as Prince Beviyard finished off his opponent. The Prince appeared to be tiring, his sword point dropping slightly. The would-be assassin tried to exploit this, coming in with a lunge that ran over the Prince's blade, but Prince Beviyard was wise to this manoeuvre. He had lured the attacker in, and as their blade ran over his, Prince Beviyard twisted his wrist, turning the assassin's blade outwards. The force of the assassin's lunge carried them towards the Prince, who stepped into their foiled attack, reversing his sabre and slamming the hilt into their face. The assassin collapsed, stunned, and Prince Beviyard leaned over them, stripping away their face covering. He blinked in surprise.

"Anyone you know?" Belasko stood over the Prince and their third assailant, a short sword in each hand.

"No. I've never seen them before in my life. They're Baskan military, though. See this tattoo?" The Prince pointed at a faded blue serpent inked on the attacker's neck. "That's the sign for one of our infantry units—I can't remember which one, though."

Belasko grunted, then turned to Queen Lilliana. It was his turn to blink in surprise as the Queen had a wicked-looking knife in each hand. She raised an eyebrow in question as, with a flutter of the sleeves of her robe, the knives disappeared.

"Parlin is teaching you well, then."

Queen Lilliana smiled. "I am ever so glad you recommended him to my service."

"Damn it," Prince Beviyard swore, crouched over the attacker he had disarmed.

Belasko joined him. "What is it?"

Prince Beviyard looked up at him, brows narrowed in confusion. "He's dead, but I didn't hit him hard enough for that."

Belasko crouched over the assassin, examining the body. A faint trail of spittle descended from the corner of their mouth. Careful not to touch anything, Belasko got closer, sniffing the air. There was a sharp acidic smell near the body, particularly near the mouth.

He sighed, standing up, grunting slightly at putting weight on his bad joints. "Poison. I don't know what kind, but clearly carried in the mouth. To evade capture and questioning? Who knows? You might have broken the capsule when you hit them, or they triggered it themselves. Either way, we'll get no answers from them."

The sounds of fighting, unheard during the frenetic moments of the attack, came from the corridors outside the royal suite. Clashing steel, yells and screams. Belasko cocked an ear at the sound, then turned to Queen Lilliana. "I was wondering why your guards didn't come in. That may be my answer. I think we should leave, but with caution. If we can get to my rooms, I can collect my own weapons, maybe find Byrta and Anerin. They'll be useful if this attack is widespread. What do you say?"

Queen Lilliana nodded. "I'll be led by you in this, Belasko." She affected a smile, although pale and clearly distressed by the bloodshed she had witnessed. "You have more experience in this sort of thing."

"Thank you, ma'am." Belasko turned to the Baskan Prince. "What about you? Are you with us?"

"Yes, I'm with you." The olive-skinned man, face darkened still by anger, fell to his knees by Queen Lilliana. "I'll give my life to protect you if need be, Lilliana. Or spend the rest of it making up this dishonour to you."

"Oh, dear Beviyard." Queen Lilliana reached out, cupping his cheek in one hand. "Let us hope it doesn't come to that. No need to talk of laying down lives, I already have a sworn Champion, but the second half of that statement is certainly of interest." She smiled again, warmer now. "First things first, let's get out of here safely. Then we can figure out who is behind this."

Prince Beviyard stood, frowning. "Yes, Lilliana, that sounds like a good idea. In terms of who it is..." His frown deepened. "Their mode of dress, the poison—it reminds me of something. From the history books. I can't quite recall it now, but give me time."

"While there's nothing I'd like more than to stand around discussing ancient history and laying down my life, we had better get moving." Belasko strode towards the door, limping slightly. *Damn foot, now is not the time.*

He put a hand to the door handle and turned to the others. "Ready? Let's see what awaits us."

Belakso opened the door and slipped through, captured short swords held in each hand. Prince Beviyard followed, then Queen Lilliana. All three stopped in shock at what they saw before them.

They had walked into a scene of chaos. There were bodies scattered across the corridor, more assassins with black face coverings mingling with the corpses of

Villanese royal guards. The sounds of battle that they had heard in Queen Lilliana's rooms were louder now but clearly came from a distance. Tanit came limping up to them, helmet askew, blood trickling down his face. Pale, in pain, he gasped, "Took us by surprise. Sorry, your majesty. We're seeing them off, pushing them into the outer chambers." He caught sight of Prince Beviyard and spat on the floor. "Should have known never to trust Baskans."

"This is not my doing, nor my father's." Prince Beviyard turned to Queen Lilliana. "I swear it, on my life and his. I don't know who is responsible for this, but when I find out, the retribution will be swift and painful."

"Be that as it may, we need to get out of here. If the palace has been infiltrated, then it isn't safe. Where can we go? Belasko, lead us to your rooms and let's gather who we can." Queen Lilliana looked at Belasko. "Well? Let's get on with it."

They made their way down the wide corridor, checking to see if any of the prone figures on the floor were only injured. Belasko's face grew more grim with every step and every dead comrade confirmed.

He turned to Prince Beviyard as they reached the doors to Belasko's rooms. "Whoever is behind this had better pray I don't get to them before you or, Aronos above help them, my vengeance will be terrible to behold."

"All right, gentlemen, that's enough posturing. Let us go inside and start to plan our next steps." Queen Lilliana gestured at the door. "Come along, Belasko, let's see what awaits."

Belasko stepped forwards and opened the door. A quick search revealed that his rooms were empty, although smashed windows and broken glass scattered across the

The Swordsman's Descent

carpet indicated that some of their attackers had tried to pay him a visit.

Belasko discarded the short swords he had retrieved from their enemies and went over to a long slim wooden chest on a table by the wall. He opened it.

Inside were his best rapier, a matching dagger, and several other knives. He pulled on his sword belt, rapier in its scabbard on one side, matching dagger on the other, then secreted the knives about his person.

Prince Beviyard had been watching the door warily, sword drawn. Queen Lilliana automatically stood between him and Belasko, maximising her protection.

Footsteps could be heard outside, boot heels echoing off the floor. Belasko and Prince Beviyard exchanged looks, and both moved to stand between Queen Lilliana and the door.

"It might be an idea to retrieve your knives, your majesty. You may have need of them yet." Belasko waited until the Queen acknowledged his request, nodding at him as she drew the blades hidden up each sleeve. She gripped their handles tightly, knuckles white, but her hands didn't waver.

Belasko drew his own blades, rapier in his right hand, dagger in his left, and stood ready. Voices could be heard now, and he relaxed slightly.

"It sounds like Byrta and some of the others," he told the Queen and Prince. "Stay wary still, until we confirm."

A figure appeared at the door. Byrta, her sabre drawn and held easily in one hand while she cleaned it with a bit of rag she'd picked up somewhere. She smiled to see them. "That's a relief; I was worried you two had got hurt in the kerfuffle. When we didn't see you..." Byrta's eyes widened at Prince Beviyard's presence. "I didn't expect to see you with this one." She strode forward, dropping the rag and raising her sword. "How dare you attack us in our quarters? Do guest rites mean nothing to you Baskans? I thought you kept to *some* of the old ways but this—luring us here under false pretences and then attacking us? Lowest of the low. Out of the way, Belasko," she spat. "I'll kill him myself."

"You'll do no such thing," said Queen Lilliana, voice clear and ringing out. "Prince Beviyard was with us when we were attacked and aided us against the assassins sent to kill us. This is none of his doing, nor his father's."

"You are right, though—Byrta, is it?" Prince Beviyard shook his head. "It's not us, but someone at court has to have organised this, or at least let them in. That they would go against the guest rites, the rules of honourable combat... It disgraces us all. But it shows that they were afraid. Afraid of the peace we have sought to bring about. We must forge ahead with the negotiations."

"No," said Belasko. Some of the students he had been training filed in after Byrta. He smiled to see them largely unhurt, although a few carried small wounds. Olbarin was with them. The Water King, Nobody, No One, and Borne were in amongst them, in their disguises as his liveried servants. Majel came next, face like thunder, although she brightened when she saw the Queen. Anerin filed in last of all, blade still in hand. His eyes lit up when he saw Belasko, and the relief therein was almost palpable.

Belasko turned back to the Queen. "Queen Lilliana, it is clear we are unsafe here. I would not be doing my duty as your protector if I allowed us to stay. We must gather our people and go." He held up a hand, stopping Prince Beviyard as he went to speak. "Negotiations should continue, yes, but on neutral ground. It is clear you can't protect us here, and those who would do us harm would find it too easy to do so if we stay." Belasko turned to their people.

The Swordsman's Descent

"Let's round up the guards that remain in quarters, then go and fetch our people from the barracks."

"I'm afraid most of the guards that were up here are dead, Belasko." Anerin had a sombre look on his face, his usual wry good humour absent. "We tried to send runners to get to our soldiers, let them know what has happened, but we're blocked in. These young people from your service were most resourceful—" He indicated Nobody and No One. "—but they couldn't get through. I'm afraid we're not going anywhere."

Someone at the back of the group started to laugh. It was the Water King, in his guise as Belasko's servant—although that guise fell away as he wiped tears of laughter from his eyes. The transformation was remarkable, as if the Water King shed the skin of the servant named Jofar in an instant. He stood a little taller but somehow seemed larger. More of a presence. "Oh Belasko, it looks like I'm about to make good on that promise I made you back in your study. I know a way out. It's tight, but we could get everyone here out of the palace."

Belasko eyed the Water King for a moment. "You know a way out of the palace from here?"

The Water King grinned. "Yes, a secret passage."

Prince Beviyard's eyebrows shot up. "You know a secret passage out of the palace? From here?"

The Water King ignored him, serious now, eyes on Belasko. "It's how I've been getting out to conduct my own parallel negotiations."

"Parallel negotiations?" It was Queen Lilliana's turn to look surprised. "Belasko, who is this man? I thought he was one of your staff."

Belasko turned to her. "He's a friend, ma'am."

She frowned. "Do you trust him?"

"With my life. I have before." He leaned closer, speaking for her ears alone. "In the past, I've mentioned help from unexpected quarters. Let's just say you're about to meet those unexpected quarters for yourself."

She looked at him for a moment, then nodded. "Very well. If you trust them, then so will I." Queen Lilliana addressed the group. "Sir, if you know of a way we can escape this chaos, then please lead on."

"I'll stay here," said Prince Beviyard. "I'll plead ignorance as to your whereabouts and do what I can to ensure the safety of your people that remain in the palace. My own squadron is here. We'll surround them with a ring of steel if we must." The Prince paused. "I feel like I should send someone with you, though."

Olbarin stepped forward. "I'll go." He bowed to Prince Beviyard. "I will represent Baskan honour in this."

"Very well then," said the queen, "we'll send word when we've reached safety, wherever that may be." She turned to the Water King. "Sir, lead on. We entrust our lives into your hands."

The Water King bowed. "I shall do all I can to deliver such precious cargo to safety, your majesty."

"All right," said Belasko, "let's go."

36

Queen Lilliana sighed, having walked through another cobweb. She reached up with one hand and tried to pull the sticky mess out of her hair. *This really is the least salubrious exit to a palace I've crept out of.* She snorted then, remembering the way she used to sneak out of her own palace at night when she was younger. The disguises and rigmarole she went through, even though a pair of palace guards always trailed behind.

The man she had thought one of Belasko's servants had led them to the entrance of a secret passageway, hidden at the back of a linen cupboard. He had stepped confidently onto stairs that descended into darkness, picking up and lighting a torch from a wall sconce. They had no choice but to follow.

She leaned forward to whisper to Belasko, who was on the step just in front of her. "Your friend—who is he that he knows of this route out of the palace? What was he talking about, 'parallel negotiations'? Who are those young people with him? I thought they were all your staff."

Her Champion, who had apparently been deep in

thought, startled at her questions. He glanced back at her over his shoulder, and she noticed the grey hair that wound through his head of otherwise chestnut brown. They glinted in the torch light. *We are all of us getting older, my Champion.*

"Their identity is not mine to give up, your majesty. I will tell you this: they are friends. They helped me during that unpleasantness with your father. Without them, I doubt I'd have survived, let alone made it into the palace to confront the King. I owe them a great deal and trust them implicitly." He paused. "Although I'd be wary of letting them too close to any valuable items."

The Water King laughed from further ahead down the staircase. He called back to them. "I'm sorry, I'm not eavesdropping, but my hearing's good and I couldn't help but overhear. They're behaving themselves while we're in good company, Belasko, don't worry." He stopped, turning on the narrow staircase. "I'm happy to supply my credentials to you, ma'am. Given the circumstances." He squinted down the way they were going. "We'll reach the bottom of the staircase soon—it widens there into a larger chamber. We can speak properly then." He turned and started off back down the staircase. They followed in silence.

It took a short while, but just as he had said, they soon reached the bottom of the staircase, which opened up into a larger chamber of natural rock. Lilliana held her torch aloft. The light from it did not reach the far wall of the chamber.

"Here, let us speak while everyone rests a moment. You three," the Water King called to Nobody, No One, and Borne. "Stand with me." He looked at Queen Lilliana as the others watched them curiously. "Your majesty, what questions would you like answered?"

The Queen took a deep breath. "First of all, who are you? Belasko, why are they disguised as your staff?"

Belasko shifted his weight from one foot to the other, wincing slightly. He sighed. "They can answer your questions themselves, but I think I should introduce you. As I said, your majesty, they are friends, without whom I likely would not be here. I owe them a great debt, a debt they decided to call in once they heard we were travelling to Bas as they had need to come here, too. Your majesty, Queen Lilliana, may I introduce you to the man known as the Water King? These two are Nobody and No One, two of his premier pickpockets, burglars, and generally useful people to have around in a pinch. The large chap is Borne, a gentle and well-read giant." There were gasps and murmurs of surprise from the group.

The Water King gave Queen Lilliana a rather florid bow. "Your majesty, it is a pleasure to formally make your acquaintance."

Lilliana found herself gaping and, with a little effort, closed her mouth. Her eyebrows climbed her forehead. She looked at Belasko. "The Water King? Are you joking?" When Belasko shook his head, Lilliana looked back to the Water King and inclined her head. "A pleasure to make your acquaintance, sir. You'll have to forgive me any rudeness. I am surprised to discover you are not a fantastical figure, a myth, but in fact, a real person. A real person who is standing in front of me. Who helped Belasko break into the palace four years ago and now helps us escape another. It's a lot to take in."

"I know. It serves my purposes to have people doubt my existence. It would make my business a lot harder to carry out otherwise." He smiled. "It does make it difficult when people learn the truth. I have to say you're coping with it admirably well."

"I'm surprisingly adaptable, sir, especially when my life is in danger. Belasko, why did you tell me nothing of this?"

The Water King answered for her Champion. "I asked him not to—one of the conditions of my aid."

"The other," said Belasko, "was that I owed him a favour which he would collect at a later date. I agreed to that, as long as the favour would not endanger the royal family or harm the Villanese people."

"It seems to be doing quite the opposite, as he has aided our escape from danger. What is your business in the city?" she asked.

"As you conduct your negotiations in the palace, I have been conducting my own in the city below, with my counterpart here." The Water King frowned. "We've been trying to come to terms over some arrangements that would benefit us both."

"The city below?" asked Belasko.

The Water King grinned at him. "It's quite impressive, you'll see. This is an ancient city, inhabited for thousands of years. What it is mostly built on is itself. Buildings from earlier eras are covered over and become the basements of the newer city above. There are catacombs, houses, whole streets running underground."

"Will your contacts here aid us?" asked Queen Lilliana.

The Water King nodded slowly. "They should do, as long as they see some advantage for themselves in it. Come, let's go see them and find out. We'll need to tread carefully though, they don't like surprises."

"How will we find them?" Queen Lilliana raised an eyebrow in question.

"Oh, they'll find us," said the Water King, "have no doubt of that. The entrances to these tunnels are closely watched, and there are several checkpoints to pass before we get into the heart of it all."

"Well then," said Belasko, "we'd best get on with it."

∽

Elsewhere, in a dimly lit room, three figures dressed in dark clothes stood in front of a desk. The figure sat behind said desk was swathed in shadow, their face unseen.

"How in the many hells did that Villanese bitch survive? Our people had the element of surprise. It should have been a slaughter."

One of those standing shifted their weight. "The swordsman was with her, as was Prince Beviyard. They complicated matters."

The shadowy figure slammed a hand down on the desk. "Three operatives were despatched to deal with the Villanese Queen while others kept her guards busy outside. Are you telling me they couldn't take out an unarmed woman, an ageing duellist, and a popinjay prince?"

Another of those stood before the desk spoke. "The Prince is far from a popinjay, whatever you think of him. He's a very competent cavalryman and good with that sabre he carries. It's not just for decoration. And we've all witnessed first hand that Belasko is not entirely pat his prime."

The figure behind the desk sighed. "Be that as it may, they should not have survived the attack, never mind escaped. Now, they are in the wind, and some of our best people are dead. How did they escape? Have you ascertained that?"

The third person in dark clothes spoke. "Not yet. It's been hard to gain access to the Villanese quarters since the attack, although the Villanese soldiers and guards are contained in their barracks. King Edyard has his guard crawling all over looking for answers."

"We'd best find those answers before they do. Our order dates back a thousand years before the founding of Bas. This city has been our home for all that time. How is there a way in and out of the palace that we don't know? Get into those quarters and find out. Take them apart if you have to." They tapped a finger on the table. "While we are looking for their escape route, we must keep searching the city—above and below. Our knowledge of this ground is unparalleled."

37

THERE WERE CURIOUS glances from the others as they continued, and muttered conversation. Anerin sidled up to Belasko as they moved on into the tunnel. He tutted and shook his head. "I don't know, old boy. Consorting with legendary criminals? At your age?"

Belasko smiled. "How else did you think I broke into the palace? I needed some assistance, which they gladly gave. They're not bad people, really, although they sometimes do bad things."

"You're going to have to tell me more about this. I know the stories, of course, but I'd rather have your side of events."

"Of course. Once we're out of this mess, I'll gladly spend our ride back to Villan telling you the whole sorry story. Hang on, what was that?" Belasko looked up and ahead, eyes scanning for movement, any threat or sign of danger.

"What? I didn't hear anything." Anerin was looking, too, now, eyes squinting into the dark.

"Shh," the Water King said, "we're near the first checkpoint. I need to listen out for the signal."

They all quietened down, Belakso aware of the sound of his own breath in his ears. His heartbeat pulsing.

Then, quiet but distinct, a tapping noise. A pattern made out of the sound of rock on rock.

The Water King kneeled down. Drawing his dagger, he began to tap out a counter rhythm, banging the pommel of its short hilt on the rocky ground of the tunnel.

Silence. Then a voice in the darkness.

"Step forward. What's your business in the city below?"

Shadows peeled away from the walls, revealed to be men and women dressed in dark tones. A young man, slim, sharp of feature, tense and full of potential energy, like a bow drawn and ready to be released, stepped forward. Clearly their leader.

"Ah, Chapman," said the Water King.

"We weren't expecting you until tomorrow." Chapman's eyes narrowed, darted to the others. "Who are all these? This wasn't in the agreement."

The Water King nodded. "True, but events in the city above have necessitated that we apply a certain, how should I put it, flexibility to our situation."

Belasko stepped forward. "I don't know exactly what agreement you had previously," Belasko said, nodding at the Water King as he did so, "but I'm sure it didn't involve us being attacked in the palace. We fought off the assassination attempt but were barricaded into our quarters. With no knowledge of who attacked us or why, we thought it sensible to flee to safety until we could get our bearings. My friend here knew of a way out of the palace, perhaps our only route to safety, and he took it. We are grateful for his aid."

Chapman looked at the Water King and raised an eyebrow. The Water King nodded. The young man whistled, turning his sharp gaze on Belasko once more. "Who might

The Swordsman's Descent

you be, then? If you're with him then you're part of the Villanese group, here for negotiations."

Belasko nodded. "Quite right, where are my manners? My name is Belasko." He bowed. "Royal Champion to Queen Lilliana of Villan, whom it is my pleasure to introduce." Belasko stood upright, gesturing to the Queen.

She smiled at the young man and his companions. "A pleasure to make your acquaintance, although the circumstances are somewhat strained. The... Water King here—" To her credit, she barely stumbled over the name. "—has our thanks for his quick thinking in bringing us here, and we will be grateful for any aid you can provide."

Chapman's eyes widened at this. He swallowed. "Right. Well. That's a turn up for the books. You'd best come with me; I'll take you to see her ladyship. She'll decide what to do with you."

"Very good. Thank you. We'll make the rest of our introductions on the way." Queen Lilliana smiled brightly, which only seemed to unsettle the young man further. He turned and led them deeper into the tunnels.

It was as the Water King had said: the city was built on itself. The tunnels they travelled cut through the rock underneath the city, occasionally crisscrossing ancient streets, working their way through what once were the lower floors of the buildings above, now forgotten basements and subbasements.

Chapman relaxed a little as they walked, answering questions when he could, shrugging when he couldn't. They passed a few people walking in the other direction, and one or two who hurried past them on their way to somewhere else. All gazed curiously at their party but said nothing beyond a muttered greeting to Chapman and his crew.

They passed the low entrance to another chamber, an

arch decorated with human bones, a grinning skull at its peak. Anerin shuddered. "What's in there?" he called to their reluctant guide.

Chapman shot a look back over his shoulder. "Oh, that's one of the old catacombs. The city's burial chambers from long ago. We don't go into those places."

"Yes, I can understand why not." Anerin shuddered again. "I've seen death, but the presence of so many dead, all gathered together... It's enough to give one nightmares."

"If that sort of thing scares you, then we'd better get you up to the city above pretty sharpish. Here, we're almost at her chambers." Chapman indicated a little further up the way, where two large doors were carved out of the rock. A number of people milled about the entrance, occasionally someone would leave and set off with a determined stride on their way into the maze of tunnels.

As they got closer, Belasko could see that the chamber beyond the door was brightly lit. They entered, and it surprised him to see a room as gaily decorated as any ballroom above ground. Chandeliers hung from the rocky ceiling, holding hundreds of candles. The ceiling itself had been carved and painted into scenes of decadent feasts, dances, hunts, and all manner of things. Mirrors hung from the walls, scattering the light from the chandeliers further around the room, which was a quiet hub of activity, an indistinct murmur of conversation filled the air. That stopped when they walked in, and those present turned to look at them.

Then they turned to look to the other end of the room, where a thin woman of middle years sat on a finely carved wooden chair on a low dais. Her olive-skinned Baskan complexion was a little sallow, as if it as turned so by much time spent underground. She wore a plain gown of grey,

The Swordsman's Descent

clearly well made, and her head was entirely bald. Her smooth scalp shone in the light from the chandeliers. An eyebrow arched, and she stood. "Chapman, you bring unexpected visitors. Come closer." She beckoned them over with long finger nails that were sharpened to points.

Their Baskan guide led them through the still-silent crowd of people and up to the dais, Belasko, Queen Lilliana, and the Water King at their fore. Chapman darted up to stand beside the woman in grey and whispered into her ear. Her eyes widened.

"Everybody out, except my guards. I must have private words with our visitors." Those gathered stood for a moment, obviously surprised at the command. The woman in grey raised an eyebrow and drummed the fingernails on her right hand on the arm of her chair. At this they all turned and hurried from the room, the low buzz of conversation returning only to vanish with them as they left.

"Please, come closer." The woman remained seated but leaned forward and beckoned them on with her finger. "Let me get a good look at you."

As they drew closer, Belasko realised that the woman's eyes too were grey, misted over with a slight film. *She's losing her sight. That's the reason for all the lights.*

The woman observed them as they came closer, a wry smile pulling at her lips. She shook her head. "To think that I should have the Villanese Queen in my presence. In my power. Her Champion, Belasko, too, and such important members of her court. The question is, what to do with you?"

Queen Lilliana stood straight, eyes bright as she locked gazes with the lady in grey. "Aid us, madam, and it will not go forgotten."

The lady in grey waved her hand. "Oh, I am sure." She

tapped her chin with one of those long, pointed nails, and her eyes narrowed as she looked at Queen Lilliana. "Don't worry. I've no intention of selling you out to whoever pursues you. Not yet. I care not that you're Villanese—countries and their squabbles matter little here. Except where they impact on business, of course." Belasko caught the Water King nodding in agreement from the corner of his eye. "There are people of all countries and none here, in my city beneath the ground. We find our own way, our own people, in time. No." She frowned. "But you are too valuable as pieces in the great game. I must ask myself how I can use that to my own advantage."

"By aiding us." The Water King strode forward. "You've already said it yourself: war is bad for business. It's too disruptive. If anything were to happen to her majesty here, the Villanese response would be fierce." He shrugged. "And if something were to happen to me, well... My people would not take that kindly at all. Would you risk war in the world below as well as above?"

She was silent for a moment. "I suppose what you say has some merit. Do they know who I am?" She nodded towards Belasko and his companions.

"No, but I can correct that if I may?" The Water King waited expectantly.

The lady in grey nodded. The Water King turned to his companions.

"Your majesty, friends, it is my pleasure to introduce the Grey Lady. She rules the Baskan criminal underworld with an iron fist, though it be clothed in a velvet glove. Grey Lady, may I introduce Queen Lilliana of Villan, her Champion Belasko, his friend and assistant Byrta...?"

As the introductions continued, Belasko found his mind wandering, taking in his surroundings. He looked up at the

Grey Lady when she turned her opalescent gaze upon him. Their eyes met, and Belasko found himself nodding—in greeting or recognition, he didn't know, but it surprised him when his gesture was met with a wink. Belasko blinked in surprise, and the look of wry amusement returned to the Grey Lady's face. He realised that she was speaking.

"And what aid might I offer you? Sanctuary? Escape? What do you need? I think our mutual friend speaks reason. It is in my interest to help you, but I must do so carefully, without drawing too much attention to myself here. My own little kingdom has taken many years to build. I would not see it fall."

"If I may," Belasko took a step forward, "if we might beg sanctuary of you, for a time, while we figure out our next steps? We were attacked and fled for our lives only a short while ago. We must try and understand what has happened, find out the fate of our people left behind at the palace, before deciding our next steps. We know too little. We must take stock of the situation."

"Very well, this I grant you: sanctuary and, if needed, my help in fleeing the city. This much I can do without arousing suspicions from the city above. Anything more risks bringing forces down upon me that I cannot counter. I have not been attacked. I cannot—no, I *will* not move more openly."

Queen Lilliana smiled, offering a respectful bow to the Grey Lady. "It is more than we could have hoped for. You have my thanks."

The Grey Lady grunted. "Don't thank me yet. You haven't seen your accommodation."

38

THE QUARTERS THEY were granted by the Grey Lady were not the sort of accommodation most of their party were used to. A small chamber with a low ceiling with damp walls carved out of the rock, they were to share this space. A separate adjoining chamber was set aside for the ladies in the party's private use. Communal privies were down the narrow corridor that led to their chamber which, Queen Lilliana couldn't help noticing, was a dead end.

I'm still not sure whether we rank as guests or prisoners, or somewhere in between. The Water King seems convinced of this Grey Lady's honour, but I think we had all best keep our wits about us.

The identity of the person she had taken to be Belasko's serving-man had been a shock. As had his friendship with her Champion. She glanced over at him now, sat on one of the low bunks that were set against the wall. Only he and his employees seemed totally comfortable in their current accommodation. The three of them conversed quietly.

The Water King looked up and caught her looking at

him. He inclined his head respectfully, a gesture she returned, which raised a smile from the older man before he returned to his conversation. *A little courtesy costs us nothing, no matter to whom.*

Lilliana became aware of a presence at her shoulder. Her secretary, Parlin, ever-present, was subtly trying to get her attention. "Yes?" she asked.

He cleared his throat. "Your majesty, I don't know if you've noticed, but Lord Anerin seems somewhat... Restless."

Lilliana frowned and directed her attention towards the noble. Parlin was right; Anerin did seem a little agitated. He was conversing with Belasko and Byrta in the far corner of the room and was getting increasingly animated. Belasko shook his head at whatever Anerin was saying, and Byrta put a hand on the lord's arm, as if trying to calm him.

Lilliana set off towards the three of them. They looked up as she approached and stopped talking. She stood for a moment, then rolled her eyes. "Well, is anyone going to tell me what that was about? Is anything the matter?"

"No, nothing, your majesty," said Belakso. "Anerin had an idea, born out of restlessness more than any reasoned thought. Byrta and I were trying to calm him a little."

Anerin snorted. "Calm me? What am I, a horse?"

"As thick-headed as one, sometimes," muttered Byrta.

"I'll have you know I've known some very bright horses in my time, but the idea itself is not foolish." Anerin appealed to Queen Lilliana. "Your majesty, I am restless, it's true. We all are. But I alone here have contacts in the city above. I know people in the city, Villanese merchants among others, who may be useful to us. We have no idea what's going on, what's happened to our forces. Are they imprisoned? Free? Alive or dead? As much as I value our unlikely ally's equally unlikely ally..."

"He's talking about you, boss," said No One.

"Unlikely, that's us," said Nobody, grinning from ear to ear.

"Hush, you two. Lord Anerin is making an interesting point, I'm sure. Eventually." The Water King gestured for Anerin to continue. "Pray, carry on."

"Thank you. Where was I?" Anerin looked a little flustered at the interruption. "Oh yes, as much as I value our allies, we don't know who we can and can't trust in this city. I have people I trust in the city above. If I can reach them, then I might be able to find out what's happening in the palace. I just need to get to them."

Belasko gave the lord a loaded look. "And I told him it was too dangerous. That those friends of his may well be being watched, and we are not in a position to draw any attention down upon ourselves at the moment."

Anerin riled at this and opened his mouth to offer a rebuttal when Queen Lilliana raised a hand, and the others fell silent. "The idea itself, properly executed, is not without merit. We will have to ask our hosts for assistance, and do so carefully, but I think it's an avenue worth pursuing."

"What assistance do you require?" The Grey Lady had appeared at the entrance to their quarters, silent as a shadow, with Chapman at her side.

Queen Lilliana turned to meet their host. "Lord Anerin here has connections in the city above that could aid us and may have information about what is happening in the palace. As a parallel to your own enquiries. We'd have to manage it carefully, but I think it is worth making contact with them. We would need your assistance to make sure it happens safely. Would you be able to grant us this aid?"

The Swordsman's Descent

The Grey Lady looked around. "Are your quarters not to your satisfaction that you seek to leave so soon?"

Anerin stepped forward and offered her his most grandiose bow. "It is nothing of the sort, fair lady. We are grateful for any space and consideration you grant us whatsoever. It is simply that I am chafing at the bit to find out more about what is happening and frustrated when I know that I am in a position to help."

The Grey Lady regarded him for a moment, a faint smile on her lips. "Oh, you are a charmer, aren't you?" She tapped her fingers against her leg for a moment before nodding. "I'll help. It would be useful to have other sources of information besides our own. We can compare what you find out with what our own operatives say. The whole truth may lie somewhere in the middle." She turned to Queen Lilliana. "What I can offer is this: we shall smuggle Lord Anerin here to the surface and on to his contacts' houses or places of business, whichever is easiest or safest to reach. But he must be guided by my operatives at all times. We shall bring him back if it looks safe to do so. If he is spotted, then they may have to go to ground elsewhere. I will not risk bringing attention down on us here." The Grey Lady held out her hand.

Queen Lilliana walked forward, took the offered hand, and shook to seal the deal. "Agreed. Anerin, you will go only to the Villanese that are known to you in the city. Avoid any Baskan contacts until we know better what the lie of the land is. Parlin will give you the name of several members of our intelligence service who reside in the city. I would ask that you pass on some messages to them. We will try to get word out of the city about what has happened and that we are, at present, safe." She looked back to the Grey Lady. "If I might have some writing material, my lady?"

The Grey Lady nodded. "Of course. I'll have some brought to you. But we must move quickly. You—" She pointed at Anerin. "—be ready to go within the hour. We'll find something else for you to wear. We don't want you to be recognised."

39

SOME HOURS LATER, after Anerin had left, Belasko, Queen Lilliana, and the Water King were discussing their next steps.

"I think we can all agree that freeing our soldiers from the palace and getting safely out of the city are our priorities," said Queen Lilliana.

"Indeed, your majesty, but I think you need to prepare yourself for the eventuality that only one of those may be possible." The Water King sighed. "Such is the lot of an old cutthroat, to think of the worst, but it may not be possible to free your people from the palace."

"*Our* people, surely?"

"Oh." The Water King blinked. "I'm not Villanese, but I will profess a fondness for the people of my adopted homeland. I'll do what I can to aid in their escape, but it may be that our only course of action is to flee and then negotiate their release later."

Belasko leaned forward. "You're not Villanese? Where are you from, then?"

The Water King smiled and tapped the side of his nose.

"Oh no, you won't catch me out that easily. That's information I've gone to a lot of trouble to cover up over the years."

"That doesn't mean I'll stop trying. I'll catch you out one day." Belasko turned to Queen Lilliana. "He is right, though, we must be prepared for that. The people in our military signed up knowing they may have to lay down their lives in your service. They would rather see you safe than imprisoned with them."

Queen Lilliana sighed. "Yes, yes, I'm sure you're right. But that doesn't mean we give up. We try, and we do our utmost. Leaving our people behind is a last resort."

"Agreed," said Belasko.

Queen Lilliana rubbed her furrowed brow. "All this is giving me a headache. We're trying to plan our next steps, but how can we without information? Until Anerin returns or the Grey Lady's people gather some intelligence we can use, we're helpless."

A moment of silence passed while Queen Lilliana tapped her chin in thought.

"I've been meaning to ask you," she said to the Water King, "what do you know of the Grey Lady? You seem to think she can be trusted."

The Water King scratched his chin. "What do I know? Precious little, in some ways, about the same amount of information that I allow to be known about me. A decade or so ago, she began to consolidate power in the Albessar underworld. No one knows her true name or what her story is, but she rules here with an iron fist. But fairly, too. I've had some dealings with her over the years and always found her to be honourable." He laughed when Queen Lilliana raised an eyebrow at that. "Yes, majesty, there is such a thing as honour among thieves. Hard though it is to believe, there has to be. Otherwise, all criminal enterprises would collapse into anarchy. So I'm afraid I know little of her, really."

The Queen sighed. "So little information anywhere. Can we at least try to identify our attackers? Prince Beviyard said one of the assassins in the palace had a Baskan military tattoo."

Belasko spoke. "Olbarin may offer some assistance there. He's only recently left the Baskan military. He might be able to give us an idea of what that tattoo means."

Queen Lilliana nodded. "Good, let's ask him what he knows." She turned to the Water King. "Would the Grey Lady be able to help us identify the attackers?"

"She may." The Water King shrugged. "There's no harm in asking."

∼

Belasko, Queen Lilliana, and the Water King were admitted to a private audience chamber, just off the brightly lit hall where they had first encountered the Grey Lady. She was waiting for them and looked none too happy about it.

"What do you want now?" she snapped. "I agreed to help you. I didn't know that would place me at your beck and call. I do have other business to attend to, you know."

"I'm sorry, dear lady, we mean no offence." Queen Lilliana smiled sweetly in an attempt to mollify their clearly annoyed host. "You have been most gracious, and we certainly don't want to keep you from your work."

"Why are you, then? What is it?" The Grey Lady's voice had lost a bit of its harsh tone, but her brows were still creased in annoyance.

"We need to identify who attacked us, and we're hoping you'll be able to help," said Belasko.

"I already told you, it was nothing to do with me. What more do you—"

"We know that," interjected the Water King, "but we're unfamiliar with any Baskan groups that may have carried out the attack. It might be that, if we describe them, you could recognise, or at least theorise, who might be responsible."

The Grey Lady, mollified again, nodded slowly. "Yes, it is as you say. Baskan politics is a viper's nest, factions within factions. There may be a detail you remember from last night, insignificant to you, that would help me guess who they were." She held up a hand. "One at a time, tell me what you remember. Every detail you can think of. Any commonality of dress, or choice of weapons may be a clue."

So, slowly at first, dredging their memories for all the detail they could muster, Belasko, Queen Lilliana, and the Water King recounted their experience of the attack. After which, the Grey Lady sat motionless, her chin resting on one hand whilst she leaned on the arm of her chair.

"Does that give you any idea...?" ventured Belasko.

"Quiet, I'm thinking," she snapped without looking up.

Chastened, Belasko looked at his two companions, shrugged, and settled down to wait.

After a few minutes, the Grey Lady stirred, nodding slowly to herself. "Yes, I think I have it. Or, rather, I might have it." She frowned. "But if it's the group I'm thinking of, they haven't moved openly for many years."

"Who is it?" asked Queen Lilliana. "I would know who attacked me."

The Grey Lady held up a single finger, forestalling any conjecture. "I can't know for sure, but from what you've said... The modes of dress and attack, the fact they carried poison to use on themselves to avoid capture. I think we are dealing with fanatics. Worshippers of the Lady of Night, the moon goddess. She is the opposite, in our pantheon, of the Lord of Morning. The god you call Aronos. I believe you still incorporate some of her aspects into your own rituals surrounding death."

Belasko, remembering the night he stood memorial over his dear friend Orren, nodded. "Yes, we do."

The Grey Lady sighed. "We're about to delve into details of both Baskan and Villanese society that are none to seemly. The Lady of Night..." She shook her head. "Her worship as part of our pantheon is quite normal, respectful even, but there are more fanatical devotees. These are the people I believe you encountered. An old order, they worship death itself. In days gone by they were considered fierce fighters, bred for war, and counted high-ranking officials and soldiers amongst their number. They were connected to underground groups in Villan, too. When religious worship in Villan moved to focus solely on Aronos, worshippers of the other gods continued in secret. Various of the gods and demi-gods were retained as saints, I believe, in your own religion. But those who continued to fully worship the old gods were forced underground. Those who worship the Lady of Night in Villan found common cause with the extremist followers in Bas. Which is, I believe, where your Champion comes in."

"That's it," said Belasko. "I knew there was something familiar about them. Dear god, I feel like a fool."

Queen Lilliana turned to Belasko, eyes questioning. "You've encountered them before?"

"Yes," Belasko sighed. "I'm sorry, your majesty, I failed to see the similarities, but it was long ago..."

"What was long ago, Belasko?"

He looked up and sighed again. "After the Last War, your

father and his generals decided to eradicate the last holdouts of the death worshippers in Villan. They had gone underground, formed secret societies, and this had persisted down the long centuries since the worship of Aronos came to the fore. Their existence was tolerated, so long as they kept themselves to meetings in basements. Their habit of dressing mysteriously and muttering incantations was considered harmless, but after the War the closeness of their relationship with Baskan groups became apparent—an obvious concern in terms of security. I was one of the officers responsible for rooting out their cells."

He was silent then, lost in thought and memory. Queen Lilliana allowed him his moment of thought before encouraging him on.

"What exactly did that involve, Belasko?" she asked quietly.

Belasko sighed. "It was none of it pleasant. We had some intelligence as to the whereabouts of various cells, so we tracked them down. We'd break into their meetings, attempt to round them up, give them the option to reform and give up their antiquated ways or…"

"Or what, Belasko?"

"We gave them up to the Inquisition." His voice was hoarse, as if something caught in his throat.

There was an awkward silence in the room, which Belasko himself broke.

"I know, I know. I regret it now, but I was a soldier, following orders. We were fresh out of a war we barely won, in which we'd all lost a lot of friends and people we cared about. So we followed our orders and did what we could to keep the country safe." He shifted his weight from one foot to the other, uncomfortable under their scrutiny. "In truth, few were ever handed over to the Inquisition. They fought like cornered animals, or took poison to avoid capture." He met Queen Lilliana's eyes. "When our attacker did the same, it reminded me of something, I just couldn't recall exactly what. It was this." Belasko turned back to the Grey Lady. "We rooted the fanatics out of Villain. I'm surprised they're still in operation here in Bas."

"Are you? You shouldn't be." It was the Grey Lady's turn to shake her head. "We are, or at least have been, a militaristic nation. The death cult's philosophy, that only through attack comes strength, has chimed with leaders in days gone by and found favour in their worldview. But they haven't been taken seriously for years, as far as I was aware their worship had dwindled down to more of a secret society. A sort of club you might join to improve your prospects, advance your career. Which is why they remain entwined with some amongst our country's ruling class, although I doubt anyone considered them a force to be reckoned with. Or thought them capable of something of this magnitude." She shrugged. "Most, myself included, thought they were a bit of a joke these days. Their time of open action long past. The things they have done these last few days..." She shook her head. "It's like something out of our old stories. They have been misjudged, to great cost."

"What about your new king, Edyard? Does he have any sympathies in this direction?" the Water King asked, eyes narrowed in thought.

"No, not as far as I'm aware. Although he's from a noble family he was a career military man, not given over to much politicking and plotting until now. He seems a plainspoken, practical, sort, I can't see him going in for secretive groups and furtive meetings. His move since taking power has been to take us away from our warlike past and try to bring about peace with our neighbours. It would certainly not sit alongside their views." The Grey Lady rubbed her chin in thought. "Which would mean their involvement makes sense. If they're trying to stir up unrest and ill-feeling between our two countries, how better than to attack the Villanese Queen and start a new war? Their actions go against King Edyard's express wishes, which would suggest they're operating independently."

The Water King grunted in frustration. "Yet again, we need more proof. More evidence. Without information, this is all idle speculation."

Queen Lilliana spread her hands in an expansive gesture. "We work with what we have." She sighed. "You're right, though. We need more information. How many of these cultists are we facing?"

"It's impossible to say exactly, but I doubt there can be more than a few hundred in the city. In the country as a whole? Who knows." The Grey Lady shrugged. "They are a secret order after all. Now then, in terms of information all we can do is wait for your man, Anerin, to return, and my employees, as well. Hopefully, they will bring us some much-needed knowledge." The Grey Lady stood. "Now, if you'll excuse me, I have other things to attend to. Please, feel free to stay and talk amongst yourselves. When you're ready, one of the people outside the door will show you back to your quarters."

40

IT WAS LATER that day—at least Lilliana thought so; it was difficult to keep track of time underground.

Funny how you take such a simple thing as seeing the sun for granted. Of living your life by its rhythms.

She sat on her bunk, her mind trying to unravel the knot of the situation they found themselves in, but was forced to give up once again in frustration.

Too many variables. Without information, we are lost.

They had been allowed to keep their weapons. Some of the warriors tended theirs for wont of anything else to do. Her secretary, Parlin, sat nearby. He was polishing one of the seemingly endless supply of knives he secreted about his person. He looked up and saw her looking at him. He smiled, and in a flutter of cloth, the knife disappeared. He twisted his other hand in an exaggerated gesture, and another blade appeared to take its place. Parlin looked back down and set to polishing this new knife.

Lilliana smiled. A little reminder to keep up my own practice.

There was a commotion by the door to their quarters. In

the blink of an eye, Parlin stood between her and the door, knives in both hands, ready for whatever came through.

Lilliana blinked. I didn't even see his hand move.

She stood and peered around Parlin. As she did so, she realised that all those who had weapons held them ready, positioned to protect her if needed. A strong feeling of grief and sadness hit her then, almost overwhelming. Lilliana blinked back tears at the thought that these people were prepared to lay down their lives for hers. She smiled to see that the Water King and his people stood slightly apart from the others but no less ready to fight.

The tension left the room when the door opened to reveal Anerin, who blinked at the sight of them all with their weapons drawn.

"Not quite the response a gentleman hopes to receive," he said, smiling. "Stand down, everyone, it's only me. Sorry for the commotion. I had to remind the guard that I was with the group."

Byrta snorted. "Announce your arrival next time. You might have walked straight in into one of our blades."

"Good to see you, too, old friend." Anerin looked around, his eyes alighting on Lilliana. "Your majesty, I should report."

"Of course. Come in, please. Join me over here. Belasko? Water King?"

The two men walked over with Anerin. Belasko placed a hand on his old friend's shoulder, giving it a squeeze. Anerin's hand moved up to briefly cover it, and the two men made eye contact and exchanged a brief smile. *Or more than friends?* Lilliana speculated to herself, trying to keep her face composed.

When they all had gathered around—Lilliana sat on her bunk, the others on chairs—Anerin began his report.

"I'm afraid to say that I don't have much to tell you. I managed to meet some of my contacts, and get your messages into the right hands, majesty, but the palace is locked down tighter than a priest's particulars. Word of what happened hasn't reached the streets, which is remarkable. The Baskans must have iron discipline in place."

"Thank you Anerin, for trying and for getting those messages out. What can it mean?" Lilliana speculated. "Does it indicate that King Edyard doesn't want war? Word getting out that I had been attacked and was now missing would almost certainly spark some sort of retaliation."

"Most likely yes, majesty," said Belasko. "I can't say that I know the King particularly well, but I believe him to be an honourable man. I can't imagine he has anything to do with the attack. In fact, he's probably trying to get to the bottom of things as much as we are."

The Water King nodded. "That fits with what I've heard of the man. I wouldn't be surprised if he was searching for us right now to try and make things right."

"Well, that's the thing," said Anerin. "The Grey Lady spoke to me when I first got back. I think she wanted to see if I'd had any more luck than her people. They've run into the same issues, but apparently, the Baskan intelligence services are combing the streets and the city above our heads. One can only assume to find us, but no one seems to know where their loyalty lies. Are they working for the palace or to their own ends?"

Queen Lilliana made a fist and punched it into the bedding of her bunk. "Ah! It's so frustrating. Thank you, Anerin, for all your efforts, but once again, our conversation is fruitless." She sighed. "Very well, we can only work with what we have. Please, everyone, settle down for the evening.

We might as well rest up. I think we'll need every ounce of energy in the coming days."

~

Belasko was readying his bunk when Anerin approached him, preparing to at least try to lie down and sleep. Belasko knew that sleep would likely prove elusive, but the old soldier in him also knew the importance of rest. He looked up as his old friend came up to him, frowning at the worry etched on Anerin's face.

"What is it? You look concerned about something."

Anerin looked up, met his eyes only briefly, then looked away. There was something furtive about his manner. Furtive and sad. "Can we speak, Belasko?" he asked quietly.

"We are speaking, aren't we?" Belasko smiled, trying to break the tension.

Anerin didn't meet his eyes this time. "Somewhere else, even out in the corridor. I have something I need to say to you. Privately."

Belasko nodded slowly. "Of course, let's go apart for a moment." Anerin returned Belasko's nod, then turned and walked towards the door to their chamber.

Outside, in the corridor but away from the door, Belasko rested a hand on Anerin's shoulder, halting him, then gently turning him around. "All right, what is it? What's the matter?"

Still, Anerin wouldn't meet his gaze. He ran a hand across his eyes, then rubbed the back of his neck. His eyes were downcast when he said, "The people who attacked us at the palace—I know who they are." He looked up sharply. "I mean, not as individuals, but their group. They are a

The Swordsman's Descent

death cult. They worship the Baskan goddess of death. They're zealots, fanatics."

Belasko's hand dropped from Anerin's shoulder. "Yes, so we've been led to believe by the Grey Lady. But if you knew, why didn't you speak out before?"

Anerin swallowed, looking back at his feet. "I didn't realise, not at first. It was a long time ago, years now. Not that I had any dealings with them, but they approached me. Several times."

"Approached you? Why? What did they want?" Belasko grunted and shifted his weight onto his right foot at a surge of pain in his left.

Anerin sighed, and when he looked up, he seemed on the verge of tears. "Why? I was struggling, Belasko. It was a bleak time in my life. I had begun to feel that if I wasn't able to live my true life, being myself, being true to who I am, then what point in living? What point in loyalty?"

"What did you do, Anerin?" Belasko's voice was low and steady, but inside, his emotions were roiling. Had his old friend betrayed him, betrayed them all? Most of all he felt sadness—sadness that Anerin had clearly been so deeply unhappy and that he, Belasko, hadn't known about it.

"Nothing, I swear. I was tempted, Belasko, oh I was tempted, if only to spite my father. But I did nothing except report the contact to the Inquisition."

"That's something, at least. But what did they want?"

"Oh," Anerin made a vague gesture with one hand, "they wanted me to join them, or at least give them information. Information and access to Villanese society. I declined as politely as I could, and they disappeared. Like ghosts."

Belasko put a hand on Anerin's shoulder again. "That's something, too. I would have thought a death cult would orchestrate a more final parting."

Anerin smiled. "I told them that I had letters placed with several factors from the family businesses. Letters detailing our meetings and their approaches, that were to be sent to the Inquisition if anything happened to me. Of course, I then went and told the Inquisition everything anyway, but it worked. They left me alone after that. Funnily enough, our old friend Ervan debriefed me himself, although he pretended not to know me."

Belasko frowned. Something in that, the mention of Ervan and their attackers, stirred something at the back of his mind.

The worried look returned to Anerin's face. "But if they approached me, who else might they have approached in Villanese society? We may have enemies where we thought we had friends."

"In that case, you definitely need to tell Queen Lilliana," Belasko said. "She has to have this information."

"I agree, of course, you're right, but I'm worried, too," Anerin said. "How did they know of my mental state at the time, that I would be susceptible to them? Did they have someone in my household? Do they still? I fear that, unwittingly, I may have endangered our mission."

"All the more reason to tell the Queen," said Belasko.

Anerin wrung his hands, anxiously pulling at his fingers. "I also fear that I will lose the trust of the rest of our party if I reveal the source of my knowledge. If they know, they will doubt me."

"I don't doubt you," said Belasko, pulling Anerin closer and putting his arm about his friend's shoulders. "I'm sorry, too, that you felt so bleak and I didn't know. Whatever happens, it has been good to see you again, to renew our friendship. Now." He released Anerin and clapped him on the back. "We must go and tell the Queen. This may shed

The Swordsman's Descent

new light on things. The rest of our party deserves to know. They may have questions for you that can help us understand our predicament better."

Anerin smiled weakly and accepted Belasko's gentle urging to walk back to their quarters. As they made their way back to the door, Anerin sighed. He was just about to speak when a commotion could be heard from further down the corridor: voices raised, doors slamming. Belasko and Anerin looked at each other.

Then came another sound: the clash of steel on steel.

"Intruders!" a muffled voice called out. "We are attacked!"

41

Anerin paled. "It wasn't me, Belasko, I swear. We were cautious; there's no way we were tracked."

"I believe you. Perhaps they found the tunnel from the palace. Come on, let's get the others and try to get to safety." Belasko clapped him on the arm and sprinted the rest of the way to their quarters.

They burst through the door to find the others already preparing to fight or depart. Blades in hand, Byrta, Olbarin, and the others formed a protective ring around Queen Lilliana. Parlin stood by her side, a knife in each hand. A blade appeared at Belasko's throat as he entered, held by someone beside the door.

"It's a good thing we're friends, Belasko. I held off a moment there. Anyone else coming through that door, and I might have had their head off."

The Water King stepped into view, removing the knife he held to Belasko's throat. He frowned. "Where have you two been?"

"Anerin has some more information for us. He just wanted to talk to me about it first. More pressingly, we need to get to safety and then we can share it. How well do you know these tunnels?" Belasko walked as he talked, going over to what had been for a short while his bunk. He grabbed his sword belt and buckled it on, settling the rapier and accompanying dagger into place. Grabbing his jacket from where it had lain crumpled on his pillow, he threw it on in one smooth movement, then turned back to face the room. "It's clear we need to get out of here. Can you help us?"

The Water King shook his head, his face grim. "I don't know the tunnels well enough, just the route from the palace to here, and I don't think we should head that way. I suggest we find the Grey Lady, or some of her people, and join them in their retreat. They'll have a few backdoors and safehouses to flee to."

"Very well, then. If your majesty approves?" Belasko raised an eyebrow, shooting Queen Lilliana a questioning look.

She threw her hands up in the air in response. "You don't need to ask my permission to save our lives, Belasko. Let's get to safety. This is more your field of expertise than mine."

"What?" he asked. "Running for my life through damp and dirty tunnels, enemies all around, ready to fight?" Belasko grinned. "Fair enough. Fun, isn't it? Come on, let's go."

Belasko, the Water King, and Anerin, led the way. Majel, Byrta, Olbarin, and the others formed a protective ring around Queen Lilliana, her secretary, Nobody and No One, and Borne. Belasko approved.

If anyone gets close enough to the Queen that she's in danger, the short blades they carry will be needed. Of course, the rest of us will be dead by then. He grinned once more. Why is it I feel so alive when my life, and those I care about, is in danger?

Anerin looked at Belasko out of the corner of his eye and saw him grinning. The other man shook his head. "An odd idea of fun you have."

"Oh, I don't know," said the Water King. "There's something invigorating about being in danger. Like swimming in a mountain lake or piloting a ship through a storm. It makes you feel alive."

Anerin snorted. "Neither of those sound appealing to me, either—one's too cold, and the other offers a high probability of drowning. I have other ways of feeling alive, thank you."

"Oh, what are they?" asked Belasko.

Now it was Anerin's turn to grin. "Maybe, if we get out of here, I can show you."

"Oho, now that sounds promising. I—"

The Water King was interrupted by a figure in dark clothing that flew at him out of a side tunnel, blades flashing in the torchlight. The Water King's own sword came up to block one, whilst Belasko lunged, his rapier batting aside the other blade before burying itself in the figure's stomach. Their attacker screamed, a horrendous sound that was neither better nor worse than the choking gurgle that replaced it when the Water King stepped in and slit their throat.

He turned and, catching the shocked look on some faces in their party, shrugged. "What? That's a kinder death and a quicker one than by stomach wound."

"Come on," said Belasko, "let's focus. We need to find the Grey Lady and get out of here. Enemies are all around. We can make jokes later."

They set off again, more cautious now, although they

The Swordsman's Descent

didn't encounter anyone else until they got closer to the Grey Lady's audience chamber. The noise of fighting was louder here, the clang of clashing blades and the shrieks of the dying and injured. The smell of the battlefield, too, made itself known. The metallic tang of blood in the air, the stench of opened bowels and spilled innards. Still, they avoided seeing any other attackers.

At the Water King's suggestion, they avoided the main thoroughfare and went instead to the small side room attached to the Grey Lady's hall in which they'd had an audience with their host a few days prior. It was quieter here, although the fighting could still be heard. Unsurprisingly, the door was barricaded closed.

Belasko banged on it with the hilt of his rapier. A voice called from the other side. "Who goes there? And if you've all got black cloth wound about your faces, me and my mates have got a bone to pick with you."

"No, and we, too, have some issues to take up with the assassins. It's your Villanese visitors. We're here to help and see if we can get out of here."

Silence. Then the indistinct murmur of voices behind the door. Eventually, the voice came again.

"All right, we're going to open the door. But be warned, we've got crossbows and a whole host of weapons in here. If you try any funny business, you'll be doing your best pin cushion impression shortly before you're butchered like a pig. Got it?"

"Of course. How could we not with such clear instructions and vivid imagery? Open up, let us lend a hand."

There was a scraping of bolts and barriers being withdrawn, a pause, and then the door creaked open. Belasko stepped in first, free hand held up high, sword held down low. He blinked as a light trained on his eyes and temporarily robbed him of his vision. When it was removed and his sight adjusted, he saw that whoever had spoken was not mistaken. A dozen crossbows were trained on him, and the people in the room bristled with blades.

"You spoke true, as did I. We're here to help and to see if we can get out of here. May we speak with the Grey Lady?"

Chapman, for it was he who had spoken, snorted. "Oh, I'm sure she'll be glad to see you. I think she wants to thank you personally for bringing all this to our door."

Belasko and the others were marched from the side room into the Grey Lady's hall. It was still as brightly lit, which seemed to have drawn the death cult assassins like flies to honey, judging by the dead bodies piled up by the barricaded main entrance. The denizens of the city below were clearly being attacked on multiple fronts. If, as the Grey Lady had said, there were only a few hundred cultists in the city then most of them were here.

Death cultists were trying to force their way in, pushed back by spears thrust through gaps in the hasty barricade, followed by crossbow bolts when they'd been pushed back far enough. It seemed like the Grey Lady's people were holding their own, but for how long?

Belasko peered at the fallen assassins by the doors. He could see that although they all wore dark clothes, they had no uniform as such. In truth, only their face coverings distinguished them from the people they fought.

Handy. You don't have to stand out from the crowd and can don, or remove, your uniform in moments.

They found the Grey Lady on her chair, sat bolt upright, issuing commands to various underlings, who scurried off to do her bidding. She turned as they approached. "Ah, you. I'm glad we located you."

The Swordsman's Descent

The Water King stepped forward. "Damn these cultists, if we brought this to your door I'll kill my fair share—"

The Grey Lady brushed aside the suggestion. "I don't blame you. A city can only have so many shadowy organisations running around manipulating things to their own ends. We've been treading carefully around each other for years, at least this brings things out into the open." She eyed them for a moment. "You look like most of you know how to use the blades you're holding. That's good. My people... Well, they're more suited to knife fights in dark alleys, not going toe to toe with people who know what they're doing. We're about to leave. If you'd come with me, I'd ask your help in fighting a rearguard action. Slow them down while we make our way to a place of safety. We don't have to go too far, and we'll be able to guarantee they can't follow us."

"How, exactly, would you manage that?" Queen Lilliana asked.

The Grey Lady smiled. "You'll see soon enough. A lady doesn't want to reveal her secrets too soon. There's no fun in that. Come on." She stood. "Let's go. Be ready to fight."

Some of her people came to her then, swords and knives at the ready, a few with spears, as she led them to the back of the room. A tapestry hung there, a hunting scene that Belasko had found himself admiring when they were first brought to meet the Grey Lady. Now she gestured, and one of her people pulled the hanging to one side to reveal a wide door.

"Handy," said the Water King.

The Grey Lady shrugged. "The best escape routes are easily reached." She turned to them as people set to opening the door. "The passageway beyond joins up with a lesser tunnel that runs almost parallel to the one that leads to the front door. From there, we can make our way to a safehouse.

I and several of my people will go ahead to ready the surprise for our uninvited guests. If you wouldn't mind closing the door behind you and being prepared for the enemies that will inevitably follow, that would be incredibly helpful." She looked at Queen Lilliana. "Your majesty, it might be wise for you and one or two of your people to come with me—to get you away from the immediate fighting, although I'm sure we will encounter some of our own."

Queen Lilliana stood straight and lifted her chin. "I would rather not be separated from my people."

"And we would prefer that you were safe, your majesty," said Belasko. "The fighting will be hard and dangerous, and I would rather you were away from it. Parlin can go with you, and Nobody and No One. They're handy enough to keep you safe until we're in a position to join you."

"I'll be going, too," said Majel. She looked at the others. "What? I'm the Commander of the Queen's Guard, I'm going to guard her."

"It's probably for the best, your majesty." Anerin smiled. "We're all loath to be parted from you, but it will make protecting you easier."

Queen Lilliana looked them over, her followers who stood ready to fight. Her shoulders slumped a little. She sighed. "Very well, there is some sense to what you say. So be it." She turned back to the Grey Lady. "Lead on, my lady. Although I trust that the rest of my band will not be far behind."

"Not far at all. I just ask that they watch our backs and give us room to work. Come with me, your majesty. I'll see you to safety."

42

AS THEY SET off, Queen Lilliana casting one final glance over her shoulder. Belasko, the Water King, Byrta, and the rest of the party who were experienced fighters set to closing the door behind them. The door was large and heavy, but it couldn't be bolted from the side they now found themselves on.

Belasko looked over to the Water King and raised his eyebrows. The other man shrugged. "She probably doesn't want to risk someone blocking off her escape route. Sensible, if not particularly helpful right now."

"There's not much we can do about it. Hopefully, the tapestry hanging in front will keep them from finding it too soon." As they set off after the advance party, their way lit by flickering torches, a great commotion could be heard from the other side of the door they left behind. Some yelling, followed by a great crashing sound.

"What was that?" asked Anerin.

Byrta frowned. "It sounded like something falling from a great height."

Belasko and the Water King's eyes met once again. "The chandeliers," they both said in unison.

"That means..." said Anerin.

"Fire," said Byrta, face grim.

"Let's move a little more quickly," said Olbarin. "There's not much to burn along this tunnel, but a fire of any size will soon use up the air."

"Come on then, let's get to it," said Belasko. Then, from behind them came a lesser crash as the door to the tunnel was thrown open. They all turned and saw figures, wreathed in smoke, outlined against the fire that already blazed behind them. There was a momentary pause as both parties took in the other, and then, wordlessly, the cultists rushed forwards.

Belasko and his group, arrayed across the tunnel, fell into defensive postures.

"We must hold them off but not allow the Queen to get too far ahead," said Belasko. "Give ground, but slowly, and don't give it cheap!"

Now the assassins yelled as they closed on the defenders, blades flashing in the dim red light of the torches and the blaze that had once been the Grey Lady's audience chamber.

"For Villan!" cried Belasko.

"For Bas!" cried Olbarin.

And the two men found themselves side by side as battle joined.

Their attackers fought with fierce skill, but Belasko and his group outnumbered them. They still found themselves hard-pressed, and the ground they gave up slowly was not given up willingly but rather taken from them inch by inch.

Belasko fought and, in that moment, the years fell from him, and he was as fast as he ever was. Tiredness and pain

The Swordsman's Descent

disappeared, though he knew from bitter experience that they would come crashing back once the thrill of the fight had worn off.

Olbarin stood on his right, Byrta on his left, Anerin and the Water King to either side of them. The rest of their group of warriors stood behind. Ready to fill a gap if any should fall, aiming careful thrusts between the front rank into the bodies of their enemies.

Byrta and Belasko fought with the easy familiarity of old comrades, the many years they had spent teaching together at the Academy meaning they could move as one. Olbarin did his best to keep up, as did Anerin—one with the energy of youth, the other with the skill and experience from years of training. But they found themselves in a supporting role, filling in around the two fighting furiously in the centre. The Water King fought with a savage economy. There was nothing flash about his fighting style, just ruthless movements intended to leave his opponents crippled or dead.

The first enemy to die fell to a swiping cut from Belasko that opened their throat. The next to a vicious thrust from Byrta that opened their belly. As they screamed and fell to the ground, their compatriots stepped over and around them, the momentary interruption of their movements allowing Anerin, Olbarin, and the Water King to press the attack, and in a few moments, all their opponents were down.

Anerin breathed heavily. "Shall we... Shall we run back and close the door?"

Belasko squinted back up the tunnel, the ruddy red glow of the fire in the room beyond suddenly cut off as, with a rumble, the timbers that made up the doorway collapsed, bringing part of the tunnel ceiling down with them.

"I'm going to say 'no', and suggest we make our way

along fairly quickly now. I'd rather this part of the tunnel didn't collapse on us, too." Belasko turned and led them down the tunnel in the direction the Queen and the Grey Lady had gone. "Come on, keep an eye out for trouble."

As they walked on, small side openings emerged as their tunnel was joined by other tunnels through the rock.

"All escape routes? I wonder," said the Water King.

"The Grey Lady seems like a resourceful sort," said Belasko. "I'm sure she has all manner of secret routes in and out of her domain."

"Just remember to keep a watchful eye," said Byrta. "There's no telling where—"

She was interrupted by a pair of cultists, black cloth across their faces, who came flying out of one of the side entrances.

Byrta sighed. "See?" she said as she leaped to meet the attackers head-on.

And so it carried on. They made their way cautiously in the direction Queen Lilliana and the Grey Lady had travelled, fighting furiously almost every step of the way.

They followed the trail of lit torches left for them. Anerin paled when he saw these led off the main tunnel and into a catacomb, its entrance made of an arch of bones with a grinning skull at the top. "I'm not sure about going in there," said Anerin.

The Water King shrugged. "The choice seems to be a dead man out here or walk amongst the dead in there. I know which I prefer."

Anerin sighed. "You're right, but the thought makes my skin crawl." He shuddered. "Let's get it over with."

They entered the catacomb, the grisly entrance leading into a series of twisting turning tunnels. The walls were all shelves and cubby holes, filled to the brim with skeletons.

Some were whole, but most were random assortments of bone all jumbled together. Each doorway had an arch of bones, and bones had been inlaid into the walls in decorative patterns. At one point, Belasko realised that what he had mistaken for a cobbled section of floor was rather the tops of skulls, interlaced in an intriguing pattern.

They finally turned a corner and caught up with their companions. All were tired, dirty, and in a few cases bleeding. Anerin had a shallow cut to his left thigh, which although not deep, was making him limp as they walked up to the others.

"Are you all right?" Belasko asked his friend.

Anerin winced. "Yes, it's not deep. Hasn't hit anything important, but by Aronos's golden balls, it burns like fire."

Belasko clapped him on the shoulder. "Bear it a little longer. We'll get it cleaned and bandaged as soon as we can. Even shallow cuts are dangerous. We don't want it getting dirty."

Belasko went to Queen Lilliana. "Your majesty, are you well?"

She nodded. "Yes, Belasko. We seem to have been travelling ahead of our attackers. It looks like you caught the brunt of their attentions."

"That was the idea. You don't know how happy I am to see you safe." He turned and surveyed their location. "The question is, now what?"

They were at the end of one of the catacombs, a large door set into the wall ahead of them. The walls and roof of the tunnel in front of the door were held up by interlaced timbers, sturdy and cunning in their construction. Belasko eyed them warily.

"They don't look like a permanent feature to me," he said.

"They're not," said the Grey Lady as she stepped forward. "Designed to be brought down if needed, but in such a way that the door is protected. A hefty push in the right place, and the tunnel in front of us will come crashing down." She looked at the Water King and smiled. "I see you made it through unscathed. I can't say I'm surprised."

The Water King snorted. "It'll take more than a bunch of idiots with black handkerchiefs to put me down. Honestly, what sort of assassins announce their presence by yelling when they attack? Bloody amateurs! Posh boys and girls playing at being killers, I'd wager, most of them." He shook his head wearily. "They really should leave it to the professionals."

"What is our next move?" asked Queen Lilliana. "Why are we waiting here?"

"We're waiting for someone. We can bring this down and block our enemies' pursuit, but it requires a certain touch." The Grey Lady squinted into the darkness beyond their torches. "He should be here any minute."

As she spoke, a giant figure loomed out of the gloom. Belasko and the others who were armed leaped to attention, their blades whistling around to face this potential new threat.

A deep voice rumbled, accent guttural, as the figure resolved itself in the circle of light from their torches. "Lady sent for me. Sorry I take a while. Had to deal with some pests."

Belasko blinked. It was the Vargossian shaman they'd encountered in the mountains. As large and formidable as he had been then, but without his white bearskin cloak. "It's you!" he blurted. "But you speak the common tongue. I didn't think..."

The shaman chuckled. "Of course, I speak the common tongue. How else could I work for the Grey Lady?"

Belasko turned to the Grey Lady. "He works for you? He came to our aid in the mountains, helped clear a path when it was covered by a rockslide."

"Yes, he was doing his job. I asked him to shadow you through the mountains and lend a hand if you needed assistance. I couldn't have our mutual friend here," the Grey Lady indicated the Water King, "getting waylaid on his way to our talks now, could I?"

Belasko turned to the Water King. "Did you know about this?"

The Water King looked shamefaced. "Well, he told me when I spoke to him in the mountains but asked me not to say anything." He sighed. "You know I used to employ a Vargossian shaman? Well, this is the one. Her ladyship here poached him out from under me. His name's Malrak."

The shaman, Malrak, nodded at the Water King. "Nice to see you, though, boss. Must catch up over a drink. What does the Lady need me for?"

The Grey Lady gestured at the arrangement of timbers that held up the tunnel ceiling. "I have need of your, um, gifts, to help bring this down. Once we're through, of course."

Malrak assessed the tunnel, lips pursed. "All right. You want me to stay behind or follow after?"

"Come with us. You might be useful in the days ahead."

He nodded. "Okay. You open door and go through, I deal with this."

As Malrak stood, running his hands over some of the timbers and humming to himself, the Grey Lady went to the door and, fumbling with a ring of keys, opened the lock that held it secure. The ring of keys disappeared, and several of her underlings pulled the door open. There was darkness beyond but no sign of intruders.

"Good, this at least is still safe." The Grey Lady gestured to the door. "Let's go and leave our shaman to his work."

Belasko turned and looked at Malrak as the others began to make their way through the door. The huge man turned to him and, winking, pulled a wineskin that hung around his shoulder open with his teeth. He spat the cork away and, lifting the bag to his mouth, drained the contents. He pulled the wineskin from his person, snapping the straps, and threw it down the corridor. Malrak hummed to himself all the while. He looked questioningly at Belasko. "Swordsman like to watch? Help me with the door afterwards?" He smiled. "There's going to be a big noise, big mess."

"All right," said Belasko, "I'd like to see this." He turned and called through the doorway to the others, "I'm going to come last, help Malrak and make sure he comes through safely as well."

Queen Lilliana, further down the corridor, nodded and called back to him, "Just be sure to make it through, Belasko. You won't be much good as my Champion buried under half a ton of rubble."

Belasko smiled, waving away her concerns, and turned back to watch Malrak work. The big man hummed to himself, and swayed as he turned to face the timbers. He stopped, turned, and called down the corridor. He was pointing at Borne. "Hey, big man, you stay, too. You might be helpful."

Borne shrugged and walked back towards them. "This should be fascinating," he said, "watching a shaman at work."

Belasko stepped back into the doorway, hands on the

door, preparing to close it quickly in the face of whatever the shaman was going to bring down on them.

Malrak was singing now, quietly at first and then with greater volume as he clapped his hands together. The sound echoed sharply down the tunnel as the shaman set those hands against one of the timbers. "Hey, big man, put your shoulder against the opposite timber and push." Borne did as he was bid, muscles tensing as he pushed against the seemingly immovable object. The shaman's touch on the timber was gentle, almost reverential, as he sang to himself.

Belasko became aware of a similar sensation to that which he had experienced in the mountains: a tension building in the air, the hairs on his arms beginning to stand up. The odd feeling that things unseen were moving just outside his vision, but when he turned to look, there was nothing there. Borne grunted as he continued to push against the timber.

Then, over the sound of the shaman's singing, Belasko heard footsteps approaching. Lots of them. He squinted into the darkness, heard the whisper of breaths and muffled voices. The ringing sound of blades leaving their sheaths joined the shaman's song.

"Faster, Malrak, faster," Belasko hissed. "Our enemies are upon us."

The shaman, seemingly lost in his trance, raised his voice, his song culminating in a shout as he slapped his hands against the timber in front of him. Dust fell from the rocky ceiling, and the timber shifted slightly.

Borne roared as he gave one last shove, and his timber moved. Malrak set a hand on his timber again and gave it a gentle push. It, too, shifted, and with it, the ceiling. A ripple seemed to pass through the walls of the tunnel. The other timbers began to shiver as the shaman, dripping with sweat, turned. "Now, swordsman, big man!" he said. "Let us go!"

He pushed Borne through the door, following after. Belasko, about to pull it shut behind them, stopped for one last look. He could see enemies approaching, rushing to try and make it to the door, as dust and rocks began to rain down. Then, with a shuddering crash, one of the timbers holding up the walls and ceiling fell in, and with a rippling motion, others raced to join it.

Belasko hurriedly shut the door, bracing against it with his back, as the tunnel shook. There was a sound, louder than anything Belasko had ever heard. It was a physical force as air rushed away down the tunnel, making Belasko's ears pop. Then silence as a cloud of dust shot in from the slight gap around the door. He began to choke as Malrak took him by the arm and helped him up.

"Well," said Borne, his chest heaving, "that was fascinating."

43

THEIR NEXT SAFE house was an old basement, long built over. At least, that's what it once had been. The original basement had been extended into an extensive suite of rooms, alternative accommodation for the Grey Lady, should she need it—as she did now. The rooms connected upwards to a series of subbasements beneath a grand house in an old part of the city, which the Grey Lady owned.

By the time Belasko, Malrak, and Borne, filthy with dust, caught up with the others, they had already started to apportion rooms and set things in action, addressing immediate concerns first of all.

"Any wounded?" asked Queen Lilliana. "We must clean and tend to any wounds."

"Mostly bumps and scrapes," said Byrta, "although Anerin picked up a nice little scratch."

"It's all right," said Anerin, indicating the cut on his leg. "Didn't hit anything major, but it will need cleaning and binding."

"Very well," said the Grey Lady, "I shall send for one of

the healers in my employ. Everyone check yourselves for any cuts. The tunnels aren't the cleanest place, and it would be easy for even a small wound to turn nasty."

"Aye." Anerin winced. "Mine burns like fire, though I've certainly had worse."

"Too much fine living," said Byrta, grinning. "All that hoity-toity nonsense of being a lord has turned you soft."

"I don't doubt it," said Anerin, smiling wanly. "I can handle a blade, but I'm no battle-hardened soldier. I enjoy my comforts and fine living, as you say, far too much for that."

"Those of us that have military experience know a thing or two about wounds, so we can look things over while we wait for the healer," said Belasko, stepping forwards. "But first, majesty, there's something you should know."

"What is it, Belasko?" Queen Lilliana looked up from where she was examining a shallow cut on the back of No One's hand.

"Information Anerin shared with me, privately, before we were attacked. We were coming to talk to you about it when, well, events overtook us."

"What information is this, Lord Anerin?" The Queen frowned. "You told us your trip to the surface was fruitless."

Anerin sighed, looking downcast. "It's not information from that trip, majesty, but from years ago. Belasko, I..." He looked up at the swordsman, eyes pleading. Belasko met his gaze head-on. Anerin sighed again and looked away. "It's our attackers, this death cult... I've encountered them before, and Belasko's right. You need to know."

He recounted the tale then, as he had for Belasko earlier, as his companions' eyes widened with every word. Once he had finished his story, only silence greeted him. Silence which Byrta broke.

"Aronos's hairy arse, you knew these people? Damn it, Anerin, what have you done?"

"Nothing," said Anerin, eyes flashing as he stood and faced her. "I rebuffed their approach years ago and informed the Inquisition. I've not heard anything from them in all the years since."

"Come now, Byrta, you know Anerin as well as I. You know him to be an honourable man." Belasko looked around the room, meeting every eye. "I believe him, and I stand by him. A dishonourable man would have kept this information to himself for fear of reprisal. Of blame where there is no fault. This information is helpful in that we now know the cult has been trying to reach out to Villanese subjects even after we thought them exterminated in Villan. Instead, it looks like we just pushed them further into the shadows. Deeper underground." Belasko snorted, looking at their surroundings. "An apt choice of words." He shook his head. "But what does all this mean?"

Queen Lilliana spoke. "I trust Lord Anerin and thank him for coming forward with this information. I know it must have been hard to do." She tapped a finger on her chin. "The question is, as Belasko says, what does this mean?" She frowned. "If they could reach out to someone of Lord Anerin's influence, then they could target anyone. How many of the disaffected or vulnerable among our people may have been seduced by this cult?"

"Impossible to know," said the Water King, shrugging. "Something to be investigated once we're back in Villan, perhaps, but there's no way of knowing. Not now, and not here. I suggest we assume they have sympathisers among the Villanese and proceed with caution."

"My own concern is that they might have agents on my staff," said Anerin. "How else would they have known about the dark place I was in, the melancholy that nearly overcame me all those years ago?" He looked pale. "What risk have I put us in by coming on this trip?"

"It's not your fault," said Belasko. "There's no way of knowing how—"

As he spoke, Anerin, who had been leaning against a wall, slumped to one side. A sheen of sweat had broken out on his forehead. He looked shocked, surprised. He looked up at Belasko. "Belasko, I, oh—" Then Anerin's eyes rolled up in his head, and he collapsed the rest of the way to the floor and started to shake.

Belasko leaped forward. "Anerin! Can you hear me?" With Byrta's help, they rolled their friend onto his back and tried to open one of his eyes. The eye rolled about madly in its socket as Anerin twitched and flailed on the ground.

The Grey Lady stood over them. "Is he prone to fits?"

"No," said Byrta, "or at least, I've never heard of him having one before."

"Quick, give him something to bite on so he doesn't put his teeth through his tongue." Belasko looked around, searching for something he could use. One of the Grey Lady's followers leaned forward, offering a length of leather strap they had retrieved from a satchel. Belasko nodded his thanks and placed it between Anerin's jaws.

The Grey Lady crouched down, peering at Anerin. She sighed. "Poison. My guess, on the blade that did that." She pointed at the cut in Anerin's thigh, then stood. "A small cut, but from the tales I've heard it's not uncommon for the cult to poison their blades. My healer is already on the way. I'll send for an apothecary I know, the best in the city. If we move quickly enough, then we might be able to save him." She looked around at all of them. "You'd best all check yourselves for any cuts made by the enemy; start cleaning them

The Swordsman's Descent

right away." With that, the Grey Lady strode from the room, calling out instructions to her followers, some of whom came and collected Anerin, bearing him away to somewhere more private where he might be treated.

Belasko looked on as his friend was carried from the room, a hollow feeling spreading in his stomach. Byrta came up to him. "Are you all right?" she asked.

Belasko sighed and shook his head. "No. I've only just found him again, after all these years, and rekindled our friendship. If he is to be taken from us so soon..."

"Hush," said Byrta, "that's foolish talk. I teased him about soft living, but the truth is that Anerin's as tough as anyone I know. He's a survivor. He will get through this. Now, we'd best do as the Lady says and start checking ourselves for injury. Let's help each other."

And so they looked each other over. There were plenty of cuts, grazes, and bruises amongst them, but amazingly, only Anerin's injury seemed to have been made by an enemy blade. The only one poisoned.

Why? wondered Belasko. *Was he targeted for his knowledge of the cult?*

Queen Lilliana spoke, pulling him out of his reverie. "Well, now we're all assured that we've not been poisoned, we should discuss next steps. What should we do?"

"Get out of this city," said Belasko without hesitation. "However we can. Free our people held at the palace and make a run for the border, fighting a rearguard action if necessary."

"I have to agree," said the Water King. "There are too many unknowns here, and the murkiness of Baskan politics is not lending itself to illuminating any of them. I second Belasko's suggestion."

Queen Lilliana looked around the room as a murmur of

assent spread through the group. She sighed. "I'm keen to get onto familiar ground, too, and agree that we must bring our people with us. The only question is how?"

She looked around again, met only by silence, for none of them knew.

44

THEY BROKE INTO disparate groups, tending their wounds and weapons while they waited on a visit from the Grey Lady's healer and word of Anerin's condition.

Belasko found himself sitting with Majel as each cleaned and sharpened the blades of their rapiers and daggers.

"'A good weapon should be a part of you and needs tending as regularly'," quoted Majel, smiling at Belasko.

"Now, who said that?" he said, returning her smile. "They sound awfully stuffy but correct."

"Oh, just a teacher I had once. A bit full of himself, but he usually knew what he was on about."

Belasko nodded. "I suppose a good teacher should be right at least part of the time."

They sat for a while, the air full of the sound of whetstones running along blades, followed by moments of quiet as they polished steel with scraps of cloth.

After a while, Belasko spoke without looking up from his work. "What do you think about our situation. Entirely hopeless?"

Majel, similarly absorbed in her work, shrugged. "Not entirely. We're a small group and so can move more easily than a larger group. It might be difficult to get out of the city, but I'm sure with the Grey Lady's connections, it could be done."

"That is the priority then—to get out of the city?" Belasko looked up at Majel, brow furrowed.

She continued polishing the blade of her rapier before holding it up to the light and looking down its length. Smiling to herself at the way the freshly oiled blade gleamed, she set it down across her lap. Majel met Belasko's gaze then. "My priority is as it has ever been: the protection of the Queen. Her safety is paramount, and our lives are secondary. All of the soldiers who accompanied us here would agree on that. At present, I can only see one route to that safety: smuggling her out of the city."

"Even if it means leaving our people in the palace behind?"

Majel sighed. "I have no desire to leave anyone behind, Belasko, but my priority is the Queen's safety. And I suspect it is yours."

Belasko nodded, returning his attention to his sword. "That it is. Although the thought of not finding out who is behind all this, of leaving our people behind, of leaving our dead unavenged... That leaves a sour taste in my mouth." He paused before holding out his rapier for Majel's inspection. "Look at this sword. It is old but well-made. A gift from Markus when he made me his successor, my favourite of all the weapons in my collection. The same one I handed over to you for safekeeping when I was put in the palace dungeons at Inquisitor Ervan's behest. Well-tended, a good weapon will outlive its master." He sighed. "I fear I am nearing the end of my own usefulness, but if I can do this

The Swordsman's Descent

one last thing, get Queen Lilliana to safety, I will give it my all. Whatever the cost." He looked up then, eyes steely. "If I am lucky enough to survive the coming days, and if any of our people are harmed further, if I find out we were lured here under false pretences and all this was an underhanded way of restarting an old war... I will return and raze this city to the ground."

Majel swallowed. "Let us hope it doesn't come to that."

"Yes, let's. I was actually starting to like some of these Baskans." Belasko held out his hand for Majel to clasp, wrist to wrist. "The Queen's safety, our ultimate goal."

Majel took the offered hand, gripping firmly as she met Belasko's eyes, leaving him in no doubt as to her own seriousness. "The Queen's safety."

They shook on it.

Belasko smiled, grim. "Whatever happens, it looks like my quiet retirement is further away than ever."

∼

The Grey Lady looked up as Queen Lilliana entered her private lounge. This safe house may be set up in the basements of a townhouse, but it's as well-appointed as any above-ground dwelling, the Queen thought to herself.

The room was furnished with comfortable and well-made furniture—not gaudy or flashy, but solidly made pieces that spoke of expensive craftsmanship in their simplicity.

"Welcome," said the Grey Lady. "Please, sit." She gestured to a chair near her own. "I thought it might be nice to talk amongst ourselves after the events of the last few days. While we rest, and before things get exciting again."

"Thank you, that would be nice." Queen Lilliana took the offered seat.

"Tea?" asked the Grey Lady, lifting a pot that sat on a small side table.

"Please," said the Queen. "I'm rather fond of a good cup of tea."

The Grey Lady nodded as she poured into two porcelain cups. "I feel the same way. There is something both refreshing and calming about it." She passed one cup and saucer to Queen Lilliana, then took up her own. They both took a sip.

"Very nice," said the Queen.

"Yes," said the Grey Lady. "It's my preferred blend. A shopkeeper here in town makes it up for me." She took another sip then held her drink in her lap. "Now tell me why, after all the trouble you've brought me, I shouldn't sell you and your people out to the highest bidder?"

To Queen Lilliana's credit, she didn't falter or show surprise. She merely smiled. "Why, my lady, I would have thought it obvious. No one will bid as high for my life as myself. Name your price, and when I have returned to Villan, it will be yours."

The Grey Lady took another sip of her tea, her eyes not leaving the Queen's face. "Yes," she said, "but your wealth is in Villan. *If* you return there, it will take time to organise. Why shouldn't I take the path to a more immediate reward?"

Queen Lilliana also took a sip of tea and regarded the Grey Lady for a moment. The older woman's misty gaze gave nothing away. "You're a woman of authority. I know something of that, as I'm sure you understand. You wouldn't have reached your position, claimed rather than inherited as mine was, if you didn't know that the more fruitful path is usually not the immediate one." She set her cup and saucer down on the side table between their chairs. "At present, we have a common enemy. The cult of the Lady of Night may have been seeking me, but they had no compunction in laying waste to your own kingdom. It is as you've said previously: a city can bear only so many shadowy organisations. I believe that the cult work against King Edyard's purposes, so are his enemy also. Assist us further, as you have already done, and when I am free, I will do all I can to set him against them. A war waged against them above ground would help you in your own shadowy battle, would it not? I am a powerful woman with many resources I can bring to bear once I am free."

The Grey Lady looked her for a moment before speaking. "Once you are free, yes." She took another sip of her tea. "Very well, I will aid you further—in return for your assistance along the lines you suggest, and I may think of a few more things besides." She smiled. "In truth, I already had designs along that path. I only wanted to see how you would react." She raised her cup in salute. "To working together."

Queen Lilliana picked up her own cup and raised it in the same way. "To working together." She sipped the tea then looked into the cup. "This really is very good, you know. I may have to get the details of the blend from you."

45

QUEEN LILLIANA HAD been shown to a private room to rest. In something approximating normality, Parlin had stationed himself outside.

He knocked on the door. "Belasko is here to see you, ma'am."

"Thank you, Parlin. Please send him in."

Belasko walked into the room and the breath caught in Lilliana's throat. He looked so tired. The grey in his hair shone in the torchlight, the lines around his eyes more pronounced.

We must all look so, after these last few days.

He bowed to her. "Your majesty, how can I help? Have you word of Anerin's condition?"

Lilliana sighed. "Not yet. The Grey Lady's healer and apothecary are still working on him. As soon as there's news, good or bad, you will hear it. No, it is not about Anerin that I wanted to talk to you."

Belasko frowned a little, deepening the lines on his forehead and around his eyes. "Then what can I do for you?"

"I just wanted to talk. I heard a little of what you said to

The Swordsman's Descent

Majel earlier. It occurs to me that the worries of these last few years have fallen heavily on you, and I wanted to see if there was anything I could do to help."

Belasko blinked, then looked away. "Thank you, majesty, but I don't think... That is to say, I serve you, not the other way around. If I have allowed things to weigh on me, well, perhaps I could have handled things better. My worries now, we have spoken of them before."

"Yes, I heard you say to Majel that you fear you are outliving your usefulness."

"I—" Belasko cleared his throat. "I fear that my increasing frailties mean that I will fail you. That is true, yes. You said as much when you told me to find my replacement."

"Belasko..." Lilliana shook her head. "You have never failed me or the Villanese people, so I hardly expect you to start now. You have more value than that which resides in your sword arm." She sighed. "Your heart, your mind— these are your true strengths. For these, I value your council more than any other. Not merely for the longevity of our friendship, but because you have a will of iron and a moral code to match. You will always do what you think is right, no matter the cost to yourself."

Belasko flushed red. "Your majesty does me much credit, and I wish what you said was true, but I worry that my actions of the last few years, keeping myself apart from people, were born of selfishness."

Queen Lilliana stood and went to him, laying a hand on his arm. "You needed time to grieve, Belasko. We all did. But there is work to be done, and I hope you will be at my side to see it through." She laughed. "After our present difficulties are over, of course."

Belasko softened slightly, smiling at her and laying his

hand over hers. "Of course, if a past-his-best swordsman can be of service, then I will serve."

She looked at him a moment, head tilted slightly to one side. Her next words were hesitant and slow, almost shy. "You know... My court is not my father's. Villan has moved on in the time since you became champion and a lot of old fashioned views are falling away. It's funny, isn't it? That those at the top of our society are the slowest to change. It seems to me that the common folk are always ahead of us on these things. More accepting of difference. Whereas we aristocracy are so hidebound by traditions." She smiled. "Taking up arms, for instance. It is rightly acceptable for a woman of common blood to become a soldier, to learn to fight, to stride about in breeches and wear armour. But aristocratic women and girls are expected to follow more traditionally feminine pursuits." Queen Lilliana laughed. "I acknowledge my own privilege, I'm certainly not bemoaning my station. I..." She paused, catching herself before she let her train of thought gather too much momentum, and gave a delicate cough. "I suppose that's my long-winded way of saying that you could live openly, freely. Not have to hide your affections away for fear of scorn or mockery. It's not the same world you grew up in. Or the court I grew up in. With time, and as the last of my father's courtiers fade away, I intend for it to change further. For the better." She gave his arm a squeeze. "Think on it, Belasko. When we get home, I would like you to be at my right hand. I need someone not tainted by court politics who will cut to the crux of the matter. Someone blunt and honest, who isn't afraid to upset people."

Belasko laughed. "If I can think of anyone who matches that description, I'll let them know there's a job available at

The Swordsman's Descent

the palace." His smile faded. "I will think on what you have said. I've hidden that aspect of my life for so long, at first out of deference to your father and because of the prejudices at court, that the idea of living openly feels a little overwhelming. I have my academy to think of, too, my students, my legacy. Can I put that aside to serve at court once more? Let us survive these next few days. I will give you my answer once we are home and safe."

~

Meanwhile, in a room deep within the Baskan palace, shrouded in gloom, a figure sat. Behind an ancient hardwood desk, their face wreathed in shadow, they looked at the three people stood before them, their faces hidden behind black cloth. Only their eyes could be seen, gleaming in the dimly lit room.

"How? How have the Villanese Queen and her followers escaped our operatives again?"

One of the figures spoke. "We don't know how they got out of the palace, into the tunnels under the city, but it seems from there that they made contact with the Grey Lady."

The person behind the desk brought their fist crashing down on it. "I know this! Didn't we then send people to flush that harpy from her nest?"

Another of the three standing figures coughed. "It seems that the Grey Lady and her people used their superior knowledge of the tunnels to make an escape. We had people in pursuit, but they brought the tunnel down on top of them."

"So, to summarise: the Villanese escaped from a perfect

trap within the palace. They fought their way through some of our best operatives to freedom underneath the city. And we have no idea of their whereabouts?"

The third figure, who had yet to speak, inclined their head. "That is correct."

"I knew this all already. I just wanted to repeat it, so you understand how great our failure is. We own this city, and we can't even capture a dozen tired, poorly equipped, and poorly prepared Villanese courtiers!"

The first figure spoke again. "With respect, some of them are very gifted warriors."

"Quiet." This came, not with a roar, but with a calm authority that was all the more terrifying. They leaned forward, bringing their face into the light, revealing sharp features. A fringe of hair around a balding head. Eyes bright but cold. "Here is what we are going to do," said Jonteer. "All of our people must be prepared for Queen Lilliana and her party to surface, at any time. We are on the highest alert, sleeping in shifts, cells staying at their chapter houses until this is all over. We will have to move swiftly, perhaps openly. Maybe the time has come to show our strength, and our faces, in the light."

There was silence from the three who stood before him.

"What?" Jonteer frowned. "You don't agree?"

They shuffled slightly. The third of them spoke. "None can disagree that we must be ready, but to move openly... We operate in the shadows—from the darkness comes our strength. The unexpected attack, death wrought in silence. Many would be wary of operating so openly. That is all."

"There is a reason I am our leader," said Jonteer. "A man of vision is required in these times. Be glad that I am here. Now, you have your orders. Make ready, lie in wait, strike when possible. And if there is any word of the

The Swordsman's Descent

Villanese Queen or her people, I want to hear it first. Understood?"

The three figures nodded, silent again.

"Good, now get out. I have to prepare a report for Count Veldar to give the King.

～

King Edyard was in his study, sat behind his desk, glaring at the papers he shuffled in his hand. He looked up at his son, Prince Beviyard, who sat opposite. "Still no word of Queen Lilliana? Nothing?"

Prince Beviyard sighed and shook his head. "Nothing, Father. No word, no news—it's as if they just vanished."

"Vanished? Leaving a trail of dead bodies in their wake, some of them members of that bloody stupid cult. How did they even get out? They must have been trapped by their attackers."

Prince Beviyard shrugged. "We don't know. One of their party said they knew a way out. We still haven't been able to find it. All I can say from my time with them is that they're a resourceful lot. Anyone who backed them into a corner would come to regret it."

"Then where are they? We don't know. We don't know anything! We don't know where they are, we don't know if they are injured, we don't know how they were attacked in our own bloody palace!" The last was shouted, frustration having built and built in the normally calm and composed former general. He let out an angry yell and swept his arm across his desk, pushing its contents onto the floor. King Edyard stopped then, putting his head in his hands as he rested his elbows on his now-empty desk. "And now I have to pick all that up off the floor."

Prince Beviyard smiled, relieved the see some of his father's normal humour returning. "Father, we have people for that."

King Edyard lifted his head and raised an eyebrow at his son. "Have I taught you nothing? You clear up your own messes in life, son. You don't leave them to other people to tend to." He sighed, sitting back in his chair. "So, how do we clean up our mess? It's a bloody big one."

"We have to find Queen Lilliana before the cultists," said Prince Beviyard.

"Do you happen to have any ideas of how to do that?" A look of weary resignation passed over King Edyard's face. "No, because we've gone over this already. We have the army and the watch scouring the streets for any sign of them. They seem to have gone to ground, and will likely only appear when they feel safe to do so. Or they have already snuck out of the city and are on their way back to Villan, most likely to raise an army. If only there was some way to get word to Queen Lilliana, let her know that we are not the enemy."

"Maybe that old ghoul Count Veldar will have some ideas." Prince Beviyard shrugged. "What? Your head of intelligence has to be good for something."

King Edyard sighed. "You're right. I'm seeing him next; he's supposed to have a report for me. Perhaps he'll have some ideas on how to find the Queen and her party." He frowned. "I just can't understand why the cult would operate so openly, why they would act in such an extreme way."

"I thought their power had mostly been political in recent years. What's changed?" asked Prince Beviyard.

"I don't know, but you're right. I thought that, too, that

The Swordsman's Descent

they were a secret society people joined to get promoted above their ability. They had influence over the old King, held too much sway. In a way, that's what led to the old war. All their nonsense about a country needing to be at war to be strong. That a country that isn't growing is dying. They fed him that by the spoonful, and it led him into ordering riskier and riskier military action."

"Did they never approach you to join them?" asked Prince Beviyard.

King Edyard snorted. "Never. I suspect they knew I wouldn't have any time for their mysticism and nonsense. No, they had feebler minds to sway."

"What now, then?" Prince Beviyard sat cross-legged and drummed his fingers restlessly on his boots. "I hate sitting here while they're out in the city, in god knows what conditions. I feel so useless."

"You and I both, son." King Edyard shook his head. "We need to take control of the situation, but for that, we need information. Without information, we cannot act."

Prince Beviyard stood. "Meanwhile, the rest of the Villanese in the palace grow restless. We can only keep them under lock and key for so long."

"I know, I know, but can you imagine if we let them loose in the city at the moment? They'd tear it apart looking for their Queen."

"Perhaps that is what is needed." Prince Beviyard shrugged. "They are wary of us, untrusting, and want to know what has happened to Queen Lilliana. I can't say I blame them. I hope your meeting with Count Veldar is more fruitful. Please pass on any information he brings you. Particularly anything I can share with the Villanese under my guard."

"I will. I'll see you at dinner." King Edyard watched his son turn and leave the room before surveying the mess of papers and writing materials that now littered the floor of his study. He sighed. "Come on, then, old man. You made this mess. You sort it out."

46

BELASKO SAT BY Anerin's bedside. The Grey Lady's healer and apothecary had done their best, working on his stricken friend tirelessly, but they had done all they could. The poison had worked on Anerin's body longer than they had, and he was gravely ill. When asked if he would survive, their faces had gone blank.

"That is up to him," said the healer.

"We have done what we can. Now, it is his own strength that will decide matters. If he is a fighter, then he may yet survive," said the apothecary.

They had left, then, providing remedies to be administered and instructions for Anerin's care. He seemed to be in a deep sleep.

You almost wouldn't know anything was wrong, except for the dark circles around his eyes and the sheen of sweat on his brow. A slight smile played across Belasko's lips. Although he had that look a time or two before, after a bout of heavy drinking.

The Villanese were taking it in turns to sit with Anerin, to offer a comforting presence if he should wake. *And to inform the others if he doesn't*, thought Belasko to himself.

Belasko looked down at his old friend. *Not so far removed from my vigil for Orren, four years ago now.* Then, Belasko had sat the death vigil beside his oldest friend. The man he loved. Who had followed him into danger and died because of it.

Shut up, Belasko, Anerin yet lives.

But Belasko couldn't help but reflect on what had brought them to this point. The events of the last few days seemed a form of madness, one none of them could have prepared for, yet still, he felt responsible.

Why? Why do I blame myself? Why have I outlived so many of those I have loved? Faces ran through his mind, friends and colleagues lost in the Last War, those who had died since. He shook his head. *Now another friend lies injured, close to death, and here I sit. Why have I survived all challengers, only to see those I care about suffer?* He sighed, frustration building. Belasko stood, and started to pace around the room. He talked to his unconscious friend as he did so, but really to himself.

"Perhaps my own actions of the last few years have led to this. Keeping people away, isolating myself, thinking I always knew best." Belasko shook his head. "I've got used to solving problems alone. It felt that way when Ervan and King Mallor turned the whole city against me. But even then I had help. From Lord Hibberth, from the Water King. From Orren..." He stood still for a moment, a surge of emotion rising up and threatening to overwhelm him. When he spoke again, Belasko was quiet. Subdued. "I've been thinking like a duellist. This isn't me alone against the enemy. Only together can we win through. I must work with the others, trust in them, if we are to survive." He walked back to Anerin's bedside, looking down on his stricken

The Swordsman's Descent

friend once more. "I can't bear to lose you so soon after being reunited, Anerin. It doesn't seem fair."

Anerin stirred slightly, as if in response to his name. Belasko leaned forward.

"Anerin, can you hear me?"

Then, slowly, so slowly, Anerin's eyes opened. Unfocused at first before they settled on Belasko's face. He smiled. "Belasko, what's happened?"

Belasko took his friend's hand. "You were poisoned, Anerin, by an assassin's blade. The Grey Lady has her healers working on you. We're safe."

Anerin frowned. "Poison? So, I'm dying."

"No, no, Anerin, you're not." Belasko shook his head. Anerin seemed not to hear him.

"I should tell you, I think, before I die..."

Belasko squeezed Anerin's hand. "Anerin, you're not dying."

Again Anerin seemed not to hear. "I love you, Belasko. I have done for years. Since we trained with Markus, all that time ago..." Anerin's eyes glazed over as he spoke, then drifted shut. He was unconscious once again.

Belasko could only look at him, heart racing. His mind whirred at Anerin's revelation, running back over their time together on this journey. The nervousness and tension he had at times felt in his old friend's company. The butterflies in his stomach when they stood close together or a farewell embrace lingered a little long.

Did I know? Have I always known? He frowned. Did I not allow myself to acknowledge my own attraction to Anerin, because of my feelings for Orren? Belasko shook his head, as if to clear his thoughts.

Then he rested a gentle hand on Anerin's chest. He felt

Anerin's heart beat, and the laboured movement of his lungs. "You will get through this, my friend. For you are a fighter, for all your lordly manner, and one of the strongest people I know. You have to survive. We have years to catch up on."

Belasko leaned forward, placing a kiss on Anerin's forehead. Then sat back down in his chair, and he did as he had so often done down the years and pushed his personal thoughts and feelings to one side. Forcing his mind to return once more to their troubles. To his duty.

How? How can we get out of this situation?

∼

The Water King wandered into the Grey Lady's parlour, looking about at the fixtures and fittings. "Very nice," he said. "Tasteful."

"I'm glad you like it. Sit, won't you?" She gestured to the chair next to hers. A crystal decanter and two glasses were on the table set between them.

"Thank you, nice to take the weight off. All this running about being chased by an ancient order of assassins is very wearing." He grinned. "These days, I usually get other people to do my running around for me."

The Grey Lady picked up the decanter. "Rum?" she asked. "I know you spent time at sea, I suspected you might like a drop."

"I have been known to partake from time to time."

She poured two glasses, set down the decanter, and passed one of the glasses to the Water King. She picked up the other and raised it up. "To profitable ventures."

"I'll drink to that," said the Water King. He took a sip of the rum and made an appreciative face. "Very nice. I may have said it before, but you keep a good cellar."

The Swordsman's Descent

"One tries." The Grey Lady took a little sip of her own rum. "I must admit it leaves a pleasant aftertaste. Unlike the trouble we've had these last few days."

The Water King sighed. "That is regrettable. Trouble like that seems to follow Belasko around; the rest of us just get caught up in it."

"Yes, what is your connection to the swordsman? I've been trying to work it out."

"I did him a favour a few years back. It was to my own benefit to help him then."

The Grey Lady sipped her drink. "And now?"

"Now?" The Water King shrugged. "Belasko's a friend. I called in that favour to be brought here as part of his retinue, and the rest unfolded as it did. Regrettable, but at least we've had the opportunity to finish our discussions and come to an arrangement."

"An arrangement that you'll be unable to fulfil if you're trapped here in a basement in Albessar."

The Water King waved away the suggestion. "We'll think of something. We won't be here long. Belasko and the others are a resourceful bunch. Between us, we'll hatch a plan."

The Grey Lady swirled her drink around in its glass, watching as the liquid flowed. "I was surprised to see your loyalty to the Villanese Queen. Pleasant though she is."

"Yes, well, needs must and emergencies make strange bedfellows." He took a sip of his rum. "I wouldn't call it loyalty, as such. I made a promise to Belasko when he agreed to bring me here, that if things went sour, I would help get the Queen to safety if I could. One of his conditions for disguising us among his staff. I gave my word, something I don't do lightly. I take my promises very seriously. And he's a friend, as I said. You know, in our business, those are important."

She looked up at him, the grey film over her eyes catching the light. "Almost as important as enemies. If less fun."

The Water King leaned forward in his chair, cradling his drink in his hands. "All this pleasant chat aside, have you had time to think over the terms we discussed? Are we agreed?"

The Grey Lady nodded. "Yes, the terms are acceptable. We are agreed. Favourable terms going forwards, and co-operation over smuggling routes, as and when you get back to Villan."

"Oh, I'm sure that won't be long. As we're such good friends now ourselves, I'm sure you'll be able to help us get out of the city if it comes to it." He grinned again and raised his glass. "To enemies and friends."

The Grey Lady lifted her glass and echoed his toast. "To enemies and friends."

~

It was a short while later that Belasko entered the main hall, as they had taken to calling the space in the centre of this new underground compound that was large enough to hold them all at once. As he entered, the low hum of conversation in the room quieted as all turned to look at him. He observed them in return for a moment, taking in the faces of those gathered. The nobles and commoners, soldiers and thieves, Villanese and Baskans. The Water King met his eye and winked. Queen Lilliana raised an eyebrow. Belasko nodded and began to speak.

"I've been wracking my brain, trying to find a way out of this mess. I know we all have. I went apart from you all,

The Swordsman's Descent

thinking while I sat with Anerin. My first thought was to call a meeting of my closest allies, the people who accompanied me here. And I realised, it wasn't by fighting alone, or dividing into little groups, that we are going to win out." He took a breath. "The habits and ways of doing things that I have fallen into in the last few years aren't going to work here. Keeping apart. Separating myself. In fact, it is only by working together, trusting each other, and using the talents of all those gathered here that we will find a way through. We are allies now, no matter our background or what brought us to this place. Grey Lady, your situation is almost as parlous as our own. You are besieged by the same sinister forces that hound and attack us, and they are allied with who knows how many powerful and influential people in the city above."

The Grey Lady nodded in reply. "It is as you say. This cult is proving most troublesome." A grim smile hovered about her lips. "Thank you for bringing them to my door."

"For that, you have our sincere apologies. But while we were their initial focus, it seems they are intent now on driving you from these tunnels. You yourself said that a confrontation between the two groups was inevitable."

"It is true. This day has been coming for some time. The events that brought you into my sphere of influence have only hastened things. How does helping you further help me with my own situation?"

Belasko smiled. "I'll get to that. Now, I have an idea, but I want to see what everyone thinks and can add to it." He turned to face Olbarin. "You were an officer of the Baskan army. Do you know anyone now stationed with the palace guard? Are you friendly with anyone who might help us or be able to provide information? And would you be willing to help us break into the palace?"

Conversation broke out around the room—people questioning Belasko.

The Water King laughed. "Is your answer to everything to break into a palace?" he called to his friend.

But Queen Lilliana seemed to understand, and a small smile found its way onto her face. "You want to free the rest of our people from the palace," she said.

Belasko nodded. "And our horses, and then get out of this city as fast as we can."

Olbarin's face paled and he swallowed. "You must be mad. It's the most heavily guarded building in the city. Getting in is one thing, getting back out another..." Something seemed to resolve itself within the young Baskan, and he nodded. "But I am willing to help you. I am ashamed at the actions of my own people. This death cult are dishonourable. I would show you that there are some Baskans who still believe in honour. I know someone who might be able to help: a member of Prince Beviyard's cavalry squadron, they might be able to get me in to see the Prince. I'm sure he'd help us." He looked from Belasko to Queen Lilliana and back again. "I'm sure they all know I'm with you by now. How do I persuade them to let me in?"

"The first part is simple," said the Water King. "Tell him you're working for Baskan intelligence and that you need to get into the palace to report to the Prince on the whereabouts of Queen Lilliana. Everyone here seems terrified of the intelligence services." He shrugged, looking at the Grey Lady. "That's what I'd do."

"Your instincts are correct," said the Grey Lady. "The ordinary citizen lives in fear of the intelligence services and will go to extraordinary lengths to aid them or avoid their notice. It has a chance of working, if only a slim one."

"Good, so it might work," said Belasko. "We'll need some help disguising our party."

The Grey Lady laughed. "Oh, that I can do. I can source some palace livery. With a wash and a brush up, we'll have you looking like you belong below stairs in no time."

"All right, what next? How do we do this?" asked Belasko.

Majel held up her hand. "I suggest that Olbarin gain access and let those of us who can fight into the palace. We'll gather what we can."

"Then split up to free the rest of our people from where they're being held, if Prince Beviyard can aid us, or give us that information," said Byrta.

"Not forgetting to retrieve the horses from the stables," said Queen Lilliana.

"Then we break out of the palace, meet up with the Queen and the rest of the party, in their own disguises, in the square outside," said the Water King.

"And we all ride like hell to get out of the city and towards the mountains, passing through our camp outside the city to pick up as many of our people, spare horses, and supplies, as possible." said Belasko.

The Grey Lady nodded. "It's mad and desperate, but it might just work. If all the pieces fall into place. I can station people along the routes out of the city, to see that gates aren't closed and make sure you can get out."

"Good," said Belasko. "I think we have the makings of a plan. Let's work quickly, flesh out the plan today, and move as soon as we can. What does everyone think?"

He looked around the room, greeted by some cautious nods and some more enthusiastic calls of agreement.

"Right then, let's get to work."

"Belasko," said the Grey Lady, eyes narrowing, "you still

haven't explained how aiding you further is going to help my own situation."

"Oh yes, I did say I'd get to that. Well," said Belasko, scratching his chin, "if we're successful and a whole host of Villanese soldiers come spilling out of the palace and start making their way through the city, that is the sort of thing that might draw out the cult. Isn't it? Perhaps force their hand, make them operate in the open. If you're lucky, their leaders might be exposed, and you can, well, deal with them."

The Grey Lady smiled now, a grim expression on her face. "Oh, I see. I'd dearly like to cut the head off this particular snake."

"Hopefully, we can provide that opportunity."

∽

The next few days were a whirlwind of preparations. The Grey Lady's people kept them fed and watered, something she was able to accomplish because as far as the city above was concerned the house on the surface from which her people came and went was the city residence of a lady of means. One who spent most of her days at her country home. The extra supplies they brought in, and the comings and goings, could be explained away as preparations for one of her rare visits to the capital. They also provided new clothes for their Villanese guests to replace the outfits they had worn on their escape from the palace. Their own clothes were laundered and returned, as fresh and clean as they could be made, or replaced for something more suitable for the hurried journey they hoped to soon be undertaking. Olbarin reached out to his contact in Prince

Beviyard's squadron, the Grey Lady sourced them disguises, and the plan was worked out to the last detail.

Of course, there were moments of rest as well. It was during one of these that Queen Lilliana and Borne discovered their shared love of books. The gentle giant had knocked on the door to the queen's room, bearing a package.

"Hello, your majesty. The Grey Lady asked me to bring you this. Clothes for you to wear tomorrow, she said."

"Thank you Borne, do come in." Queen Lilliana went over to Borne as he ducked his head to fit in under the low door frame. He handed the package to her and waited while she examined it. It was reasonably large, the contents wrapped in rough cloth and tied with string.

"Bear with me while I open this." She crossed over to the bed against the far wall and dropped the package onto it. Borne looked round him while he waited, patient and curious as ever.

"I suppose this is smaller than you're used to, your majesty."

The stone-walled room, although well appointed for where and what it was, was definitely on the cosy side. It was simply furnished, bed, chest, a table with two chairs, a narrow wardrobe. The furniture that was there was well made.

Queen Lilliana looked up from where she was struggling with the knot on the package. "Hmm? Oh, yes, but anything will serve. I'm just grateful for a place to rest my head at the moment. Survival is more important than luxury."

Borne smiled. "Then you've read the work of Alvarus, the Navician philosopher, your majesty? Of course, that idea was key to several of his texts."

Queen Lillian blinked in surprise. "That's right, I have. What do you make of him?"

The big man shrugged. "Well enough, although he's a little stark for my taste. I like my philosophy to have a dash of poetry to it too."

"I'd forgotten, when Belasko introduced you he said you were well read. I'm sorry we haven't had much time to talk during this whole business Borne, old tomes and ancient philosophies are two of my favourite subjects." The queen frowned at the knot she was trying to unpick. "If you don't mind me saying so, I wouldn't have expected the same from someone in the Water King's employ. You're full of surprises."

Borne gestured to the knot Queen Lilliana was still struggling with. "Would you like to borrow my knife, your majesty? It would make quicker work of that."

"That's alright, I have my own." With a flick of her wrist a narrow dagger appeared in the queen's right hand, which she used to deftly cut the string around the package. With another quick movement the knife disappeared once again. Queen Lilliana laughed. "I don't know why I was trying to untie it. One of my old nursemaids had a tendency to collect old bits of string and cloth to reuse. Funny how these things rub off on you."

Borne smiled. "Yes, it is. I have to admit you've also surprised me, your majesty. I wouldn't have expected a queen to keep knives up their sleeve."

"Yes, well, one can't be too careful." Queen Lilliana unwrapped the parcel and took out the contents, laying them out on her bed. A hooded travelling cloak, an unassuming but well made dress with panelled skirts for riding, and several smaller items. "This will do, this will do nicely. Please relay my thanks to the Grey Lady."

"Yes, your majesty." Borne turned to leave, and was half out the door, head lowered to avoid that low frame, when the queen's voice stopped him short.

"Borne, one moment."

He turned back to look at Queen Lilliana, still half out the door. "Yes, your majesty?"

She looked up at him, a speculative look on her face. "While I wouldn't want to come between you and your current employer, I have been looking for an archivist for the palace library for some time. I'm wondering if that is something that might interest you? When we're all safely back in Villan."

Borne frowned. "I owe the Water King a great deal, your majesty, but I'd certainly love to see the royal library."

"Well, once we're all home I'll ask Belasko to facilitate a visit. You can have a tour of the library, we can discuss our favourite works and debate the merits of different philosophers and poets, and see if it would be a good fit. If you're interested, perhaps we can come to an arrangement. With the Water King's blessing, of course. What do you think?"

A smile crept across the big man's face, and he brushed his shaggy dun-coloured hair out of his eyes. "I think that would be marvellous, your majesty."

"So do I, Borne. So do I."

∼

Belasko went to see Anerin later that night, the night before they were due to carry out their plan. His old friend looked much better, although he had dark circles under his eyes and had lost some weight. He smiled weakly when Belasko entered and sat on the chair next to his bed.

"I'm happy to see you. What's going on?"

Belasko returned his smile. "Oh, not all that much, really. Tomorrow we're going to use a contact of Olbarin's to break into the palace, free our people, and ride hell for leather for the border. There may be some fighting involved." He shrugged. "Just another day, really."

Anerin laughed, struggling to sit up in his bed. "For you, maybe. All this excitement has been a bit much for me. I'm feeling somewhat fatigued."

The smile left Belasko's face. "Being poisoned will do that to you. Anerin, I'm sorry, but you're still too ill to travel. You'll have to stay here. The Grey Lady has agreed to shelter you until you're well. Depending on how things go tomorrow, she will also aid you in your return to Villan if needed. If things go well, that will hopefully be in due splendour with the acknowledgement of the Baskan court. If not... Well, you will just have to travel in a more sneaky style than that to which you're accustomed."

Anerin swallowed. "Of course, I understand. I wouldn't want to be a burden."

Belakso reached out and took his hand where it lay on top of the blankets. "You're no burden, Anerin. We don't want to risk your health when you're still recovering. You're in no fit state for a pitched battle. Hopefully, it won't come to that, but you never know. The Water King and his people are going to help us carry out our plan and then come back here once the rest of us are out of the city. His smuggling contacts will come in handy if you need to take a more obscure route over the border."

"You're going about things backwards, Belasko." Anerin smiled. "Armies usually try to get into enemy cities, not escape them. You're a military man, you should know that." He looked down, suddenly embarrassed. "I need to apologise for what I said the other day. I thought I was dying and—"

"Wanted to tell the truth, after a lifetime of being forced to live a lie by your family. I understand." Belasko squeezed Anerin's hand. "Don't apologise. We have a lot to talk about when we get back to Villan. Years to catch up on. Perhaps it's time I set duty aside and lived at least a little for myself."

He paused, hesitant, then leaned forward, tilted Anerin's chin up with a finger, and kissed him on the lips. It was a shy, delicate kiss, and after a moment, Anerin returned it warmly.

Belasko smiled, eyes closed, resting his forehead on Anerin's. "Where on earth have you managed to get cloves from?"

47

THE DAY AFTER Belasko's conversation with Anerin, hearts racing, he and his companions waited outside a servants' entrance to the palace. Olbarin led the way, fumbling a key out of his purse with trembling hands. Belasko laid a gentle hand on his shoulder. "It's all right, be calm. We all know what we're about."

Olbarin shook his head. "It's not that. I'm prepared, I know we all are. It's just..." He held up the key. "What if I've been given a false key? What if the old friend I met up with is working for the intelligence service, knows I'm not, and has set us up? We could be about to walk into a trap."

Byrta leaned over Belasko's shoulder. "The boy has a point. We're taking a lot of risks here."

Belasko swallowed. "I know. We all know that. But if we don't at least try to free our people, and just snuck out of the city in the dead of night... I don't think any of us could forgive ourselves."

Byrta grinned. "I know. The danger doesn't bother me. Just making sure we all understand." She looked up at Olbarin. "Come on, my young Baskan friend. Let's open that

The Swordsman's Descent

door. The longer we stand here, the more suspicious we become."

Olbarin looked at the faces of those assembled, took a deep breath, and nodded. He faced the door, placed the key in the lock, and turned it.

Belasko realised he was holding his breath until the tumblers of the lock opened with an audible clunking sound. He let out the breath in a sigh. "All right, let's go. Once we've determined it's not a trap, we'll set off on our different missions. Everyone has the routes Olbarin gave them memorised? Good."

Hands went to weapons secured under their livery as Olbarin pushed the door open to reveal an empty corridor.

They slipped in on silent feet and, meeting eyes one last time, nodded and went their separate ways.

Olbarin led Belasko and Majel to where the Villanese were being kept, while Byrta, Nerys and Sysko went to free their horses. A greater force, led by the Water King, went to secure the gate they would use to make good their escape. For their plan to work, time was of the essence. Any resistance they encountered had to be quickly neutralised before any alarm could be raised. Although, if Prince Beviyard was as good as his word, then they should encounter no trouble. All knew their tasks and what was required of them, and they set out with grim purpose.

As Olbarin, Majel, and Belasko crept through the halls of the palace, they all slowed.

Something's not quite right, thought Belasko. Something's off. What is it?

"Where are all the people?" asked Majel.

"That's it. I knew something was strange. Where are all the servants, the guards?" said Belasko.

Olbarin shrugged. "It's early. I've not spent that much

time in palaces. Would there be that many people around at this hour?"

"There are always people busy in a palace, boy, even in the dead of night, making preparations for the next day. Always guards, too. I have an odd feeling about this." Majel frowned, looking around them.

"I agree, it is most odd. Perhaps the guards are focusing their attention elsewhere, not expecting trouble inside the palace? I've taken advantage of that sort of lapse myself," said Belasko.

"It could be," said Olbarin. "I think we should just count ourselves lucky, do what we came here to do, and get out as quickly as we can."

"Is that right, Baskan?" hissed Majel from between her teeth, rounding on Olbarin. "Or perhaps you've set us up?"

Belasko stepped in between them, quick to defuse the situation. "Majel, calm your temper. Olbarin has given us no reason to doubt him. For this to work, we need to trust each other. We can't fall at the first hurdle. Particularly when that hurdle is things going our way."

"It's all right," said Olbarin, "I understand. You're in the heart of your historic enemy's lair. This is strange for all of us. But I promise you, I have not betrayed you."

Majel sighed, taking a step back. "You're right. Both of you. I'm sorry, tensions are running high, that's all. Ignore me. Let's go save our people."

～

Byrta, Nerys, and Sysko made their way to the stables. They, too, found that their route wasn't barred, and no one was guarding the entrance to the stables.

Byrta frowned. "This is odd. Why haven't we seen anyone?"

Sysko shrugged. "I don't know. Let's not look a gift horse in the mouth."

Nerys nodded. "Agreed, let's get into the stables and ready our mounts as best we can."

Byrta nodded to Sysko, who pushed open the wooden door of the stables where they knew the Villanese horses had been taken on their arrival. They hoped they were still there. The three of them walked through, stopping short at the entrance.

Byrta blinked. The stable block was large, ordinarily a busy place, but other than the sounds of the horses in their stables, shuffling their hooves, nickering or snorting to themselves, happily munching their hay, it was silent of activity. But that wasn't what caused the three of them to stop in their tracks.

"They're ready. All of them," Byrta whispered.

It was true. All the Villanese horses had been made ready. They were saddled, their saddlebags in place, ready to ride out.

"Okay, now that *is* odd," said Nerys.

Sysko looked to Byrta. "What do we do?"

She swallowed. "What we came here to do. We check over the horses, get ready for the others to appear, and pray this miracle is a sign of Aronos's favour and not that we're walking into a bloody great trap."

∼

Belasko, Olbarin, and Majel stood outside the door to the barracks where the remaining Villanese had been placed.

The courtiers, lords, ladies, and soldiers were all bedded down together.

"I still think it's odd that we haven't seen anyone," said Majel.

"Oh, it's definitely odd," said Belasko. "The hairs on the back of my neck are standing up. And why aren't there any guards on this door?"

"It's locked," said Olbarin, pointing to the large metal key that stood in the lock.

Majel snorted. "Trust me when I say that isn't enough to keep the royal guard behind a door." She looked at Belasko and shrugged. "Either they'd have picked the lock or broken the door down by now if they wanted out."

"The question then is why haven't they wanted to leave?" asked Olbarin.

"Because they've been well-treated," came a voice from down the corridor. "And they don't want to go anywhere without their Queen."

The three of them whirled around to face the sound, hands reaching for their weapons. None relaxed when they saw it was Prince Beviyard who had spoken.

He held up his hands. "That's all right. I wouldn't be too trusting in your shoes." The Prince walked closer. "I've more than kept up my end of the bargain. I had your routes cleared of staff." Prince Beviyard smiled. "Royal status is good for something after all."

Belasko relaxed, taking his hand from his rapier's hilt. "Then you have our thanks."

"Don't mention it." Prince Beviyard paused. "Just tell me you can get Queen Lilliana to safety."

"We're going to give it a damn good go," said Majel.

The Prince smiled. "Good." He looked up and down the corridor. "I'd better go. My father doesn't know I'm doing this. Take your Queen and your people to safety. My squadron stands by to assist if you need it." He turned to go, pausing for a moment to look back at Belasko. "Tell Queen Lilliana that I look forward to continuing our conversation." Then he walked down the corridor and was gone.

Belasko looked to the others, then reached for the key. Grasping it in one hand, he turned it slowly, the ancient metal protesting, until the tumblers clicked. The door sprang open with a push to reveal a sea of curious faces, weapons at the ready. A sea of faces that broke into smiles, a chorus of people talking over each other.

Questions came at them from every angle as Belasko and Majel were surrounded, embraced, clapped on the shoulders. Too many questions to be heard clearly, or understood, until Lord Beggeridge pushed himself to the front of the group.

"Belasko, what is the meaning of this? Where is the Queen?" He looked at Olbarin. "Are you in league with the Baskans?"

Belasko snorted. "Hardly. Look, the events of the last few days have been confusing, to say the least." He turned to address all those he could see. "Rest assured, the Queen is safe." There was a cheer in response to this, one that carried on down the barracks as people at the back of the group turned to whisper Belasko's words that they might be carried to all the Villanese people gathered there. "We are here to rescue you. Although I am surprised to see you're not guarded." He frowned. "And that you've been allowed to keep your weapons. What is going on here?"

"We're not prisoners," said Lord Beggeridge, "and we've been treated well. The Baskans told us there was an attack from an unknown source, that the Queen escaped, and we've been placed here for our own safety. Difficult to argue with an overwhelming show of arms." He shrugged. "They've been very reasonable about it, particularly when some of our soldiers wanted to set out and comb the city for the Queen."

"An understandable instinct. The Baskans have told you true, there was an attack on the Queen. Some of us made it to safety, although the same forces that attacked us have pursued us. We know who they are—a Baskan cult of their goddess of death—but not who leads them or their larger goal. Other than to sow division between our peoples." Belasko addressed the crowd once again. "I am not one to look good fortune in the eye and wish it were not so. All of you, make ready to leave, for we do so as soon as we can. But quietly!"

The Villanese sprang to, racing off to gather their things. Lord Beggeridge watched them go, then turned to Belasko. "You'll have to tell us what has happened. We've been cut off from information these last few days."

"So have we, my lord, so have we. We know who attacked us but not why. I promise, the Queen and I will tell you all that has befallen us when we have time. For now, let us move with speed. Gather your people and your things, for we must fly this coop."

Lord Beggeridge nodded. "Very well." He turned to go, then paused before turning back. "Thank you, Belasko, for coming back for us."

"You're welcome, my lord. I'd never have forgiven myself if we didn't at least try to free our people." Belasko grinned at the elderly lord. "Even you, your lordship."

Lord Beggeridge laughed. "It's good to see you haven't lost your sense of humour or impropriety, you impudent wretch." But he was smiling, too. "I shall do as I am bid and gather my things." He turned again and went into the crowd.

The Swordsman's Descent

～

They filed through the palace, moving as quietly as a gaggle of courtiers, squadron of cavalry, and other heavily armed soldiers could. Belasko led the group, with Majel and Olbarin. Lord Beggeridge and Baroness Morlake walked alongside them at the front.

"Despite assurances, I really am worried we're walking into a trap," said Belasko. "For the way to have been left so clear for us? We've still not seen a single person. Not a guard, a servant, anyone from the royal household. Even with the Prince's intervention, it is beyond odd."

"Perhaps our Baskan hosts would rather see the back of us," mused Baroness Morlake. "Perhaps they would rather we set off home to Villan, rather than have a large armed force within their city walls that are increasingly anxious as to the fate of their Queen. As far as they know."

"It's possible," said Majel. "They don't know what we've been up to, any more than we've known what's been going on above ground."

"Above ground?" asked Lord Beggeridge, a puzzled look on his face.

"One of those things I'll have to explain when we have more time, my lord," Belasko said. "Perhaps you are right. I can't trust to that, though, so everyone be at the ready."

"I don't think I could be any more ready, Belasko," said Olbarin. "I feel like I'm about to jump out of my skin."

Belasko laughed. "Oh, you'll get used to that once you've got a few more sneaky life-or-death missions under your belt. Wait, these are the stables, aren't they?"

They had emerged under a portico that led into a courtyard. A stable block made up three sides of the courtyard; the fourth was open and led to a gate.

"This is them," said Olbarin. "Let us see if our luck holds."

He led them across to a side entrance, knocking on the door with the agreed-upon signal. The door opened to reveal Byrta, whose face broke into a wide grin.

"Come in, come in," she said. "All is ready." She peered over his shoulder. "Oh good, you've brought everyone."

"How did you get on?" asked Belasko as he walked into the stables. "You can't have had enough time to—" He stopped, blinked, then turned to Byrta. "How? They're all saddled and ready. By Aronos's golden balls, you've worked a miracle."

She shrugged. "I'd love to take the credit, but, bizarrely, they were all ready and saddled up when we got here. They've been well-tended, too, I'll give the Baskan grooms their due. Bloody odd."

"It is," said Majel, looking at Belasko. "But it matches our experience elsewhere in the palace and what the Prince said. The way has been left clear for our escape."

Byrta shrugged. "I think we just get the hell out of here and thank our lucky stars and our friends in high places."

"I agree, but I think we still need to proceed with caution." Belasko tuned and called to the mass of people behind them. "Those of you who have them, look to your horses. Find them and prepare to leave. We ride out as soon as you're able." He turned back to Byrta. "I don't suppose you got our horses ready?"

She rolled her eyes. "When I found myself with an unexpected amount of free time, I did gather all of our horses together, yes. They're ready to go."

"Good. Now, let us hope our other friends have had as easy a time of it securing the gate."

The Swordsman's Descent

They lined up in the courtyard, cavalry at the fore, foot soldiers arrayed behind. With their infantry, engineers, palace and royal guard, they had just under four hundred troops. There were several empty saddles, a bitter reminder of the loyal guards lost in the cultists' attack on the royal quarters.

Belasko climbed up into his saddle, not quite as gracefully as perhaps he once would have done, and winced as he put his weight on his bad foot to do so. He stood in his stirrups, turning to take in the whole group behind him. He raised his arm, in signal and salute, sat down, and put his heels to his mount's flanks. The rest of their group set into motion behind him. Majel had found the rest of her remaining guard unit and led them, walking the Queen's horse alongside her own.

Belasko approached the gate. He stopped and called up. "Hello in there! How goes it?"

The Water King leaned out of an open window in the gatehouse, picking his teeth with a thumbnail. "It's gone suspiciously well. The gate was left unguarded. We figured out the mechanism and have been sat here playing dice, eating dried beef, and waiting for you to turn up."

"How much have you won?" asked Belasko.

"Everything but their teeth," replied the Water King, grinning.

"More fool them for playing with your dice. We've had a similar experience. Even with assistance, everything seems too easy."

The Water King nodded, stroking his beard. He raised an eyebrow. "Trap?"

"Almost certainly."

"Oh good," said the Water King, "I was worried I wasn't going to get to bash any heads today. Shall we open the gate?"

"Could you? Thanks awfully."

"My pleasure. See you down there in a moment."

Lord Beggeridge was looking at Belasko with a puzzled expression on his face. "Who on earth is that? What a strange manner he has with you."

"Oh, him? He's an old friend, my lord. An eccentric one. Ah, he's made good on his promise."

With a rattling of chains, the gates swung open. Belasko turned to face them all.

"Shall we? Follow me."

48

QUEEN LILLIANA WAITED across the square from the gate they were hoping to see their people emerge from. This wasn't the grand square by the main entrance to the palace, but it was large. Businesses and taverns lined the three sides that weren't the palace walls, and a few stall holders were setting up for their day of trading around the edge of the square. The people there were cloaked and hooded against the chill, which aided Queen Lilliana's disguise.

Queen Lilliana, Nobody, and No One made their way around the square, making a show of examining the limited wares on display at that time of the morning as they gradually moved towards the gates. Nobody's hand flickered out as another early morning shopper walked by, only for them to look up in surprise when they found the Queen's hand clamped around their wrist.

"You've got good reflexes, your, um, ladyship," said Nobody.

"Thank you, but remember what your master said," she

hissed between gritted teeth. "Nothing to draw attention to ourselves. Particularly the picking of pockets." This last, the Queen whispered.

Nobody sighed. "All right, if we must be so boring. You've got to keep your eye in, you know, or you lose the knack."

No One piped up in agreement. "They're right, um, miss. A body's got to practice."

"Then you can practice when we're not in the middle of an escape attempt."

"Hardly worth the bother, then," said Nobody.

"Yeah," said No One. "Where's the fun in that?"

"I wouldn't know," said Queen Lilliana, "as I've never picked a pocket."

Nobody's expression perked up. "Have you never? Oh, well, that might be fun. To teach you."

Queen Lilliana laughed at the thought. "I'm not sure that would be—oh."

"Look," said Nobody. "Something's happening."

They all turned towards the gate, which, slowly but steadily, had begun to open.

~

Belasko rode out at the head of the Villanese force, his eyes scanning the sparse crowd in the square. Looking for...

Ah, there she is.

A hooded woman, who could only by Queen Lilliana, flanked by two slender figures that must be Nobody and No One, had broken into a run as they rode out of the gate. Other people around the square, the Grey Lady's forces, also swung into action, keeping other people back so they wouldn't impede the Queen's progress, and clearing the exit they planned to use.

Queen Lilliana's and Nobody and No One's paths diverged as they crossed the square, as Queen Lilliana ran towards Majel, who was leading the queen's horse, and Nobody and No One ran towards the Water King, who was leading their horses.

As they mounted and took their saddles, Belasko gave a shout and set his heels to his horse's flanks. His horse reared, as if for dramatic effect, then set off across the square. As the others followed on behind, Belasko leaned down and patted his mare's neck. Whispering in her ear, he said, "I see I'm not the only one with a flair for the dramatic, old girl."

He turned in his saddle to address the Queen, smiling. "Everything is going to plan so far, your majesty. What say we hurry up and get out of this city? If we keep a good speed, we could be back on Villanese soil the day after tomorrow."

Queen Lilliana opened her mouth to speak, eyes smiling, but stopped short. Her face fell as Belasko became aware of the sound of many hooves approaching.

Belasko swivelled around to see, from the other avenue that opened into the square and luckily not the one they hoped to leave by, a mounted force approaching. They were followed by infantry. There were perhaps five hundred of them in total. He squinted at the person riding at their front, making out a slim figure with a balding head.

"Jonteer," he said to himself. Belasko took in the people he rode with, many of them with their faces covered, some wearing black armbands, and turned back to Queen Lilliana. "At least now we know who's in charge of the death cult that has been pursuing us."

"Or at least allied with them. A member of Baskan intelligence. No wonder they were able to gain access to the palace. What now, Belasko? Do we still ride for the city gates?" A frown creased Queen Lilliana's brow, but she did not look downhearted.

"We can try, but we might have to shed a little blood first. I think we—" He was interrupted by Olbarin, who started swearing vigorously. Belasko turned to the young Baskan. "What is it? Apart from the obvious."

Olbarin shook his head, face darkening with rage. "That's Jonteer, all right. And the man riding at his right-hand side? My old friend, the one who helped us get into the palace. He was working for the cult, and he set us up. I'm sorry, Belasko." He squinted again. "And the woman on his left is Emilynn, the Prince's banner bearer." The young man shook his head. "We are betrayed, and it is my fault."

"Nonsense, you couldn't have known. I'm sure—" Belasko was interrupted as Olbarin wheeled his horse around, a determined look on his face.

"I'll be back," the young man called over his shoulder as he galloped back through their forces and into the palace through the gate they had just opened.

"I thought a great many things about that lad, but not that he would be guilty of cowardice," said Majel, frowning after their young Baskan ally.

Belasko coughed, a wave of disappointment washing over him. He shook his head. "Never mind. I'm sure he will be back. I don't think he'd desert us. Nevertheless, we should deal with the pressing problem that's approaching from across the square. Majel, if you'd give the order?"

She nodded, taking up a horn that hung from her saddle and blowing a long note followed by a short one. "Battle positions!" she cried, as the Villanese formed up to face their attackers.

Jonteer gave his own signal, raising his sword as he stood in his stirrups. He brought it down to point at the lead group of Villanese. The mounted force he rode with increased their speed from a trot to a gallop, then broke into a charge, and the infantry that followed began to run.

The Villanese responded in kind. Their cavalry, Byrta at their head, swept around the royal guard that now surrounded Queen Lilliana, Belasko, Majel, and the rest of the royal retinue, and their infantry took up defensive positions.

"What now?" said Majel. "We can't fight a pitched battle in the middle of a hostile city. We're outnumbered by the people that attack us now, never mind all the other military units stationed in the city."

"A fair point," said Belasko. "We'll have to think of something."

The cult's cavalry were charging straight for them. A group of Villanese infantry had placed themselves between the two. Byrta's cavalry came around in their own charge, heading straight for the Villanese cavalry. At the last moment, they split into two groups, flowing either side of the Baskans, who ploughed on straight ahead and onto the waiting spears of the Villanese infantry.

Obscured from the Baskans' view by Byrta's cavalry charge, the Villanese had set themselves ready with long spears, and the Baskan cavalry charged straight onto these. The air was filled with the sound of injured and dying warriors and horses, as some of the Baskans, having avoided the spears, closed on the Villanese and began to reap their revenge.

Battle was well and truly joined as Baskan and Villanese blood mingled on the cobbles of the square.

∽

The fight flowed backwards and forwards across the square. Although the Villanese were outnumbered by the cultists, their military discipline meant they were more than holding their own against skilled individual fighters that clearly weren't used to fighting together.

As the battle in the square played out, the royal guard kept a tight protective circle around Queen Lilliana. They were trying to manoeuvre around so that the Queen's party could make good their escape down their planned route while the rest of the Villanese forces held off pursuit.

"It won't be long, your majesty, then we should be able to make our move," said Belasko.

The Queen's face was pale. "What about the rest of our people? How will we bring them with us?"

"We won't, ma'am," said Majel softly. "They will keep our pursuers busy, so we can get you to safety."

If anything, the Queen's face paled further. "But they'll die. We'll be leaving them to their fate. We can't—"

"We must, your majesty." Majel shook her head. "My foremost duty, Belasko's too, is your protection. All those gathered here have sworn their lives in your service; they knew that might mean their deaths. They will buy us the time we need. We need to be ready—"

She was interrupted by the sound of another horn, a bright and brassy note calling from across the square. They all looked up.

Prince Beviyard rode through the open gate and into the square at the head of his squadron, Olbarin to his left

The Swordsman's Descent

blowing the horn, Ambassador Aveyard to his right. Prince Beviyard grinned as he stood in his saddle, raising his sword high as Olbarin blew a third and final note, and then he and his squadron of cavalry charged, right into the rear of Jonteer's forces.

All was chaos and confusion in the square, blood and curses in the air, as it became impossible to know friend from enemy. Jonteer's forces turned to face this new threat, trying to fight on two fronts.

"Now!" shouted Belasko. "Sound our retreat. Aronos bless that mad Baskan Prince, he's bought us some time. We have to take our chance and take it now."

Majel nodded, blowing a series of notes on her horn. The royal guard that were mounted, and the cavalry that Byrta led, broke away from the fighting and formed up around the Queen. They started to move towards the exit they had been originally aiming for. The infantry, breaking free where they could, took up defensive positions by the exit. As the Queen and her party moved through, they closed ranks, denying access to anyone following.

"Wait, what about the infantry?" asked the Queen, a puzzled look on her face.

"The mounted party can move quicker without them, ma'am," said Belasko. He sighed, shaking his head. "I had hoped we could all make good our exit from the city together, but as the fighting has started, they will stay behind to protect our backs. They're to initiate a staged retreat towards the gate and hold it against the Baskans if needed. We'll leave with a smaller force of mounted guards and soldiers. I—"

The sound of galloping hooves came from behind, stopping Belasko short. He turned to look over his shoulder as a lone figure that had been let through the Villanese forces came riding up to them. It was Olbarin.

"I told you I'd help you get away," he shouted as he got closer. "You'd better not leave me behind."

At a nod from Majel, the royal guard parted to allow the young Baskan through.

"That was well done, Olbarin, fetching Prince Beviyard," said Belasko. "I'll admit, I thought the worse of you when you rode away, but I'm glad you did. Forgive me for thinking you had been struck by cowardice."

Olbarin shook his head. "That's understandable. I didn't have time to explain. I know the barracks where the Prince's squadron were staying was close to their stables, and that they were standing ready to move quickly. Only a few words from me, and they sprang into action." He turned to address Queen Lilliana. "The Prince bade me tell you this, your majesty: the attack on you was nothing to do with him or his father, and they will stop at nothing to root out the people responsible. Peace remains their true goal, and they hope the negotiated accords can be signed once current events are settled."

"Jonteer rather tipped his hand as to who was responsible," said Queen Lilliana, "but I appreciate the Prince's words. Let's get out of the city, and I'll think of a suitable response later—although if talks are to resume, I would expect it to be on neutral ground."

"The Prince was very angry at the actions of the cultists, your majesty," said Olbarin. "I think he will stop at nothing until they have been driven from Baskan society."

"That's what we thought we'd done in Villan," said Belasko. "But it turns out we only pushed them further into the shadows."

The sound of fighting faded behind them as they rode.

The Swordsman's Descent

The Grey Lady had been as good as her word: the streets were clear, and they made good progress. There was the occasional flash of movement as a curious resident looked out of a window, but the locals all seemed to sense that there was violence in the air and kept themselves to themselves.

"There we are," said Olbarin, "the gate. It's open and unmanned." He frowned. "I wonder how the Grey Lady managed that."

"Professional secrets," said the Water King. "She'd never tell you. But I reckon she's called in more than a few favours this day. We owe her. Something I don't think she'll let me forget. Speaking of which…" He beckoned Nobody and No One over. "Time we went our own way. We'll stay here, as agreed, and bring Lord Anerin home when he's well enough, by any means necessary."

He brought his horse up alongside Belasko, and held out his hand. Belasko clasped it. "Goodbye, Belasko, and good luck. See you when this is all over." The Water King looked over at Queen Lilliana. "I'd appreciate it if the royal party wouldn't mind forgetting my existence. It's so hard to be a mythical and mysterious presence when people know you're real." He grinned. "Of course, do feel free to embellish the stories about me to your hearts content, the more outlandish the better." The Water King stood in his stirrups and essayed as good a bow as he could manage on horseback. "Your majesty, it's been a pleasure to make your acquaintance."

She respectfully inclined her head. "Likewise, your majesty."

The Water King grinned, then turned and rode his horse into a dark alleyway, Nobody, No One, and Borne following behind.

"Now let's get out of here," said Queen Lilliana. "I think

I've had enough of Baskan politics for now. Let's go home." She tried to force a smile, but it didn't reach her eyes, in which sadness lurked.

Heavy is the burden of leadership. Of friendship too. Belasko thought of Anerin, left behind in the care of the Grey Lady, and wondered if he'd ever see his friend again.

The Queen looked up and caught Belasko's eye. He gave her an understanding look and a sympathetic smile. One she returned, a little more genuine than the last, before turning her attention back to the road ahead.

49

AMBASSADOR AVEYARD STOOD in the middle of the square, surveying the remnants of the battle that had taken place around her. Dead and dying people littered the square, Villanese and Baskans bleeding together. A voice from over her shoulder startled her.

"What has happened here?" King Edyard asked, a sad look on his face as he took in the sights.

"Battle, Father," said Prince Beviyard as he strode up.

"I can see that. I'm not so old I've forgotten, son." The King's face was pinched, his tone waspish. "But battle with whom, and why?"

"I helped the Villanese to leave with Queen Lilliana, and Aveyard's secretary led a force of cultists that attacked them. That young man who was supposed to be in my cousin's employ, Olbarin, then came to find me. Begged me to bring my squadron to bear, to aid in Queen Lilliana's escape. Aveyard happened to be with me, so joined us, and we came to help."

"Glossing over for a moment the fact that you helped

them escape, why would Aveyard's secretary confront the Queen?" King Edyard looked puzzled now.

"It would seem," said Ambassador Aveyard, "much to my surprise, that Jonteer is in command of the Order of the Lady of Night. That they were behind the attack on Queen Lilliana, as we suspected."

"And the Queen is now where?" asked King Edyard.

"Riding hell for leather for the border, I'd wager," said Prince Beviyard.

"I'd take that bet," said Ambassador Aveyard. "With Jonteer and the remnants of his forces in pursuit."

"Then what are you doing standing here?" King Edyard grabbed his son by the arm. "If Queen Lilliana gets back to Villan without a full explanation of what happened here, it could mean war. And all our efforts would be for nought. Ready fresh horses, including mine, and as many soldiers as we can bring. We ride in pursuit."

"Yes, Father." Prince Beviyard bowed, then ran off to carry out his father's doing, calling orders to his squadron on the way.

Ambassador Aveyard eyed her uncle. She knew the old man well enough to know that he was furious. A slow-burning sort of anger that, when it erupted, would be terrifying to behold. She was glad it wasn't aimed at her.

"Uncle, you do realise that Jonteer and his people, the cultists, are between us and the Villanese?"

"Not for long, niece, not for long." There was a fierce glint in King Edyard's eyes, and Ambassador Aveyard felt herself shiver.

~

They rode as hard as they dared for the mountains and the easiest route back to Villan. They had to spare their horses —if any pulled up lame it would be disastrous—yet they had to make the border as fast as they were able. It made for a tense journey, worsened by Byrta's discovery that they were being pursued.

She had been riding ahead, scouting their route and keeping an eye out for trouble, when from the top of a rise, she had glanced back and seen dust clouds in the distance behind them. Byrta put a looking glass to her eye, muttering to herself. Then swearing. She had ridden back to rejoin the others.

"There are two large groups following us," she reported, "and I know not who. Only that there's a lot of them, and they're mounted."

"Are they together?" asked Majel.

Byrta shrugged. "There seems to be some distance between them. It could be that one pursues the other as they pursue us, or it could be two different groups with a shared purpose. All I know is that they're behind us, and that's not good."

"It could be Prince Beviyard," said Queen Lilliana, "or it might be the cult."

"Or some other player we've yet to face," said Belasko. "What about up ahead?" he asked Byrta.

If anything, her face grew yet more grim. "Bad news there, too, I'm afraid. There seems to be a large military group camped along the road a few miles ahead, between us and the camp we used before entering the city. There's no way of knowing if it's a group loyal to the cultists, or a regular Baskan military unit on manoeuvres. Either way, I don't think they'll take too kindly to a large group of heavily armed Villanese riding through their camp."

"We're stuck then," said Queen Lilliana. "Danger ahead and behind and nowhere to go."

Olbarin coughed. "That's not quite true. There is another road, a track really, up ahead. If we follow that, it joins up with another road, not so easily passed as this one, but it leads to the mountains. I normally take it at a more leisurely pace, but a day's hard ride will get us there."

"Where in the mountains?" asked Belasko. "It's no good to us if there's no route through. How do you know of this road, anyway?"

"Somewhere you've been before, Belasko. But I don't think you spent long on the Baskan side. There's a monument there, up in the mountains, to the Baskan soldiers that fell nearby. I visit it yearly to pay respects to my father. That is how I know of the road. The one that leads to Dellan Pass."

Belasko felt a chill run through him, and he shivered, the hairs on the back of his neck standing on end. He was aware, too, that the others were staring at him.

"I'd hoped to never visit that place again," he found himself saying, "but if it's our only way through to Villanese soil... Let us ride for Dellan Pass."

∼

Jonteer rode at the head of a column of mounted warriors. They were a mixed bunch: commoners and courtiers, soldiers from different branches of the Baskan military, all united by their membership to the cult of the Lady of Night. This was what remained of their strength from the capital city. He was their leader but, as had been pointed out to him, that role was one of first among equals. If the gamble he had taken, bringing them into the open, failed, then he

The Swordsman's Descent

wouldn't keep hold of the position for long. Or his head, for that matter.

They were pushing their horses as hard as they dared, trying to keep up with the smaller group of Villanese ahead of them. They had trackers ranging out in front of their main party, trying to ensure the Villanese didn't catch them out with some trickery.

One of these trackers appeared along the road, riding back towards Jonteer. He wheeled his horse around and fell in beside the nobleman, his horse's flanks heaving. The tracker seemed a little breathless, too.

"Well?" asked Jonteer. "What is it?" His tone was waspish, but knowing that King Edyard's troops were in pursuit only increased the tension of the situation. "I assume you have something to report?"

"Yes, sir," said the tracker. "It appears the Villanese have left the main road, taking a side route up to the mountains."

Jonteer frowned, swaying in his saddle. "There's no other direct route up to the mountains off this road. Unless..." He blinked in surprise. "They mean to connect up to the road to Dellan Pass."

"That would be my guess, sir," said the tracker. "It would be their only way back onto their own ground without riding many miles out of their way."

"They don't have the supplies to manage that," said Jonteer. "They'll be looking for the most direct route possible."

A voice came from behind him. "Why did we allow the Prince to ready their horses for them again, Jonteer? You must remind me. Whatever the reason, the strategy now seems poor." It was Baron Sottomey, a noble who outranked him at court but was beneath him in their order. Something he seemed to have forgotten, perhaps sensing

Jonteer's position was delicate and that he may take advantage.

"The idea, dear Baron, which you agreed to not so long ago, was to allow them to ride out of the palace so that we could confront them in the streets. Such an abuse of our hospitality, to ride out as if at war in our capital city. To then shed Baskan blood... Well, it would force an outright war."

The Baron sneered. "But you didn't take the possibility that Prince Beviyard might interfere into account. There was no back-up to your plan. Now, war may very well occur, not least with our own people, but the Villanese Queen and her people have got away."

"Not yet," said Jonteer, a tone of steel in his voice. "We ride for Dellan Pass."

50

THE VILLANESE RODE for Dellan Pass. They were quiet beyond necessary conversation, for all knew that much was at risk. They also felt the sting of abandoning those at their camp outside the city, adding to the tally of people left behind them in Albessar.

Earlier, Belasko had told them what he remembered of Dellan pass. "The pass is a much more direct route onto Villanese soil, but we'll be pretty far from civilisation on the other side. Although there's a garrison stationed about a day's ride away. The terrain is passable on foot, but we won't be able to get the horses through. The pass narrows to a switchback, there's no way to get our mounts around that."

Queen Lilliana frowned, reaching down to touch her mount's neck. "Are you sure, there's no way?"

Belasko shook his head. "I'm afraid not, your majesty."

"Surely that's madness," said Majel. "Although our pursuers would be in the same position, casting ourselves adrift in the mountains on foot seems like a terrible idea. It doesn't matter if we're on Villanese soil if we're swarmed by Baskan cultists."

"Ah," said Belasko. "You wouldn't be cast adrift, so to speak. After the Baskan's failed invasion attempt, we built a small fort at the mouth of the pass on the Villanese side. A wall across the pass with a few buildings beyond, and a large signal pyre. It's been empty for years, the gates left open in this time of peace, but you should be able to get in, hunker down, and light the pyre. If the Villanese agents Anerin met in Albessar managed to get messages out then all of the border garrisons will be poised for action. When the garrison I mentioned before see that pyre lit they'll come running to investigate."

"Can we hold the fort though, if need be?" asked Queen Lilliana.

Belasko nodded. "It was built to be held by a small force. The wall isn't wide, the numbers we have here should be sufficient to close the gate and defend the wall long enough for the garrison's forces to arrive." He smiled. "I don't think our pursuers will have stopped to pick up siege ladders on their way."

Majel shook her head. "I don't like it, Belasko. This plan has far too many 'shoulds' and 'I thinks' in it." She sighed. "I don't see that we have any option though."

Queen Lilliana looked at them both, then nodded. Her mind was clearly made up. "We will do as you say Belasko, as it seems the only course of action available to us." The faintest smile quirked her lips. "Next time we come on one of these expeditions we really must have our escape routes thought out in advance."

After that conversation Belasko lost himself in thoughts of the past. This would be the first time since that fateful day, all those years ago, that he had returned to the place that made his name. That made his legend. He knew legends were nonsense, but certain achievements and

The Swordsman's Descent

events had raised him up in others' eyes and he had always tried to live up to that. Now, tired, in pain from a dozen old wounds and injuries, he wondered if it had all been worth it.

Olbarin seemed sombre, too. Belasko could guess at the reason why. The lad was about to visit the site of his father's death, in the company of the man who had killed him.

"Are you all right?" he asked the young Baskan, as softly as he could over the sounds of an armed group riding hard.

Olbarin sighed. "It's always difficult, visiting this place. I never really knew my father, and this is where he was taken from me. The last time I was here was when I pledged to track you down and defeat you in single combat, avenging him." A sad smile worked its way across his features. "The fact that I'm returning *with* you is so bizarre that I can't fathom it."

"It's been an interesting time, that's for certain. We've spoken before, about your father, about the events of that day, but I can tell you this, Olbarin: all the Baskans I faced that day were brave and did their duty. As you have done yours, if in unexpected ways. Your father would be proud of the man you've become."

Olbarin dashed away sudden tears with the back of his hand. "Thank you, Belasko. I don't know why but, coming from you, there is something comforting in that." He sat up straighter in his saddle. "Look, a scout."

One of the cavalry officers they had set to scouting galloped up, overtaking the column and falling in alongside the Queen's party.

"Report," said Queen Lilliana. "Does it go well?"

The scout nodded, her long hair tied back in a tail that bobbed as she did so. "Yes, your majesty. We near the plain that marks the entrance to the pass from this side. As we've gained a bit of height, I've been able to look back using my glass, and can see that the cavalry have begun their rear-guard action."

Byrta and the other cavalry commanders had stayed back, aiming to slow their pursuers with surprise attacks.

"How are they doing?" asked Belasko.

The cavalry woman shrugged. "It's hard to say from this distance, but they're slowing the first group of pursuers and managing not to engage them for long. Sweeping attacks to their flanks before disengaging and disappearing again." She frowned. "I'm not sure how long their horses will be able to keep it up for, though. They're having to use them pretty hard."

"Long enough, hopefully," said Majel. "If we're nearing the pass then, Aronos willing, they've given us enough time."

"Let us ride, then," said Belasko, "while our brothers and sisters buy that time with their lives, we had best make the most of it."

They rode on, grim, determined.

~

It was a short while later that they arrived at the entrance to Dellan Pass. It was much as Belasko remembered it: sparse rocky ground with little growing, flat and wide enough for an army to muster, and a crevice in the sheer grey cliffs that led to the pass beyond.

One thing had changed, though. In the middle of the plain, aligned with the entrance to the pass, stood a stone column. Elaborately carved, it stood as high as a city wall.

"The monument to the Baskan dead," Belasko said.

"To the dead," said Olbarin, "and to the death of Baskan hopes in the war. This was a turning point, Belasko,

The Swordsman's Descent

although I know any war contains many of those. Without the defeat that day and the breaking of General Edyard's great gamble, we might have won."

"It would have been a close-run thing, Olbarin, I know that for certain. If we had the time I'd stop and pay my respects. Instead we must forge on."

They rode quietly for a moment, the column looming in the distance.

Belasko could hardly take his eyes off the monument, taking in the great height of it as they rode along. After a time he bowed his head and closed his eyes. *So many dead, so many I have killed over my life. And for what? I'm sorry to all those soldiers who never made it home. To their families. We were all just doing our duty, but that doesn't make it right.* He was surprised to feel the start of tears behind his eyelids. Belasko wiped them away with the back of his hand, then opened his eyes and looked over at Olbarin.

"Taking someone's life, however noble you're led to believe your purpose is, is a great weight, Olbarin. A stain upon your soul." Belasko voice was quiet, hoarse. "Imagine how heavy my soul must be, how stained. I can feel it, some days." He coughed. "You know, I've never liked killing. I'd be extremely wary of anyone who does. It's just been my gift, perhaps a curse, to be good at it. To be fortunate, if you can call it that, to have survived when others fell." He twisted in his saddle to face the young Baskan. "If I have any advice for you, it is this: don't be a killer. If you must take a life, it is a last resort, in protection of your own life or others. Do something good with your life. Raise a family. Grow things. Put some good into the world, however you choose to do it. Be defined by the life you lead, not by those you've taken."

Olbarin stared at him, Belasko's words taking him by surprise. "Belasko, I wouldn't view yourself so harshly. As difficult as it is for me to say, I think you have done good in this world. How many lives have you protected? How many others have you raised up, sought opportunity for? You even did it for me. You couldn't help yourself."

Belasko gave a wry smile. "I couldn't. I didn't want to see a life wasted. That's why I didn't kill you that day." He sighed. "I've grown tired of killing, although I fear we'll have more to do this day." He looked ahead. "Ah, here we are."

The mouth of the pass was ahead of them, Belasko and Olbarin rode closer to the others.

"Belasko, you know the pass. Are you absolutely sure we can't get through with our horses?" Majel asked.

Belasko shook his head. "I'm afraid not. Once the pass narrows to that switchback I mentioned; it's single-file through there and not wide enough. When the Baskans tried to come this way in the war they only brought infantry. We'll have to take what we can carry from the packs and set the horses free, discard what we don't need before we make our way through to the fort. Move quickly, though, time is of the essence. Oh, bring as many of the discarded packs as we can carry. I have an idea."

They sprang into action, relieving their mounts of their burdens and sorting through the packs as quickly as they could. Within half an hour, they were ready, and set their horses free. It was hard to see the animals go, the steeds that had carried them so faithfully milling around, unsure what was happening. Nosing forlornly at the scrubby ground of the pass. Belasko yelled and tried to scatter them, the others joining in, and gradually the horses moved away.

They set off into the pass. It wasn't long before they reached the switchback, where Belasko had held his ground all those years ago. It was hard going even getting the packs through, but they did, everyone discarding the excess packs

The Swordsman's Descent

they had carried at the point where the pass widened a little.

Belasko made sure everyone else was through before finding the Queen at the head of their group. "This is it," he said. "You're on Villanese territory now. Just keep on going to the fort at the mouth of the pass. The gates should be open, hole up in there and light the signal bonfire. The local garrison will send troops to investigate. All you need do is hold the fort until they arrive."

"That sounds suspiciously like you're not coming with us," said Majel.

Queen Lilliana frowned. "What are you up to, Belasko?"

He shook his head. "If the Baskans go any further on from here, then it would be an act of war. I don't know if they'd actually risk that, but I don't want to leave it to chance. Someone has to stay and protect the pass, buy you some time to get to the fort and ready your defences. It might as well be me—with a small force, though, I'm not doing it alone this time."

"No," said Queen Lilliana, "I won't allow it."

"With respect, Lilliana, my Queen, it is not yours to allow. My oath binds me to your protection above all else, even your own protestations." He looked out over the rocky ground of the pass. "I'll stay with any that would stand with me and do my duty one last time. We'll hold them off as long as we can." Belasko looked around at all of them. "Just know that staying likely means death. For me, it is perhaps fitting. Enough people have cursed me, said I should have died here. I don't normally go in for talk of fate, but perhaps that's why I survived. So I could return, now, and protect my Queen's life."

He turned back to Queen Lilliana. "Before we came on this trip, you asked me to name my successor. Well, I've chosen." Belasko looked over at Majel. "Sorry, old friend, it's you. You've shown you have the skills with a sword and, more importantly, the will and heart to protect your Queen no matter what. I hope you'll accept."

Majel frowned. "It's not anything I've ever wanted, Belasko. I know the role of Champion sets you apart from others, leads to a life alone."

Belasko shook his head. "That's how I've done it. That's how Markus explained it to me. But perhaps it doesn't have to be that way. Take the role, make it your own. Do with it as you will. All that matters is that you do your duty."

Majel nodded. "All right, you old bastard. You've caught me. I accept."

Belasko walked over to her, holding out his hand for her to grip. She clasped hands, pulling him into an embrace.

"Don't be in such a hurry to die today. You might surprise yourself."

He laughed. "I'll do my best."

"You always have," said Queen Lilliana.

Belasko went to her, dropping to one knee. "I know it hasn't been easy these last few years, but it has been my honour to serve as your Champion, Lilliana. And a greater honour to have known you. To see the girl you were become the excellent queen you now are."

She pulled him up and into an embrace of her own. "Try to live, Belasko," she whispered in his ear. "Remember what I said in the Grey Lady's den. I have need of you, not just your sword arm."

Queen Lilliana let go of him then and stood back. "If we have to part, I would prefer to take time over it, but I fear we must go."

"You must," said Belasko, nodding. "Now, who will stay with me?"

51

OLBARIN WAS ONE of the people who volunteered to stay, to Belasko's great surprise.

"Did you not hear my emotional speech to you as we passed the monument?" he asked the younger man.

Olbarin smiled. "I did, and I would like to take that advice, but I think I have to help here first." He looked around at the pass. "If you feel it is fitting that you die here, perhaps it is fitting that I do so, too. Give my life where my father fell, but in defence of peace and not making war. If we survive this day, slim though that chance may be, I will put your advice into practice."

There were four others who elected to stay and help hold the pass, including Nerys and Sysko.

Belasko looked at them and the others who had chosen to stay. He nodded. "Very well, let's get started." He pointed to the switchback. "As you have experienced for yourselves, that is single file only. We don't have the equipment to make a proper fortification, but desperate times and all that. We'll use the discarded packs we've brought to make at least an obstacle for the Baskans to deal with. Let's start piling them up."

They set to, doing what they could with the packs to make something that would inconvenience anyone approaching from the other side of the pass. Vertiginous walls of stone rose high above them as they filled the packs with loose rocks scrabbled from the valley floor to weigh them down, then stacked them up as high as they could. Their improvised fortification, if you could call it that, came to about waist height. Enough to give anyone approaching them difficulty.

Little grew here beyond scrubby brush and low-lying weeds. Belasko stopped, wiping his hand across his brow. Although the air was thin and cold he had worked up a sweat. He was trying to ignore the pain in his foot, the aching of his joints, the tiredness from being on the run, that lay just underneath the surface. His hands were stiff, but he knew he could still hold a blade. At least today.

He looked at the others. "Here's what I propose: they'll have to approach single-file, so we'll take turns facing them one at a time as they round the corner. We rotate, so no one fights for too long, and we all get the opportunity to rest. Hopefully, that will keep us fresh enough to hold them off for a while. If they break through, pushing us back into the wider part of the pass, well..." He shrugged. "We fight side by side, back to back, and do not sell our lives cheap. Agreed?"

The rest of those who remained nodded amongst themselves. "It shall be as you say, Belasko," said Nerys. "Who knows better than you what tactics will work in this place?"

They rested then, and prepared themselves as best they could for what was to come. A short while later, they heard

The Swordsman's Descent

the sound of many feet, approaching footsteps echoing off the walls of the pass.

Belasko insisted on taking the first turn at the front. As the first Baskan rounded the corner, the black cloth across the lower portion of their face giving them away as death cultists, they stopped short at the obstacle in their path, surprised, and Belasko lunged forwards. His opponent desperately parried the blow, but with a sweeping riposte, Belasko opened their throat. The killing had begun.

Belasko felt the bonds of time blurring, and he found it difficult to say if he was awake or dreaming. A nightmare from his past, it seemed, as he killed and killed again.

There was a brief pause in the fighting, and Sysko tapped him on the shoulder. Belasko stepped back, breath heaving in his lungs, and walked away down the pass to the back of their group. He heard the clash of blades and knew that the fighting had started up again.

Belasko dropped his rapier and dagger to the ground, slumping to sit on a large rock, and put his head in his hands as he tried to get his breath back.

I can't do this. I'm too old, too worn down. How the hell will we hold long enough?

He looked up as footsteps approached, crunching in the gravel. Olbarin stood over him, holding out a water skin. "Here," said the young man, "you look like you could do with this."

Belasko nodded his thanks, taking the water skin and a long sip from it, before handing it back to Olbarin. He stood and, long experience teaching him not to let his muscles get tight, started to stretch.

"I've not seen the like," said Olbarin.

"What, someone stretching?" asked Belasko, a wry smile on his face.

"No, your fighting. Your technique, speed, skill with a blade... You must have been something to behold in your younger days." Olbarin was smiling now.

Belasko laughed. "Oh yes, I'm old and slow now. What you see is the result of a lifetime of training, of pushing myself." Belasko pulled his sword arm across his chest, easing the tightness in the muscles along the back of his arm. "All of it bloody exhausting."

Sysko came to join them, his time at the front over for now, and reached for the water skin. "These Baskans are giving us some good sport, but we're holding our own."

"More than holding our own, as we've yet to lose anyone," said Olbarin.

"We do have the advantage," said Sysko. "They're coming to us around a blind corner into an obstacle. Still, we can only hold them for so long."

"I'd best go, get in line. It will be my turn to face them again soon enough." Olbarin nodded to them both, then turned and took his place behind Nerys.

And so it went for a few hours. Their system worked, but all began to tire. To slow. Wounds and shallow cuts, hastily bandaged, began to appear, and all knew that, eventually, they would fail. The six of them could not hold back the few hundred cultists indefinitely. One of the guards who had opted to stay took a savage cut to the thigh before despatching their opponent. They limped back to safety as someone else took their place, and started trying to bandage the cut and stem the flow of blood. Shortly after that, the other guard took a backhanded cut across their sword arm that opened it to the bone. Now only four remained that could fight.

"How did you do this all day?" gasped Sysko, chest

The Swordsman's Descent

heaving as he tried to get his breath back following his latest stint facing the Baskans.

Belasko shrugged. "I was younger then, but I still don't know to tell you the truth. Listen, we're holding as long as we can. That's all we can hope for."

"No, all we can hope for is that they'll tire of this sport and bugger off, although I fear that is unlikely."

"Well," said Belasko, "stranger things have happened. I remember, once I—"

He was interrupted by the sound of horns from the Baskan side of the pass. Belasko looked up. "What is that?"

The horns came again, faint but unmistakable, and then the distant roar of voices, followed by the sounds of battle joined.

"I wonder what's going on out there?" said Sysko.

"I don't know," said Belasko, "but we have to deal with what's going on in here."

Their own fight with the Baskans carried on, although the flow of enemy warriors slowed to a trickle and then stopped.

They all stood there for a moment, looking at each other.

"Whatever's happening on the other side of the pass seems to have caught their attention," said Olbarin.

"Shall we go see what it is?" asked Sysko.

Belasko frowned. "It could be a trap. I'm wary of giving up our position."

"I can go," said Nerys. "I'll make my way to the other side, see what's going on, and come back to report."

"All right," said Belasko, "you do that. We'll hold here for the time being."

So Nerys went, clambering over their improvised barrier and the bodies of dead cultists beyond it. The atmosphere in the narrow gulley was tense as they waited. Belasko paced back and fore whilst they waited for Nerys. At the sound of footsteps, all whirled around to face the switchback, blades drawn, as a voice called out.

"It's only me," said Nerys, face peering around the corner. She grinned. "You're going to want to see this. Come have a look. It's safe. For now."

So, making their wounded comfortable first, they did as they were bid and set off to see just what was happening on the other side of the pass.

∼

King Edyard rode at the head of a column of cavalry. Ambassador Aveyard rode to his left and Prince Beviyard to his right. They approached the plain before the entrance to Dellan pass cautiously, wary of any traps set for them by the cultists they pursued.

As they rode onto the plain, the memorial built there was illuminated gold by the rays of the sun. He stopped, bringing the column to a stuttering halt. Then the Baskan King began to laugh.

They could see that the cultists had been massed at the entrance to the pass, dismounted in order to make their way through. Their numbers diminished further by the battle in the city square, what had seemed a small battalion was now no more than a few hundred cultists. Those that remained were backed up, milling around. Clearly something in the pass was holding up their progress.

The King laughed again. "He's doing it again, the mad Villanese bastard. He's holding the pass. Let's help him this time. Those men and women down there are traitors—I would see them dead. Except their leaders. Bring them to me."

Prince Beviyard nodded. "As you say, Father. Let us take the fight to them." He gestured to the stocky man who had replaced Emilynn as his banner bearer, and he blew a long note on the horn. The cavalry began to form up for a charge. The cultists, now aware of their presence, were in disarray. Some ran for their horses; others tried to form up infantry lines. Desperately trying to ready a defence against the much larger force bearing down on them.

The banner bearer blew another note, and the cavalry began to move. A trot at first, rising to a canter, and then a gallop. Prince Beviyard, grinning, raised his sword, and a third and final note blew. The Baskan cavalry roared, crashing into the broken lines of the cultists. Battle was joined.

∼

When Belasko and the three others emerged from the pass, all was chaos before them. All that was immediately clear was that two Baskan groups were engaged in a bloody battle. After a moment, Belasko was able to pick up several distinguishing features. Some wore black face coverings or armbands, presumably cultists, and others wore normal Baskan uniform. After surveying the battle for another moment, his long experience of war allowed him to read the scene like an expert tracker.

He pointed. "I think the cultists broke ranks and discipline when they ran up against us in the pass. They were milling about out here when the larger force of Baskans struck in a mounted charge. That's why this has turned into such a melee. Who are the other Baskans, though?"

"It's Prince Beviyard's squadron, plus some others," said Olbarin.

"How can you tell?" asked Belasko. "The uniforms?"

"Yes, there are several units here." He squinted. "And there's the Prince himself." Olbarin pointed at the thick of the action.

"Is anyone tempted to sneak off while they're fighting each other?" asked Sysko.

Belasko frowned. "The Prince and his allies have taken the battle to the people who were trying to kill us. There are two things to say about that: I've never let others fight my battles for me, and anyone killing the people who were trying to kill me is probably my ally. The cultists are canny fighters. Even with greater numbers, Prince Beviyard will be hard-pressed to win the day conclusively."

"Why do I get the feeling you're going to suggest we charge those murderous Baskan cultists?" asked Nerys.

"Because I am." Belasko gave a savage grin. "I can't ask any of you to join me, you've done more than anyone could have wanted, but down there is the person who's responsible for putting us through hell these last few days. Who's responsible for the death of my friends. I'd like to find them and ask them a few searching questions. There's just the small matter of this battlefield in the way. A battle in which a few extra blades might make all the difference."

"I'll join you," said Olbarin. "Those people have dishonoured my country. I'd like to take them to task over that."

"For honour?" asked Sysko.

Belasko shook his head. "For duty." He hefted his sword.

"For duty!" cried the others.

And they charged the nearest group of cultists.

As they limped towards the enemy, exhaustion and small wounds slowing them down, Belasko could make out

The Swordsman's Descent

the sound of hoofbeats getting closer. He looked up as a squadron of cavalry, led by a whooping figure, swept around the battle and turned, approaching their group from the rear.

Belasko smiled. Byrta. You always know how to make an entrance.

His old friend approached, cantering alongside. "Nice of you to show up," she called across to him.

"I'd yell something witty," he replied, "but I need all my breath for running."

She grinned in response, raised her sword in salute, then swept it down. "Charge!" she yelled. Byrta and her cavalry overtook Belasko and his warriors, smashing into the Baskans they had targeted, who were frantically trying to turn around to face this threat from another front.

Belasko and his group arrived moments later, throwing themselves into the battle.

∽

It was bloody work, and the world shrank to the immediate threats around them. Despatch an enemy, protect yourself and your comrades. They fought as a group, as best they could, but in the confusion of conflict, they found themselves fighting alongside the Prince's forces at times, and then the Villanese that Byrta had brought with her after fighting their rearguard action.

Sysko went down, a thrust from a Baskan cultist opening their belly. Nerys avenged them, fighting furiously over their dying friend, savage and fierce even as tears ran openly down their face.

Nerys nearly fell, as she dropped to her knees to cradle Sysko's head in her hands. A Baskan soldier saved them, parrying the attack they hadn't seen in their grief, before despatching their attacker.

Belasko and Olbarin arrived then, and fought alongside the unnamed Baskan soldier, defending their grieving friend. When Sysko breathed their last, Nerys stood and composed themself.

"Thank you, I shouldn't have lost control like that," she said. "Now, let's kill some more of these bastard cultists. We have another death to avenge."

They fought on and on, through exhaustion and out the other side. Belasko, already weary from the events of the last days, joints ablaze with pain, found himself staggering from fight to fight. Only a lifetime of training, and his still fast reflexes, kept him alive. That and his remaining friends.

In the midst of the chaos, Byrta came face to face with Emilynn. Neither woman said a word, although Byrta grinned as they set to. It was a stunning display of swordcraft and horsemanship combined, as their sabres struck faster than some eyes could follow, and they manoeuvred their horses around each other. It was almost as if they were dancing, until Emilynn's horse slipped slightly on a muddy bloody bit of battlefield. It was all the opening Byrta needed. As Emilynn's arms went wide to keep her balance, she struck with a savage cut to the inside of Emilynn's sword arm that severed tendons and caused her to drop her sabre as she gritted her teeth against the pain. Byrta pulled up and back from that stroke, drawing her blade across Emilynn's throat.

The Baskan looked faintly surprised as blood fountained from the wound, and she slipped from her saddle, one of her feet catching in the stirrup. Emilynn's horse panicked and galloped off, Emilynn's corpse dragging along behind it.

The Swordsman's Descent

Byrta nodded. "Now we know who's better," she said to herself before rejoining the fray.

After a time, and it must have been some time as the sun was lowering in the sky, there came shouts. Horns were blown, and most of the remaining cultists stepped back from the fight, lowering their weapons. Others, a minority, carried on the fight, which continued in pockets across the plane, but they were surrounded by the other Baskan forces present, and their defeat seemed inevitable.

Belasko looked around him as cultists dropped their weapons, and saw in the distance King Edyard's banner. He turned to those he had with him, those who had survived. "Shall we go have a chat with the Baskan King? I'd like to find out what the bloody hell has been going on."

"You speak for all of us there, Belasko. Let's go," said Olbarin, who had already started walking towards the King's standard.

52

THEIR WAY WAS barred by Baskan soldiers as they approached.

"Let them through," called a familiar voice. "They're the reason we're here. Or part of it."

The soldiers lowered their spears, letting Belasko and his companions through. They could see the one who had spoken, King Edyard.

He beckoned them over. "I'm glad to see you survived, Belasko, all of you."

"Yes, we're also glad to have survived," said Belasko. He turned, indicating the battlefield. "What the hell has been going on in your country? No disrespect, your majesty, but these cultists seem to have had the run of your palace, not to mention the city, and have been able to act with impunity. It's only through sheer luck that Queen Lilliana, or any of us, are still alive. We came to you to bring an end to wars between our people. A fresh one nearly started."

"I think you're the sort of person who makes his own luck, Belasko, but you're right." King Edyard shook his head. "I

The Swordsman's Descent

didn't realise the depths to which this cult would sink, the reach of their influence. I misjudged them; thought they were stuffy mystics more interested in arcane rituals than bringing about real change. And for that, I apologise. My blindness to their mission, and my misplaced trust, almost caused something terrible to happen. I can't apologise, there aren't words, but I will do whatever must be done to put this right."

"You can start by asking him some hard questions," said Belasko, pointing to the figure of Jonteer, who was being led up in chains. "That erstwhile secretary seems to have been leading this group and the one that attacked us in the palace square." He turned back to the King. "We owe your son and Ambassador Aveyard a debt of gratitude. Their intervention at the behest of young Olbarin here—" He clapped the young Baskan on the arm. "—allowed us to make our escape."

"You can pass on your thanks in person later. And that man will pay for his crimes." King Edyard's eyes gleamed. "His head will adorn a spike above the palace gates before long, as a warning to other traitors. After he's answered some of those hard questions you mentioned."

Jonteer was brought before the King. He laughed at the sight of Belasko, before spitting at the ground before Belasko's feet. Jonteer turned to King Edyard. "You can't help yourself, can you? Even now, you're associating with this Villanese peasant and attacking true patriots."

King Edyard eyed the failed cult leader. "Patriots, are you? You attack a visiting sovereign, cause bloodshed in my palace, in the streets of our capital, almost setting war in motion in the process, and call yourselves patriots? You're criminals—Jonteer, is it? Nothing more. You have no glorious purpose other than your own vanity. You have gambled and lost. Your life, as well as your hope." He peered at the other man. "Why? Why have you done this?"

"Why?" Jonteer laughed, but there was no humour in the sound. "You would have weakened our country permanently. A country that stands still, that does not conquer and subjugate its neighbours, is dying, if not already dead. Of course, we wanted to start another war, you idiot. That is the whole point."

"If I'm the idiot, why am I still standing here in my crown while you have failed and are about to experience a short but extremely painful future?" King Edyard waved a weary hand. "Get this fool out of my sight. Take him for questioning."

The King turned back to Belasko, pinching the bridge of his nose in a gesture of tired frustration. "Belasko, as you held the pass I take it Queen Lilliana has gone on ahead? Could you catch up to her? Tell her what has happened here and bid her return?"

"Perhaps. She hasn't gone as far as you may think, I sent her to occupy a fort at the other end of the pass. Why would the Queen return, though? I bid her to stay put until reinforcements arrived and she was safe."

King Edyard looked out across the plane. "You know what has happened here today? For the first time in our history, Baskans and Villanese have fought alongside each other. Against a common enemy, for a common goal. The accords we negotiated are complete, finalised the same day you were attacked in the palace. I think it would be fitting to sign them here and now."

"Amid the sounds of the dead and dying? The stench of a battlefield?"

King Edyard smiled, but there was no humour in it. Only sadness. "What better place to seal a peace than surrounded by the folly of war? A reminder of what we are working to prevent."

Belasko sighed. "Very well, I will try. I will go to Queen Lilliana, and if she agrees to return, then we shall. If we haven't returned by tomorrow morning, I would ask that you give my compatriots supplies, so they may return to Villan as well." He paused. "Two of our own were wounded in the fighting to hold the pass, I'd appreciate it if your medics could tend to them."

"Of course," said King Edyard. "You have my word."

"No," said Nerys, "we're going with you, Belasko."

Belasko shook his head. "No. Stay, rest. Let me go to the Queen." He turned back to King Edyard. "You just so happen to have copies of those accords here, with you now?"

The King shrugged. "I'm a strategist, not an optimist. I had hoped to catch up to Queen Lilliana and sort things out without all this bloodshed, but at least that is resolved for now. Come, Belasko, let us work to prevent more wars. We have supplies at the back of our column, I'll have someone bring you water and food so that you may break your fast as you go."

∼

Belasko pushed hard to reach the Queen as quickly as he could, once he had wound his way through the narrowest parts of Dellan Pass.

It took some time, picking his way across the rocky and uneven ground, before he saw the wall of the fort. Lining the wall that stretched across the mouth of the pass, silhouetted against the setting sun, were a number of soldiers and other people. It could only be them. Smoke from the signal pyre billowed into the sky behind them, alerting those for miles around that something odd was happening here. Belasko picked up the pace.

Those atop the wall readied themselves, weapons raised, wary.

"It's me, it's Belasko. Wait, I have news!"

Those atop the wall lowered their weapons slowly as a slender figure with golden hair pushed to the fore. It was the Queen.

She wore a quizzical look on her face as he approached the wall. "Belasko, I'm glad beyond telling that you are here, alive and well, but what of the others? What is happening?"

Belasko stopped beneath the wall, a wave of fatigue washing over him as he did so. He blew air out between his lips, then looked up to his monarch. Squinting against the setting sun as he did so. "That's a long story, and time is short, so I'll try to be quick."

He told them. How they had held the pass, how King Edyard's forces had attacked the cultists, and ultimately how the cultists were defeated. Of King Edyard's request.

Queen Lilliana blinked. "That's a lot to take in, Belasko." She called down from the wall. "He wants me to return, after all that's happened?"

"Yes, your majesty. I know it sounds mad, but I believe you'll be safe. I believe, too, that the King really does want peace, and is prepared to face the enemies within his kingdom to achieve it."

The Queen nodded as she pondered what he had said. Eventually, she sighed. "I set out to foster peace and, despite all that has happened, that is still my goal. Open the gates, let Belasko in. We shall return. We'll have to camp here for the night, though. We're losing the light."

"It looks like it will be a clear night and a full moon. If

we go carefully, slowly, we should be able to walk back and arrive long before dawn."

Queen Lilliana winced. "It would have to be slowly in any case. None of us have any speed left in us."

"Then let us go."

The gates opened, and Belasko strode through. Nodding to those he knew while all that accompanied the queen gathered up what little they had with them. Then, weary, sore, and tired to the bone, they set off back through Dellan Pass.

~

It was the middle of the night when they arrived back on the Baskan side of the pass. An effort had been made to clear away the dead, bodies stacked high in piles, while work had begun on vast communal graves. The site was torch-lit and soldiers carried on their grim work in shifts. It was clear where King Edyard had made his camp, and they strode towards it.

Baskan soldiers turned to watch them as they passed—some Villanese, too—waving and calling out cheers for the Queen and Belasko.

They approached King Edyard's camp, and he came out to meet them with Prince Beviyard and Ambassador Aveyard. The King bowed deeply to Queen Lilliana. "Your majesty," he said.

She returned his greeting, offering a stately incline of her head. "Your majesty."

He looked at her. "The events of the last few days pain me. That your people came to harm in my palace, in my city, when we have been working so hard to foster better relationships between our two countries. That traitors and conspirators could have cost us everything... I cannot apologise enough for that. But those traitors are in the open now. We will track them down, root them out, and end their influence in Baskan life forever. I swear it. I hope Belasko told you of my request?"

Queen Lilliana nodded before walking closer to King Edyard. "It would be easy to lose trust in you, in your stated goals. But the sight of Baskan and Villanese soldiers having fought together, having died together... That gives me hope in our common purpose. I agree that it is fitting that we sign the accords here. The other matter we discussed," she glanced briefly at Prince Beviyard and, although her expression did not flicker, there was a warmth to that look, "can be decided another day. You have the accords ready?"

"I do. Your majesty?" King Edyard held out his arm. Queen Lilliana took it, laying a hand in the crook of his elbow, and he led her over to a table under an awning where everything they needed was prepared.

They both took up pen and ink and, in a moment, signed both copies of the accords. By the light of torch and flame, in the dead of night, the Dellan Pass Accords came into being.

53

IT WAS LATER the next day, after all had been given a chance to rest and refresh themselves, that Belasko was summoned to the tent King Edyard had given over to Queen Lilliana.

Parlin smiled as he opened the tent flap, beckoning Belasko to go in. He entered, pausing momentarily when he saw that only Majel and the Queen were present.

Queen Lilliana looked up from pouring out three glasses of wine and smiled. "Thank you for coming, Belasko. I wanted to take a moment to discuss our next steps."

Belasko sighed. "Your majesty, can I stop taking steps for a moment? My feet feel like they're about to drop off. I don't think I've ever felt so exhausted in my life."

"Of course, please sit. Over here, I've chairs for all of us. Majel, here's your glass, Belasko, here's yours." She passed them their glasses as they walked by her to the seats she had indicated. They both paused, waiting on formality. Queen Lilliana waved her hand, frustrated. "Please, just sit."

They sat and enjoyed a moment of companionable silence. One that Belasko broke.

"So, next steps, your majesty? What did you have in mind?" he asked.

But it was Majel who answered. "As you survived, once again and against the odds, you old goat, do you want your old job back?"

Belasko snorted. "Aronos, no. If the events of the last few days have shown me anything, it's that it's time to retire. I'm happy to be on hand to advise you, Majel, if you want, but it's time to pass the role of Royal Champion over to younger hands."

"Then you'll do as I asked? Return with me to court and serve as my adviser?" Queen Lilliana asked, eyebrow raised, but a delicate fragility about her expression told Belasko that this was important to her.

He sighed. "I will serve, your majesty, however it please you."

Her smile then was brilliant. "Good. It might please you to hear that Anerin is recovering well. Prince Beviyard brought word from an, as he put it, 'unknown source', and I plan on asking him to serve in a similar role on my council. He's so widely travelled that his input and insight into our dealings with other nations will be invaluable. So you'll have at least one old friend knocking about the palace."

Belasko returned her smile. "More than one, majesty, more than one." He frowned. "What else? I know you and the Prince were having, um, *discussions* of your own. Will they continue?"

Queen Lilliana blushed slightly. "Once we have all had time to recover and grieve our lost friends, I think so. Yes. But in Villan this time."

"I'm glad to hear it," said Majel. "I don't fancy setting foot on Baskan soil for a long time after this."

Belasko raised his glass. "I'll drink to that." He took a

The Swordsman's Descent

long sip of his wine. "Do we know what King Edyard is planning to deal with these cultists? There are surely more out there."

"King Edyard is returning to Albessar, determined to root out the cultists and cement his hold on the throne. He's tasked our former ambassador, Aveyard, to help as his new head of the intelligence service. Count Veldar has been removed from that post. Either he didn't see the cultist's schemes coming, or he was in league with them. Either would be reason for him to lose his position, and one for to him lose his head along with it. No one seems to know whether or not he was part of this cult, another question King Edyard is seeking to answer."

Belasko nodded. "Oh, Aveyard will hate that. She loathes politics and the layers of secrecy within Baskan society." He frowned. "Actually, she might just be the right person for the job. We'll be getting a new ambassador to Villan, then?"

"Oh yes," said Majel, "ably assisted by your young friend, Olbarin. The Baskans have all been very impressed by him, so the King has given him a new commission in the army and diplomatic corps. His first duty will be to serve at their embassy in Villan."

"Good, the lad has a lot of promise." Belasko swirled the wine in his glass. "Everything seems to have worked out well. I wonder how long that will last?"

Queen Lilliana made a sound of frustration. "Don't question it, Belasko, just enjoy the moment."

So, with good company, and good wine, he tried to do just that. But something niggled at the back of his mind. Pieces of information that he had picked up in the last few days but not had the time to think about started to fall into place. Belasko frowned in thought as Queen Lilliana and Majel chatted.

The Queen noticed his expression. "Belasko, what is it?"

"I'm not sure, your majesty. I'm just putting together some information that Anerin gave me." He looked up at her. "I need to speak with Aveyard, check something with her. Then I have some questions for her former secretary."

~

Jonteer was being kept in a bare tent, the only furniture a chair that he was sat in and a small three-legged stool opposite him. Shackles at his wrists and ankles connected to the legs of the chair, then to a stake in the ground in front of him. He had been stripped, thoroughly searched, and redressed in some spare uniform that was too big for him. He wasn't getting away anytime soon.

The former secretary, Baskan intelligence officer, and cult leader looked up as Belasko let himself in. He was battered and bruised, one eye starting to swell shut, a split lip with a dried trickle of blood running from it. A faint smile played across his lips.

"Ah," he said. "I wondered when you might visit. The King already had some people attend to me, ask me some questions."

"I'm familiar with those sorts of people, having sat where you sit now in the past. It's not a lot of fun, is it?"

Jonteer shrugged, chains jingling. "I've had worse."

Belasko looked at him for a long moment. Jonteer's eyes met his, never wavering. There was still an air of amusement about him. "I must say you seem in good spirits for someone who is sure to be executed."

The Baskan laughed. "You forget, I worship the Lady of Night. Death herself. I do not fear her embrace."

"That must be nice. Personally, I find a healthy respect

The Swordsman's Descent

for life, along with a fear of death, is an excellent motivator. Both to stay alive and to not make mistakes."

"Mistakes?" Jonteer arched an amused eyebrow, then winced slightly at the pain.

Belasko picked up the three-legged stool and looked at it, then laughed when he sat down. "Sorry, this is all rather reminiscent of something for me. Where was I? Yes, mistakes. Being so assured of your own cleverness that you leave a trail of clues behind you, believing everyone else so dimwitted that they could never connect them."

Jonteer was silent then, still, all traces of amusement gone.

Belasko leaned forward on the stool, intent on the man opposite him. "I'll put the pieces of information in front of you and see what you make of them. Tell me what conclusion you'd draw from them." He began to tick things off on his fingers as he counted. "Firstly, years ago, my friend Anerin got himself into a little bit of trouble on a visit to Bas when the peace between our countries was still a delicate thing. He was questioned by the head of Baskan intelligence. A service you work for—I'm assuming you did then, too."

Jonteer remained silent, watching Belasko warily.

"Second, a while after that, he was approached by members of the cult of the Lady of Night to act as a spy for them in the Villanese court. Approached by the cult you are a member of and until recently led. Third, Anerin reported this approach to the Villanese Inquisition, who sent another old friend, Ervan, to question him about the contact with your cult. Ervan, who had reason to hate me. A hate that consumed him. Fourth, Ervan, at the behest of King Mallor, poisons Prince Kellan, the heir to the Villanese throne. Poison always seemed an odd choice to me, for Ervan was a swordsman. Finally, on the day that Ervan poisoned the Prince, there was a visitor to the palace kitchens that aroused suspicion at the time. You. You were there on the day that Prince Kellan was murdered."

Now it was Belasko's turn to smile. "Can you see where I'm going with this?"

"Oh, well done, Belasko." Jonteer's returning smile was a cold, dead thing. He held up his hands. "If I could applaud your discovery, then I certainly would."

"Did you help Ervan to poison Prince Kellan? Was he part of your death cult?"

Jonteer laughed. "You're so close. But you need to take it back further."

"Further?" Belasko frowned.

"Yes, back before Lord Anerin's little indiscretion. Ervan wasn't the only one with reason to hate you."

Belasko's frown deepened. "What have I ever done to you?"

"To me, personally? Nothing. To my people? Everything." Jonteer sneered. "You idiot. Did you not think there would be repercussions to your day at Dellan Pass all those years ago? While Bas was at war, while we were growing, we were strong. As soon as our nation stopped expanding, we started to decline. A decline that started with our loss here. With you. That ultimately led to us losing that war."

His face contorted with anger. "Then to add insult to injury, you hunted my brothers and sisters, my fellowship of the Lady of Night, and exterminated them in Villan. Of course, we wanted our revenge. After he debriefed Anerin, Ervan reached out to us. He was intrigued by the nature of our order. I met with him, told him how we may, in time, be able to help him get the revenge over you that he so craved. But it would take time.

"Ervan, through his aristocratic background, could get access to King Mallor. Over the years, he drip-fed the idea of poisoning Prince Kellan to him. Oh, Mallor had no faith in his son and wished him out of the way, but Ervan helped set his feet on the path to murder and made him think it was all his own idea.

"Then, when all was ready, I helped procure the poison from a member of my order working as an apothecary in Villan and delivered it to the boy Ervan had manipulated into putting it into the Prince's food." Jonteer chuckled. "He thought he was spoiling it to make another member of the kitchen staff look bad. I brought it to him in the guise of making sure the kitchens were adequately prepared to make some traditional Baskan dishes for an upcoming feast.

"It was Ervan's idea to pin the blame on you, hiding that letter in the Prince's rooms. Mallor was easily swayed on that one as well. He had no great love for you once you started to outlive your usefulness." The humour once again fell from Jonteer's face. "It was all set up beautifully. Only you had to go and ruin things by not playing along and half figuring things out."

Belasko stared at Jonteer. "Yes. Sorry if I ruined your schemes there. I know now that you were behind the attacks and pursuit once we got to Albessar. What about the attack by those bandits? And earlier, the lone assassin. Was that you as well?"

Jonteer nodded. "Oh, yes. We thought we'd try and kill your Queen, and when our initial attempt didn't work if Prince Beviyard was caught out instead, then that would be all for the better. One would be the spark that could reignite war; the other would help destabilise a king who sought to take our country away from its true purpose."

"So, all this was about war, then?" Belasko shook his head. "It amazes me that anyone can hunger for it so."

"Of course, it was about war, you idiot!" Jonteer shouted. "What else is there for a country that would be strong?"

"Looking to the health of its people? Increasing their prosperity and happiness? There are many ways to be strong, Jonteer. Although, it must seem strange for a man of violence such as me to say it, war should be a last resort, not a guiding principle." Belasko turned and called over his shoulder. "Have you heard enough?"

Jonteer frowned, confusion writ large on his face. "What?"

"We're in a tent, Jonteer, the sound carries. You've just confessed all. You didn't think I'd be the only one listening, did you?"

The tent flap opened, and King Edyard and Queen Lilliana walked in. King Edyard was stony-faced, Queen Lilliana's expression unreadable, but her eyes were cold. Belasko knew her well enough to know that the touch of colour in her cheeks indicated a high anger.

"Oh yes, I'd say we heard enough," said King Edyard.

"Almost too much," said Queen Lilliana. She turned to the King. "We'll need more information from him. I must root this cult out of Villan once and for all."

"The revelation that one of their own not only murdered Prince Kellan but was also the agent of a foreign cult may be the final nail in the Inquisition's coffin," said Belasko. "We can rid ourselves of that vile institution at the same time."

"That's something," Queen Lilliana said. "Something else good that has come out of all this."

King Edyard nodded. "I'm so sorry that any Baskan played a part in your brother's death. As far as I'm concerned, it's death for this traitor. Once we've got all the useful information we can out of him."

"That should be fairly straightforward, your majesty," said Belasko. "Just let him run away with his own cleverness. In a bid to prove how intelligent he is, he'll confess everything." He turned back to Jonteer. "Or will that trick not work a second time?" Jonteer only glowered at him in response. Belasko turned back to the others. "Come, let us leave Jonteer to come to terms with the fact that he's not as clever as he likes to think."

They left, Belasko holding the tent flap for Queen Lilliana, then King Edyard, before letting himself out. He didn't turn to look back at Jonteer as he left.

Once outside, they exchanged a few words with the duty guards, then began to walk back across the camp. King Edyard stopped. "Thank you, Belasko. Jonteer's actions have given me the leeway to push for root and branch reform of Baskan public life. That confession is the end for the old way of doing things." He sighed. "Such a lot to do, and I'm not getting any younger. I shall bid you two goodnight and go in search of my rest." He bowed to Queen Lilliana. "Your majesty." Then he reached out and took Belasko's hand, clasping his wrist in the warrior's grip. "Belasko." With that, the Baskan King turned and walked away. Belasko and Queen Lilliana watched him go.

"What shall we do, Belasko?" Queen Lilliana asked.

Belasko smiled. "Now? I'm going back to bed. I'm absolutely exhausted. You must be, too. Tomorrow? Carry on. We now have to see how far into the Inquisition this cult's influence may have spread. On top of everything else. More than enough to keep us busy."

"Very well, tomorrow is another day, and we've lots to do."

"And no rest this side of death."

Queen Lilliana and Belasko carried on their way back to the Villanese part of the camp. "If we could make sure that whatever happens next involves less running around in fear of our lives, that would make me happy," said Queen Lilliana.

"I can't promise anything, but I'll do my best," said Belasko.

∼

THE END

∼

BY THE AUTHOR

The Royal Champion Series:
Prequel Novella: The Swordsman's Intent
Book One: The Swordsman's Lament
Book Two: The Swordsman's Descent

AFTERWORD

If you've enjoyed this adventure and would like to be kept up to date with the my news (as well as receiving a free copy of *The Swordsman's Intent*, the prequel novella set 15 years before book one of this series, short stories and exclusive content) then make sure to sign up to my newsletter at gmwhite.co.uk.

ABOUT THE AUTHOR

G.M. White lives on St Martin's, in the Isles of Scilly, with his wife and son. Like many people on the islands he wears a few different hats. Now a full time stay at home dad, he also works several part time jobs, is on the local Coastguard rescue team, sits on the committee for St Martin's Island Hall and Reading Room, plays cricket (poorly) for St Martin's Cricket Club, and somehow finds time to write.

ACKNOWLEDGMENTS

Writing this book has been a longer journey than anticipated, and a harder one in many ways. Part of that is to do with personal things, adjusting to being a stay at home dad for example, getting my ADHD diagnosis last year, losing a family member to covid, and part of it working against the backdrop of a global pandemic

So thank you to all of you who have championed me and supported me these last two years. Because it is nearly two years since my last publication, The Swordsman's Intent, and twenty months since I started working on The Swordsman's Descent. (The Swordsman's Lament took eleven months from plotting to publication, for example.)

There were a few missteps along the way, but Belasko and I found the right path in the end and I hope you enjoyed his latest adventure.

I have to thank my wife for all her support, and for accepting the fact I spend so much time with the imaginary people I invented.

My son, Teddy, for being a beacon of joy. Being your dad is a privilege, even on the difficult days.

All my friends and family that have been supportive, listened to me blather on, and let me bounce ideas off them.

Marthe Broadhurst, without whom this book would have taken even longer to write.

Kristina Adams, whose workshop on character arcs

helped me realise and correct an early misstep with my plotting.

Mark Stay and Mark Desvaux of the Bestseller Experiment podcast for their support and encouragement of writers everywhere and the community they have built.

The members of the BXP Team, that community that has grown up around the podcast, for their support, advice, feedback, and so much more.

My fellow Word Racers: Andrew Chapman, Rachel Howells, Robyn Sarty, Tom Foot, Josh Atkinson, Paul Ardoin, Angela Nurse, Gavin Ralph, Laura Regan, and Steve Gowland. Thank you for the accountability, the friendship, and the trash talking.

My editor, Vicky Brewster, for once again helping me shape my narrative with her insight and advice, and for asking all the right questions.

My beta readers: Julian Barr, Will Leggatt, and Steve Gowland. I've been fortunate to have Julian as a beta reader for all my published work, and Will and Steve joined the team this year. To all three of you, your feedback, thoughts, and suggestions all helped make this book so much better.

I know I'll have missed someone out, so if I have and you're reading this: thank you. You know who you are.